RENTED SILENCE

To Give Voice,
You Must First Survive

"Silence is the mother of truth."
—BENJAMIN DISRAELI

RENTED SILENCE

To Give Voice,
You Must First Survive

Lucia Mann

INSPIRED BY TRUE EVENTS
Revised Edition
Previously sold as *Beside an Ocean of Sorrow*

Grassroots Publishing Group

Grassroots Publishing Group™
9404 Southwick Dr.
Bakersfield, CA 93312

10 9 8 7 6 5 4 3 2

Second Edition 2016

Printed in the United States of America

ISBN: 978-0-9794805-9-1

Library of Congress Control Number: 2015956869

Cover & book design by CenterPointe Media

Dedication

In memory of my mother, Maria Picasso, and grandmother, Raphaela G., the two women who served as the impetus of this story.

I have used my imagination to bridge gaps, without departing from the tragedy that was my life, my mother's life, and my maternal grandmother's life.

Acknowledgments

I am indebted to the many wonderful souls who lent support and provided confidence in my ability to weave the fabric of this story. With gratitude beyond mere expression, I thank my editor and publisher, Nesta Aharoni, for believing in me. Ruth for being the best proofer ever! I thank my husband, Hector, who suffered my writer's tantrums good-naturedly. Last, but not least, I thank my gifted daughter, Charlotte Miriam, whose ode to *Rented Silence* adorns this book.

Table of Contents

PART TWO

Lynette Hallworthy-Martinez

Historical Fact

Before 1850 about 10 million African souls who crossed the Atlantic as slaves were shipped in British vessels.

Who owns a life that is not their own?

Listen while I begin ...

An era has gone, and with it came songs about a time of changes,

But out there somewhere I can solemnly swear there are people still kept in cages.

These bars you can't see, but there they are, a disposable race to some.

Oh, but beware of the secrets they share; soon it will all come undone.

There's the one that got away, and you know what they say, she's a little unwell.

Here is a warning: the weather is storming, brewing some evil from hell,

Lives are lost but not in vain, their blood the same, the journey is far from ended.

Another warning to you, just know what to do because The Devil can be befriended.

Hope isn't set because we soon forget what life has truly shown.

While truth gets unfolded, again you are scolded: The Devil takes care of his own.

Those souls he takes he always breaks; they will never again be whole.

As long as you fight, with all of your might, it will soon take its toll.

A soul born, a soul damned, a soul destined to live in this life of violence.

Another soul will change what once was and give voice to this Rented Silence.

–CMR

PART ONE

Intandane
(The Foundling)

"The worst sin toward our fellow creatures

is not to hate them, but to be indifferent to

them: that's the essence of inhumanity."

—George Bernard Shaw

## CHAPTER ONE

The Union of South Africa, British Commonwealth, Late Christmas Day 1945

"It is as natural to die as to be born; and to a little infant, perhaps one is as painful as the other."
—Francis Bacon

The newborn was barely alive. Her tiny heart thumped in erratic fits against her rib cage. Her lungs gasped for air under a burdensome yoke. As life ebbed from this helpless, abandoned baby, droplets of blood from her crudely severed umbilical cord spattered on the lifeless body of her twin sister, who was buried beneath her. For these tiny, unwanted humans, who had been discarded like dirty rags, death was inevitable, perhaps even preferable.

God, where art thou?

Out of nowhere a gale-force wind swooped across the arid soil, swirled into a mini-twister, and encircled the shallow gravesite, scattering its feeble, corn-husk covering over the parched ground. Afterward, the blustery emissary of unknown origin evaporated—its merciful task having been fulfilled.

The baby's eyelids were shut tight against the dusting of red dirt that layered her ashen face and long blonde eyelashes. The premature girl's blue lips slowly parted, her lungs sucking hungrily at the oxygen that suddenly flowed. Re-energized, the traumatized infant flailed her arms and legs until she wailed herself into a spent silence. With her last ounce of strength, she drew her knees to her chest and balled her tiny fists under her chin. Then, once again, she became still. A heavy shroud of *hush* cocooned this child of unimaginable misfortune. However, her struggle for mortality had not gone unnoticed.

At the edge of the cornfield where the newborns had been buried, a scruffy wild dog, shoulder blades protruding from an emaciated frame, crouched behind dense savannah grass. Her tick-infested ears twitched and her black-and-pink mottled nose quivered. Sniffing the air cautiously, this creature of the wild rose onto all fours. With swollen teats hanging low, the heavily pregnant animal slunk head down toward the babies' burial site.

CHAPTER TWO

 Servants' Quarters,
Hallworthy Estate, 1945

"Fear is the parent of cruelty."
–J.A. Froude

I n the pre-dawn hours of that same day, another one of Destiny's
children was fighting in her own way to survive. It was 4 A.M.,
and Anele Dingane, age twenty-seven, had been awake for hours.
She was exhausted, but afraid to close her eyes. Whenever she did,
horrid scenes—disturbing flashbacks—threatened to murder what
was left of her sanity, to crush her fragile psyche. It was like trying
to fight one's way through dense cobwebs.

In a dilapidated servants' shanty on the Hallworthy sugar plantation, Anele lay on her back bathed in sweat. A hand-me-down
Victorian-style nightgown clung to her feverish flesh. She let out a
soft, defeated sigh. She wanted to forget, not to relive, resurrected
nightmarish reflections. She rarely had such sleepless nights. Most
nights she fell quickly into an exhausted sleep after working seventeen grueling hours as the head cook at the mansion—a place she
longed to be wiped off the face of the earth.

It was an evil place. It was cursed, for sure. She believed that thousands of ghosts—restless slave spirits—roamed the estate grounds
and the dozens of corridors running through the palatial home built
by Lord Nigel Hallworthy in the middle of the nineteenth century.
Lord Nigel, a distant cousin of Queen Victoria, was also the grand-

father of the present owner, Lord Alan. Anele wanted *him* wiped off the face of the earth more than she wanted anything else. Without a doubt, Lord Alan, her *owner*, carried deep roots of sadistic evil that could be traced back to his relative, Lord Nigel.

Lord Nigel was born Frederick Otto Wettin in Germany in 1819. At age twenty, sporting his recently inherited title, he was a ladies' man. Winking at women and clicking his heels came naturally to him. He was handsome, tall, and slim. His blond hair was always parted on the side, and his matching moustache, neatly trimmed. His good looks often brought furtive peeks, not only from unattached women, but from married ones, as well. But it was his piercing, cobalt-blue eyes that caused the ladies to swoon. One woman remarked: "They are hypnotizing. They reach into my very soul."

Nigel had limitless wealth, having inherited a stately home in Yorkshire, England, and vast lands in South Africa and Germany.

And he was no stranger to death. When his mother died giving birth to him, his father, Wilhelm Otto Wettin, wasted no time in marrying a wealthy widow, Duchess Elizabeth Victoria Hallworthy, from Yorkshire. After their marriage, Wilhelm adopted his wife's name and became Lord Hallworthy. With his new English title, Wilhelm topped off the family fortune by selling chunks of Elizabeth's land to wealthy Germans. However, he didn't live long enough to enjoy the fiscal returns. Shortly after Nigel's eighteenth birthday, Wilhelm and Elizabeth were crushed to death in a freak carriage accident.

In the years that followed his parents' death, Nigel, the new Lord Hallworthy, developed an appreciation for quality clothing. He dressed only in the finest fitting frock coats, each adorned with stylish wide lapels. His outfits were punctuated with gold watch chains; low-cut vests; checked trousers; and fine, white dress shirts.

Nigel was debonair and business savvy, like his father. He instigated a plan designed to continuously increase his inheritance. In the fashion of nineteenth-century noblemen, Nigel built Hallworthy manor in South Africa. The structure was completed in 1867 by indentured servants and Italian stonemasons. The inspiration to build the three-story stone residence came to Nigel after he had visited a wealthy plantation owner in Mississippi. That grand mansion was fronted by stately Greek columns eight feet in circumference. It boasted several large balconies and umpteen chimney stacks. The interior was rich in splendor. It featured oak flooring, twenty-foot ceilings, an intricate plaster frieze, hand-carved marble mantles, and Italian-designed chandeliers. Nigel became a permanent resident of Hallworthy Manor after the death of his wife, the Duchess of Dorchester. She died of consumption in England during the construction of their new home. Peter, their only child, joined his father in South Africa after his mother's death.

Lord Nigel's nineteenth-century "hotel" was built on a rugged hill abutting a backdrop of mountain scenery, the Valley of a Thousand Hills. Magnificent, landscaped gardens surrounded the residence. The air hung thick with the perfumes of croton pseudopulchellus (a small shrub decorated with delicate lemon-colored flowers), pelargonium, arum lilies, daisies, and impatiens. Bordering the mansion's semi-circular brick driveway were a number of giant protea—South Africa's national emblem.

Fluent in German, Russian, and French, Lord Nigel was a shrewd businessman. Ardently wishing to keep his fortune rolling, he offered his residence to other royals as well as to additional crème de la crème who came to Africa on hunting expeditions. Lord Nigel had the ideal place for their amusement, and they paid well for it.

Thousands of hectares in size, Nigel's game reserve was tangled woodland populated by herds of deer and foxes, and even a few lions brought in for the kill. For his most special guests he offered another prized "hunt," steeply priced, of course. Hunting down the "odd one" was even better sport than shooting wild, exotic animals.

A distance from Nigel's home, several brick-and-stone outbuildings stood forlornly against the opulent setting of the manor. But there was one stone-brick-and-wood structure that no one dared speak about. For all intents and purposes, the shack had been built to house bloodhounds. At least that's what Nigel had told his builders. But this barn-like structure was never touched by dogs. Instead, wretched creatures—African men, women, and adolescents of both sexes—were housed within its musty walls.

The string of people who inhabited the shack had been rounded up from remote villages on Nigel's orders. He referred to the captured souls as *savages*. Despite the fact that the slave trade had been outlawed in 1807, many years earlier, Lord Nigel's suppliers continued to bring him "unpaid workers." Some of these victims tended to the vast estate. Others became house servants. A number of young girls were used to satisfy guests. And certain African men wearing metal dog-collars with Nigel's name etched into the surface were set "free" in the reserve for the guests' sport.

Lord Nigel, a remorseless liar, had no conscience. He was unrepentant. He thought himself above the law.

One afternoon, with his loyal German shepherd, Fritz, lying on the floor beside him, Lord Nigel wrote in his diary:

"To convert a savage to the proper English way of life is impossible. Even the strongest of us cannot bear their odor. I cannot have savages, who have no decent heart, living in proximity to my house, upsetting my guests. Africans are not entirely human. They are just apes."

In his twilight years, Lord Nigel was declared insane. He died some years later under mysterious circumstances. Was it suicide? Was it murder?

A rusty, blood-stained, iron collar was found on his deathbed.

By 1945, at the end of World War II, Lord Nigel's stately hunting grounds were long gone, replaced with sugar cane fields. But the ghostly cries that had come from within the slave building and the rundown gamekeeper's cottage had not been purged by closing of the hunting reserves. The gamekeeper, himself, had been found one day hanging from a ceiling beam.

Now, lying motionless on a lumpy, straw mattress she shared with two other female servants, Anele covered her ears. She didn't want to hear the desolate cries of past captives, but she did. She envisioned their wretchedness. She felt their pain. She felt their terror. She wanted to shut out the heart-rending echoes of the dead, but the more she tried, the more they haunted her. Like all of the earlier unfortunate people, she, too, was a slave who had suffered abundant horror in her life.

Anele felt bitterness rising in her throat, not just for herself, but for the many crushed souls of her race, and for the immense human misery and injustice they suffered when one human being owned another. The land of her birth had run red with the blood of brave African warriors fighting white invaders. But now the whites dominated the land and treated her once proud and independent people like beasts of burden, devoid of human dignity. Years after her capture, Anele was nothing more than an expendable *ape*.

Lives full of promise blown away by the hand of a slaver.

Anele's inner voice cried out: *Why do I still tremble like a frightened child at the sight and sound of these white people who think they own my black skin? Who treat me with less respect than a wild cur?* She threw back her head. *There were times I could have escaped.* But the idea of running away like a scared rabbit was contrary to her nature; she carried the blood of brave Zulus, not of cowards. Though courage ran deep in her veins, so did shame. A train of guilt and disgrace kept coming. She could never return home to her village in Zululand. No tribal suitor would touch her now. Not after a white man had repeatedly defiled her. She had given birth to *his* child, an event that would forever hold a painful darkness in her soul.

Anele turned thirteen in the spring of 1931. One late afternoon, looking pea-soup pale, she threw down the potato peeler and rushed out the side door of the Hallworthy kitchen holding her hand tightly over her mouth. The sound of violent retching permeated the humid, seasonal air. Lately, she couldn't hold down her food. The Hallworthy cook, a grey-haired woman named Lamella, who always had a cheerful grin on her lips, was not smiling today. She stared as her young helper wiped her soiled mouth on her sleeve. There was no doubt in Cook's mind. "Dear God," Lamella murmured noiselessly.

She had lost count of the number of black girls who had become pregnant by Lord Alan or his father, Lord Peter, before him. At about Anele's age she, too, had been the victim of Lord Peter's lust for dark, tender skin. Mercifully, her three babies had been stillborn.

Cook gently placed her hands on Anele's shoulders. "Listen carefully to what wise Lamella is going to tell you. No interrupting. You are pregnant, child, but you are not to blame. The rule here has always been," she swallowed hard, "that no indentured servant is allowed to bear children."

Anele scowled at Lamella, who immediately asked, "Do you understand, Anele?"

Anele wanted to gnash her own teeth to powder. "I'm not going to have a baby," she rejoined. "I have an upset tummy. That leftover egg pie you made was too rich."

Lamella shrugged. "After work I will take you to Kabila, the birthing woman. She doesn't live far from here. She will give you some herbs so your baby will not be born."

After a moment of silent contemplation and realization, Anele stamped her foot. She was young but not unaware. She had seen the signs of pregnancy on the women in her village.

"Old woman, hear me. Nobody is going to kill my baby! I *want* my baby, even though it belongs to the white devil. I *will* run away and have it! I *will* take good care of it! I *will* be a good mother!"

Lamella clucked her tongue. "Don't be stupid, girl. Where will you run? You can't go home to your village with a white man's baby inside you. You'll be turned out, and then where will you go? You need *money* to survive in the world outside of this place. You can hardly take care of *yourself*! No. You cannot give birth. It is against the rules."

Anele answered, defiantly, "I know several fieldworkers who have had the master's babies and are raising them."

"That's different," Lamella argued. "They don't work in *this* house."

"Then I'll leave here and go work in the field!"

Cook finally snapped. "I've heard enough!" She grabbed hold of Anele's shoulders and shook them before continuing. "Anele, you will do as you are told as long as you are under my wing, or you'll end up like your sisters." Cook loathed speaking about Anele's twin sisters, but she had no choice but to shock her into reality "Dead, child. As dead as this lamb I'm cooking."

A moment later Anele's sobs echoed throughout the scullery. Lamella wanted to cry, but she knew her tears wouldn't save this poor girl. She hoped that Kabila would, once again, perform a miracle.

That evening, after their work was done, Lamella marched a crestfallen Anele to the midwife's hut, almost two miles away. Kabila patted Anele's cheek, then handed over a pouch, and instructed, "Child, boil water, then add the herbs I've given you. Drink it when it has cooled. In the morning, your troubles will be over."

Anele was enveloped in suffering and tears.

The African midwife's foul-smelling, bad-tasting abortion concoction failed. Anele hid this truth and her swelling midriff by wearing one of Lady Ethel's discarded front-lacing corsets. Eight months later Anele, barely more than a child herself, gave birth, all alone in the servant's shack, to a six-pound baby girl. Lamella was not present at the time. She had left early to buy special food items for an upcoming birthday celebration, and she wasn't due back for a while. That happy day Anele tenderly gazed at her precious, light-skinned baby. Her heart spoke to her: *My baby girl fills a big hole in my life. I will be a good mother to her.*

Anele named her baby girl, Thaka-Zhana, after her twin sisters, and she couldn't have been more content. But that was not to last for long. Trouble was lurking out of sight. Anele's birthing cries had been heard by a passing fieldworker who had snuck up to the shack and peeked through a hole in the doorway. The seventeen-year-old boy then rushed back to the sugar-cane field and alerted his boss.

Immediately, Alan mounted his steed and galloped toward the servants' quarters. He was an ill wind that never blew any good. His face was red with anger as he strode toward the bed where Anele and her baby were cuddled up. He spoke with bullets in his voice. "You can't keep the child, Anele. Give it to me."

Alan stretched his arms toward Anele. Fear closed her mouth tight for the longest moment. Then she tearfully pleaded, "Please don't take my baby. I'll work harder for you, Master. The baby will be no trouble. I'll ask Kabila to mind her during my work hours."

Alan's mouth curled back contemptuously. "You know the rules, Anele. No husbands or children are allowed to live on my property without my permission. Do not make me take the child by force …" His words were cut short by a presence more ominous than his threatening words.

Like a raging windstorm, Lady Ethel, Alan's mother, gripped her car keys as she rushed into the room. "Damn you, Alan!" she shrieked. "This is the last time I'm going to tolerate your despicable behavior! I'm sure your wife won't be too happy with another half-caste bastard running about the place. Now pass me that child!"

With a clenched jaw Alan lunged at Anele. When she clung harder to her child, he grabbed a piece of wood by the doorway and marched back to the bed. In a demonic voice he snarled, "It looks like you are not giving me many alternatives."

The blow to Anele's head knocked her unconscious.

Alan's lips warped into a satisfied smile as he lifted the baby from

Anele's limp arms. He handed the wailing infant over to his mother. While fiercely grasping the writhing newborn, the sharp-tongued, cold-hearted woman gestured toward Anele as she ordered Alan, "Take this black bitch to the hospital. I'll call ahead and make the necessary arrangements." With that *dark* ending, the roaring cyclone that was Alan's mother stormed out of the shanty with the baby.

Poor Anele was none the wiser. She was in a twilight world of unconsciousness. The brief joy she had experienced had already vanished. Alan, with his psychopathic blood still boiling, threw her into the trunk of his mother's Bentley.

Anele wasn't aware of her body being thrown from side to side as the vehicle sped for miles along dirt roads. She would have tried to escape if she had had a clue that she would soon be "unloaded" at a "For Blacks Only" hospital about thirty miles from the estate. Or if she had known that a tidy sum of money had changed hands at the hospital. The director was more than pleased with the Hallworthy "donation."

Tubal ligation, surgical sterilization, was performed on Anele. Her fallopian tubes were burned so that sperm could no longer reach the fertile eggs that would continue to be released from her ovaries.

An hour after the surgery, Anele opened her eyes and looked around the unfamiliar setting. She cried out, "Where am I?"

The room was empty.

Just as she was about to call out again, an excruciating pain drew her knees up to her torso. She reached down and clutched her abdomen. Her bloodcurdling scream shattered the stillness of her room and brought a tall, dark man to her side. The surgeon's eyes were kind, but his words spoke a cruel truth: "Child. You are in a hospital."

"Why? What have you done to me? Why do I hurt so much?"

Anele's memory was on hold. She couldn't remember why or how she had arrived.

Dr. Buthelezi looked away from Anele's probing, pain-filled eyes. With his head lowered, he spoke to her. "Child, I'm not sure if you will understand what I am about to say, but I had little choice but to operate on you and surgically ..." He took a deep breath before finishing. "I'm afraid you will never bear another child."

It took a split second before the past events and current reality hit home. A tidal wave of sorrow drowned Anele's heart. She was sentenced to an infertile life for the unforgivable and irresponsible crime of having being born in a country that felt no pity. She crossed her hands over her heart and wept for what seemed forever. Still sniveling, the broken-hearted girl came to the realization that she would never see her daughter crawl, walk, or talk. She would not see her grow into a fine young woman, marry, and have children of her own.

Anele's heart-rending sobs pierced Buthelezi's heart. Some days he wished he had not chosen this profession. Other days he longed to be Caucasian instead of black. And still other days he wished he were dead. This was one of them.

He had to wonder if a *white* professional would have been so intimidated—so *bullied*—into performing Anele's cruel surgery. But what choice had he been given? Alan had threatened to kidnap his wife and children, to hold them captive until the surgery was done. "Do as you are told, kaffir," he had said, "or they will suffer! You have no idea what I'm capable of." Buthelezi did what he had to do—protect his loved ones above all others. Of course, his action was contradictory to the medical oath he had sworn. But unethical practices continued, with his involvement or without. That's how it was on the godforsaken Dark Continent, where skin color took precedence over every other consideration.

The surgeon clasped Anele's hand and spoke to her in a soft, placating voice. "Take my advice, child. If you wish to survive in this cruel world, you must learn to make the most of your life. You are young. Try to forget. Forgive the evil some men do, and move on."

Anele wanted to punch him in the mouth. His words were platitudes. Forgive the unforgivable? *Never!* If she'd had a gun, she would have shot them all: the doctor, Alan, his wife, his mother, and the snitch who had squealed on her. She would have gladly danced a jig atop each of their graves.

Two days later, Lord Alan turned up at the hospital to take his *ape* home. Still consumed by post-operative pain, Anele had a hard time climbing into the trunk of the Bentley. No black person was allowed to be seen in a white-owned vehicle. That's just how it was. Alan's loathsome, inhumane treatment of his servants was not about to diminish—not until hell froze over. Throughout his life, he would show no remorse.

When Anele was finally released from her moving dungeon and deposited in front of her modest shanty home, she grabbed Alan's arm with a fierce grip. "Master, where is my baby?" she asked tearfully. "You have taken away my woman's parts. You can't take her, too."

As if she was nothing but muck stuck to his boot, Alan roughly removed her grip and replied, "What baby? No baby was born here. That's all there is to it! Be back at work tomorrow morning sharp."

At that moment Anele longed to die. Her perseverance shattered, along with the hope she harbored for her baby. She couldn't handle adversity anymore. Yet she had to ask herself why Alan hadn't left her at the hospital, or, worse, killed her. Hadn't her twin sisters met their death at his hands?

The ghastly thought brought Anele to her knees. She pounded the dry earth and screamed, "Their death was my fault. Please forgive me. Come in spirit and tell me what to do, I beg of you."

On that ill-fated day four years ago, Anele and her sisters did not know they were about to meet the Devil himself: a dyed-in-the-wool racist who had no regard for people, though they breathed the same air he did. As if it were yesterday, Anele's mind swept back to the day she and her sisters had the misfortune to set foot on the unhallowed Hallworthy grounds.

 # Anele Dingane
Tswanas Kraal, February 1927

"The most common trait of all primitive people is a reverence for life-giving earth ..."
–Stewart Udall

Tswanas Kraal, a remote, black African settlement, sat in the province of Natal near its northern border with Swaziland and Mpumalanga. It was home to fifty-odd Nguni-speaking Zulus. The rural tribe lived a simple life just as they had done before the English and Dutch settlers inundated their homeland decades ago.

"Kraal," a Dutch word, is also used in African English to refer to an enclosure surrounded by a fence of thorn-bush branches, a mud wall, or other fencing, roughly circular in form. The Zulu tribes-people's primitive lives in Tswanas Kraal would be turned upside down before this day was done.

It was a blisteringly hot day in Zululand. A naked girl, tall and slim, her body wet with perspiration, emerged through the doorway of her family's hut which resembled an upside down basket. Her large, dark eyes, the color of ebony pearls, searched the enclosed compound. She huffed. Where were they? Her twin sisters, Thaka and Zhana, aged fifteen and measuring less than five feet tall, should have been at the fire pit already. It was one of their duties to collect firewood for the cook's campfire meals.

The attached-at-the-hip sisters were nowhere in sight.

Anele, age nine, released a disgruntled sigh. She wanted to tell them that she was feeling better—that the fever caused by the black widow spider bite had broken. She spotted Mercy, the village cook, scowling with her hands on her hips.

"Mercy," Anele shouted, "have you seen Thaka and Zhana?"

The robust, healthy woman in her fifties responded snappily. "No, I haven't, and I can't say I'm happy about it. I had to send another girl to collect wood so we can eat tonight."

The mere thought of food prompted Anele's next question. "What are you making? I'm hungry."

Mercy heaved a long sigh. "That's a good question. I'll make whatever is caught. And if I don't get firewood, no one will eat!"

Anele made an "ugh" face. She hoped it wasn't monkey meat again. This malodorous meal didn't sit well in her delicate stomach of late. However, she was old enough to understand that the recent drought had starved most of their crops and livestock, mainly the Nguni cattle, which were decorated with enormous horns and creamy coats spotted with fine rust speckles.

The daily task of providing food was left to the tribesmen and their sons. With their slingshots and spears in hand, they left the compound well before sunrise and made a four-and-a-half-mile trek to the protected game reserve. When they were lucky—when their presence was not detected by a patrolling warden—the village poachers targeted a dainty gazelle, gutted it on the spot, and hauled it back to the kraal on a reed stretcher. But lately, the patrols had been stepped up, so they hunted for whatever unfortunate creature happened to cross their path. So monkey meat was likely the menu of the day.

Little Anele headed for the dense shrubbery behind the circle of their mud-and-dung huts. Her hunger and her wonder at the whereabouts of her missing sisters had been replaced by the pressing need for a bathroom break. As she neared the latrine, a hole in the ground, her legs came to a grinding halt. She tilted her head, and her brows suddenly knotted. She heard soft-spoken voices coming from behind a tall, concealing clump of dry grass. Anele's frown deepened. There was no doubt in her mind. She could recognize those two voices a mile off. What were they doing hiding behind the grass? What were they whispering about? Why weren't they out doing their chores? What strange behavior, indeed.

Although Anele's curious nature favored barging in and demanding answers of her sisters, she instead patiently crouched down and strained her ears. Seconds later, she clamped a hand over her mouth. Were her ears playing tricks on her? She strained harder. No, they couldn't be! Were her diminutive sisters, Thaka and Zhana, *really* planning to *leave* home without a word to anyone? How could they? They knew the rules—an unmarried girl had to ask permission from her father to leave the village for *any* reason.

Their father, Naboto Dingane, was the chieftain of the village and a relative of King Dinuzulu and Queen Nobuntu, a former child slave on the Hallworthy estate during Lord Nigel's reign. Naboto was a stickler for tradition. He had made it clear on more than one occasion, "Until you marry, you will obey me in every way, or I'll take a stick to you."

Anele crept closer. She didn't want to miss a word.

Thaka asked, "What if the storyteller who visits our village has made up the tale of riches to be had in the big city for those of all skin colors?" Her sister answered, "Didn't you see the storyteller's fine clothes? It must be true. But I have to ask you, Thaka, how else are we going to get money to buy more cattle to replace our loss if we don't try?"

"Okay. Let's do it!" Thaka confirmed excitedly. "We will work hard and bring father lots of money to buy goats, cows, sunflower seeds, millet, and vegetables." She scratched her head before adding, "But sister, we don't know the way!"

"I have a rough idea where to go," Zhana commented. "I remember the storyteller drawing the way in the dirt for all to see." She lowered her eyes, hoping her sister wouldn't see the deception. She hadn't a clue.

"What if we get lost … or worse?" Thaka said with worry in her voice. "We could be eaten by a lion or leopard!"

Their ongoing to-and-fro jabbering was lost on Anele. Her mind raced like a thoroughbred until an idea popped into her mind. She too could help, could join them on their crusade. Without further ado she rushed into their hideout, causing the twins to jump upright.

"I heard everything," Anele blurted, her face flushed with excitement. "And I'm coming with you. I can work, too."

Zhana, the firstborn twin, her brows raised high and her cheeks flushed with annoyance, argued, "Don't be so bullheaded. You're far too young. We've heard from travelers passing through that the *umlungu*—the white-skinned tribe—only hire strong boys and older girls to work in their fields."

She turned and smiled mischievously at her twin. "We might even find husbands."

Identical and inseparable, the gods had not bestowed the twins with comely features likely to excite would-be suitors. They were not pretty or tall or slender like Anele. They were short, almost dwarf-like, with mottled facial skin and bellies swollen like watermelons. Despite their unattractive physical traits, suitors were available. But much to their father's annoyance, both girls balked at accepting conventional marriages. The twins were adamant. "We will not marry unless identical twin brothers come along."

The two girls were the only twins for miles!

The sisters now spoke in unison. "Little sister, we both agree you cannot come with us. You must stay and take care of our widowed father. He is much too sick to be left alone."

Chief Naboto, having taken to his bed—likely from a lack of nourishing food beyond his daily ration of monkey meat—was counting on his remaining three daughters. Five of his other daughters had already married and relocated to other villages. His only two sons had died from disease. He depended on the three sisters to care for him: bring him food, empty his urine pot, and fetch him beer made from the Marula tree fruit.

Although Anele was normally innocent and sweet, her bullheaded anger spoke volumes this day. Of course she loved her father. But why should she be the one to take care of him? Why did she always allow the headstrong twins to ruin her life?

Anele, now a spitfire, stamped her feet. "There are plenty of single and married women to see to father's needs. There is Matudia. Yes, she is the oldest woman in the village, but I've seen the way she looks at father with love-struck eyes. And then there is Mercy, the cook. She has been a widow for far too long. And I better tell you, Mercy is going to whip your hides."

Zhana, the temperamental one who demanded full attention, made an angry face. "Our father's private life has nothing to do with us. *You* must stay behind."

"Please, please, please, let me go with you," Anele pleaded.

"No."

Anele's eyes slanted. "I'll go and tell father," she threatened. "Then you'll be beaten and tied up like the goats."

Zhana lunged at Anele. With her hands on Anele's throat, she growled, "I'll see to it that you won't see another day if you dare tell father."

Thaka, the meeker of the two, came to the rescue. Softly, she said to her angry sister, "If I make her promise, I know she won't tell father."

Anele slumped to the ground. A pool of urine gathered at her feet. Shame, mixed with rage, brought on a rush of words. "I hate you, Zhana! I hate you, Thaka," she spat, rubbing her neck. "You're bad. I hope you *never* come back!"

Anele would regret those words to her dying day.

Before daybreak the next morning, with her naked upper body exposed to the rising sun, Anele stealthily followed the twins. After walking for what felt like hours, she slipped on a precarious, protruding rock and tumbled down an embankment. Her loud shrieks stopped the twins in their tracks. Zhana kicked the dirt like a bull ready to charge. "She's in for a beating!" she raged. "That stupid child has followed us!"

"No, sister," Thaka countered adamantly. "I won't let you beat her. I'm going back to see if she's all right."

Thaka found Anele sprawled in the dirt, her beaded grass skirt wrenched down to her ankles, her bare bottom exposed.

Thaka bent down and saw that Anele's injuries were only minor grazes to her forehead, knees, and elbows. Nothing serious, she concluded, except for their predicament. What should they do? Take Anele back? Thaka shook her head. Without having asked for Naboto's permission, that would be awkward. Their father would beat them *all*, for sure.

What concerned Thaka most was the real reason she did not want to go back—their father's undying hatred for the white race. He had voiced it often. "No child of mine will ever slave for white devils. I would rather starve first."

Naboto's raw hatred was more than justified.

When Naboto was thirty years old, he led his tribesmen into battle against the Voortrekkers—Dutch colonial settlers. The Zulu call to arms to fight the invaders was answered without question. Every able-bodied man and boy swore to defend his homeland. Each one marched from the kraal with their heads high. Tragically, the brave warriors were ambushed near a mangrove swamp, and the skirmish took its toll. They fought courageously, but, unfortunately, their *assegais,* native spears, were no match for the rifles of the usurpers riding horseback. The small band of village fighters found themselves trapped. One by one they dropped and were trampled by horses. Naboto was the last man standing, and he was shot in his right leg. As he fell sideways, another bullet struck his upper body. He crashed to the ground, bleeding profusely. Moments later, triumphant Dutchmen shot anyone who twitched. Naboto feigned death. He lay face down on the bloody ground and waited for them to leave. After a long period of anguished quiet, Naboto called out, "My brothers, speak to me. Are any of you alive?"

He received no answer.

Naboto called out again.

The breath of silence met his ears.

Was he the only survivor?

The injured Naboto had to think fast. He would join his fallen brothers in death if he did not escape the area. He was about to stand up when he saw them—many pairs of glowing eyes shining from jungle predators anxious to pounce on fresh kill. He used his spear as a crutch to help him rise, gritting his teeth through excruciating pain.

It seemed to take him forever to travel the short distance from where he had fallen to the dense undergrowth adjacent to the killing field. Thorns and branches attacked his flesh as his eyes scoured the area for a safe place to rest until daylight. Naboto reasoned that the night scavengers already had enough food. They would not be hungry enough to chase after him.

Naboto found a deep cavity in a decaying tree trunk. He packed his wounds with damp tree moss and hunkered down. Outside his resting place, the din of the scavengers grew louder, followed by the night-splitting roar of a dominant lioness summoning her pride. Naboto hung his head in sadness—and anger. The thought of his people being torn apart made him livid. He cried out for revenge. "Ikloba, Dark Spirit of the Invisible Kingdom, strike the *umlungu* from our land with your tongue of fire. Sweep them into the ocean with your breath. Bring disease to all those who have spilled the blood of our brave warriors."

At first light, Naboto repacked his wounds with river mud and headed home.

In the weeks that followed his safe return, and after the witch doctor had removed the two bullets, Naboto slowly recovered. But nothing could soothe his wounded spirit. He had imbibed all the terrors of war and lived. Thoughts of the massacre and the guilt of being its sole survivor tormented him for the rest of his life. Over the years, Naboto grew bitter. He obsessively hated every white-skinned person—and with good cause.

The late afternoon sun beat down like a copper mallet upon the bare heads of the three silent sisters walking single file. Lagging behind, Anele was deep in thought. Then with lightning speed she dashed to the front. She avoided eye contact with the mean twin, Zhana, as she apologized. "I'm sor*reeee*," she said in a melodic voice. "I'll watch where I'm going so I don't fall again. And if I do trip, you can leave me. I'm sure some animal will find me tasty."

Thaka smiled, but Zhana did not. The unsmiling twin simply urged, "We must keep going before we lose too much daylight."

Time is of the essence. But they would come to wish it wasn't!

It took the sisters five long days to reach the Valley of a Thousand Hills described by the storyteller. They had walked during the day and slept in the boughs of tall Mountain Karee trees at night. Having consumed their meager rations of dried monkey meat, their bodies suffered pangs of hunger and thirst. It was Thaka who spotted the fast-flowing irrigation ditch paralleling the rows of tall sugar cane plants. "Water, water!" she cried.

The girls drank until their stomachs rebelled. Then nature called. They squatted in the open, and emptied their overflowing bladders, but their release was cut short by deafening sounds. Now upright, their bodies stiffened and their ears cocked. What was that thunderous, fast-approaching noise? It sounded louder than village drums? Terrified, the twins stood like statues, but not Anele. She wasn't going to wait and see what it could be. She flung herself into the water ditch. Flat on her stomach, she clung to the mossy embankment as if her life depended on it.

Lord Alan, the twenty-one-year-old grandson of Nigel Hallworthy, rode atop a tall, seventeen-hands-high black stallion. Foamy saliva dripped from the horse's bit. The young man halted his steed within inches of the twins. With his jaw jutting, he yelled in a refined British accent, "Get off my property, *now!* If I catch you stealing sugar cane, I'll shoot you!"

Alan had a commanding presence. He was almost drunk with power.

Naturally, the twins couldn't understand what he was saying. But the white boy's tone and gestures didn't need translation. Fearful, the twins screamed at the top of their voices, "God of the Zulu people, help us!"

Out of sight, Anele just cupped her mouth. She was a mere girl and had never heard such a raw fear being raised to the heavens. Anele was too afraid to peek out from her hiding spot. Thoughts of her father and the friends she had left behind popped into her mind, but they could not help her or the twins out here. Oh, how she wished she had never heard her sisters whispering in the bush. Right now even a monkey stew was more desirable than the immediate unknown.

Kelingo, age sixteen, was working nearby in a cane field when he heard the ruckus. Many other workers lifted their heads but chose not to venture away from their work. But this was not the case of young Kelingo. From childhood he possessed a natural, highly curious nature. Dropping his hoe, he made his way toward Lord Alan to investigate. When the twins saw another black approaching, they spewed out their native tongue as if from a burst drainpipe. Kelingo would be their life preserver, or so they thought.

Kelingo had no problem understanding the twins' tongue, since most of the workers on the Hallworthy estate were of Zulu origin. But there would be a shocking discovery many years later that would place Kelingo in the very same kraal these girls escaped from.

Kelingo nodded to the twins and then turned to face their challenger. "Boss, they are not here to steal. I think they want to work."

Alan gave the girls a dead stare, his lynx eyes hidden behind sunglasses. He began to check them over as if inspecting cattle.

The twins stared up at the sun-bronzed, blond young man. He had pronounced, high cheekbones and a deceptively youthful appearance. But lurking behind his striking good looks was a malignant side—inherited evil, twisted DNA.

The brutal legacy of the Hallworthy line lived on in its new lord. *An apple does not fall far from the tree.*

Alan pointed with his riding crop, saying, "Okay. You girls follow me. I'll give you some hoes, and you can begin work."

His mouth opened wide in surprise when Anele's head popped up from the ditch.

Alan said to Kelingo, "I don't want the kid. Look at her. She's stick thin. She wouldn't last a day in the fields."

Kelingo translated.

Zhana gasped. Then in a wobbly voice she pleaded, "Please. My little sister may be thin, but she is as strong as a bull elephant ..."

Zhana was cut short by a jab in her ribs from a frightened Anele. "Sister, I want to go home. I'm scared of the white man."

Zhana stressed harshly, "You wanted to come with us, stupid girl!"

Anele stamped her foot and hissed, "If I were older, I'd slap you, Zhana."

"That's never going to happen, puny child," the twin countered.

Alan's laughter sounded like a hyena. The girls didn't know Alan was fluent in their language, and for the moment, he wasn't going to let on. He said to Kelingo in English, "Tell these ignorant bush girls that I'm in a good mood today. The skinny one can labor at the house, if my mother has work for her. If Mistress Ethel says no, then send her off. I don't want her hanging around here being useless. Is that clear?"

With his eyes cast downward, Kelingo simply said, "Yes, Boss."

Kelingo went over to Anele and placed a firm grip on her upper arm. "You have to come with me," he said.

"No, I won't," Anele shrieked, trying to unfasten his grip with her right hand.

Kelingo tightened his grasp.

The twins looked anxiously at their struggling sister until Zhana spoke up, "Where are you taking her, black brother?"

"To the master's house," was his curt reply.

Somehow Anele freed herself. She gripped her mean sister Zhana's hand with such ferocity that the twin cried out, "You're hurting me! Do as you are told for once. You wanted to help and so now's your chance. I should take a stick to you. Go and work in the white man's house so we all can earn money. Remember?"

The tender-hearted Thaka touched Anele's cheek. "Don't fret yourself, little sister. We will see you when our work is done."

Wise for her age, Anele's gut instinct told her otherwise. She gave Alan a hostile stare, then in a war-like stomp, marched toward his horse and boldly spat a glob of phlegm onto Alan's riding boot. Taking a deep breath, she made herself clear in a penetrating voice that could have scared wild animals. "Ugly, ugly white ... *umlungu!*" she bellowed. "You can't make me go where I don't want to go. I won't be separated from my sisters. I will work with them."

Alan's face grew as dark as a summer storm. Now was the time to let them know that he understood their language. He turned to address Kelingo, who stood silently to the right side of his steed. "This skinny insect has the nerve to spit and talk to me as an equal?" he roared in Zulu. "How shall I teach her a lesson, Kelingo? Should I whip her? Or blow her head off?"

Before Kelingo had a chance to respond, Anele grabbed hold of the dangling rein and began yanking the steed's head down. Then, with a balled fist, she punched the creature on the nose. The target of her wrath was less than happy. The Arabian thoroughbred snorted, reared, and bucked, nearly throwing off its rider. Alan, his jugular vein pulsating, quickly tightened his grip on the reins. "Whoa!" he commanded.

While calming his steed, Alan bawled at Anele, "Black bitch! I've a good mind to get down and knock the shit out of you. Or better still, shoot you."

Anele did not need a translation. "You hurt me, white man," she retorted, "and I'll run back home and fetch my father. He is a Zulu warrior. He will chop you up with his long *assegai*. You'll bleed like a pig from his spear."

With malicious intent Alan maneuvered his horse. Anele's little body was lifted off her feet. All eyes were on the flying girl, who hit the earth with a mighty thud. Back in his grandfather Nigel's time, a Shongweni girl her age had experienced comparable Hallworthy brutality.

Alan's cobalt-blue eyes glared murderously under his sunglasses. He dismounted as if he had all the time in the world and strolled over to the sprawled child. With his abdomen pulled in and his chest expanded with power, he raised his leather crop over his head and brought it down across her bare shoulders. Anele's shrieks of agony pierced the humid air. She tried to crawl away, but Alan's riding boot pinned her skinny frame down. In uncontrolled rage, he began whipping her.

With tears rolling down their cheeks, the twins dropped to their knees in painful, inescapable helplessness. The brutal flogging was nothing like what *their* father doled out for disobedience. It looked as if the young white man intended to beat Anele to death.

The braided whip gripped in Alan's hand continued to rain down, sending Anele's blood-curdling screams to the heavens. A flock of nesting sun birds joined in the din and then flew shrieking into the sky.

Thaka's gentle heart could take no more. The gentle twin rushed toward Alan, latched firmly onto his extended arm, and begged, "Please, *umlungu-man*, stop! She is only nine summers old and such a foolish child. She did not mean to harm you or your beast."

Alan's dark, thunderstorm face warped into a grim demonic scowl. He slapped his blood stained crop against one boot and glared at Thaka with a "how-dare-you-interrupt-me" look.

Thaka, who would not have said "boo" to a goose, snatched this brief interruption to reach down and, with a mighty shove, push Anele out of harm's way. Alan's next strike hit Anele's rescuer full in the face. Blood poured from Thaka's gashed cheek. Her screams scattered every living creature nearby. Her frantic, high-pitched screeching could be heard for miles.

Kelingo clenched his fists behind his back in powerless fury and focused his eyes on the ground. His facial muscles twitched as if the lash had cut into his own skin. He heard the whip crack again, but not a corresponding scream from Thaka. Instead, he perceived the accelerating sound of feet pounding the dry ground.

Running as fast as their short legs could allow, the twins sprinted toward the dense sugar cane fields where Kelingo had been working. To onlookers, they looked as if they matched the speed of cheetahs.

Hunger for freedom, they knew, hurt more than hunger for food.

Kelingo hung his head. He dreaded what would happen next, but it was inevitable. He had witnessed many a scene like this before—poor black folk who had stepped onto Hallworthy soil without permission.

He stood rigid and watched Alan gallop after the girls with one finger on the trigger of his rifle. Then, leveling his weapon, he aimed. A thunderous *boom* was followed by repeated *booms*!

A plume of smoke curled from the rifle's muzzle.

Thaka and Zhana lay dead, each one shot in the back of the head execution style.

Anele jumped to her feet. She had never heard gunfire before, yet her instincts told her it was bad. She would have run and met the same fate had it not been for Kelingo.

His arms stretched wide as he blocked his master's aim. He pushed the girl, who had blood trickling from her bare skin, behind his thin frame. "Please let her live," he begged Alan. "She is just an ignorant bush girl. If you let me, I'll take her to the house just like you asked."

In a chameleon switch, Alan smiled warmly, as if he had merely been out for an afternoon ride. "Be a good girl and go with Kelingo," he said to the quaking Anele. "Forget what has happened here and you'll be fine. Work hard for Mother and you'll be rewarded."

He addressed Kelingo. "After you have dropped the *ape* at the house, I want you to get your brother and clean up that mess over there," he said pointing backward.

Kelingo's questioning brows prompted Alan's retort. "I don't care! Bury them … burn them … whatever."

Alan scratched his chin. "On second thought, fling them down the old water well," he said dryly. "You know where it is, Kelingo."

Without a backward glance, the Devil's new playmate, a born killer, rode off.

High above the horseman and his racing stallion, a dark cloud streaked with red—a veil of blood—began to form.

With her shoulders sagging, chin drooping, and dusty feet dragging, Anele walked beside Kelingo away from the grisly scene. The grim words she spoke to her sisters at the kraal played heavily on her mind. *"I hope you never return,"* would torment her for the rest of her life.

In time, Anele would wish she had died along with her sisters.

When the Hallworthy cook heard the side door open, she stopped kneading the bread dough. She stared at the entering pair as if they were two-headed creatures. Cook wiped her hands on her apron before confronting Kelingo. "Why have you brought this filthy girl in here?"

"I was told to bring her here."

"And who told you?"

"Lord Hallworthy."

Cook squinted. "Tell me what happened."

Scene by bloody scene the field worker related the heinous events.

Cook sighed. She had known the horrible Hallworthy boy from birth. This was not the first time she had heard of his murderous ways. As the privileged son of a titled family, he got away with all of his crimes. He would *never* face charges. No one *dared* report him.

Back in the 1840s, a black solicitor named Kadir Yar'Adua had *dared* to confront Alan's grandfather, but he had failed. His legal action had led to the deaths of three innocent people. In those days, slaves were dispensable. They all had expiration dates stamped on them from the day they entered the Devil's domain.

These days were not much different.

At age thirty-five, Alan's father, Peter Hallworthy, who had been living in England, inherited the Hallworthy estate. His maternal grandparents were glad to see the back of him and his new bride, whom they detested. When the couple decided to move to South Africa, Peter's inlaws confided to a family friend, "They deserve each other. Both are sick in the head."

Alan was an only child, by his mother's choice. After a difficult birth, Lady Ethel vowed never to have another baby.

She kept that promise, remaining celibate until she died.

Ethel Hallworthy had no natural maternal feelings. She rarely saw her son, Alan, who stayed on the third floor in the same bedroom Nigel, the boy's grandfather, had occupied. When Alan started displaying dysfunctional behavior at age three, as had his father, she washed her hands of him. He was raised by black nannies during his developing years. His unfortunate caretakers were bitten, scratched, slapped, and kicked by him. And naturally, the little white boy's words were always believed by his parents.

"She hurt me, Mother."

"Nanny pushed me, Mother."

"She looked at my pee-pee, Mother."

But it was his sadistic cruelty to animals that turned even the most hardened of stomachs. Lady Ethel's toy poodle, its tongue missing, was found floating in the pond.

The family cat, eyes gouged, was found hanging in Alan's closet.

Pet rabbits were dismembered.

The apple doesn't fall far from the tree.

Even though Peter defended his son's behavioral problems, his wife had the last word. Alan was sent away to an expensive private boarding school. He had been there barely a week before his parents were summoned by the school authorities.

It seems the school, too, wanted to wash their hands of this malicious boy.

During his short enrollment at the school, the Hallworthy heir had repeatedly stabbed a white female teacher who had reprimanded him for disruptive behavior in the classroom.

He had stripped a fellow student and locked him in the bathroom.

He had thrown his food in the face of another student.

The school suspected that he was behind the massacre of their chickens. Each one's throat had been cut. In the end, a large amount of money exchanged hands. No charges or written reports were filed. After being expelled, Alan was homeschooled by a local tutor. The headstrong, disturbed boy refused to turn a tutorial page.

By the age of fourteen, the natural born sadist found his true passion. His father appointed him overseer of the Hallworthy plantation. Empowered and following in his grandfather's evil footsteps, Alan reigned supreme over the *apes* his grandfather Nigel had bequeathed to his father, Peter.

Alan's sadistic, psychopathic, power-hungry inheritance had played out with the twins and Anele in February 1927.

Cook sighed. How many poor souls were dotting this massive estate in unmarked graves? She looked around to make sure no one else was listening, then whispered to Kelingo, "He should be dragged through the field and flogged." Her eyes narrowed with fury as she added, "or worse."

Kelingo bobbed his head in agreement. He spoke with urgency when he said, "I had better return to the fields before *he* takes it upon himself to shoot *me*, as well."

Before Kelingo left, he had something to say to the sad-eyed child.

"I'm sorry that you had to go through all this, being so young and all. You will be safe with Cook here. You can trust her. She is one of us."

The traumatized girl didn't respond. She was floating in a silent, numb world of her own.

Cook's ample bosom rose up and down as she heaved a mighty sigh of resignation and regret. There was nothing she could say or do. There was *nothing* that could be done to make the hellish ordeal the child had undergone any better. But Cook could relate. Like her grandmother, who had labored as the estate's seamstress, Lamella, an indentured servant, had worked at the manor from the age of ten—without pay and against *her* will.

Lamella took Anele by the hand and led her through the servants' entrance to the outside washhouse a few feet away. The fieldstone building had sealed windows and a low, sloped roof. A steady plume of smoke from a crackling fire spiraled up through a brick chimney. In the far corner, a huge copper pot boiled on the hearth. The heat in the room was worse than any African summer Anele had ever known.

"This is where you will wash the dishes, pots, pans, and table linens," Cook said in Zulu. "You will also sleep in here until Lady Hallworthy says it's all right for you to share the shack with me. But first, it's time for your bath. You smell worse than the hog I butchered yesterday."

Cook lifted the heavy cauldron from the hearth, poured the boiling water into the plugged stone sink, and retrieved a bucket of cold water sitting near the doorway. Wordlessly, she removed Anele's sodden, blood-spattered grass skirt, lifted the feather-light child into the sink, and reached for a bar of carbolic soap. With a deep sigh, Cook returned the odorous object to its holder. *No. I can't put her through more pain,* Lamella thought. The soap had antiseptic properties, but the carbolic acid would sting the girl's raw whip wounds.

Anele winced when the jug of warm water cascaded over her back, but she did not utter a word.

"You are a brave child," Cook commented. "In time your wounds will heal, but not your memory of this awful day."

Anele remained silent.

After the cleansing, Cook scratched her head. What could she put on the child? "Ah, I have just the thing," she muttered. She went to a large laundry hamper and rummaged through it, finally extracting a garment. She guessed it would be far too big for the girl, but the discarded cotton petticoat that had belonged to Lady Ethel was better than nothing. When she put it on Anele, it hung like a drape past the girl's feet. Under better circumstances, Cook would have laughed. Instead, she nudged the child and pointed, saying, "Sit there on that stool."

Anele did as she was told.

Then, with a wordless don't-you-dare-move-a-muscle glance, Cook said, "I'll be back in a moment."

Cook slid the bolt that locked the wooden door.

On the second floor of the manor house, the kitchen servant found Lady Ethel tending to an array of flowering potted plants. A look of displeasure darkened Ethel's pasty face. She slapped her cook across the face and spat, "How dare you come here without my permission!"

Her cheek smarting, the servant rushed to explain. "Mistress,

I'm here because something terrible has happened."

Lamella related the graphic details.

The poker-faced Lady Ethel simply retorted, "Where is the child now?"

"I've locked her in the washhouse, Lady Hallworthy."

"Keep her there until I've had a word with my son."

Ethel beckoned with a wave of her hand. "Follow me."

From a writing desk in an adjacent room, Ethel removed an indentured work contract and backdated it by a month. "Have the child place her mark here and bring it back to me," Lady Ethel ordered. "It will prove that she could not have been anywhere near the fields when all this happened. I'm not going to be concerned with this *problem*. No one has ever come here inquiring about missing black relatives." Her eyes seemed to bore through Cook. "And if you know what's good for you, don't breathe a word of this to anyone."

The indentured contract that Lamella grasped in her hand stated that Anele would work for the Hallworthy plantation until such time as her owner saw fit to release her. Food and lodging would be provided. Food would be nothing more than table scraps, and lodging meant a cold dirt floor in the washroom.

The cook's heart grew heavy as she approached the washroom with the contract. The sound of mournful weeping was more than her tender heart could bear. "Don't cry, child," she said, taking the girl in her embrace. "I'm going to take care of you. I won't let any more hurt come to you."

Although heartfelt at the time, it would be a promise Cook could not keep.

In the pain-melting warmth of Cook's embrace, Anele's voice murmured softly, "I want to go home to Tswanas."

"Oh, sweet child, you can't."

"You can find the way to my village, old woman."

"Not so much old! And even if I did know where you lived, I couldn't take you."

"Why?"

"Because, child, many have tried and failed." Cook shook her head. "We would end up like your sisters or left hanging on a tree. So let's have no more about running away!"

In order to turn the conversation to a more pleasant subject, Cook said, "You must be hungry. How would you fancy a nice warm bowl of vegetable soup and a glass of fresh goat's milk?"

"No."

"It will do you good to eat, even a little."

"No."

"Child, when did you eat last?"

Anele remained tight-lipped.

Cook sighed as she removed the document from her apron pocket. Guided by Cook's hand, Anele hesitatingly placed her mark on the dotted line. The indentured Hallworthy servant let out another deep sigh, folded the work contract, and put it back into her pocket. She patted Anele on the shoulder. "There are some old sheets in the corner," she indicated. "Lay them on the floor and get some sleep. I'll look in on you later."

Lamella left Anele in the sealed room while she busied herself in the kitchen. An extra pair of hands would be welcome. She was behind schedule for this evening's meal. When she finally completed the cooking, washing up, and cleaning, it was past ten o'clock at night.

Before departing for her hovel, Cook poured a glass of milk and filled a bowl with vegetable soup for Anele—leftovers from what was served earlier.

She found the girl curled up in the straw-lined laundry basket. "Ah, poor child," she murmured. She placed the soup and milk nearby, just in case the girl woke up and was hungry enough to swallow her anger and pride.

Lamella returned to her workplace at five the next morning, unlocked the washhouse door, stepped in, and scratched her chin. She noted the empty glass standing in the middle of the floor, but she saw no sign of the child. Where was she? She couldn't have gotten out; the windows were sealed and the door was bolted fast. Anele, hiding behind the open door, innocently pounced upon Lamella and pinched her generous behind. Cook let out a shriek. She grabbed Anele's shoulder and scolded, "Child, you nearly scared me half to death! It seems you are rested and ready for work. It will take some of that silly energy out of you."

Anele's long workday began inside the washhouse. She also started work at five in the morning and slaved in the merciless heat until late at night. Because Lady Ethel had not yet given permission for Anele, a manor prisoner, to join Lamella in the servant's shanty, Anele slept on the floor of her workplace.

Anele was no stranger to hard work or harsh conditions. As a young child she had worked with her sisters and other women of Tswanas in the cornfields. Traipsing to and from the manor's kitchen with heavy trays of dishes, pots, and pans was a challenge for a nine-year-old, but it was the washing and starching of table linens by hand that she hated most. The gooey starch stuck to her fingers, and the smell caused her to sneeze constantly. But Anele was not one to grumble.

Hard work helped stem the tide of anger that threatened her relentlessly. Although not a day passed that Anele didn't miss her father, sisters, and village life, she endured the hardships of indenture.

Several months passed.

Her life went on.

On a windy fall morning several months later, Anele's mentor and friend, Lamella, set her to work washing the breakfast dishes in the newly installed scullery off the kitchen. Anele was happy she did not have to go outside to the old washhouse. With only a cold-water faucet in the new scullery, water for cooking and washing had to be boiled. It was Anele's job to make sure the kettle on the kitchen range was always hot. On this particular day, Lamella was rubbing lard over a leg of lamb when, out of the blue, a stabbing pain rippled through her chest and took her breath away. She sat down and waited for the discomfort to subside. She assumed her distress was the result of excessive and prolonged pipe smoking. Smoking was how Lamella chose to momentarily "forget" her circumstances. Every moment she could, she filled her clay pipe with the tobacco she grew outside the shack and enjoyed a smoke.

As soon as Anele stepped through the door after hanging laundry outside, Lamella called her over. "Child, Cook doesn't feel so well. Would you like to help me?"

"What is it you want me to do?" Anele responded helpfully. Even though she loved the old woman who had taken her under her wing, you could see on Anele's sour face that she hated every moment she spent in the whites' world slaving for them.

"Sweet, sweet child," Lamella said, "I know that you are not happy to be here, but I am blessed to have you in my life. I'd like you to place the potato pan on the stove and fill it with cold water. When it begins to boil, add a spoon of salt and the washed and peeled sweet potatoes."

Lamella gestured with her finger. "There, in the bucket. Can you do that?"

Anele gave an "of course" nod.

The water-filled pot weighed more than Anele, yet somehow she found the strength to lift it to the back plate of the coal-burning range and add the potatoes without disturbing the now dozing cook. A few moments later, Anele prodded a potato and frowned. She didn't want to wake Cook, but she was unsure of what to do, so she tapped the woman's shoulder. Lamella bolted upright. "What is it? How long have I been asleep?"

"Not long. I don't know when they are done."

Lamella's eyes twinkled with mirth. "The knife should slip easily through the potato."

Anele rushed over to the stove and stabbed one. "No," she said, "the knife sticks."

Cook clicked her tongue and laughed, "Silly, ignorant girl! You have a lot of learning to do."

Sometime later Anele tried again. Unable to contain a surge of victory, she shouted, "They're done! They are definitely done!"

The chef's face—as broad, plain, and dark as the bottom of a burnt pie pan—broke into a grin before she said, "I'm coming."

Lamella was making her way to Anele, who was waiting at the stove, when she heard behind her the swishing sound of taffeta material and smelled the strong odor of Lily of the Valley cologne. Lady Ethel strutted like a peacock into the kitchen. Above her long, shiny skirt was a frilly-white-lace and chiffon blouse decorated with dainty pearl buttons. The garment looked uncomfortably tight, as if it would strangle the large woman should she attempt a deep breath. An oval diamond brooch reflected the colors of her blue and green skirt.

With her mouth agape, Anele stared at the tightly corseted figure whose constricted waistline looked deformed. She did not know whether to laugh at the outrageous attire or be frightened because, as soon as the woman entered the kitchen, Cook's cheerful face stiffened like a starched shirt collar.

Lady Ethel glanced at her cook and then glared at Anele, who was standing by the stove rigidly holding a wooden spoon that was pointed upward. Ethel's eyes were large and her expression demonic when she shrieked, "Go to the scullery, you filthy savage! Since when did I give *you* permission to cook *our* food? God knows *what* is under your filthy fingernails!" Her heavily rouged cheeks reddened even more as she turned on her cook. "Lamella, you of all people should know better than to let this heathen near my stove!"

In the short period Anele had been at the manor, she had been able to grasp quite a bit of English. Stepping boldly forward with hands defiantly on her hips, she spat back, "Don't shout at Cook! She is sick today. I am helping her. That's all."

Lady Ethel's eyes took on an evil glint that could have opened the gates of Hell.

She marched over to the range, raised the pan to chest level, and, with a mighty swing, flung the contents at Anele. The terrified girl tried to duck, but it was too late. The scalding water struck her with such force, it sent her reeling backwards. The back of her head struck a metal bin used for discarded vegetable peelings. The mistress of the house stood over the scalded child as if she were a game trophy. "That will teach you to be flippant," Lady Ethel ranted. "You will show me respect, girl, or I will fetch my son, whom you know well enough by now. He will skin you alive if I tell him you had the cheek to talk back to me." Snapping her mouth shut, Lady Ethel turned on her heels. Her pointed, ankle-laced boots thudded out of the lower level kitchen.

All of the color faded from Anele's face. White as a sheet and unaware of how serious her third-degree burns were, she placed a hand on her scalded neck. When she withdrew her hand and noticed the tiny piece of pink skin stuck to her palm, she screamed, "Namandla, God of the Zulus, please help me! I'm dying!"

In this household there would be no skin grafting to treat Anele's severe burns. After all, she was nothing more than an injured *ape*!

Lamella, her shoulders drooping, had been standing in a fog of grief throughout the entire ghastly event. When the fog lifted, her dazed mind tried to unwrap what had occurred. Her senses were awakened by penetrating screams coming from her helper.

Lamella rushed to the sink, ran cold water, and then knelt beside the wailing child. Dipping the corner of a rag into the bowl of water, she gently placed it on the girl's burned neck. Anele let out a scream that reverberated like boomeranging Ping-Pong balls hitting brick walls. Cook's good intention had caused the ice-cold water to seep onto Anele's scalded left nipple, which was smarting as if from a painful sunburn.

Anele took a deep breath and then innocently remarked, "Cook, I think the bad, ugly white woman has blistered my womanhood."

"Whatever do you mean?"

Anele's pain-filled eyes guided Lamella's. Anele pointed to her chest, saying," Look at my breast. It is thick with burned skin. How will I be able to give milk to my children when the time comes?" She closed her crying eyes and then hugged herself.

Lamella's tears flowed like buckets of rainwater. "Oh, it's my fault," she whispered, "I should never have asked you to do my work. Take your arms away so I can get a closer look."

"No." the defiant Anele retorted.

The girl rose unsteadily from the floor. Her only thought was to flee from this horrible place. But first she had to stop the unbearable pain. She rushed outside. With her eyes darting frantically, she found a fishpond not far from the manor's washhouse. She raced toward it, slid down a steep embankment, and flung herself into the water. Thank goodness it wasn't too deep because she couldn't swim. The cold water first stung and then soothed Anele's burned flesh, but not her anger. Her hate-filled heart was bursting with a blaze no amount of cold could extinguish.

Still immersed in water up to her neck, a shudder worse than any she had known sent shivers down her spine. Anele knew that she would never feel safe again. She told herself that she must get as far away from this dreadful place as possible. She must! Could she remember the path she took to get here? She doubted it. Her home was in the heartland of the Zulu kingdom and might as well have been at the end of the earth. Without someone to guide her, she knew she could never find her way home. But she made a promise to herself—she wasn't going to give up trying.

While tiny goldfish swam around Anele's scalded body, she sobbed into her hands. She tried to make sense of her life so far. She wanted to blame the twins. But deep down, she knew that she alone was to blame. Had she stayed home and not attached herself to her runaway sisters, none of this would have happened.

A large bullfrog hopped onto a lily pad and snatched a hovering insect. It eyed the person invading its feeding ground before it disappeared into the murky water. Anele never saw the amphibian, but she did see the image of her father's face during one of his passionate "I-hate-the-white-skinned" tirades. Anele had never understood his wrath ... until now. She felt an eerie chill creep over her, and her angry heart spoke. "My father is right. All *umlungu* must be fathered by evil spirits."

Demonic possession, malevolent preternatural beings, had inhabited the bodies of the Hallworthy clan for generations. These dark entities would continue to rule supreme on the unhallowed Hallworthy grounds until an illegitimate descendant not guilty of Hallworthy transgressions would send them back to hell, where they belonged.

In the meantime, Anele would be forced to exchange her adolescent years for a life of adult slave labor.

Human beings take no note of time but from its loss.

 Present Day, December 25, 1945

"My painful past is a nightmare from which I am trying to awake."
–Anonymous

On this festive Christmas day the twinkling stars looked like billions of tiny eyes mocking her and telling her that she, alone, was responsible for her entrapment. Why had she been so stubborn? Why had she been such a willing victim?

Ah, if only ...

Anele ran a chapped hand across her disfigured, chocolate-brown face. It was hard to imagine that she used to be a stunning African beauty. Even though she was only in her late twenties, the ravages she had suffered during these long years on the Hallworthy estate had forever destroyed the spirited child she once had been. She had aged a lifetime. Since shortly after her enslavement at a young age, she had carried pink scars and welts, the result of a Hallworthy punishment. Her burn marks were not a pleasant sight, but other factors played a role in her unattractiveness, as well. Gum disease had reduced her even, white teeth to broken stumps. Premature, snow-white threads streaked her bushy black hair. And she carried more pounds than her tall frame was comfortable with thanks to the manor's starchy, leftover European food.

The most unbearable thought, though, was that, like all African maidens, she had longed for a traditional Zulu wedding, a good and hard-working husband, and, of course, many children. The dream of one day snuggling her own little ones on her lap was long gone.

After Anele had been collected from the hospital, eighteen long years ago, and unceremoniously dropped off at the shanty, Alan had yelled from the car window before speeding off, "Don't go stirring up trouble, Anele. Your baby is gone." As he wagged his finger from side to side, he said, "If you know what's good for you, you will keep your mouth shut." He added commandingly, "I'm giving you the day off, but you'd better be back at work on Monday."

Anele had wanted to spit in his face. She had hoped with all her heart that his car would crash into the nearest tree and kill him dead.

Anele stood staring into space for the longest time before she realized the stark truth. She was only half a woman—forever childless. But what brought on her worried frown was this question: *Would he continue to rape me*? She no longer had a big belly to get in the way of his forceful lust.

Thank the gods, her question was answered.

The day after Anele returned to work, she learned from Cook (who didn't miss a word of gossip) that Alan's lust had been diverted to a younger girl who had recently come to the plantation looking for work. Although Anele would no longer suffer the physical torture, the psychological torment continued. *Wog, nigger, black whore, bitch,* and *bloody ape,* were among the crude obscenities Alan constantly hurled at Anele when their paths crossed.

Life went on.

One sunny summer day a year later, Anele heard a rumor that caused her heart to jump for joy. Could it be? Could her baby girl be alive? Not dead, as she had suspected? The idea sounded too good to be true. But the young sugar-cane cutter (Alan's latest victim) was adamant. "Honest, Anele, as the God Namandla is my witness,

I saw it with my own eyes. The old white woman from the big house handed your baby to the Nigerian priest's wife."

"What priest?"

"Father Batuzi."

"Father Batuzi! He's a Catholic priest! They don't marry! " Even though Anele had refused to attend the white god's teachings, she was aware they were held once a month on the plantation and led by the Father.

"He *does* have a wife," the fieldworker argued. "I met her at Bible class last week. Her name is Nyasha, and she's from Nigeria."

Anele scratched her head. "How do you know the baby was mine?"

"No one else birthed that day, Anele. You were the only one."

While her heart performed somersaults, Anele ran as fast as her legs could carry her to the makeshift church at the edge of a banana field only to learn from the priest's helper that Father Batuzi and Nyasha had left two days earlier for Nairobi. Anele threw herself onto the dirt in front of the abandoned home, and cried, "I will never forget you, my child. If it takes me the rest of my life, I *will* find you, daughter."

Even in this merciless world of hate, racism, and inhumanity, hope is often planted in the dark. When dawn arrives, miracles begin to grow.

From that moment on Anele's deep wounds continued to tear her apart. She felt painfully alone with her thoughts. In those dark hours, Cook increased her wretchedness by telling her, "Whether you like it or not, *he* owns you. If you wish to survive, to tell your tale to someone who will listen—and that's a fat chance—you have no choice but to accept your lot."

Anele had persevered. She had tried to get on with her "lot," tried to be jolly. Smiles and laughter didn't come easily to her in her oppressive, white-dominated world. How could she ask her "owners" to back off? She was just an *ape*.

Now, on this Christmas morning in 1945, Anele's throat tightened with so much bitterness she could not swallow. *Why*, she beseeched from the roots of her soul, *did the Gardeners of Life plant my seed if my life has no purpose?* For her, "life" meant nothing more than survival—or self-destruction. What could she do to make all the hurt go away? Would her pleas to her god make an iota of difference to her plight? Would He even hear her? Did He even give a damn? She decided to give Him one more chance.

She prayed silently: *"Namandla, Zulu God of the Invisible Kingdom of Spirits. I beg you to take this yoke off my neck. This isn't living. I'd rather be dead."*

Unlike the incandescent, starlit heavens, Anele's brown eyes held no sparkle. She tried to repress past thoughts, but could not. She felt tears roll down her face and into her ears. Sorrows marching in battalions infested her, not allowing her any respite. She focused on yesterday evening, Christmas Eve. The scene had been surreal.

It was 7 P.M. sharp when the bell above the door leading into the mansion's brick basement rang several times. It was time to serve the specially prepared meal to thirty-nine-year-old Lord Alan Percival and his wife, Corrie (South African born of Dutch parents), eight years his senior.

The menu began with cream of tomato soup, roast chicken, roasted new potatoes laced with fresh mint leaves, cinnamon-glazed baby carrots, and Brussel sprouts cooked in lemon juice. Dessert was a traditional English trifle made from thick custard, diced fresh fruit, sponge fingers laced with Sherry, and topped with fresh whipped cream.

Anele, dressed in a crisp uniform, stood to the side of the long walnut table and awaited further instruction. Without looking up, Lady Corrie raised her hand and said, "You can leave now. I will dish up. I'll ring when we are done."

With her head lowered, Anele turned on her heels. She shook her head from side to side. Never did a "thank you" or "this meal looks delicious" ever pass the mistress's lips. That's how it was. That's how it would always be. *All upper-class white people are gratitude-challenged*, she thought. *But just once, wouldn't it be a joy to be appreciated?* That was never going to happen in this house.

Anele went downstairs to supervise the younger kitchen staff: fourteen-year-old Maekela, a slender cheerful teenager with curly black hair, gleaming brown eyes and a mischievous grin. Her younger sibling Isona was the opposite. She was short, rotund, and sullen. Never a smile creased her lips.

In Anele's absence, the girls had been instructed to scrub clean the pearl-grey enamel pots, wipe the counters, and mop the kitchen floor, just like she had done in years past.

The teenagers were hard at work, busy drying pots and pans in the whitewashed scullery, which housed two deep stone sinks. Behind them sat a recently purchased gasoline-powered washing machine, which had brought some happiness to Anele's dreary life. No more washing and wringing by hand. Next to that labor-saving device was a treadle sewing machine in a walnut frame. This was Anele's only worldly possession. She had no idea that before the day was done, this contraption would open the gates of hell.

While her helpers did their chores, Anele took the opportunity to rest her aching back. She eased her ample derriere into a wooden rocker. A grimace pinched her face as she undid the laces of her undersized plastic shoes and released her sockless swollen feet. Oh, how she had wanted to fling those shoes into the garbage can along with her outdated servant's garb: a black A-line dress with long sleeves and lace cuffs, a white cotton apron, and a mop cap—impractical clothing that proved unbearable in the heat both outside and inside the kitchen, where temperatures often reached over 100 degrees. But the lady of the manor, Corrie, had made it clear: she was not going to spend a penny on lighter uniforms. "You'll wear what I tell you to wear," were her final words.

As the manor's ancient floorboards creaked beneath the rocker, Anele cupped her chin in her hands and wondered why she had been waiting so long to confront her mistress about her overdue wages. She didn't know what to do. Should she dare go up to Lady Corrie's private quarters, the forbidden place? Anele shuddered as she recalled what her predecessor, Lamella, had once told her: "Whatever you do, *don't*," she stressed, "*don't* venture upstairs to their quarters or you'll be taught a lesson the hard way." Lamella had sighed deeply before she continued. "The day you arrived here, Lady Hallworthy screamed at me for disobeying the rules. She then slapped me hard across my face several times. I never went up there again."

From a bevy of housemaids over the years Anele had also learned that Alan and Corrie had separate bedrooms, living rooms, and libraries. It was certain there was no love lost between this husband and wife. Anele had witnessed them hurl hundreds of angry tirades at each other across the dinner table.

As Christmas Eve darkness descended outside the manor, Anele grew jittery with angst. She rocked faster, causing the floorboards to groan in protest. She didn't give a hoot about her obnoxious employers or their dysfunctional marriage. She wanted only what was hers. A contemptuous smile pulled her lips upward. If she thought she could get away with it, she'd murder them in their sleep. Or better yet—the picture forming in her mind brought on a sardonic grin—poison their food. That premeditative possibility of a crime wasn't far from the making.

The bell was ringing. The meal had ended. It was time to clear the table.

Anele jumped to her feet. She slipped her shoes back on and called out, "Maekela and Isona. Stop what you are doing! Get the clearing trays and follow me."

In the second-floor, wood-panelled dining room, the twenty-foot banquet table stood abandoned, except for the clutter of dinner plates, side plates, tureens, sterling silver cutlery, and crystal champagne flutes. Only the finest dinnerware, accompanied by hand-sewn linen tablecloths and napkins, was used for every meal. The extravagance and the upstairs location of the dining room—instead of it setting, sensibly, closer to the kitchen—had baffled Anele for years. Repeatedly traipsing up and down a long, grand staircase with serving trays was exhausting for all of the help. The dumbwaiter had been out of service for umpteen years. They couldn't be having money problems, could they? That last thought prompted her to caution her helpers. "Be extra careful. Don't drop a thing or the lady will have a fit, and you won't see any wages for years."

Upstairs, Maekela's impish eyes twinkled with mischief. She bent her knees in a mock curtsy and responded to Anele, mimicking a posh English voice. "Yes, my lady. You tell us this every day, and we haven't broken a dish yet."

"Cheeky monkey," Anele laughed. She watched the girls place trays of dirty dishes and uneaten food on their heads. After they exited the dining room, Anele set about doing a task that her mistress insisted be performed after every mealtime, polishing and buffing the table. After this back-breaking chore was done, Anele placed the final touch on the center of the table—a huge crystal vase filled with fresh flowers. Tonight it was a colorful display of bird of paradise.

The weary cook gave the room a final look before she flicked off the light switch.

Downstairs, Maekela was at the sink up to her elbows in soapsuds. Isona was rinsing dishes. Anele leaned against the old doorframe and watched them. What should she do? Have them finish off their chores or send them off to bed? After a few seconds of contemplation she made up her mind. Yes. It would be wiser to send them off. If something went wrong ... Anele inhaled sharply. She didn't want to think of the possibilities.

Anele had been taking care of the two orphaned girls for over a year. Her protective, maternal love for them would not allow her to expose them to anything dangerous. She almost felt as if the girls were hers, replacements for her childless heart. She approached Maekela. Removing the scrubber from the older girl's hand, Anele said, "Leave that. Take your sister and go to bed. We have to be up at four in the morning to get the Christmas food underway."

Anele's request drew a deep frown from Maekela. "Is something the matter, Anele?"

"No. Of course not," Anele replied glibly. "And since when do you question my orders? Now, run along, you two." Playfully, Anele slapped Maekela's backside and added, "Get going before I change my mind and find something else for you to do."

With joyful hops and skips the girls threw their aprons into the laundry hamper, kissed Anele on her uninjured cheek, and danced out through a side door into the dark of night, beginning the long trek back to their shack. They didn't need an oil lamp to guide them. They could walk the well-trodden trail blindfolded.

Standing in the middle of the kitchen, Anele glanced up. The clock struck nine. Was it too late? No. She didn't think so. The owners' upstairs lights were usually seen blazing until after midnight. Anele hoped this night wasn't going to be an exception. And yes, the risk was worth it. She put on a clean apron and said softly to herself, "It's now or never."

Anele climbed the imposing, unending staircase. When she reached the top floor, she was in a part of the house that was unfamiliar to her. She had no clue which rooms were which. Her heart stopped. Lord Alan was the last person she wished to encounter on this night or any other night. He was a monster of the worst kind. The thought of bumping into him sent a rush of shivers down her spine. Her impulsive bravery threatened to give way. She wanted to turn on her heels, but she couldn't move. Her legs had turned to cement blocks.

You have to do it, her inner voice urged. *You know you deserve the money. They owe it to you.* Without her due, she wouldn't be able pay the white store owner for the secondhand sewing machine he had sold her almost two years ago. He had given her until Boxing Day to come up with the money. "Not a day longer," he had said. "I'll not give you another chance to pay your debt."

Now Anele could kick herself. How she wished she hadn't placed her mark on the buyer's agreement, which had been witnessed by her master. This long-term debt commitment—ten years—not only kept her legally chained, it also forced her to beg for her pittance of a wage from Lady Corrie, who was a force to be reckoned with in any circumstance.

Wilhelmina Corrie van Hoof was born in Cape Town in 1898. She was the second child of Dutch colonists, Wilhelmina and Ambroos van Hoof. Her father was a wealthy diamond dealer. To say the least, she was an ugly baby; she had nothing like the porcelain features of her older sister. At birth Corrie's head was large, almost misshapen. Her nose was bulbous, almost Negroid. And her lips were paper thin. Nevertheless, she did have an unusual asset: exquisite irises that resembled shiny purple grapes. Her intelligence was also in her favor. Over the years she had completed secondary school and attended a Natal university, where she studied economics. After she graduated from college, she became a forceful personality who spoke and acted her mind when the need arose.

Corrie had no real friends. Boyfriends? Non-existent! That is until the day an eligible young man knocked on their door. It was her mother, Mrs. Wilhelmina van Hoof, not Corrie, who was thrilled and relieved by the caller. Corrie's father was not as enthusiastic. He knew what fueled young Alan Hallworthy's interest in his unattractive daughter. It was common knowledge that the Hallworthy Estate was in serious financial crisis. Lord Peter, Alan's father, a chronic alcoholic, had frittered away the family's wealth by gambling. It was his wife, Lady Ethel, who set in motion the scurrilous plan to hold on to the estate. Alan was her sacrificial lamb. But Ethel Hallworthy wasn't the only crooked player. Corrie's mother was a step ahead of her. If Corrie's ample dowry served as bait to hook a suitable husband and spare the family the shame of spinsterhood, then so be it.

Naturally, Alan had stomped and raged at the suggestion of marriage to Corrie. "Never in a million years!" His father had begged him to be reasonable for all their sakes. And his mother had given him little choice. She had plenty of "dirt" on her son, enough to put him behind bars for an eternity.

Alan had made a face of utter disgust when he heard about the arrangement; nevertheless, he agreed to court and wed the unappealing heiress. He did it for his father, whom he was fond of. Alan was devastated when in 1926, shortly after shaking his father's hand in a loyal commitment to honor the deal, the penniless Lord Peter died of congestive heart failure. For as long as he lived, Alan never forgave his mother.

Alan kept his promise to his father but vowed that the marriage would be in name only. No real man would sleep with Corrie without first getting blind drunk. Yet drunkenness did find its way to Corrie's frame on occasion. She didn't complain when it happened, but, thankfully, never conceived a demon heir.

Like Roquefort cheese, Alan and Corrie's mutual hatred was well aged by time and circumstance. It reeked of their foul tempers and sadistic temperaments. Alan found he could not easily cut their legal shackles. Corrie had insisted on joint ownership of the estate, contingent upon settling considerable restoration costs. There would be no divorce, she'd insisted. And she took it upon herself to run the financial and operational management of the estate's affairs.

With an iron will and a tight fist Corrie governed the manor house and newly built sugar refinery while her husband supervised the day-to-day running of the sugar plantation. Corrie had informed her household staff, "From this day forward you will be compensated for your services." But her words had been hollow.

Under Corrie's brutal control, household servants were worked for food and lodging only. Eventually, they were paid a trivial wage. Anele's pay was five shillings a month (about one dollar in today's currency). But even that amount became an empty promise. Lady Corrie held the staff's wages "in trust," which kept them in bondage. If her indentured servants ever decided to leave, they would be penniless. Where could they go with no money in their pockets? They could not afford travel, food, or accommodation. Nor could they seek employment elsewhere. Nothing had changed since the legal slave-trade days. No *black* on the estate was a free soul. That's how it was under Corrie's reign. And that's how it would continue to be well into the future. White-skinned folk had relentless, heartless control over their *primates.*

But Anele was a testimony to the human spirit. With her stomach as tight as a sailor's knot, she approached the glow emanating from the bottom of a dark, oak-framed door. Taking a gamble, she knocked gently three times, praying it was Corrie's door.

"Come in, Alan," a strong voice answered. "The door is unlocked."

Relieved to hear Corrie's voice, not Alan's, Anele walked shakily into the room and stopped mid-step on Corrie's blue, wool rug. She clasped her nose to hold back a sneeze threatening to escape. The room smelled of old things. When Anele looked around, she saw a sitting room cluttered wall-to-wall with Victorian objects. Several tripod tables were adorned with porcelain figurines set on hand-crocheted doilies. Two large, brocade Chesterfield sofas were well placed, and a walnut, long-case grandfather clock mournfully kept time. In the center of the room was an Adams marble fireplace flanked by aspidistras in large brass pots. The only modern acquisitions Anele noticed were an electric phonograph, playing an RCA Victor recording of Jeanette MacDonald's *Smoke Gets in Your Eyes,* and a black cradle telephone resting on a rosewood occasional table.

Anele winced when her eyes connected with Corrie's. The Lady, wearing a green housedress, was reclining in an oversized armchair. A cloud of cigarette smoke spiraled above her head. She sported a fashionable 1940's Veronica Lake hairdo. A curled lock of henna-dyed hair dangled over an eye. Corrie had not changed from ugly duckling to swan. She was pockmarked from a bout of adult chickenpox, and at five-foot-four in stocking feet, her body overflowed like bread dough that had risen too high and needed pummeling.

Lady Corrie glared angrily at her servant, who instinctively stared at her feet. An eerie silence filled the air. Fingernails tapping on the side table punctured the hush. Anele felt her legs tremble. She feared they would give out at any moment.

Lady Corrie stubbed out her cigarette before straightening her back. Then, in a flash, her heavy-set frame sprang from the chair. Face-to-face with her servant, she shrieked, "How *dare* you, Anele! You have been here long enough to know the rules. You are *never* to come upstairs to my quarters."

Anele could not keep her nose from twitching. The overbearing odor of Gardenia cold cream wafted up unpleasantly to her nostrils, threatening to make her sneeze. Instead, with her mouth as dry as cinder, she stammered, "I'm s-s-sorry to disturb you, Mistress. I know I sh-shouldn't be up here, but ... c-could, c-could I please have my wages tonight? You see, the man I bought my sewing machine from is hounding me ..."

"Ouch!" Anele cried. Her shoulder hurt from the violent jab. Was a slap across the face to follow?

Fortunately, Corrie's response was verbal. "Are you drunk? How dare you ask me for money! I paid you and the girls only last week. Now get out of here before I yell for the master. If *he* finds out that you are badgering me for more money, he'll hang you up to dry."

Her voice shaky, Anele countered, "Maybe it s-s-slipped your mind. Honest, I tell no lie. I haven't been paid in three months."

As if she had eaten something sour, Corrie's face contorted. She gave her servant a direct look and said, "One more word and you will be fired. You ungrateful *wog*! You'll not find employment anywhere, not if I can help it. Now get out of here! Don't ever again come to my quarters unless I summon you!"

Anele was itching to continue this argument, but she thought better of it. It was madness. She curtsied and said, "Very well, my Lady."

Anele walked out of the room and closed the door. It took every ounce of her willpower to not slam it shut. Yes, she was angry—she felt enough rage to punch a hole in the wall—but what would that accomplish? Corrie's threats were real—one of them for sure. No one else in the entire region would employ her if Corrie let her go. Her employer would spread horrible lies about her, making it impossible for Anele to get work, food, or shelter. And worse, she could end up in jail based on a false accusation concocted by that Dutch shrew. Although she wasn't going to get a penny for her labor, Anele had no intention of losing her source of bread and butter—work, leftover food, clean drinking water, and a leaky tin roof over her head. The alternatives were bleak. She knew that countless numbers of her people went hungry, even starved to death. Many slept under makeshift shelters in the bush.

Back downstairs, Anele started toward the scullery that housed her only possession. She felt the hot tears sting her tired eyes. Five long years of making payments to the Hallworthy finance company was more than she could bear. Tomorrow her sewing machine would be repossessed. She thought of the girls and how they would react to the loss. "Oh," she whispered, as she recalled how the sisters, one afternoon off each month, strutted around the plantation like peacocks showing off the new outfits and matching hair bows Anele sewed for them. Now they would be robbed of even that small pleasure. She was beyond understanding anything. Nothing had changed since the slave days.

It was well past midnight before Anele left the spotless kitchen behind her and headed toward the shanty she called home.

 Hallworthy Manor House, Early Christmas Morning

"Only when you drink from the roar of silence shall you sing."
–Anonymous

Anele felt anything but merry on this "festive" December day in 1945. Her thoughts remained on cold-hearted Corrie, even though she was a *saint* compared to her predecessor, Lady Ethel. Four and a half years after Ethel had permanently disfigured Anele when she was a child by throwing a pot of boiling water on her as punishment, Ethel died in a car accident while on her way to visit friends in Port Elizabeth.

Behind closed doors, Lamella and Anele had rejoiced, holding hands and performing a gleeful "ring-around-a-rosy" dance in the kitchen.

The crowing of a cock brushed away Anele's reflections. She sighed heavily. It was time to get ready for work. It would take her forever to get going today. She was drained, emotionally and physically.

Anele reached for her uniform and underclothes: a pair of rayon briefs with ribbed leg bands and a camisole that she tucked underneath. She glanced at the two sleeping girls, their bare arms wrapped around each other. She decided to let them sleep a while longer while she dressed herself. She tiptoed toward the doorway. A drowsy voice stopped her in her tracks. "Is it time to get up, Anele?" Maekela asked.

"No, it's not," Anele answered. "I'm just going to get a breath of air. That's all. Be quiet, or you'll wake your sister. I'll tell you when it's time to get up."

Outside, patches of mist hovered on the hillside looming high above the shack. Summer's dark, rain-laden clouds obliterated the stars that had shone so brightly on Christmas Eve. Anele felt her tired legs give way. She slumped on the hard ground. Leaning her bare back against the outer wall of the shack, she buried her face in her palms. She could have wept with exhaustion. How was she going to cope physically with another long workday, especially with the hard work that went into the Christmas fare preparations? A thought did cross her mind. Thankfully, Corrie wouldn't be poking her nose in the kitchen until much later in the day. Earlier in the week she had informed Anele that she and Alan would not be on the premises for a good part of Christmas day. Although she didn't give her servant a reason, last night at dinner Anele had overheard Corrie say to Alan, "You don't have to come. You can go wherever you want, but I have to make an appearance. After all, she is *my* mother."

Anele had learned through the gossip grapevine that Corrie's mother had been placed in an old people's home after her husband, Mr. Van Hoof, had died. Alan had made it clear, "She's not living here. And I'm not paying a penny for that old bat's accommodation."

"I have never asked that of you," Corrie had retorted. "But you forget, dear heart," she had added sarcastically, "It's *my* money that keeps you and this place afloat."

Corrie's other words of yesterday suddenly flashed into Anele's mind: "Make sure Christmas dinner is ready exactly at seven o'clock. You know how Lord Alan hates waiting for his meal."

Still slumped on the dry earth, Anele suddenly gasped with an abrupt realization. *They aren't here. They have gone to sort out accom-modations for Corrie's mother and are not due back until mealtime.* Finally, opportunity nudged Anele to consider an escape. *Think fast,* she said to herself. *It's now or never.*

Anele got to her feet and dressed hurriedly, knowing she had to move quickly, before she lost her nerve. She questioned whether her bid for freedom would be in vain. Could she possibly get away with it? What would happen if they caught her? Would she go to prison? Or would she meet the same fate as her sisters—shot to death?

"Procrastination" wasn't in this uneducated servant's vocabulary.

Smiling wryly, Anele wrapped a bright-red, fringed headscarf over her knotty hair. She was as ready as she would ever be. But just as she was about to leave, a dose of sadness sprinkled her heart. She desperately wanted to whisper "goodbye" to Maekela and Isona, but she couldn't bring herself to do it. Anele knew what it felt like to not say goodbye to a loved one. After all, Lamella's disappearance had left a hole in *her* heart.

One day, many years ago, when Anele was a mere slip of a girl, she awoke to find the cook, Lamella, missing from the bed they shared. Anele's solitary washroom abode had been exchanged for Lamella's shanty the day after she suffered scalding burns at the hands of Lady Ethel. Anele hurried to the manor kitchen assuming Lamella had already left for work. But Cook wasn't there either. However, Corrie, clad in a brown, V-neck frock, was. The lady of the house said snap-pily, "I've been waiting for you." She handed the perplexed Anele the week's menu instructions. "You are the cook now."

Anele brows shot up. "What! Where's Lamella, Mistress?"

Corrie looked down at her feet and replied, "She wasn't in the best of health, you know. So I gave her permission to return to her home, to die in her own bed."

Anele stared into the woman's cold, soulless eyes. Not for one moment did she believe Corrie's pathetic explanation for the missing cook. It was a downright lie. Lamella had been close to Anele, as close as a natural mother and daughter could be. Lamella would never have left the estate without saying goodbye to her. So why had Corrie made up this ridiculous story? Had something terrible happened to her best friend? The march of time would solve this mystery one day.

In the days following Anele's appointment to her new position, she demonstrated that she had learned much from Lamella and could tackle any menu demanded of her. But working alone in the kitchen preparing elaborate meals was back-breaking. There wasn't a day that went by that Anele didn't miss her only friend. Lamella's sudden disappearance had left her heartbroken. She had never felt so lost. That void began to fill when Lady Corrie, accompanied by two shabbily dressed girls, announced, "I've brought you some helpers, Anele. They are to share the shanty with you. If they give you any trouble, take a stick to them."

Anele loved Maekela and Isona from the moment she set eyes on them. They were like a breath of fresh air. But they came with a tragic tale, a riveting journey. The sisters (both with Alan's cobalt eyes and light, curly hair) had been wandering around the estate for weeks after their mother, a fieldworker, had died of sunstroke. At least that's what some people said. Others suspected she had been killed by the father of her children. And who could that be?

Why Corrie had rescued her husband's teenaged offspring was a puzzling question. Was it out of compassion? Did she have an ulterior motive? Unbelievably, there *was* a soft side to Corrie. She had a weakness for *these* orphaned children. *He* wasn't going to violate *these* youngsters, his own offspring, while they were under her roof. Corrie's inclination would manifest itself again with another one of Alan's half-caste children in the not too distant future.

On this Christmas Day morning, after a moment of soul searching, Anele made the decision not to reenter the shanty, but, instead, to make her way to the manor to supply her journey. She shut her eyes for an instant and prayed Maekela and Isona wouldn't take the brunt of what she was about to do—pick up the shattered pieces of her life and escape from the estate. She took several deep breaths, trying to quell the butterflies fluttering in her belly. She stated aloud, "Why didn't I do this before now."

With her jaw set tight and her lips compressed, Anele picked up the corner of her dress, clenched the material tightly in her right hand, and started running. It wasn't bravery propelling her legs. It was fear.

Halfway down the path leading to the manor, Anele's lungs overheated. Panting, she rested her back against a gum tree. As she gathered her thoughts, she shook in fear. She hadn't thought it through. Her blood ran cold. *What if they did not go to Corrie's mother's side? What then? Will my bid for freedom be in vain? Not entirely,* her inner voice rebutted. *Even if they are inside, they are never up at this hour. A bomb couldn't wake the pair of them this early!*

Anele walked on, quickening her pace. She barely noticed the day beginning to stir with life: cocks crowing; brightly plumed parrots swooping down on sluggish insects, guinea fowl darting for cover, and toads croaking their mating calls. Walking from her shack toward the manor, she could see the alley of oak trees that led to a house that had seen better days. The mansion had been neglected since Alan and Corrie took over. The Greek columns surrounding the structure were cracked and in need of a coat of paint. The intricate wrought-iron balustrades on the balconies were obscured by thick, dead ivy.

The once magnificent dwelling looked ghostly in the dark morning mist. But it was the thought of another dwelling place that made Anele shudder from head to toe. Lamella had told her about the manor's diabolical slave history. Saddened by the story, Anele had once visited the slave building, which now lay in ruins on the northern edge of the estate. She had fled the place within seconds, later telling Lamella that she had *heard* the woeful, haunting cries of the dead—the ghosts of men, women and children who had been trapped within its walls. She also said she heard a pack of dogs barking.

Now, Anele's fearful thoughts were elsewhere. Her heart thumped against her chest as she hid behind an oak tree and peeked out at the manor. The house was in total darkness. Not even the wall-mounted light fixtures that came on from dusk until dawn were alit. But the total darkness didn't mean the owners weren't there.

Stealthily, she dashed down the oak tree alley and weaved around large sculptures until she came to the garage. Pressing her face against a side-wall windowpane, she made out the dark shape of a half-ton navy-blue pickup. The spot where the brand new 1945 black Ford coupe was normally parked was empty. She let out a sigh of relief. They *had* left. They definitely would have used the Ford coupe to drive to Corrie's mother, not the half-ton.

Anele decided to cautiously approach the manor's kitchen. Her forehead beaded with nervous perspiration as she slipped the heavy brass key into the antique door lock. Once inside she tiptoed across the kitchen floor and headed toward a heavy, oblong rug that had been strategically placed to conceal the trapdoor that lead to an underground cellar—another place forbidden to the servants.

Anele wrestled with a heavy trapdoor bolt. With a loud creaking of its hinges, the door opened into a cold, dungeon-like space. She gaped at the overstocked shelves extending from floor to ceiling. There were hundreds of canned goods: vegetables, jams, butter, pickles, and relish, as well as large bags of cornmeal and an assortment of bagged dried goods. Lady Corrie was carrying on Lady Ethel's hoarding obsession by stockpiling food. Anele wondered why white people squirreled away food they didn't use. The waste was wicked, especially when so many black folks were hungry.

The concrete cellar floor was icy cold on Anele's bare feet as she sought specific foods for her travels: cornmeal, dried milk powder, two cans of condensed milk, several jars of jam, and a handful of deer jerky strips. She managed to squeeze all that, plus three bottles of imported English beer and several beeswax candles, into an overflowing picnic basket. She couldn't wait to drink one of the "whites-only" beverages instead of the *umncindo*—a strong beer made from sourdough—that the fieldworkers drank. A cynical thought popped into her head. Once she got far from here, she'd make a toast to her employers' bad health.

The smiling rebel was about to leave the cellar when she heard a faint rustle. She looked around and spotted a scurrying gray mouse. Instinctively she reached for the broom resting by the door. Then her heart softened. "Help yourself, little creature," she said to the rodent, while its beady, black eyes flashed with fear. She watched as it disappeared through a hole in the baseboard.

"Eat whatever you like before someone finds you," Anele whispered on her way up the cellar ladder. After she climbed out of the dingy hole, she let out a sigh of relief. She set her heavy basket down, closed the trapdoor, and arranged the rug so it didn't appear to have been disturbed. She didn't realize how much time had passed until she glanced over to the double window above the sink. Surprised, she thought, *I couldn't have been down there that long.*

Fingers of bright sunlight were poking through the ivory net drapes. That was her cue to get going, and quickly. Although it wasn't unusual to be in the kitchen well before the girls, Anele wanted to be long gone before they arrived. She couldn't bear to see them break down when they learned of her disappearance. But Anele first had one more thing to do.

She opened the refrigerator and took out the fresh stuffed turkey covered with thick, fatty bacon. She placed it on the butcher's block. Then, from under the kitchen sink, she retrieved a dark blue box containing insecticide. Her fingers pummeled a handful of dry powder into the stuffing. "If it doesn't kill them," she scoffed inwardly, "it will at least keep them in the lavatory for days." But the death of the evil couple would have been more rewarding to the servant, whose life they had stolen.

Now she felt better!

She was ready to leave this awful residence forever. It had been a place to work, a place to live, a place to die, but nothing more. She grabbed a handful of notes and some loose change from the copper teapot's grocery money and stuffed them into her skirt pocket. She stepped out of the door and tossed the kitchen key into thorny shrubbery nearby. Then she lifted her heavy basket of provisions and positioned it on her head. In perfect balance Anele set off thinking that the best route to take was through the overgrown bush rather than on the riskier back road that led from the estate.

Anele was indentured and her work contract had been signed. She knew that without travel documents from her owners, she might face scrutiny by the white police officers who often patrolled the back roads. God knows what would happen if they searched her and found the wad of bills in her pocket. No black person ever earned that kind of money, not even after years of labor. There were times when Anele had been tempted to steal from her owners in order to hang on to her precious sewing machine, but that didn't matter now. The ugliness must be left behind.

Wary as an alley cat, she walked onward, hacking through thick foliage with a butcher's cleaver. When she passed the old slave ruins, she bowed her head. To relieve her fear of being invaded with sorrowful voices again, she began humming an African tune that Lamella had taught her. It was about freedom from white oppression.

As she chopped away at the bush, she began a steep uphill climb, happy at last to feel the warm sun on her back. She looked heavenward and noticed a sky suffused with an artist's palette of vibrant colors. It was an awesome sight for a servant who had spent all of her days laboring indoors.

Further along the trail Anele noticed several creatures enjoying the sunshine: green salamanders basking, a harmless garden snake wiggling out of its dead skin, a red-and-black bird swooping down on a grasshopper. She delighted at the sound of a songbird's joyous trebles.

Before long Anele's legs began to ache and her mouth began to grimace. She was used to climbing stairs, but not with a laden basket on her head. Her plea to the Zulu God was softly spoken: "Namandla, God of the Zulus, help me. I want to make it back home safely and get good medicine for my aches and pains." After that, as a distraction from her discomfort, she thought of her father, Naboto. *Was he still alive? Had he missed her? What did he look like now?* The more she tried to conjure up her father's image, the more her heart ached. There wasn't a day she hadn't missed him and her village. But it was her twin sisters she missed the most. How was she going to break the news of their awful demise to her father? It was something she would have to face if he *was* still alive.

For now Anele hoped she was heading in the right direction. Then she remembered Kelingo, the young, black field worker who had dragged her to the manor all those years ago. When he spotted her in the back garden one day, he had pointed in the direction of the Valley of a Thousand Hills and said, "Up there and a good way beyond, that's where the Kingdom of Zululand is, the beating heart of Africa." He sighed. "Never, *ever* forget your roots, young Anele of the Tswanas tribe. They will help you survive the dark days to come."

Christmas's afternoon sun, as warm and soft as a whisper, fell upon Anele's weary body. She had been walking nonstop since well before sunrise. Fortunately, she had not encountered any police patrols. However, Anele had been given the "look-over" by a Bantu woman on the backroad who had stared at her as if she had two heads. Anele frowned, but then the proverbial penny dropped. Her maid's uniform *was* a dead giveaway.

A little ways onward, and not a soul in sight, she undressed behind a large boulder and wrapped the floral fabric intended to become manor drapes around her body. This colorful makeshift outfit, knotted above her breasts, made Anele feel more like the African she was and had forgotten how to be.

Anele tucked her former attire into the food basket and, barefoot, plodded onward. Soon a lack of sleep, growling hunger pains, extreme thirst, and excessive heat seemed more than she could handle. But could she risk stopping? Was she a safe distance away? She hadn't a clue. So she decided to walk on until she dropped. Surrounding her were miles of red soil, empty corn fields covered with daisies, clusters of large-leafed fig trees, and, in the distance, a prominent outcrop. Anele wondered if the outcrop was far enough away for her to rest awhile in its shadows. Her ponderings were halted by a thirst that was attacking her parched tongue. A big slurp of beer would go down well right now. But she overruled the force of her thirst and decided to keep moving.

Farther on Anele spied what looked like the thatched roof of a traditional Zulu homestead. At last she could rest and even share her food with the residents. But before heading to the home, she needed to relieve herself. She was just about to squat when she happened to glance at the trail winding behind her. What she saw caused her deep concern. What *was* that swirling mass in the distance? Could it be a funneling sandstorm, an event that was common during summer months?

A prickly feeling ran down the back of Anele's neck. She suspected the swirls were made by horses. As her body froze and her blood ran cold, her thoughts warned her: *Run, woman! Run!* But Anele couldn't move. She felt as if she were mired in quicksand. In desperation, her mind raced, leapt, and darted like a scared jackrabbit. Was someone tracking her? Was it the police? Was it the Bantu woman? Had she informed the police? Was it Alan? Had he been at home all along and seen her leaving the grounds? No. He definitely would have taken chase at the beginning of her journey. Then who were these horseback riders? As far as she knew, no blacks owned horses in these parts. An adrenalin rush, a surge of strength and energy, finally spurred her into action. She gripped her basket of provisions with both hands and ran through a deserted cornfield toward the Zulu hut. Would the occupants take pity on her?

To Anele's dismay, the abode was empty—abandoned. Just as well, she reasoned. It was much too obvious a place to hide. Her eyes darted from side to side, searching for a safer hiding place. Could the outcrop she saw earlier conceal her? She backtracked a bit and made a beeline for the rocky formation. Panting like a dog, she reached the base of the outcrop and looked up. There was an opening halfway to the top. But how on earth could she get there?

Where there's a will, there's a way.

But the heavy basket of provisions didn't yet match the adage, until she came up with a solution.

Fashioned from the floral curtain fabric, Anele placed a strap across her forehead. The heavy load rested on the upper part of her bare back, kept in place by the strap. The design enabled Anele to climb and grip rock ledges with both hands. When she reached a narrow fissure, she made a disgruntled click of her tongue. "Oh, this is not happening!" A slim child would have had no problem, but Anele would.

Understanding that size and time were not on her side, Anele shoved the food basket in the crevice as far as it would go. Naked, she slithered into the rock formation and immediately wished she hadn't. The overpowering odor of animal feces assailed her nostrils with such force, she almost gagged. Her immediate thought was, *I hope the creatures that made this disgusting stench aren't waiting for me in here.*

The size of her refuge was not what she had expected. After living in a "closet" for so many years, the cave looked to be the size of a palace and was, gratefully, dark and quiet. Another pleasant surprise was the density of the dried bracken sticking up from the lower ledge. The vegetation would make her hiding place more difficult to detect. Anele crouched. Her heart pounded as her arms locked over her body in a nervous embrace. She waited.

A horse neighed directly above Anele, causing her flesh to tremble in fear, her stomach to flutter, and her head to feel like it was frozen. The top of her hideout began to reverberate with the movement of horses. Anele shrunk back against the cave's rough wall. The color drained from her face, and the hair on her neck stood as upright as a pig's bristles. There was no mistaking that malevolent voice. It was Alan Hallworthy's. He would show no mercy. A scream silently ripped through her throat.

On the flat plateau above Anele, a hand gesture from the sour-faced Alan brought the other riders to a halt. Above the din of the milling horses, Alan's voice boomed. "The rotten bitch is here somewhere. I'm going to find her. And when I do, I'll break her neck, so help me God."

Anele was too scared to breathe.

The next voice was also unmistakable. "Why are we searching out here in the bush?" Lady Corrie asked. "Wouldn't it make more sense to check out the Durban docks?"

"The tracker found her footprints leading up here ..."

Corrie cut in, "We should search the docks, not here."

Alan exhaled loudly before giving a intimidating reply. "Woman, are you bloody deaf? Why the hell did you come along just to stick your nose where it doesn't belong? My affairs are not yours!"

The insulted redhead countered angrily, "Oh, yes they are! I've had to put up with your nonsense for years. And, my dear, I wouldn't want to miss out on the fun. It seems it's the only pleasure I get, seeing you go insane like this."

"Shut up, Corrie!" Alan growled. "You are a feeble-minded excuse for a woman."

Their eyes locked like horns for the longest moment.

In her mind's eye, Anele could see the stubborn jut of Lady Corrie's jaw and her lips drawn tight with anger. From the sharpness of his tone, Anele could also imagine the ugly contortions etched on Lord Alan's striking features. Anele wondered why Corrie had put up with Alan's despicable behavior for so long.

Corrie knew why she had sold herself to this devil, but now, if she were able, she would gladly sell her soul again to be free of him.

In the desolation of the valley's wilderness, Alan sat high on his black Arabian horse. He was of two minds: shoot his abominable wife and say it was a hunting accident, or throw her down the well on his property that served as a human boneyard. Corrie's high-pitched "bastard" broke his murderous thoughts. "Only yesterday I saw you chasing after that young fieldworker." She bit her lip to refrain from adding: *another child hardly out of puberty whom you would have put in the family way.*

Alan swatted a fly and laughed. His dry cackle was as humorless as a crow's. "Yeah, I know the one," he bragged. "She shot off like a racehorse, didn't she?"

Corrie steered her mare closer and glared at her husband. "Don't tell me that the bitch you kept in the cottage can't run like that Bantu field girl who birthed the bastard girls, Maekela and Isona. Then tell me, dear husband, why is *this* plaything so important?"

Alan's face flushed dark red. "Shut your mouth, Corrie," he spat, "or I'll shut it for you."

Corrie whined, "Why are you taking your anger out on me? *I* didn't leave the door open for your precious Italian *thing* to escape."

"She's not Italian." Alan corrected. "She's Sicilian."

Corrie made a clucking, agitated sound and said, "It's all the same, isn't it?"

The snarl on Alan's mouth expressed how he felt.

Below them, Anele's lips moved silently: *Thank the gods. I'm not the one they're looking for.* She hoped that the young foreign girl, Maria, was long gone, heading homeward, like she was.

Alan reached out and roughly grabbed the bridle of Corrie's horse. Corrie wrinkled her nose. Alan's mouth and riding gear reeked of whisky. "I have needs." Alan's upper lip curled derisively as he said, "And as sure as hell, I will never touch you again, drunk or not! You make me sick! If my mother were still alive, I'd kill her for making me marry you. Get out of my sight. Go home. Let me get on with what I have to do."

Alan raised a fist and continued ranting on another subject. "I know who helped Maria escape. It had to be Anele. As God is my witness, she will vanish from the face of the earth when I get back home."

The normally impenetrable Corrie was taken aback, stung by his loud, heartless words. She gasped and clutched at her throat. But molten anger soon flooded her veins. How dare he speak to her in that despicable manner! She wanted to crush his head like a soft-boiled egg. Whatever glimmer of obligatory marital commitment she might have once nourished for him died like the last rays of the sun. She'd had enough. It had gone on too long. She was aware Alan had a sick appetite for young girls. Some were just children. Disgusting!

Acknowledging the power of her awareness of Alan's repulsive tastes, Corrie said gloatingly, "Husband, dear, as you normally never set foot in the kitchen, let me be the first to tell you that Anele has run away—with my grocery money. To top that, we won't be having a turkey dinner this evening. Maekela and Isona can't boil an egg, let alone prepare a Christmas meal. And I'm damned if I'm going to cook for you!" The sound of Corrie's victorious laughter echoed across the valley. But she wasn't finished. "I spoke to *your* bastard child, Maekela. She saw Anele get up well before dawn. It seems Anele told her to go back to sleep."

"*What?*"

"My dear, do I have to spell it out for you?"

"Why didn't you tell me this earlier, before we set off?"

"Because all you were interested in was finding Maria."

Fuming, Alan exhaled so sharply it lifted the hair on the horse's mane. He stared straight ahead.

Fear sprouted roots down to Anele's feet. She could not move or breathe.

Corrie found it difficult to breathe, as well. The long horse ride had worn her out. All she wanted to do was to go home and relax, have a few more martinis, smoke some cigarettes, open the only Christmas presents she ever received—those given to her from her family—and eat an alternative meal, one she'd have to prepare. Maekela and Isona had few culinary skills. The thought of not having a traditional meal waiting for her riled her, but she decided to break the icy tension. "Alan, I could kill Anele with my bare hands. She is nothing more than an ungrateful, bloody, *wog* thief!"

Alan wasn't smiling, even though he liked it when his wife took his point of view. He patted his horse's neck, and, through tight jaws, threatened, "Not if I get to *her* first. If I find the fat black bitch, I'll put a bullet between her eyes. So help me God, I will."

It was by no means an idle threat. Corrie had seen firsthand what happened to people who had crossed paths with her husband. She, too, was afraid of him at times. This was one of those times. She spoke in a pacifying tone. "My dear, why don't we concentrate on finding Maria, before she blabs to whomever will take her seriously. You could end up in jail. Good lord, no. I wouldn't want that to happen!" she ended glibly.

Alan jeered. "Who on God's earth is going to believe anything that crazy bitch says? I'm a Hallworthy, for God's sake. I practically own the Port of Durban, the police, judges, and over a thousand *golliwogs!*"

Wisely, Corrie remained silent but her thoughts ran rampant. Who was he kidding? She held the purse strings. He didn't have a dime to his name. He didn't own a damn thing except the slaves. And they weren't getting paid. She was dying to give him a tongue-lashing, but in the back of her mind she knew it was pointless to argue with the Devil.

As though punctuating Alan's anger, white knives of lightning split the sky, followed by drum rolls of thunder. Corrie's spooked horse reared, and she was sent flying from her saddle. There was no knight in shining armor to help her up, so she dusted the dirt off her riding pants and demanded, "For Christ's sake, Alan! Let's go home. A bad storm is coming. And there is always tomorrow."

Without even a nod, Alan rotated in his saddle and ordered his workers, "Turn around. It's time to go home. Follow me."

The posse galloped homeward.

The sound of retreating hooves was music to Anele's ears. She was safe, at least for now. To cheer herself, she pulled out a bottle of beer. The warm alcohol trickled down her throat like nectar from the gods. Within seconds she was lightheaded. She slouched against the wall to get some long overdue shut-eye. As she began to doze, something seized her arm. It felt like the grip of a bird of prey's talons. Anele drew in her breath and tried to scream, but the only thing that came out was a rasp of shocked terror. A sibilant voice pierced the tomblike quiet. "*Ees* okay, Big Mama," said a reassuring voice. "The *bastardo... ees* gone."

Anele gulped in relief. There was certainly no mistaking *this* accented voice. Anele had taken enough food trays to the gamekeeper's cottage to recognize that lilt. Had Maria been here all along? Why hadn't she said anything? Anele fumbled in the dark and snatched Maria's arm. The girl shrieked in the same broken English she had used since she met Anele. "You make me hurt!"

Outside, on the ledge, Anele looked her over from head to toe and then into the haunted green eyes of the pregnant thirteen-year-old white girl. Anele's heart went out to her. By the look of her dirt-encrusted pink dress (an outfit Anele had sewn for her), Maria had been traveling for some time. And the rest of her body was beyond filthy.

"Let me go," Maria screamed, trying to pry Anele's fingers from her forearm.

"No! " Anele said. "You nearly scared me to death!"

Maria whimpered, "I no mean scare you, Big Mama."

"Well, you did!" Anele countered. "My heart almost jumped out of my chest!"

"I no mean ..."

"Maria, I set you free *yesterday*. You should be long gone by now. I showed you which way to go to the docks."

Maria clutched at Anele's waist. "I run fast from *di diaula* (white devil) Big Mama. He tried to kill my babies and me. The *bastardo*, he beat me bad. I scared. Not know way to big ship to take me home to Sicilia. Then I see *diaula* on horse. I run. I hide in hole here."

Anele was astonished. "You mean to tell me you've been here the whole time?"

With her bottom lip quivering, Maria nodded. "Yes, Big Mama. I think I'm lost in this land until I see you coming up the hill. I not know you run away like Maria. My heart knows you're sad like me, no? You, too, run like me from the *diaula*, no?"

Anele sighed. She knew little about the girl's background, but she could recall the day she met her, as though it were yesterday. Anele's memory drifted back to the unforgettable spring day Maria had arrived on the Hallworthy Estate.

On that fateful day, when Anele was outside hanging laundry, a shabbily dressed foursome arrived at the manor's back door—a stunning teenager flanked by a thin man of about forty, a short woman of similar age, and a handsome, dark-haired young man. Anele couldn't take her eyes off the olive-skinned girl. She was the most beautiful white girl she had ever seen. Her waist-length black hair, glistening like polished ebony, was as thick as a horse's mane, and the unadorned cotton dress she wore matched her emerald eyes perfectly.

The older man spoke first. "Signóra, where is the *proprietario* of this plantation? We need work."

Anele did not recognize the accent, but she did recognize danger. *Ah, these foreigners,* she thought. *They'd be better off starving to death than coming here. The girl is far too lovely. Alan will devour her faster than a fox in a henhouse. Predators recognize an easy mark.* Anele's expression spoke volumes. She cautioned the older man. "Take your pretty daughter and go quickly. There is no work for you here. The refinery owner isn't hiring now ..."

Anele heard the fast-approaching clatter of hooves. In her tortured memories, that sound was painful. It was even worse than the loud door-knocking she had often heard at three in the morning, not knowing who, or what, was awaiting her.

All heads turned as the rider came to a halt. Anele's heart skipped a beat at the barely concealed lust lighting Alan's eyes as they devoured Maria's beauty. With his focus glued on Maria, he said, "What do you want? Are you looking for work?"

Cesare Girrdazzello nodded eagerly. "Si, sir. Raphaela, my wife," he said, pulling the petite woman up close, "is a hard worker. My son

Paolo," he pointed, "he strong boy. We work hard for you, Signóre."
He made no mention of his daughter.

Alan removed his sunglasses and looked the family over. "Are
you Spaniards?"

"No, Signóre. We are from Sicily."

"You're a long way from home. What brings you here? Or
shouldn't I ask?"

Cesare explained, "We have bad times from the war. We need a
new start in this land."

Alan ignored him and nudged his steed closer to Maria. "You're
such a pretty girl. What's your name? How old are you? Do you have
a boyfriend?"

Maria shrank behind Cesare. He quickly explained, "She doesn't
talk, Signóre. She has … how you say? …" he tapped at his head,
"… brain sickness. *Ees* no good in the head," he ended. Was that
the truth? Maria's family assumed she was suffering from amnesia.
Before the malady arose, however, she had been able to understand
some English, even though no one knew where she had learned it.
The reason Maria shrunk behind her father was not because she
didn't understand the man's words but because she didn't feel comfortable with the man's questions.

"What a shame," Alan said, in a voice that could melt butter.
"I'm sure I'll be able to find her something to do. Now, are you and
your family prepared to work for food and lodging only?"

Cesare frowned, scratched his chin, and responded, "Do you
mean … work for *no* money, Signóre?"

"Yes," Alan said icily. "That's exactly what I mean. If you don't
like the idea, you can find work elsewhere. But I assure you, not too
many white folks are hiring refugees, especially the illegal kind …"
he paused long enough for Cesare and his son to exchange worried
glances, "… which you most probably are. You get my drift?"

The baby-faced Paolo, who didn't look much older than Maria, was worried that Alan would change his mind, so he stepped forward and in good English said, "It is okay, Signóre. Your offer of food and a place to sleep will be fine."

While the family grouped and conversed in their tongue, Alan took hold of Anele's arm. He pulled her aside and whispered, "Take the girl to …" he hesitated briefly before adding, "… the-you-know-where. Put her to work. Give her some cleaning cloths. See that she scrubs the place from top to bottom. I'll take her parents and brother over to the stables. They can stay there for the time being."

His chilling orders were as clear as a spring snow thaw. The "you-know-where" was a place Anele dreaded. To her, and many others, the old gamekeeper's abode was a house of horrors where abominable atrocities that laid bare the darkest of human behavior were committed. She knew every inch of that hellhole. She had suffered untold terror and torture there. The depravity still lived in her soul—forever a scar. Alan had killed not only her spirit, but that of countless others, as well. Anele didn't want to see another young girl ruined, so she tried to wrangle her way out of going.

"But, Lord Alan, you heard the man. She's sick in the head, and she doesn't speak English," or so the servant was led to believe. "How will I make her understand?"

"She's not bloody blind!" Alan roared. "Show her what to do, stupid!"

Later that night, locked in the gamekeeper's cottage, with no savior in her corner, Maria joined other young plantation victims—she was brutally raped.

The next morning Alan sported a deep scratch on his cheek and a smirk on his lips. He handed Anele the key to the cottage and ordered, "Take her some food." He didn't have to tell Anele to keep her mouth shut. His piercing, evil glare said it all. Anele felt sick to her stomach. She yearned to take the butcher's knife she held in her hand and plunge it into Satan's sidekick.

A few minutes later, Anele placed a bowl of porridge, a slice of marmalade toast, and a glass of milk on a tray. When she reached the cottage, she removed the key from her pocket and unlocked the heavy oak door. Her heart almost wrenched out of her chest when she saw the half-naked Maria restrained to the room's brass bedposts. Anele had been there herself. Without saying a word, she placed the tray on the end of the bed, sat next to Maria, and untied her restraints. Even if Maria could have spoken good English, no words could possibly soothe what had been done to her.

Wide-eyed with fear, Maria's arm sprang up and sharp finger-nails sank into Anele's neck. Anele screamed. The scalding wounds she bore were still tender after so many years. Wincing in pain, Anele grabbed Maria's arms, pinned them to her sides, and scolded, "Why did you do that? I'm not your enemy, you stupid girl! I'm the only friend you'll ever have here." She released the struggling girl and tried to hand-feed her. The petrified teenager clenched her teeth and jerked her head away.

As silently as she had entered the room, Anele left, locking the door behind her. With her head as low as it would go, the servant repeated, "My spirit no longer lives in the house of yesterday ... my spirit no longer lives in the house of yesterday."

Back in the kitchen, Anele tried not to think about Maria. But all she could see were the girl's pain-filled eyes. What could a lowly servant do to help? Absolutely nothing! So she went about her work as if nothing had happened, until she heard tapping. She looked out the window. Raphaela Girrdazzello was standing on a tree stump in order to reach the glass pane. Using hand gestures, the woman asked after Maria. Anele raised her hand in a "wait-there" sign. She had to think fast. She certainly couldn't take the woman to the cottage. What else could she do? Then an idea popped into her head.

Anele left the confines of the kitchen, took hold of Raphaela's arm, and, without a word between them, led the woman to the front entrance of the manor. Anele knocked sharply and then dashed away to hide behind a pillar. Raphaela was left standing at the door.

"What the bloody hell do you want?" Alan shouted, looking Raphaela over as if she were merely a blot on the doorstep. "Shouldn't you be working?"

Anele could hear Raphaela's Sicilian tongue going hell for leather, then Alan's reverberating hyena laughter.

"Good Lord, woman!" he said, "I haven't got a clue what you are saying. You better learn English fast because I'm sure as hell not going to speak bloody Sicilian."

"Maria … Maria, I need look at her. Look at her now!" Raphaela stressed, doing her best to get her message across.

His eyes, full of deceit, narrowed. "You can't come in contact with your daughter, not at this point. I noticed some sores on her legs, so I got my doctor to check her. She is contagious. Do you understand what I'm saying? *Contagious!* She has a bad blood infection. I can't have her working in this condition alongside you or my other fieldworkers. You can see her when she is well."

Anele's insides trembled. She could envision his wagging finger. She tilted her head to one side and heard Alan's warning, "Don't go near the cottage. Alfred, my overseer, has instructions to shoot."

Anele did not hear Raphaela's response. Perhaps she did not understand him, or she understood only too well. After the front door slammed shut, Anele shot back to her workplace.

The next day, Anele was stunned when she learned that the Girrdazzello family (parents and son) had vanished without a word to anyone. It was a mystery. But it left food for thought. Had Alan silenced them for good?

Later that day Anele did her best to gently tell Maria that her family had up and gone without a word. The blank expression on Maria's face caused Anele to release a sigh that soon turned into a gasp. Maria's English words took Anele by surprise.

"Big Mama, you no lock door. I …" she pointed to her body "… I want to run away."

"You *do* understand English. Why didn't you speak to me earlier? Never mind. You have your reasons." Anele lowered her head and responded truthfully. "Oh, child, if only I could. But *he* would hold me responsible. I don't have to tell you that he is evil and capable of anything."

On the rock formation, Maria, looking heavily pregnant, was hunkered down with Anele—two sad runaways. If Alan found them, without a doubt he'd blow off *both* their heads. Anele looked at Maria and felt pain for the pitiful expectant mother. Maria's matted hair was a bird's nest. Her lovely face and eyes were blackened and swollen from cruel punches.

Anele blinked. Then her eyes widened like saucers. "Dear God of good Zulu hearts!"

"What is it, Big Mama?"

"Maria, can't you feel it?" She pointed. "That's fresh blood I see trickling down your legs! Does your belly hurt?" Anele counted on her fingers. "If my memory serves me, you're at least eight and a half months."

Maria's mind, contained by a fractured wall, chose silence as her response. Numbness was the only way she could handle her pregnancy.

To Anele, Maria seemed not to comprehend what was happening to her. Or did she?

Anele released an exasperated sigh before she revealed, "I was younger than you when I delivered my own baby—by myself. Back then I was fearless. Now I'm not sure if I'll be capable of delivering yours." She shook her head and finalized her decision. "No. It's out of the question. I will have to find a midwife. There has to be someone living around here."

Maria's face scrunched in pain.

"Do you have hurt in your belly, Maria?"

Maria still didn't reply.

Anele tenderly squeezed the girl's hand, her voice soft and motherly. "Don't worry, child. I'm going to get help." Maria grabbed Anele's hand and kissed it. "Big Mama, you are a nice lady, but you please not go back to bad sugar place. Don't worry for me. No *bambinos* ... babies no more."

"Of course, I'm worried. You and your baby may die if I don't get help. And no, I'm definitely not going back to the *sugar place*."

"No. I no die. Me *libero* ... how you say? Yes, me *free!*"

Anele rubbed her forehead thinking that somehow she had to get the pregnant girl to listen, to lie down so that she could check the position of the baby's head. Maria took hold of Anele's hand and placed it on her swollen abdomen. "See, black Mama, I *libero*, free. No more *demonio* babies. No *diaula sangu*." She ended her outpouring with a troubling statement: "The Devil's blood no more in me."

Anele scrunched her forehead. "Missy Maria Girrdazzello, I've no idea what you're rambling on about, but you need to lie down, not stand up. It may help the blood loss."

Maria made an angry face. "My name is Maria Picasso Genovese. No say "Girrdazzello" name. Not my *familiare*. Those bad people bring me here to this country."

"What are you babbling about, Maria?"

"Paolo ... he stole me from Papa and Mama in Sicilia." To blot out the memory, she covered her face with her hands.

Anele had no doubt that this young girl was mentally and physically crushed, just like she had been at her age. Anele shrugged. She would not dwell on the past because she had a more pressing concern in the present: the baby's safe delivery into the world. Anele made eye contact with Maria and asked her, "How long has your blood flowed?"

"I don't know!"

Anele knew she was lying. "Lie down," she ordered, "so I can check you."

"No."

Maria began to sob. Her heart carried more sorrow than any young heart should ever have to. A long and tortuous road had brought her from a home nestled in the shadows of Mount Etna in Sicily to the dark shores of Africa. Maria Teresa Picasso Genovese *was* her real name. She was the only daughter of Sofia Maria Picasso, a Spanish-born socialite, and Don Alberto Vincenzo Genovese, a wealthy landowner and a reigning regional Mafia boss.

Maria had to get her story out. "Paolo Girrdazzello stole me from my papa for big kidnap money. My papa would not pay. Paolo was mad. He sold me to German man. He sent me to bad death camp in Poland. After the war, I not know my name or where I come from. Paolo, he saw me in the camp. He scared that I tell the story what he did to me. His Mama and Papa, they bring me here to dark land by boat. They are bad, bad people, the Girrdazzello. I remember ... I remember." Maria's amnesia-frozen mind finally unlocked the awful truth and caused her to sob uncontrollably. Anele, whose heart was breaking, flung her arms around Maria and said, "Please don't cry."

Anele clung to Maria until her cries shrank to a whimper. Then, using the hem of her floral outfit, she dabbed the girl's tear-streaked cheeks and commiserated. "I'm so sorry to hear that you have had so much hurt in your young life, but we have to deal with what is happening now, Maria. Listen to me, please. First babies don't always come out quickly. If I can't find a birthing woman, I'll come straight back and help you myself."

Maria picked at the tip of a mud-caked fingernail and pretended not to have heard. Anele stared at the girl's nails. "Maria, how did your nails get so filthy?"

Puffing out her cheeks she replied, "Me no say."

Anele let out a frustrated sigh. Did she mean she wouldn't say, or couldn't? Anele suggested, "If you like, you can change out of that filthy dress. I've a uniform in my basket for you to put on. I also have some food. Are you hungry?"

Maria's eyes were vacant, her mouth mute.

Anele was worried about leaving the girl alone in the approaching darkness, but what else could she do? She couldn't take her along, not in her condition. Anele informed her, "I'm setting off now, Maria. With a little luck I'll have help with me when I return."

"I say again," Maria huffed, "I no need birth woman."

"Yes, you do! What if something goes wrong? The baby could be stuck?"

"I tell you last time, Big Mama, the babies ees *morto* … they are dead!"

"Your baby, *not babies*, is going to pop out before the full moon shines tonight."

Maria laughed. "Too late, the babies have gone … babies die. I make sure."

Uneasiness swelled in the pit of Anele's stomach. Something wasn't right. It crossed Anele's mind to continue her homeward journey—to leave the befuddled white girl and let her birth her baby alone. But Anele knew she'd never be able to live with herself if she abandoned the helpless girl. Except for her swollen stomach, Maria looked dangerously thin. Would her baby be born alive? What Anele didn't see was the ribbon of blood flowing from Maria's inner thighs.

Anele had a change of heart. She tilted Maria's long face to meet hers. "Child, I've decided *not* to leave you here alone. But I'm going to need your help. Does the pain come one after the other?"

"Me no say."

"What am I going to do with you?" Anele said. Then using an eating gesture, fingers to her mouth, Anele asked, "Are you hungry, Maria?"

"No want to eat, Big Mama." Maria made a sucking noise with her lips. "Drink."

"Would you like some sweet condensed milk? I stole it from the *bas-e-tar-do's* house."

Maria's pitiful face lit up like a moonbeam. She loved Anele's pronunciation of the word for bastard. "No. Want water. And Big Mama, the pain, I tell you, *ees* gone for good."

"No, it's not gone for good. The pain is going to get much worse."

Maria shook her head and smirked. Anele sighed in response. "Okay, Maria. Here's what I'm going to do. I saw a rainwater barrel near an abandoned homestead. I'll get enough for you to drink and to wash the baby when it comes."

Maria puckered her lips amusingly. Her funny face reminded Anele of Isona and Maekela, whose laughter often overruled the seriousness of their situation. "You cheeky monkey," Anele said. "I bet you understand everything I say. Am I right?"

Maria's broad grin was her only response.

Back to business, Anele thought. "Come along, mum. It's time to lie down."

Maria followed Anele deeper into the cave. Once there, Anele lit a candle, spread out her uniform on the cold ground, and pointed for Maria to sit down on the uniform and use the picnic basket as a backrest. Anele smiled when she was satisfied that the mum-to-be was comfortable. "I'm going to go for water. It's not far so I won't be long. Just lie still. I'll be back before you know it."

Anele headed toward the cave's opening with an empty beer bottle in her hand. She wiggled out of the crevice and climbed down the rock formation. At the bottom she became besieged with concern. Could she deliver Maria's baby safely? What if it was breech? What if it got stuck? What if Maria, who barely weighed ninety pounds, had no breast milk? It seemed unlikely from her worn-out appearance that the new mother could produce a drop. But they had some lifesavers in the basket: a packet of dried cow's milk and a tin of condensed milk, just in case. Only time would tell how her other worries would resolve.

Anele was thankful for the hundreds of fireflies that were flashing their lanterns in the diminishing daylight. She retraced her steps to the abandoned home and water source and bent down. As she was scooping the discolored water into the bottle, she heard a peculiar sound. She tilted her head to the side and heard what sounded like a kitten mewing. A few seconds later the sound grew louder. Now it struck a note that resembled a faint human cry. No. It couldn't be.

Anele carried on with her task, but a loud rustling followed by a thin wail stopped her in her tracks. With a rock in her hand, she went to investigate. She nearly jumped out of her skin when a scruffy wild dog sprung to all fours and bared its razor-sharp teeth at her. Anele quickly lowered her eyes and backed away. Taking this as a sign of submission, the dog sat back on its haunches and returned its attention to a cornhusk mound.

Anele's taut muscles relaxed a bit. The dog was only doing what any other mother would have done: protecting her young. "It's okay, little mother dog," Anele said in a soft, comforting voice. "I'm going. But you should have found a better place to have your litter than out in the open." Anele began whistling, to show the dog that she was not afraid. She had only walked a few steps when she heard what she thought was a weak human cry.

It couldn't be …!

Seized by an unknown fear, Anele grabbed two large stones and hastily retraced her steps. The dog was pawing at something. Anele walked toward the critter. Nothing could have prepared her for what she saw.

With a massive surge of lava-hot adrenalin, Anele aimed the rock. It struck the wild animal between the eyes. The hungry critter yelped but was not about to leave. Snarling, it stood its ground. Anele snarled back. "Go. Get gone. Shoo. Go away!" The next projectile tore open the skin on the dog's scalp. The yelping bitch shot off into the bushes.

Anele looked down into the compost pit. Her blood turned cold. "Dear God!" she shrieked. Dropping to her knees, she lifted a tiny, feeble form. With a rush of tears clouding her vision, she did not notice a second baby. The lifeless body of the second twin was lying more deeply under the same layer of pawed dirt and compost that had previously covered the two of them. Anele's heart beat so fast she thought it was going to pop out of her chest. She pulled out a long length of the horse grass that was cloaking the gravesite and used it to tie the baby's mangled umbilical cord. Then, using her headscarf, she wiped the dog's drool off the infant's ashen face. There was no mistaking the parents of this abandoned infant: Maria's dark olive skin and long lashes, and a Roman nose with a bump on the bridge. Tiny wisps of flaxen blond hair and a high forehead and cheekbones identified the father.

Anele nestled the cold-to-the-touch newborn between her breasts and, supporting the baby's head, raced back to Maria's shelter. At the entrance she hollered, "Maria. Come out here *now!*"

No response.

"Maria. I know you're in there," Anele yelled. "How could you do such a terrible thing? Your baby is alive!"

Deathly silence.

Anele was angrier than a wounded wasp. She slithered into the cave.

Empty.

Not only was Maria gone, but also the makeshift bedding, basket, and money that Anele had hidden in the uniform's pocket. Speechless, she stood in the cave stunned. Then Maria's words replayed in her mind. *"I'm free. The Devil's blood is no longer in me."* When had Maria given birth? Anele could only guess. But why didn't Maria tell her?

Anele's hands reached for the baby lodged between her breasts. The child was as still as death. Anele laid her ear against the infant's tiny rib cage. At first, she heard nothing. Her heart jumped with joy when she finally heard a faint heartbeat.

A fierce urgency possessed Anele. Not wanting to rely on the Zulu God, Namandla, who had turned a deaf ear to her over the years, she beseeched the dark side of African culture—the Guardian of the Underworld. "Great Ngewele, with your powers, make this child live, even though she is *umlungu,* the pale color of the ones I hate. But she didn't ask to be born or to be left to die in such a horrible way."

Anele's angry tears fell onto the baby's tiny face. There was one more deity to try. "Please, God of the white people, let this child live." Anele's heart missed a beat as she watched the girl child gulp air and then curl a tiny finger around her own. It was a miracle. *Who* had answered her plea? That was a question that only *time* could answer.

Anele cradled the baby, kissed her cool forehead, and whispered tenderly, "It looks like I'm your mother now. Grow strong for your *Umama*. Fight, little one, as hard as you can. We both have a lot of living to do."

Without warning a second deity-inspired miracle took place.

A lifesaving milky substance began to flow from Anele's nipples as she cradled the child. Thrilled, Anele coaxed the newborn to her breast. The baby suckled greedily. At that moment, life couldn't have been sweeter for Anele. Mantled in a garment of fate, Anele felt blessed. No more would the emptiness of her womb cry out to be filled. With the trill of a songbird, Anele's tune floated up to the heavens. "Great Spirits of the white people and of black skins, I thank you for the channel of peace, love, and forgiveness. From the ugly darkness you have shown me the light of joy. I will forever sing your praises."

If Anele could have peered into the murky waters of the future, she might not have prayed so fervently for the gods to spare this *in-tandane* (foundling) whom Anele named Shiya—the forsaken one.

 Tswanas Kraal, Five Days Later

"Oh let not Time deceive you."
–W.H. Auden

Miles away, the Tswanas tribe members were going about their daily routine, tending to crops and small gardens, milking cows, and performing other mundane chores. They were blissfully unaware that before the sun became level with the horizon their lives would be turned upside down.

A tall, stooped old man paused at the kraal's gate to retie the homespun blanket that had slipped off his waist and exposed his nakedness. He was the village chieftain, a man of tradition and culture, but he was intolerant of the endless prattle of women, the boisterous shrieks of children, and the incessant barking of village dogs. Chief Naboto, his leathery face molded by old age and harsh elements, was not happy. His features scrunched up like a deflated ball as he sucked in his cheeks. "Why are things not made easier for the old?"

Finally, he headed toward his favorite resting place to enjoy his customary afternoon nap away from the kraal's hustle and bustle. He reached a solitary baobab tree. According to African myth, the baobab was accidentally planted upside down by the nature gods. This legend explained the look of the tree's odd shaped branches. Locally, the baobab, an ancient giant, was known as the "dead rat tree," named after the hairy, rodent-shaped fruit it bore.

The old man and the tree had long known each other. He revered the tree. He had climbed it in his youth, shared passionate moments underneath its branches, and marked diagonal lines on its bark after the birth and death of each of his children.

Naboto leaned his gaunt frame against the thick trunk, stroked the greyish bark, and greeted his friend. "*Ingundane abafileyo,* I've come to take my rest with you." Then he turned away from a long line of memories and spread his blanket over a carpet of brown, crinkly leaves. Comfortable under the tree's leafy canopy, Naboto shut his wrinkled eyelids and, within seconds, started to snore. Oblivious to the approaching evening shadows, he slept on until he was rudely awakened by a shrill voice.

"Chief Naboto. Chief Naboto. Wake up!"

His body jerked to alertness. He squinted. A ponderous shadow holding a blazing reed torch loomed over him. He recognized her. "What is it, Vimbela? Why have you come to my private place?"

"Chief, I h-have just c-come from the-the village," stammered Vimbela, trying to catch her breath. "Granny Matudia said to find you here."

"Can't a man have some peace? Tell me your message, brainless girl."

"It's past the time of crows!" she yelled. "The night is as black as their feathers. You must listen!"

"You don't have to scream. I'm not deaf."

"Yes, you are!"

Naboto sighed. "I'm not going to argue with you, girl."

"I don't care, old Chief," was her impudent return. "I have an urgent message for you!"

"Well, what is it?"

"Anele, your daughter, is coming."

Naboto slapped the side of his head in disbelief. "Brainless girl, it cannot be her."

"Wrong. Wrong. Wrong," Vimbela blustered in a singsong voice. "Matudia is a wise woman. She knows where people are without seeing them. She says that Anele does not walk with the dead, and that *you*, a gifted man with the spiritual insight of the ancient spirits, already know this. Your daughter is alive. Come, old man, and see for yourself."

Naboto rose. "*Indulo injonga*," he muttered, telling his old bones to "not let me down."

Vimbela lowered the torch and started to giggle.

"Now what is it, girl?"

She pointed at his drooping genitals, one testicle hanging lower than the other. It brought a toothless smile to his lips.

"Child, you have the innocence of a baby. Now pass me my blanket. We must make haste."

Having been wrenched so abruptly from his dream world, Naboto's shaky legs could not match Vimbela's pace. It took some effort to keep up with the lively girl, so he gripped her arm to slow her feet. Naboto's ankle adornments—pod-beads containing seeds—rattled and clinked rhythmically as a backdrop to Vimbela's cheerful tune. He recalled that Anele had loved this particular song. After a few more verses, the jingle no longer triggered happy memories. It ushered him back to the day all three of his daughters, the last of his children, went missing—eighteen years ago.

Eighteen years ago the sun rose, gleaming like a polished gold coin. Mercy, one of many meal-makers, sent a little girl into Naboto's hut. When the child returned, she told Mercy, "Thaka, Zhana, and Anele are not there. It is only the old chief who sleeps inside."

Mercy stomped into Naboto's hut and woke him with a loud complaint. "How am I supposed to prepare the food if your daughters don't do their part, as they have been told? When I see them, I'm going to take a stick to their behinds."

As the day turned to night, a perplexed Naboto summoned the *Imikhuba,* the local witch doctor, to help him solve the mystery. The revered soothsayer arrived within minutes. He squatted beside the chieftain and etched secret African symbols on the dirt floor with a stick. He then lifted his goat horn which was filled with magic stones. With a swoop of his hand, the seer threw the contents of the horn onto the dirt. He studied the stones methodically before he said, "Your daughters are gone from Tswanas. They left before sunup."

"Why? Where are they? Please, tell me more."

"The magic stones bring bad tidings. Are you sure you want to know the truth?"

"Yes, Great One."

"Your twin daughters are in the Invisible Kingdom of Souls, shot by a white man's steel bullets. And your last child, the one you named "Enough," is enslaved. The *umlungu* own her now."

Alone in his home, Naboto buried his head in his hands and wept.

As Anele approached the village, fingers of campfire smoke snapped Chief Naboto out of his reverie. Vimbela rushed through the compound shouting delightedly, "See. I told you I'd find the old chief in the dark. He is not happy."

Naboto shook his head. Vimbela could make a mountain shake

with her yelling. He was hardly through the village gate when a throng of women and children surrounded him. Some older women in the crowd who had known Anele as a child began whooping and hollering jubilantly. It was all too much for the old man's ears.

"Be still!" the chief commanded. "Calmness brings harmony to our souls; the wild chatter of monkeys does not. Go about your business. Leave me with mine," he ordered, lowering himself into a bamboo chair outside his hut. Was it *really* Anele? Why had she never tried to get word to him in all these years? What did she look like now? Would he recognize her? Was she in good or frail health? Was she married? Did she have children with her? His nephew and dear friend, Tekenya, handed his uncle a clay jug filled to the brim with strong beer and said, "For your heart to sing with joy."

Hardly a drop of beer had passed the chief's lips when a sharp-eyed boy, loud with triumph, shouted, "Chief, *she* is here! I can see her. Your daughter comes!"

A pack of village hunting dogs sprinted to the gate barking ferociously. Undaunted, Anele simply shooed them away. With a sleeping Shiya strapped and hidden in the folds of the material on her back, Anele pushed her way through the crowd of villagers who threatened to squash the baby with their enthusiastic welcome. Anele didn't recognize any of the faces. Had she been gone that long? She smiled contentedly.

Anele was thrilled to arrive home safely. She had made a long, perilous journey to get here, mostly through wilderness fraught with hungry critters: leopards, lions, jackals, and other feral hounds, all looking for an easy meal. The smell of baby was delectable to these creatures.

Many times Anele had wielded the butcher's cleaver like a warrior, daring her predatory attackers. But it wasn't the animals of the wild that worried her most; it was the tribal folk she encountered along the way. At first they had been friendly, until they noticed the *unana*—white baby—strapped to her bosom. One curious woman flung a question at Anele. "What are you doing with a white infant so far from the white townships?"

"You have horse blinders on?" Anele retorted. "Can't you see my baby's dark skin?"

"Since when do Zulu women give birth to blond-haired babies with green eyes?"

When they are raped by a white man! Anele's silent response echoed in her mind.

After that encounter Anele did her best to avoid settlements along the way. Now, in the twilight, the village where she had lived the first nine years of her life seemed unfamiliar. Without thinking, she asked in English, "Is my father, Chief Naboto, still here?"

Her question was answered by blank stares. Anele clicked her tongue in stupidity and repeated the question in their language. Someone touched Anele's arm and said, "Come. I will take you to him, special daughter of Chief Naboto"

With her arm linked in Anele's, Vimbela led the way. Anele's heart fluttered with love at being home again, seeing her father rising from a chair and stretching out his arms. Feeling joyful, she thought, *Thank the Great Spirit! He is still alive!* When she spoke aloud, her grateful heart missed a beat. "Father, it brings me great joy to find you alive."

"Anele, Anele, Anele," Naboto repeated. "It is good to be called 'father' again. There is no doubt you are the daughter of Tuttia. Her remarkable eyes shine through you. But I'm surprised to see you have the wrinkled face of an ancient one. According to my markings on the sacred tree, you have seen only twenty-seven summers. What has happened to you to make you look like an ancient one? And why do you bear such terrible scars?"

Anele took hold of her father's hand and said, "Let us go inside. I have many things to tell you."

As an amber glow emanated from lanterns filled with pig oil, eerie shadows were cast against the hut's oval walls. To aid his dimming eyesight, Naboto lit a third, larger lamp. Standing inside the hut where she was born, a knife of grief twisted inside Anele. How could she tell her father what had happened to her sisters or of the loss of her child or of finding Shiya? Would he order her and the baby to leave Tswanas, like Lamella had predicted? Anele sighed. She doubted that his hatred of white people had diminished with time. She was bringing a white man's infant into his home ... Naboto broke into her thoughts. "Daughter, you may have my *ndlunkulu* until a new hut can be built for you."

"No, Father. Don't give up your hut for me. We can share it, like we did when I was a child. I can sleep on the floor."

"Anele, you'll do as you are told. I'll sleep in Tekeyna's hut. He has had two empty beds since his wives have died."

For an instant, the past collided with the present. Anele let herself wander back to a time she thought had been lost forever—her father's no-nonsense ways. She hugged her father with her last bit of strength and said, "Father, I have missed you so much."

Naboto's dull eyes clouded. "But why did *you* leave ..."

Shiya's infant wail stopped the chief dead in his tracks. Naboto burst into delighted laughter. "I'm a happy man. You have brought home a grandson, yes?"

Without waiting for Anele's reply, Naboto hobbled toward the doorway and announced for all to hear, "My daughter returns with my grandchild. We must celebrate! Bring more beer to my hut." Anele rushed over to him and firmly clasped his arm. "Please, Father, no celebration, not yet. I'm too tired for that. And I bring to you a granddaughter, not a grandson."

"Girl ... boy ... it doesn't matter. You bring home a child of my royal bloodline."

Anele sighed. "Please, Father, I need you to ask for a nursing mother to come quickly. I have no more milk." Anele's miraculous milk flow had stopped hours before she arrived at the kraal.

"Does your husband follow? Do you have other children? Where are they?"

Questions, questions, questions, Anele's exasperated mind screamed. It was too much and too soon. "Father, I'll answer anything you wish to know later, but first my baby must be fed."

"Go and fetch a nursing mother to my hut," Naboto ordered a little girl standing in the doorway gawking at Anele.

Shiya's tiny chest heaved between wails. Somehow Anele had to muster the energy to care for the baby. "Hush, my precious miracle baby," Anele crooned, holding Shiya tightly against her chest. "Milk is coming." As though she had uttered a magic mantra, the crying stopped and the baby drifted back to sleep. Anele gazed lovingly at her newfound child, whose lips were twitching and eyeballs rolling in innocent dreams.

Touched by the tiny infant's will to survive, Anele wondered how long the girl had lain in her cornhusk grave with her umbilical cord ripped and bleeding. Anele could only guess. Had it not been for her miraculous but meager breast milk, the poor child would have died long before now. A proud radiance flushed Anele's face. She had saved this child. And it didn't matter if the baby was Zulu or not. She would love Shiya and raise her as though she had been born from her own body. The loss of her own child fourteen years ago was never far from her mind, but she chose now to concentrate on today.

A wholesome village girl, her breasts enlarged and nipples erect, entered the dwelling. A warm smile lifted her full lips as she spoke.

"Welcome home, daughter of Chief Naboto. My name is Umia. Like you, I have just given birth. I drink the milk of the goat to make sure my breasts are full. You should try it. It will help your own milk flow."

Umia lowered herself and sat cross-legged on the dirt floor, stretching her arms to receive the baby. Anele handed her the swaddled bundle. Immediately, Umia's happy-to-help look vanished. Wide eyed, she stared at Shiya and screamed. Outside, sitting in his chair, a drunken Naboto slept through the mayhem.

Umia leapt to her feet, sending Shiya rolling across the floor like wind-blown sage. That action was followed by a duet of Umia's horrified wails and Shiya's outraged shrieks. Anele used one hand to grip Umia's arm firmly so she could not flee and the other to sweep up her infant. A quick look confirmed Shiya was not hurt, only traumatized.

Anele ordered, "Umia, you will feed her *now*!"

Umia, arms crossed defiantly across her bosom, gave Anele a defiant look. The young girl glared stubbornly and said, "No. I will never let the lips of an *umlungu* suckle on my nipples."

"You'll do as you are told, or I'll strangle you."

Umia shook her head. Anele tried a softer approach. "If you have a good mother's heart, Umia, feed my baby. She is hungry."

Umia's sigh was compassionate. "Okay. I will do it, but only once."

Anele guided Shiya's mouth to the girl's swollen breast, but the baby's pursed lips struggled to grasp the nipple. It was obvious Umia was not going to help. Anele was at her wits end and was beyond being nice. She squatted and squeezed Umia's nipple so firmly a spray of milk splashed onto Shiya's face. The baby's tiny mouth finally latched, and she sucked greedily. Umia looked away. Soon a healthy pink glow spread over Shiya's naked body. Her sparkling emerald eyes closed slowly, then opened abruptly when a loud noise pounded her delicate ears.

Now it was Umia who let out a piercing shriek. "May the Great Spirit of all Zulus protect my good heart," she cried. "This baby has the most frightening eyes I've ever seen." She reached for Anele's hand, clasped it, and pleaded. "Daughter of Chief Naboto, I've done what you asked. Let me go now. I must feed my own child, a baby boy born just before you arrived ..."

All eyes turned. There stood an inebriated Naboto. He was draped in leopard skin, feathers, a bone anklet, and neck adornments, and was holding a long-handled *assegai*. Proud of his bloodline, Naboto had always claimed to be a descendant of the Zulu king, Dingane, half-brother of King Chaka, who ruled the once vast dominion of the brave Zulu nation. He was also related to King Ninuzulu and Queen Nobantu, a former child slave on the Hallworthy planation during Lord Nigel's time. Now, unsteady on his feet, he approached Anele and the child. "By the power in me as Chieftain of Tswanas," he slurred, "I have come to evoke *Ukuvikeleleka*, the God of Protection, over the new life that carries my royal blood. The child must be safeguarded against harmful spirits."

Nobody made a sound. But many intense eyes, including baby Shiya's, were glued to the man.

From a calfskin pouch strung around his neck, Naboto removed bone fragments (supposedly belonging to his ancestors) and placed them in a symbolic order on the floor of his hut. He began chanting an ancient rite. When he finished the mantra, he turned and ordered Umia, "Hand me the child."

Umia smiled with relief as she thrust Shiya into Naboto's outstretched arms. Her voice was cutting. "Your protection isn't going to work, old man. We are all going to die. The Fire God is going to roast our village because of your stupid daughter! She is no better than the brainless one, Vimbela. I'm going to put hot beeswax on my breasts to kill the taste of the evil one. I wish Anele had never come back. I wish she had stayed with the *umlungu*."

Naboto grabbed the girl's arm. "What troubles your brain so, young mother? Your words sting like the venom of a snake."

"You'll find out yourself, blind old man." With that said, Umia sprinted away.

Anele had been away for some time, but as far as she was concerned, Umia had broken a cardinal tribal rule, to treat the chief with respect. Naboto was still head of this village, and she felt the need to say so. "*Ubaba*, how dare she talk to you in this manner? You should take a stick to her bad mouth. Get me another nursing mother for my child's next feed. I don't wish to see that silly girl again."

Naboto didn't reply. His attention was on the infant writhing underneath the blanket. His voice was fatherly. "Do not fret, little one. I'm not going to hurt you." He uncovered Shiya and let out a gasp. His pupils grew large and droplets of saliva dribbled down his chin. He faced Anele and said angrily, "You're no daughter of mine. No child of my loins would deceive me so. The blood of this baby does not run in my family. Nor is it of your making, Anele." He tossed the wailing infant. Anele caught Shiya in midair and held the distressed child to her breasts. Anele had forgotten how embittered her father was against the whites.

Naboto continued to rant. "Madness has filled your head like the maggots of all dead flesh. Your lies have injured my heart, Anele. You are not the daughter of Tuttia, an honorable woman. She gave her life for your unworthy self." He took a deep breath and swallowed a mouthful of spit. "You have darkened her pure spirit. Worst of all, you have disgraced your own soul by possessing a child not of your birthright. Where is the white mother of this infant? Or have you stolen the blood of another?"

Anele didn't look up. She buried her head in Shiya's softness and remained silent. Naboto glared at his daughter, daring her to defy him. What he said next surprised Anele. "I've shed many tears for all my lost children, especially you, named 'Enough,' my last born. Yes, I know what happened to the twins. Thankfully, you never met their fate, and I ached through you to have grandchildren to carry on our family blood. Now I am faced with an *umlungu* baby who has the bad blood of all whites. This child has no right in my village. And it never will as long as I have breath in my body." He slapped his thigh. "I must leave here before I murder you with my own hands."

The chief's blood was still boiling when he left the hut and shuffled past the campfire where the women were gathered. At the top of his voice he yelled, "None of you are allowed in my hut. Keep away. That is an order." Without a backward glance, he headed toward the gate.

"What happened?" a young woman asked. "The Chief has the rage of a bull elephant."

Umia, her eyes red from crying, had the answer. "I'll tell you why our chief has murder in his eyes."

Men, women, and children gasped in disbelief. The sound of incredulous hissing grew louder than crackling fire as Umia ended her story. One woman was skeptical. "Are you *sure* it's a pure *umlungu* baby, Umia? Could Anele have been *taken*, forced to lie down with a white man?"

Umia cut her off, "Go and see for yourself, if you don't believe me. The baby's skin is pink as a pig's, and her eyes are the color of green plant dye. Not one drop of good African blood is in that baby. I can assure you, it is pure *umlungu*."

One young girl asked, "Do you think Anele stole this child?"

Umia clucked her tongue. "How else did she come by it?"

Old Mercy, who had known Anele as a child, cried out, "Merciful Great Ancestral Spirits of the Zulu people! That's never been heard of here. What's going to happen to us if the whites find out?"

Umia glanced furtively over her shoulder and whispered, "Nothing if we do something about it."

"What you do mean, Umia?"

"Anele and the baby must die."

Naboto disrobed a few yards outside the kraal. He flung his royal attire to the ground and walked on. Thankful for the full moon and starlit night, he was able to cross the field of sisal without stumbling. Up ahead a rock formation resembling the outstretched wings of a gigantic bird loomed eerily. Naboto, deeply spiritual, believed that this outcrop was a gateway into the Spirit Realm. As the old chief neared this sacred place, what appeared to be disembodied, red, glowing eyes studied his approach. "Creatures of the night," said Naboto, "I do not fear you. Find something tender to eat. This old body of mine will only give you indigestion."

Naboto forced himself onward until his feet breasted the summit. There, his hands on the crook of his back, Naboto inhaled a deep breath of cooling night air. He raised his outstretched arms and said, "Namandla, God of the Invisible Kingdom, your humble servant, Naboto Dingane of the Tswanas tribe, calls upon you. Give me the strength and wisdom of the *ibuthos,* warriors of old, who died fighting for our land. Let them appear in my dreams and help me fight a battle I know is sure to come. Without their guidance, the *umlungu* will kill us all."

Naboto cleared his throat. "Sadness and anger fill my old heart.

I did not see in my dreams the terrible deed my last-born child has done. Why did she steal another's child? Is she without a womb to carry her own? But why, Great Spirits, did she take an *umlungu* baby? This is not only shameful, but also inexplicably dangerous."

The stars twinkled coldly as he shifted from leg to leg awaiting a response. Moments, feeling like hours, passed. Naboto grew impatient. "Ancient Spirits, I need a sign, an indication that my pleas to you do not go unheard."

Something as cold as a mountain brook brushed across Naboto's face and the old man's leathery features cracked into a broad, toothless smile. He said, "Beloved wife, Tuttia, I sense that you are close to my wretched old body. Good woman once on earth and now in spirit, my heart is full of shame and sorrow."

Naboto knew that the dead can influence the affairs of the living. But asking a woman's advice, dead or alive, was taboo. Just in case a male from his village had followed him, he whispered, "Wife, I need your wisdom to deal with the grave situation that our tribe must face. Please tell me what has to be done."

Silhouetted against the moonlight, Naboto lowered himself slowly onto a flat stone. With his bony back resting against a boulder, he closed his eyes. His mind lifted with warm thoughts of that happy day so long ago.

On a summer's evening long ago, the Tswanas tribe was busy preparing their chief's wedding to Tuttia Umdanuna, a young girl from the neighboring Mtunzini village. Voices of jubilation filled the air. Hunters returned with ample fresh kill of impala and oryx. The women prepared gallons of beer while the children scattered wild flowers in the matrimonial circle drawn by the witch doctor. The seventeen-summers-old groom noted that everyone was excited, except his bride, Tuttia. Still shy of her thirteenth birthday, she entered the matrimonial hut with the married women, who, while chattering and buzzing like bees, began preparing her in accordance with tribal rituals. The women recognized that the girl's solemnity suited a funeral rather than her marriage. Tuttia pressed her hand over her aching heart. She was not joyous about joining the other married women of the African bush.

While being rubbed down with sheep fat and oils, Tuttia stood still and remained as silent as a tree stump until an elder began shaving *all* her body hair with the razor-sharp tip of a spear. The bride pulled back and cried, "Why do you do this, old woman?"

"It's the Tswanas custom."

Tuttia let out a glum sigh.

Moments later, a crown of aromatic and colorful wildflowers was placed on the bride's head. It overpowered the foul odor of the sheep fat emanating from her body. Tuttia was given a beaded straw skirt, a carved bone-and-bead necklace, and large hooped earrings. After a final critical inspection from the women, Tuttia was pronounced ready.

At the nuptial circle the groom was handed a mug by the local witch doctor, who said, "Naboto of Royal blood and Tuttia, daughter of Umdanuna and unknown father, drink the elixir of all life. On this your wedding night, new life will be certain."

Naboto took a sip and handed the drink to Tuttia. She downed the rest in one mighty swallow, gagged, and then complained, "It is bitter and smells worse than cow dung."

The witch doctor's eyes grew wide. "You weren't supposed to drink it all!" he said.

Naboto puffed out his chest and laughed, "I don't need the whole elixir to prove I'm a man. Take my bride to my hut," he ordered. "Make sure she is properly prepared for the stallion of this village."

The menfolk partied until the beer ran out.

Sometime after midnight, Naboto staggered into his hut. The nimbus of the yellow flame radiating from the lamp exposed his naked flesh. Tuttia scooted to the top of the straw mattress.

"Wife, are you ready for the father of your children?"

"You smell worse than wild pig meat!" came a muffled voice from under the blanket.

Smiling, Naboto fell upon the straw mattress and claimed his Mtunzini bride.

In the years that followed, Tuttia became a dutiful wife. She bore him eight children; the birth of the last, Anele, would take her life. The night of Anele's birth, beneath a dusting of stars, heartbroken Naboto took the newborn to the sacred outcrop. Like his ancestors before him, he held her up and announced, "Namandla, I name this child Anele—Enough. Protect her, Great Spirit. Give her strength." Naboto sighed heavily with grief. "My beloved wife, Tuttia, I will forever see your image in her eyes. You are gone from me in flesh, but in spirit you will always remain within both our hearts."

The first rays of sunlight danced over Naboto's eyelids and woke him. He rose and attempted to loosen his stiff neck. Soon his mind flooded with anguish: *What have you done, Anele? These old bones were prepared for death, ready to join your mother, brothers, and twin sisters. How can I now leave this mortal land a free man? Anele, Anele, Anele. You have to return the child to its rightful white tribe or you and I will surely die a horrible death. Our spirits will not fly free. The*

thought of not reuniting with his darling Tuttia wrenched Naboto's heart from his chest. He bowed his head and let the tears fall.

Suddenly an eagle swooped down from the sky, its mighty wing-span stretching to within inches of Naboto's head. The bird released a deafening screech and then soared upward. The old man stretched his crooked fingers and bent to pick up a fallen tail feather. His heart quickened. This was the sacred sign he had been waiting for.

With renewed strength Naboto hurried from the rock as fast as his legs allowed. A few yards from the kraal Naboto felt a pain worse than bullets and dropped to the ground. His dull eyes tried to focus on the sacred bird that had landed only a hand's breadth away. With enormous effort Naboto lifted his head. The molten eyes of the majestic bird fused with his. It was telling him ... it was telling him ... Naboto's eyelids closed for the last time. The revered eagle of the African plains screeched loudly, circled Naboto's dead body, and summoned the undertaker birds while it soared into the blood-red sunrise.

The buzzards tore ravenously into the lifeless yet still warm flesh of the spiritual man who had been the Royal Chief Naboto Dingane.

Back in the kraal, Natu, Umia's ten-year-old brother, had an impish smile, knowing full well that he was supposed to get per-mission before leaving the compound that early. Carrying a rusty spoon in his hand, he climbed over the gate. He planned to dig for worms early, before the sun drove them deeper into their tunnels, or dig for ant pupa in the many mounds dotting the area around the settlement. Today his older brothers were going fishing at the river, and he wanted to join them. If he offered them juicy worms, he felt sure they would invite him to come along. The thought of fishing with his brothers propelled his legs faster, and he dashed toward a nearby ant mound.

Natu rubbed his runny nose with his hand and began digging

through a thick layer of sand to reach the pupa. The soldier ants appeared in droves and attacked his busy fingers. After several painful bites, he moved his location. That's when he saw the vultures. They were diving into what he imagined was an animal carcass. He thought, *Dead creatures have maggots—even better fishing bait.*

The ugly birds dashed skyward as he approached.

What Natu saw caused him to drop his spoon and tin and take off like a rocket. The slapping of his feet and his frantic cries alerted the villagers. Natu flapped his arms as if trying to scatter the buzzards. He finally managed to get some words out. "The Chief lies dead outside the kraal. He has a big hole in his face and no eyeballs." Natu's body was shaking against his mother's hip.

"Are you sure, son?" Natu's father asked.

Natu nodded.

"Come show me where this body lies."

Minutes later, Natu's father confirmed. "Yes, our chief lies dead."

The rapid, high-pitched tongue-clicking and the ritual loud wailing for the dead brought Anele to the door. "What's happening? Who's died?"

Little Natu was the first to speak. "Your *Ubaba* has been eaten!"

Anele fiercely grabbed Natu's arm. "What did you say?"

The little boy cried out in pain, bringing his mother to his side. "Let go of my child, Anele!" she insisted. "He tells no lie. Go and see for yourself. Your father is dead."

The reed stretcher was lifted high as it neared the gate.

"Put it down!" Anele screamed. "I want to see."

She pulled back the blanket covering Naboto's body. The scavengers of the African plains had not only plucked out his eyeballs and tongue, they had nearly stripped him of his flesh. With her face frozen in shocked disbelief, Anele cradled her father's bloodied head saying, "Father you cannot be dead! No! This is not happening! You can't be gone, not so soon! I've been home less than a day! And there was so much I wanted to tell you about Thaka and Zhana. How brave they were. How I survived the dark days ..." She began to sob.

Vimbela strode through the crowd, hunkered down, and in her simplistic way said, "Your father was a *very* old man, as old as the stars. It was his time. Be happy for him. He's gone to a better place. Our ancestors will take care of him now."

The matriarch of the village, Granny Matudia, stroked Anele's tear-stained cheek. "Last child of Naboto, you must let the burial women do their duty. It is custom to bury him before the setting of the sun."

Anele rubbed the tears from her eyes and nodded in agreement. She tried to get up, but her body remained glued to the dusty soil. She was weighted down by sorrow. Vimbela noted her efforts and came to her rescue. Her powerful arms lifted the sobbing Anele and led her back to Naboto's hut. Inside, Anele flung her body to the ground and began pounding her fists into the dirt floor. "I've had more unhappiness than a heart can hold," she wailed. "This pain is too much to bear."

Expressionless, Vimbela went to the makeshift crib—a wooden orange crate lined with calfskin—and lifted the sleeping baby. The teenager said to the prone Anele, "Sit up and hold your baby. Be strong for your *umlungu* child. She needs you now more than your dead father does. Wailing and pounding fists will not bring back your dead *Ubaba*."

A solitary tear rolled down Anele's cheek and fell on Shiya's forehead.

"I love you with all my heart," Anele said, "but I can't be a mother to you at this moment. I must first grieve my loss. Vimbela mind my baby, please."

Outside, the sun was as intense as the accusations being flung, mostly by the younger generation. "If *she* hadn't come back, our leader would still be here."

"Yes. He was in fine health until she came."

"The shock of her stealing a white child is what's killed him."

"She is to blame for his sudden death."

One voice shrilled over the rest—Umia's. "The Chief is gone. Why don't we chase Anele and the white baby from our village? Or, better yet, let's do what we discussed last night, kill …"

Umia was cut short by a mighty shove from Granny Matudia, who had just walked out of her hut.

"Get on with your chores, you stupid girl. Who gives you the right to judge Chief Naboto's daughter! Go or I'll take a stick to you!"

Matudia, her age unknown, had not been present to welcome Anele home. She had taken to her bed with severe stomach cramps and diarrhea, which she blamed on undercooked goat's liver. She had not taken kindly to people wandering in and out of her hut gossiping about Anele and the white baby. Matudia had chosen to ignore the village prattle until she was well enough to find out for herself.

Matudia covered Naboto's desecrated face with his blanket. To the two elderly women wailing tribal death cries she ordered, "Burial women, you must now prepare our chief for his journey to the afterlife." To the oldest of Natu's brothers, Kumdi, she said, "Carry Chief Naboto to his hut and place him on his bed."

Kumdi nodded. Then the matriarch turned to young Natu and said, "Go to the sacred cave in the hill, Twazli's home, and tell him to come quickly. We need his 'passing over' powers."

The dust from Natu's racing feet swirled into a mini-twister.

Meanwhile, Kumdi, a strapping teenager, lifted Naboto in his arms as if the old chief weighed nothing more than a handful of grain, and carried him into the hut. He placed Naboto on the bed, glared contemptuously at Anele, and left.

Anele stroked her father's cold forehead and tenderly picked off the blood-encrusted leaves that had stuck to his mangled flesh. She whispered, "Father, my heart is like a swollen river. It overflows with loss. It was the hope of seeing you again that kept me from losing my sanity during my enslavement. The wisdom you instilled in me as a child—to look evil in the eye and conquer it—is how I survived those dark days. I'm sure you are watching over me with your all-knowing and all-seeing eyes, so my words of sorrow will not go unheard."

Something on the bed caught her eye.

Anele picked up the eagle's tail feather that had been found near her father's body. *Funny*, she thought. *It looks similar to the one I found lying near Shiya's crib last night before I went to bed.* Was it a coincidence? Was there symbolism to the two feathers?

Anele reached for the crib plume, which was lying on a small, handcrafted table. She tucked both feathers into a little lock of what was left of Naboto's knotty hair. "*Hamba kahle, Ubaba*," she said in her native tongue. She then spoke in English. "Goodbye, my beloved father. May your spirit soar peacefully with the sacred eagles until the day we are reunited in the Invisible Kingdom of Souls. Hug my mother, brothers, and, especially, Thaka and Zhana. Tell them I love and miss them dreadfully." Anele kissed her father.

Matudia entered the hut and gently touched the grieving woman's shoulder. "Anele, daughter of our dead leader, the burial women have work to do. Leave the hut so that they can begin."

"No. Not *now*, Matudia. I want to spend more time with my father."

"This is your right, Anele. But maybe you have forgotten the bad flies that feed on the dead and then bring sickness to the living. This is why we must hurry to bury your father."

Anele, her patience strained to the limit, snapped. "Get out, Matudia! I will summon the burial women when I'm done speaking to my father."

Matudia, her face sullen, left the hut. She wasn't happy. How dare the *umlungu*-brainwashed woman speak to her like that? After all, she was the matriarch, the wise woman, and a powerful soothsayer. Given Anele's tragic circumstances, Matudia forgave her this time, but she would never allow Anele to shout at her again. Vimbela wasn't happy, either. To disrespect the wise woman was bad. Vimbela loved Matudia, who had cared for her since she was a child, and she felt sure Anele was in for a tongue thrashing from the matriarch when all this was over.

After Anele left the hut, she watched from a distance as the women removed items from their baskets. While chanting a "passing over" litany, a tune about the soul being free of the cumbersome flesh vessel, the women cleansed Naboto's body with boiled river water. They plugged orifices with beeswax, and sealed his empty eye sockets and mouth with a resin-like mixture. They dressed Naboto in his royal attire and then nodded to each other. They were done. The oldest woman said to Anele, "Daughter of Naboto, your father's spirit is already in the Invisible Kingdom. His flesh is ready for the Sacred Worms."

Anele bowed her head.

The villagers entered the hut a few at a time to pay homage to their chieftain. Those who were inside when the centenarian witch doctor arrived scrambled out when his cane pushed back the door blanket. With a bleating goat by his side, Twazli approached the bed. Anele pinched the skin on the back of her hand to make sure she wasn't dreaming. It had been a long time since she had encountered a witch doctor, a highly respected and feared magician in African culture. She blinked several times. Yes. She was sure he was the same mystical man from her childhood—a man she had watched with awe perform a "miracle" that brought back to life a calf that had been mauled nearly to death by a leopard. Her heart skipped a beat. Could Twazli's supernatural powers bring her dead father back to life? Anele shook her head. What was she thinking?

Fierce candlelight reflected the witch doctor's nightmarish figure.

At least seven feet in height, Twazli's gangly limbs were gnarled like the boughs of an ancient tree. A white, powdery substance was plastered on his face, which accentuated his sunken red eyes. Dried chicken feet dangled from his enlarged earlobes. An icy chill crept into Anele's veins when the witch doctor entered the hut. She smiled uncertainly, but he did not return it. "I would like to be left alone with your father," the venerable man insisted.

Anele was taken by surprise when he spoke. She wasn't expecting a boy's softness in his voice. If anything, she had expected his old vocal cords to croak like a toad's. She made a hasty exit.

A half hour passed before the witch doctor beckoned Anele. Away from the curious onlookers, his remarkably strong hands closed firmly around her fingers. She felt a tingling, electric sensation. "I have spoken to your father's earthbound spirit," he said. "He warns you to return the *umlungu* child to its own people before it's too late. The sacred eagle messenger told him of the consequences of keeping a white child here." Twazli's bushy eyebrows furrowed. "Daughter of Naboto, many here would gladly hand you a child born of their ripe bodies to mend your emptiness. You cannot keep what is not your blood!"

Anele made brazen eye contact. "If you are as gifted as you claim to be, then you will know the circumstances of how I came upon this child. Her mother is probably dead by now."

Twazli's eyes bored into hers. "Yes, I do. I am blessed with the insight of the Ancients," he stated snappily. "I know the *lungu*—little white person—is a *shiya*, a forsaken one. But she does not belong among our people. She is to be raised by her own blood. You must return her to the man who sired her."

"I can't do that. The man is evil."

"I know that, lost daughter of Naboto. But many will die by this white man's hand if you don't heed my warning."

"You are wrong. No one is going to die. Lord Alan doesn't know of this place. Nor does he know his offspring lives."

"You're a good-hearted woman, saving this child's life, but in so doing, you have forever condemned her pure spirit and physical body to a life of untold sorrow and pain. You should have left her for the jackal."

Anele gasped at his heartless remark. Then a shiver of fear ran down her spine. She reached out for his bony hand. "Please, Great Man with All-Seeing Eyes, explain what you mean by this."

He yanked his hand away and waved it over her head, as if in benediction. "Heed my warning. Leave the child in the white township, or take her to the jungle for the beasts to devour. Either will be more merciful than what I have predicted. If you do not, your fate and hers will be worse than the sinking of a deadly serpent's razor-sharp fangs into your flesh."

Twazli, his pet goat nudging his hand, left the hut.

With her insides on edge, Anele cracked her knuckles. Had she forgotten how powerful this man was? Hadn't she been told as a child that his powers came from the underworld, a dark place where grotesque entities danced with flames of fire? The witch doctor's dire predictions and the horrible thought of Shiya lying in a field somewhere ripped to shreds were too much for Anele's disturbed mind. Following tribal tradition, she threw back her head and keened her heartbreak, repeatedly slapping her chest like a gorilla until she collapsed. When Anele opened her eyes, Vimbela was staring at her. "Get up, *Umama* Anele. The burial party is ready to take your father to the Sacred Hill."

Naboto's modest wooden casket was hoisted in the air by the strongest of the men. On the way to the burial site, the funeral entourage swigged beer, danced, and sang happy tunes, as was their tradition. At the burial ground, wolf spiders weaved gossamer threads and warbling birds flew from thorn branch to thorn branch. Circling high above, the sacred eagle soared.

According to tradition, Naboto's coffin was lowered vertically into a six-foot hole that faced north. Before the earth was replaced, Anele placed a handful of tobacco leaves that had been soaked in acacia tree oil and her father's favorite clay pipe on top of his closed casket. Granny Matudia flung baobab leaves from his favorite tree and a few stones from the Sacred Rock. Natongo dropped a corked jug of his best brew of *imfuka* to finalize his cousin's passing over. These gifts, symbols of mortals, were to ease Naboto's transition into the world of spirits. Now it was left to the gravediggers.

Matudia touched Anele's solemn face. "You shed no tears. This is good. Your father is smiling at you."

"Can you see him?"

"Of course, I can. I have ancient, spiritual gifts."

"I wish my father knew how I regret not running away from the white man's place sooner."

"He knows that, child. Don't blame yourself for the evils of others."

Anele's heart spoke silently. *I will always love you, Ubaba. One day we will be together again.*

Circular garlands woven from aromatic, yellow wildflowers that resembled dandelions were placed on the burial mound. Their stunning color was deceptive, though; they were extremely poisonous. The village men took turns urinating around the grave's perimeter, their urine acting as a territorial marker to prevent creatures from digging up the body. Naboto lay in the heart of the mountain terrain he had once played in as a boy. A few yards away from him lay his beloved wife, Tuttia, her arms folded across her chest in death's embrace. A decorated stone, faded by many seasons, marked her resting place. Also on this sacred hillside, cloaked by tall thorn bushes, was the unmarked grave of Vimbela's son.

All of the mourners, except Anele, returned to the village. She remained seated on the dirt beside her father's grave. She had so much to tell him, but mental fatigue got the better of her. She buried her head in her folded arms and closed her eyes. Within seconds she was fast asleep. As time passed, curtains of multicolored light flickered in transient patterns across the darkened sky. The loud, haunting call of a wild creature snapped her awake.

After tripping repeatedly over tree stumps and rocks, she finally made it home. It was passed midnight. Not a soul could be seen around the kraal. Anele found Vimbela breastfeeding Shiya.

"I was worried that you'd been eaten," Vimbela said.

"I'm here now. So there's no need to worry your pretty head. How is my baby doing?"

"The way she guzzles, I'm going to run out of milk."

Anele did not know at this time that just before she arrived home, Vimbela had given birth to a stillborn child. Anele had naturally assumed that Vimbela's "I'm going to run out of milk" comment meant that she wouldn't have enough milk for her own baby.

As the weeks passed, Anele's life grew blissful, the rosiest it had been in a long while. To improve her lifestyle even more, she decided Naboto's mud hut, the dowdy home of her childhood, needed a makeover. The dirt floor was carpeted wall to wall with braided reed-matting. A window was cut into one side of the structure and covered with the drapery material Anele had stolen from the manor. A pinkish plant dye enhanced the woven door blanket, and surrounding the renovated home, wildflower seeds were sprouting. Anele's rope-fashioned washing line stirred the most interest from the other villagers. Anele showed the women how to hang clothing with the wooden pegs she had made, and they were delighted. No more laying out their laundry on rocks to dry.

Of all the village women, Mercy was the most pleased. Anele's culinary skills introduced novel flavors. Anele added wild herbs to meals and prepared sweet desserts made from dried acacia leaves and honey. Although Anele eventually became generally accepted by the villagers, a few did shun her. Umia was as cool as a cucumber. "I don't like you, *umlungu*-loving woman. I'll never be your friend."

"That's fine, Umia. I don't need your friendship. I have plenty of friends."

The two women avoided each other the best they could in the confines of the small compound.

But that was about to change.

One peaceful morning all the villagers, except Umia, ate heartily of Anele's corn and mealie-meal patties drenched in honey. Mercy smiled at the cook. "These are delicious. I'm glad to see that your appetite has returned. You've hardly eaten a morsel since coming here."

"It's a new day, dear Mercy. My father wouldn't want me to be sad, and I have made him a promise. On every full moon I will visit him and tell him news of his granddaughter."

Some frowned at her statement, as if Anele were out of her mind. But no one said anything to her. The promise had already been set. Or had it?

 The Witch Doctor's Warning

"Beware the ides of March."
—William Shakespeare

The burial garlands had long withered. Anele was pleased to see that her father's grave had remained untouched. The tribal urination had done its job—it had kept Naboto's resting place free from desecration. Anele removed a sleeping Shiya from the comfort of Vimbela's blanket carrier and held the child's drooping head over Naboto's grave. "*Ubaba*, I wish to reintroduce you to Shiya, the forsaken one. She's not of my blood, but she is the only child I'll ever have, as I'm sure you already know. Watch over Shiya as she grows into a fine Zulu maiden." Anele firmly pushed Shiya's tiny hand into the grave dirt. "My beloved *Ubaba*, Shiya greets you with the hand of pure love."

Shiya woke up and shrieked. Vimbela rolled her eyes and protested. "Don't make her cry so. She's too little to know our customs. Anyway, she's *umlungu!*"

Anele gave Vimbela a "who-the-hell-are-you" glare. "Vimbela, I know how much you love Shiya, but don't ever question my actions again."

Vimbela made a rebellious face, then bent and snatched the wailing baby from Anele's grip. Vimbela's voice was icy. "You can stay here all you want and talk to the dirt, *Umama* Anele, but I'm taking Shiya home."

Anele shrugged and let Vimbela march off with Shiya. What was the point of scolding the well-meaning, simple girl? She was as innocent as a child.

Anele remained at Sacred Hill for no less than an hour.

As Anele approached the village gate, Granny Matudia marched toward her. "Come with me," the matriarch said, latching onto Anele's arm. "Your presence is needed at the tribal meeting."

"Matudia, I'm exhausted from my long walk. Do you really need me?"

"Yes. There are those who are not happy with your father's successor."

"Who is it?

"Kumdi."

"Umia's brother!"

"Yes. He's not fit to lead us. He thinks only of bedding girls, rather than of the welfare of our people."

Anele lost her words but not her thoughts. *Will my opinion make a difference?* No. She didn't think so, and she said so. "If my father chose this young man, he must have thought highly of him."

Matudia shook her head in disagreement and said, "I don't think your father was in his right mind when he selected this awful boy."

Anele delicately removed the old woman's hand from her arm and leaned against the wall of the cattle shed. Something told her Matudia was only beginning to get her point across. "Kumdi has slyly taken married women to his bed. This doesn't sit well with the elders of the village who know of his wrongs. If the husbands of these women learned about his behavior, blood would rightly flow."

Anele made a "whatever" face before she responded. "Matudia, it won't be the first time married women cheat on their husbands. I blame the women for allowing Kumdi to bed them. Regardless of his sexual activities, the time has come for a spirited young leader like Kumdi to lead this tribe, even though, personally, I don't like him. With all due respect, Matudia, I don't believe anything I might say would change the voting. I'm sure whoever takes my father's place will do a good job."

Matudia, muttering inaudibly, turned her back on Anele and headed toward the communal fire pit.

Anele entered her hut, poured herself a generous beer, and elevated her tired feet.

As the full moon climbed toward the heavens, the whole village gathered around the fire pit for the meeting. Sitting on upturned logs, the elders waited for Kumdi to exit his family's hut. After a time, Kumdi sidled up to the group wearing a lion's pelt over his shoulder. His two pregnant wives walked behind him. Young men, mostly teenagers, raised their spears and in unison voiced their approval: "Kumdi for our leader!"

Kumdi smiled broadly. He lifted his spear in the air and declared, "I will honor my duty as newly appointed chieftain of the Tswanas tribe. I will bring about great change."

Nobody, especially the males, could have imagined what was to follow this oath.

The women, who outnumbered the men, joined hands and drew closer to Kumdi. They moved like stalking predators. When they were inches from him, an elderly woman spoke up. "I don't like you and never have."

With his eyes blazing, Kumdi thrust his spear within inches of the woman's heart and threatened, "Be quiet or I'll spill your blood, old woman."

Gasps. Retaliatory shouts. Then the village women circled Kumdi. Again he threatened. "Come an inch closer and blood will spill." He turned to the men, who were sitting with stunned expressions. "Are you going to let your women disrespect me?"

Now retaliatory shouts came from the men. A scuffle took place, a free-for-all. Fathers, husbands, and brothers attacked their women with spears, fists, and rocks. The night air filled with helpless screams.

Hearing the ruckus, Anele rushed outside. She was confronted by a young girl, no more than twelve, whose cheek and nose were bleeding profusely. The frightened girl grabbed Anele's hand and pleaded, "Help me, daughter of Chief Naboto. He is bad. He wants to kill us."

"Who did this to you, child?"

"I don't know," she replied honestly. The girl tugged at Anele's hand. "Come see for yourself."

The scene around the campfire looked like a boxing ring with too many contestants, and Kumdi's voice outdid all others. "Men, kill any woman who dares to lay a hand on your body."

Something inside Anele snapped. She balled her fists. All she could see was Alan Hallworthy's face the day she had first met him. She knew what had to be done. She picked up a stone, ran toward the fire pit, and hurled the rock into the flames, sending cinders shooting into the air like a fireworks display. The mayhem abruptly stopped. Many faces, some bloodied, stared at her. "Have you *all* gone crazy?" Anele shouted.

Silence.

Kumdi straightened his lion's pelt and made eye contact with Anele. "Do not interfere in our business, *umlungu*-loving woman! You don't belong here. Return to the white man's world, and take the pale child with you. That is an order!"

Anele could feel her blood pressure rising. With temples throbbing, she rushed toward Kumdi and grabbed his neck in a fierce lock. Even though she was strong and had a robust frame, she was no match for the muscular boy. He gripped her fingers and bent them to a breaking point. Anele cried out as the joint in her index finger separated under pressure.

"I warn you, woman," Kumdi spat, "don't ever lay a hand on me again!"

Ignoring the pain in her injured finger, Anele lifted a burning piece of wood with her good hand and advanced toward Kumdi. He inched away from the flame-wielding woman. Cornering him, she hissed, "I carry the royal bloodline of the Dingane family. Don't ever lay a finger on me again! I have the rightful vote in the leadership of this ..."

Like moths to a flame, the battered women swarmed around Anele. Their voices came one after the other. "Anele is our true leader!"

"We want Anele to be our chief,"

"She *is* of royal blood."

"Throw Kumdi out of the village!"

"Cut him bad and leave him to die in the jungle."

All eyes turned to Granny Matudia as she said, "As matriarch of this tribe, I declare that Anele will rightfully succeed her father."

There were gasps from all of the men but Kumdi. With clenched fists he fired, "Ancient woman, you cannot override tradition."

"Yes, I can. She has royal blood. You and the men will have to get used to it. Anele is the chieftain of the Tswanas tribe. This meeting is ..."

Vimbela pushed past Matudia. The old woman had to catch herself from falling. Shiya's wet nurse faced Anele. "I tell the truth, words from my heart," Vimbela declared. "What you don't know is that Kumdi is my half-brother. He is bad, like they say. He put the baby in my belly before you came back. And Kumdi laughed at me when it died."

Anele put a hand over her mouth, looked at Vimbela, and then over at Kumdi. He immediately reacted. "What lies you tell. You are a crazy, brainless girl."

"I'm not lying. You're a bad brother."

"I never touched your ugly body."

"Yes, you did."

Anele had heard enough. She threw another rock with all her might, hitting the boy square in the forehead. Kumdi dropped to the ground. He lay motionless as blood gushed from his head wound. Vimbela laughed as she waited to see if he would get up. When he didn't, she spat, "Kumdi, you are worse than a deadly snake. All those times you made me lie down with you and caused me terrible pain. I'm unfit for marriage now."

Kumdi's wives, who had not participated in the earlier melee, glared at their sprawled husband, but neither said a word.

"I'm happy now, *Umama* Anele," Vimbela said. "He deserved a good beating. I go now to feed Shiya."

"I'm coming with you," Anele said. "I've nothing left to say or do to this awful boy."

With their backs turned away from Kumdi, the two women didn't see him get up. He grabbed a hunting knife from his hip strap and lunged at Vimbela. Were it not for Anele's quick action—body slamming the wielder of the weapon to the ground—Vimbela would have been stabbed. Again overlooking her own injury, Anele hollered, "Brave women of Tswanas, I need your help. Hold this snake called Kumdi while I teach him a lesson he will never forget."

They happily obliged.

Kumdi was pinned down under the weight of an obese woman until his hands could be tied. Then a bombardment of stones came at him fast and furiously. The humiliated young man finally crawled to the safety of his family's hut. The rest of the men followed suit. There were too many women throwing rocks for their liking.

At midnight Matudia initiated Anele with the blood of a new-born calf. As she smeared the substance onto Anele's cheeks and arms, the matriarch declared, "Your father is proud of you. He visited me while you were having the confrontation with Kumdi. You will make a great chieftain, he said. But he has a warning. He tells you to get rid of the white child or you'll not see your twenty-eighth year of birth on this earth."

Anele shook her head. "Let's not think of doom. Tomorrow the sun will shine on all of us. Today we women have rewritten tribal history."

Anele, her head held high, walked in victory to her hut.

The next day an ear-splitting drumbeat of thunder and an awesome display of lightning slashed through the dark morning sky. Vimbela hid her head under a blanket while Shiya shrieked. Anele rushed to the crib to console the shaking child. "Hush, little one. It's only a storm."

Shiya, nestled at her mother's breasts, drifted back to sleep until torrential rainfall sounding like battalions of marching soldiers pounded the tin roof. Shiya awoke once more, and it took quite a while for Anele to soothe her. Unbeknown to the occupants of the hut, there was a worse storm on the horizon for mother and child.

Shortly after a breakfast of millet, Anele received a visitor, the little girl with the bloodied nose who had asked Anele for help. "Chief Anele, you have to watch yourself."

Anele frowned.

"Late last night," the girl said, "long after the ceremony was over, I overheard Umia telling Kumdi, "I'll not rest in this body of mine until Anele and her *umlungu* child are dead."

"Really!"

"Yes. I tell no lie. Kumdi and Umia are going to kill you and your baby and flee the village."

Anele patted the girl on the back. "Thank you for telling me this, child. Can you ask Umia and Kumdi to come to my hut?"

When the brother and sister arrived, there was poison in Umia's voice as she protested her innocence. "It's a lie," she insisted.

Anele sighed then said, "As chief of the village, I am ordering you and your brother to pack your belongings and leave Tswanas for good. You are no longer part of this tribe."

If looks could have killed, Anele would have been struck dead. But she remained unruffled. "Look, Umia, I have no objection to your parents or your younger brothers staying here. Make sure they know this."

Brother and sister looked at Anele with contempt. "You'll regret coming back," Kumdi said. "I'll make sure of it."

"You don't frighten me, *little* boy. Go before I have you chased out."

Kumdi stood like a gladiator, hand on his knife sheath. "You haven't heard the last of me. I'll seek Twazli's underworld powers to destroy you, stupid *umlungu*-loving woman! What if you have stolen this child from a white woman? If I tell on you, I will be rewarded, don't you think?"

The evicted pair stormed out of Anele's hut.

This would not be the last that the villagers would see of the humiliated wannabe leader. His return would bring shocking consequences, for he would play a part in the nightmare of all nightmares.

Afterward, Tswanas tribe would never be the same.

During the weeks that followed the troublemakers' departure, Anele's strong leadership helped her tribe grow with the times; men and women now worked side by side planting sugar cane, millet, yams, and tobacco—crops that were profitable commodities on the open market. Anele wanted to improve her village with the monetary return—build homesteads that could house large families, place corrugated roofing on the cattle sheds to protect the animals during monsoon weather, and even build a schoolhouse. Yes, Anele reasoned, she *could* bring about these improvements.

Five blissful summers and winters had passed. Anele's power had grown in leaps and bounds. No more naked villagers. Women wore colorful skirts, halter tops, and cotton undergarments fashioned from the finest woven cloth and hand sewn by Anele. Men, both young and old, wore green plant-dyed pants and short-sleeved shirts.

A small schoolhouse had been erected at the far end of the newly fenced kraal. The delighted children wore uniforms: white blouses and navy pants or pleated skirts. Sister Babavana—a black nun from a missionary in neighboring Swaziland, whom Anele had met at the marketplace—volunteered her scholastic skills.

The nun raised a subject with Anele that required some thought. What did Anele think about the Catholic religion being taught in the classroom? Anele decided that as long as the parents didn't object and the nun didn't try to enforce the Catholic faith on the children, it would be okay. Anele still had a sour taste in her mouth over what she had heard about Father Batuzi "stealing" her infant child from the Hallworthy manor, "marrying" Nyasha, and then leaving the area. Anele stressed to the nun that the children of Tswanas should also be taught the cultural history of the many brave Zulu warriors, past and present, and their battles for freedom.

Unfortunately, the nun couldn't keep that promise.

Four months after starting her teaching post, Sister Babavana ended up in a bloody battle of her own. While she was on vacation in her hometown, two rival factions clashed. During the ordeal, the nun was raped and stabbed to death.

The village schoolhouse now stood empty, and the children were heartbroken.

Anele was unable to find a replacement, so she took over the classroom herself, telling the children many stories about their heritage. The villagers became more and more in awe of their leader, until a certain incident changed their hearts.

On a hot Sunday afternoon in November 1955, Anele, Vimbela, and five-year-old Shiya joined the other women on their daily trip to the river inlet to wash clothes and collect water for cooking. Anele's heart brimmed with motherly love at the sight of her adorable, angel-faced daughter boisterously frolicking in the murky waters with the other children. Shiya was slapping the water and shrieking out of pure fun. Her curly blond hair was glistening with water droplets. Her once fair baby skin shone in a dark suntan that blended well with the skin tones of the other children. She had grown quite tall, a Hallworthy trait.

For some unknown reason, Anele's thoughts switched suddenly to Kumdi. She regretted not trying to make peace with the scorned young man. His parting words, shouted for all to hear, still haunted her: "What if Anele's child is stolen from a white woman? I'll get lots of money if I tell where she hides it." Anele continued with her washing. Surely, Kumdi had uttered only idle words of injured pride, or she would have heard about it by now.

Not long after the siblings had departed, word came that Umia had sought refuge in neighboring Mtunzini. However, Kumdi had not joined her, and his whereabouts were unknown.

Anele pounded her family's clothing on the rock and dismissed all thoughts of Kumdi, Umia, and evil Alan. It was too splendid a day to dwell on worthless people.

But there was one man who made her heart flutter. Tekenya, age fifty, was the village goatherder. He had been her father's best friend as well as his blood relative. Tekenya had pledged his love for her on the day of Naboto's funeral. Anele had been flattered but wasn't ready to commit to marriage. Tekenya had agreed to wait.

Anele began humming a lively tune as she attended to her washing. She only looked up when she heard Vimbela's high-pitched squealing. Vimbela was giddy with excitement at the sight of the tadpoles darting between her legs. The now eighteen-year-old, gripping the tail of a small, silver fish said, "Look what I have caught, *Umama* Anele. It can go in the dinner pot tonight."

"Catch lots more, Vimbela. They will make a good feast." Anele smiled fondly at the girl whose mind was not much older than Shiya's. Anele adored Vimbela, who was born with Down syndrome, a common infliction in the area due to inbreeding. On the night of Kumdi's melee, Anele had vowed that no man was ever again going to take advantage of Vimbela's innocence. Not if she could help it.

From Granny Matudia Anele had learned that the gentle, sweet girl, then barely twelve, had given birth to a malformed, blind baby boy with an enormous head and twisted limbs. Mercifully, the infant had lived only a few minutes. For hours Vimbela had clung pitifully to his limp body. In the end the infant had to be removed from her by force. That night the heartbroken young mother, her breasts throbbing with unreleased colostrum, slept beside her baby's hillside grave.

The next evening, old Matudia proceeded to the hillside grave-yard. Once there, she comforted the weeping girl saying, "We all have times in life that are not easy. I know you will overcome this loss. I hope your heart finds a way to see the good that life still has to offer you. Those we love never die, child. They just depart before we do. Be strong, girl, because you are needed now. You are the only child brave enough to fear no creature of the night. That is why I need you to go quickly to Naboto's 'rat tree' and tell him ..."

From the moment Vimbela first breastfed Shiya, the simple girl had become devoted to the "shared" baby. That strong bond would manifest itself this very day.

When Anele's laundry duties were done and she was ready to leave, she called out. "Shiya and Vimbela, it's time to go now. Umama has lots to do."

Suddenly, Anele clenched her teeth so as not to cry out. She couldn't believe her eyes—nor could the other women or wide-eyed children who stood frozen beside Shiya in the shallow water. Loud gasps rose above the sound of the flowing river as some villagers pointed at the child. Gripped tightly in Shiya's fist was one of Africa's most aggressive and feared snakes—a black mamba. The venom this creature held in its hollow, hypodermic fangs was highly toxic and would deliver a slow, paralyzing death.

Little Shiya looked as if she hadn't a care in the world. Grinning mischievously, she proudly announced, "Look, *Umama*, "I've got a big stick."

It seemed an eternity before Anele's vocal chords could function. With enforced calmness, she ordered, "*Shiya*, listen to me. Put it down. Stay very still and don't move. It is not a stick! It's a bad snake. Please, my child, listen very carefully to your mother."

Anele took a deep breath, fighting to control panicky words that could terrify her child. "Precious little girl, drop the stick and stand very still."

Shiya tossed the snake high, caught it on the way down, and then draped it scarf-fashion around her neck. She squealed in enjoyment at this new game. The snake didn't seem to mind a bit. Its forked tongue flickered at the child's face; then it uncoiled and slithered into the shallow water, disappearing under mossy vegetation.

A superstitious woman seized the moment. "These dangerous snakes have killed many people with their deadly poison." She shook her head and ended, "Why not *her*?"

Another woman nodded her head and pointed a shaky finger. "Does an evil *umlungu* spirit from their underworld possess her?"

"Maybe she *is* an evil spirit sent by the whites' god," another ventured.

"I don't think so," another disputed. "I think this child is a gift from our gods to protect us from harmful snakes."

Anele ignored the irrational prattling. She waded into the river, grabbed Shiya's arm, and yanked her onto the muddy bank. "You are a bad girl," Anele admonished. "The next time I tell you to do something, listen to me or I will beat you."

Shiya's bottom lip trembled. "I am not a bad girl," she pouted.

"The stick snake is my friend. He was happy to play with me. He told me he would not bite."

The rambling of a child was one thing, but disobedience was another. Anele gripped Shiya's shoulders forcefully and responded. "If you *ever* disobey me again, you'll be in for a spanking. Do you understand, Shiya?"

Shiya whimpered.

Vimbela's legs shot from the riverbank. She confronted her adopted mother. "*Umama* Anele, she is a little child. How is she to know about nasty creatures that can harm us if you don't teach her? You should not make her cry so."

"How many times do I have to tell you, Vimbela," Anele responded coldly. "You are *not* her mother. Please do not tell me how to raise my child."

Vimbela's bottom lip drooped lower than Shiya's. Vimbela countered angrily. "You're a bad *umama*. I like you no more."

"Yes, bad mother," Shiya repeated.

Anele chose not to respond to either of them. Instead, she took Shiya's hand and walked back to where she had left her washed laundry. Anele placed the basket on her head, gave Shiya a "follow-me" look, and started taking long strides. As Anele headed back to the kraal, Shiya's little legs raced to keep up. "*Umama*, wait for me."

Anele's mind was preoccupied on the walk back to the village. In her heart she agreed with the simple but wise Vimbela. How could Shiya know about the dangers that lurked around them, especially the "big five": elephant, rhino, buffalo, lion, and leopard? *Had* she been too harsh?

Anele stopped walking, put the laundry down, and waited for Shiya to catch up to her. Anele lifted the out-of-breath child onto a tree stump. The mother squatted and tried to make her daughter understand about dangerous wildlife—other poisonous snakes;

tsetse flies that carried a sleeping sickness; and dangerous spiders, especially the black widow, one of which had poisoned her blood shortly before she had run away with her twin sisters. "You see, Shiya, darling, there are many creepy-crawlies of the bush that can harm not only little children but *Umama*, as well. So we have to be careful at all times. Do you understand what I'm saying, child?"

Bewilderment wrinkled Shiya's nose as she darted her eyes everywhere but toward Anele. Nothing her mother said had convinced her. Hadn't the snake played with her? But to be on the safe side, the bright child decided not to rile her mother further. She simply nodded.

A few minutes later the trio entered the compound. Granny Matudia hurried to Anele's side. The matriarch had to know the truth from the source. "The young ones ran from the river to tell me of the snake. Is it true?"

Anele nodded. But she was in no mood to discuss the incident further. She wanted to let the matter lie, but it was clear that wasn't going to happen.

A group of mostly elderly men—with Tekenya, her wannabe lover, among them—surrounded Anele. The goatherder's shoulders were stiff and his voice was hard. "I speak for our people. The magic stones must be read by Twazli. Only he can assure us why the serpent of a slow death has spared this child. Many lives have been lost to snakes. So we are all asking, is she a good spirit or a bad spirit?"

A man whose mind was already made up pointed a finger at Shiya and declared, "She's an *Idimoni*—an evil spirit—all right, hiding in a white child's body. The *Imikhuba* will know, for sure."

Shiya tugged at her mother's skirt and shakily said, "I don't want the witch doctor to come. He scares me."

Anele's heart melted when she saw the fear expressed on her daughter's face. The mother tried to assure the frightened child. "It's okay, little one. There's nothing to be afraid of. As chieftain of the village, I'm not going to allow it."

Matudia, shook her head in disagreement and said, "This time you have little choice, daughter of Naboto. It has always been our custom to call the *Imikhuba* when we need answers to troubling, unexplained happenings. This is definitely one of them."

"Do what you have to do, Matudia. But I won't let the witch doctor in my home. If he has to read the stones, then he will do it outside."

Her insistence on reading the stones outside would not be taken lightly by the medicine man.

With Shiya and Vimbela clinging to her skirt, Anele walked away and headed toward the wash line outside her home. Her household chores had to get done, regardless. Upon reaching the line, she turned to Vimbela and said, "I'll hang up the clothes and you take Shiya inside. It's time for her nap."

Within seconds, Vimbela was back. "*Umama* Anele, come quick. Shiya is shaking real bad. She looks sick."

Had the snake bitten Shiya after all?

Anele dashed inside and examined Shiya.

Satisfied that there were no fang marks, Anele rocked Shiya on her lap and sang a song: "A little baby I named Shiya freed my soul from the village of hate. She came into my life and healed my troubled mind and childless body. At each tender smile my heart now rejoices with so much love for you."

Shiya's pale face broke into a wide smile. She hugged her mother and drifted into sleep. When Anele looked down at her child, a worry line creased her forehead. She wrestled with a disturbing thought: *Had she created the protective shield around her child? Had her plea to the Dark Gods of the Underworld been ...?* Anele swept the troubling questions away.

The sun climbed an hour higher in the sky.

Without announcement and against her will the witch doctor entered Anele's house. He was followed by Tekenya, the goatherder, who held a tree branch in his hand. Tekenya avoided eye contact with Anele. Vimbela squealed in fright when the two men entered the hut, and burrowed her head under a blanket. The memory of the witch doctor's visit five years ago, when he warned Anele about keeping the white baby, was still fresh in her mind.

Anele, also reflecting on that time, felt a strangling fear such as she'd never felt before; it gripped her throat so tightly she could barely swallow. Could this overwhelming emotion have something to do with Twazli's previous counsel? Her inner voice cautioned, *Tread carefully, Anele. Don't provoke him this time.* But her direct-approach nature got the better of her. "I don't want Shiya to wake and see you. You can read the darn stones outside. Not in here."

Twazli glared at her. "The child of *umlungu* blood will not hear or see me. I have seen to that."

Anele gasped. "What do you mean? If you've harmed …"

"Silence!" he roared. "You speak when I tell you to. I'm here at the request of the elders. The casting of the ancient stones of my forefathers will not alter what I have already predicted."

"I *never* asked you to change our future. Nor did I ask you to come here. Shiya is *not* an evil spirit, and your stones will prove this. Go ahead. Let's get this over with for once and for all."

Twazli sat cross-legged on the hut's floor. With the overgrown nail of his right index finger he traced a circle in the dirt. He gestured to Tekenya for the tree branch and placed it across the circle. What he did next was shocking.

The ancient man took out his long, shrivelled penis and urinated on the bark. Anele made a face of disgust and then refocused on what he was doing.

Twazli began chanting the ancient rites for truth. Then he threw a pink magic stone onto the floor. He explained that if the stone rolled out of the urine-sealed ring, trouble would befall the person.

The stone fell within the circle.

He threw another stone.

It too landed safely.

He threw a third. It bounced out of the ring and rolled across the room. The witch doctor let out a squeal that sounded more animal than human. The goatherder stepped forward and asked, "What do you see, honorable *Imikhuba*? Tell us now."

Twazli inhaled sharply before saying, "I see the fires of the damned spirits consuming this child, the one who has been named Shiya. The vengeful breath of the Dark One will deliver a white messenger. And the Dark One will also send one of us, a black traitor. Blood will flow from head wounds, holes not made by spears but by round balls that fly from fire."

Anele forced a chuckle. Her lack of respect brought Twazli face to face with her. He poked a gnarled finger into her upper arm and said, "Your father must be crying. You have brought the anger of *Ikloba*, the Dark One, not just on yourself and the white child but on all the Tswanas people."

"I long ago left this nonsense behind," Anele said, moving defiantly away from Twazli.

"Stupid daughter of a great and noble man, you may mock the words of the great *Imikhuba*, but it's our right to have the child tested."

No one noticed Vimbela shaking like a leaf. *No, no, no*, her head screamed. Certainly, she had witnessed the witch doctor bring a dead goat back to life, make a crippled man walk, and cause other unexplainable events, but she just couldn't let him take *her* baby away to be tested! Not wanting to wait around, Vimbela removed

Shiya from her crib and snuck out the door while the others were distracted.

Anele had had enough. Through clenched teeth she ordered, "Get out now, or I will throw hot pig oil on all of you." She swung the oil lamp back and forth like a pendulum.

The men stood their ground. A mere woman was not going to take this moment from them.

Twazli placed a trio of bongo drums between his knees and began tapping the warrior beat from drum skin to drum skin. As the rhythm increased in intensity, Twazli's painted face twisted in a wry grin. "This is a man's domain," he declared. "Women should have no say in it. I order that the child be taken to the Sacred Rock to spend the night. If she is not a bad seed come to lure our people into the dark cave of no return, no harm will come to her."

"You are *insane!*" Anele shouted. "To leave Shiya on the rock for the night is madness. Hungry wild creatures will eat her, you dung-for-brains man."

"The Ancients will close the mouths of beasts if the child is pure, but, if she is not …"

Anele was relieved to see Granny Matudia enter. Anele looked pleadingly into the old woman's eyes and said, "You have to stop this insanity. He wants Shiya to go to the Sacred Rock. Stay there the whole night."

Matudia wrung her broad hands. "Anele, Vimbela tells me that you are brainless, like her. What did you expect? That the snake incident would just go away? We are ancient people who respect the Imikhuba's judgment. But it seems that you are no longer one of us."

Anele stared at the matriarch. Her last words stung the worst.

Twazli made a loud guttural sound like a strangled goat and addressed the matriarch. "Matudia, good sister of mine, your words are sound. But leave us now. I've important work to do."

Matudia made a hasty exit. Anele felt afraid and called after her. "Matudia, come back! I'm the chief. You don't have to listen to him!"

Twazli's thin lips parted and erupted into braying laughter, as though a demon within him exulted. With gloating scorn, he said, "No woman mocks the Great One. Unbeliever, be warned." He began mumbling incoherently.

Anele was spellbound. Her skin tingled as though a thousand ants were crawling over her flesh. In front of her, manifesting themselves at Twazli's feet, were grotesque miniature beings. They had misshapen heads, fire-red eyes set into sunken sockets, and deformed, claw-like hands and feet. Twazli bent low to hear their high-pitched, squeaky message. After a second or so, the witch doctor simply nodded in agreement.

Twazli made eye contact with Anele and relayed *their* words. "My friends from the underworld tell me that I look weak in their eyes for the disrespectful words of a woman who dares taunt me. They confirm that the forsaken one is indeed a reincarnated bad seed. No serpent power can protect her in this life or the afterlife. They will welcome her should she die this night on the Sacred Rock."

Hot fury flowed over Anele and swept away her fear. Ignoring the ungodly eyes staring up at her, she adopted a warrior's stance of defiance, slapped her chest several times, and spat into Twazli's face.

Tekenya gasped in horror. Anele had broken a sacred tribal rule—spitting in any form was taboo. And not just at the witch doctor, but at young or old, male or female, and even animals. Anele had committed the highest insult. She could face death by stoning—a Tswanas custom.

Meanwhile, Anele's inner voice reasoned, *Stoning for spitting was part of the old ways. Surely it no longer existed in these modern-day times.*

She was never more wrong.

Twazli turned to the goatherder. "Anele must be punished. Correct?"

Tekenya nodded in agreement. Anele was flabbergasted. Was that cold, flat voice coming from the man who had fervently pledged to love and protect her? Only yesterday Tekenya had begged her to marry him. Anele gave her would-be suitor the evil eye, and turned on the witch doctor. Her voice communicated her disgust. "I ask you not to harm me or my child. At first light, I will take Shiya *and* Vimbela and leave Tswanas for good. If we are gone, there will be no cause for you to fear. I will say this: I wish I'd never returned to the village of my birth," Lord Nigel's words spilled from her mouth, "to be among savages, *apes*, who have no hearts."

The witch doctor smirked. With a wave of his hand, the wicked entities vanished into thin air. Twazli's eyes, deep and dark as bottomless pools, locked on Anele. "The running days are over, Anele of Tswanas. Before the sun dances over the Sacred Burial Hill, your fate will be set. Nothing you can say or do now will affect that outcome. You should have listened to me, brainless daughter of a good man." He turned his back on her and headed for the doorway. Before following in the witch doctor's footsteps, Tekenya, his hands clasped as if he were about to pray, whispered to Anele, "I nodded in agreement, but I didn't really mean it."

"Oh, yes you did!" Anele raged. "Now get out before I throw you out."

Tekenya, his chin nearly touching his chest, hurriedly left the hut.

An eerie shroud of silence surrounded Anele's home, inside and out, until Vimbela rushed in. Words spilled from her tongue, "*Umama* Anele. I listened by the window. I fear the *Imikhuba's* intentions."

Anele stroked the trembling girl's cheek. "Everything is going to be all right," Anele assured. "You're coming with me and Shiya. We will leave in the morning. We'll go to Mtunzini, where my mother Tuttia and my grandmother were born. We will be welcome there."

"But how will we take care of ourselves, *Umama* Anele?"

"Don't worry. You can mind Shiya while I work the fields."

"What about Umia, Shiya's first wet-nursing girl? She lives there. She hates you and Shiya. She told me so. She might take a knife to your heart."

"No, she won't. The Mtunzini women couldn't stand Umia's ugly ways, and they have chased her and her children from their village."

"But Anele, what if …"

"That's enough, Vimbela. I've lots of things to do before we leave—like preparing food for our journey, packing clean clothes, and retrieving the money I've hidden near my father's favorite tree. Why don't you take a nap? You will need your strength to help me with Shiya. The rainy season is upon us, and it could be dangerous to cross the mountain rocks on foot to Mtunzini."

That night Anele slept fitfully.

 # Abduction, 1950

"Silence comes from the cage you were held captive in."
–Anonymous

The next day Vimbela, piggybacking Shiya, walked quietly beside Anele as the three of them started their journey to a new village. Behind them, the tribe was sleeping. It would be several hours before the sun rose.

Suddenly, the two women stopped in their tracks. Vimbela was the first to say something. "What *is* it that makes the ground shake so badly?"

The rumbling noise became louder. Anele, too, was perplexed. "I don't like the sound of it."

Shiya peered over her caretaker's shoulder. The five-year-old innocently added, "Maybe lots of elephants have run away from the jungle."

In a millisecond it came flooding back. *No! It can't be!* Anele's head screamed. How could a jeep have gotten through the narrow, single-track, rocky mountain pass to reach the village?

When blinding lights stabbed through the darkness, Vimbela dove behind a pile of firewood stacked against the fence. Unknown to Vimbela, Shiya's face struck her backbone. The girl seemed to know not to cry out or wipe the blood off her battered top lip.

The camouflaged vehicle barreled through the village's fence, snapping it as if it were made of matchsticks. There wasn't yet enough daylight for Anele to make out the faces of the occupants of the vehicle, or of the four horsemen following. She also jumped behind the firewood. Hunkered down next to Vimbela and Shiya, her thoughts went into overdrive. *Who are they? Could they be game wardens? What do they want? Had one of the villagers been poaching in the nearby national game reserve?*

Before it screeched to a halt, the jeep careened through patches of garden and knocked over a large cauldron hanging in the fire pit. With their tails tucked under them, the village dogs yelped and slunk behind the huts.

Startled villagers illuminated by the vehicle's headlights peered out of their doorways. Most had never seen this or any other mode of modern transport. Or white men on horseback. The horsemen dismounted and formed a single line, their revolvers at the ready. Then they turned toward the tall man stepping from the jeep. He had a rifle slung over his right shoulder. From the rear of the jeep, another man appeared. He was a lanky and shabbily dressed black man. A floppy hat obscured his features.

The tall man roared in Zulu, "Where are Anele and the kid?"

The man's strident demand froze Anele's bones. She knew that razor-sharp voice all too well. She clamped her hand over her mouth and wondered: *How did he find me?* Zululand was a vast area, over ten thousand square miles. *And kid!* How could Alan Hallworthy possibly know of Maria's child?

Alan aimed his weapon at the person nearest him—a fifteen-year-old boy. In an intimidating tone he said, "Speak up, *kaffir*, or you're a dead duck."

The teenager's eyes grew as large as a moon. Natu was speechless.

Alan let out a disgruntled sigh and beckoned to the black man wearing the floppy hat. "Go and get the bitch. You said you knew which hut she was in."

"Yes, *baas*. Right away, *baas*. I know exactly which hut Anele and the child sleep in."

The betrayer's voice floated on the wind. It couldn't be? But it *was* him—*Kumdi!* How many pieces of silver was her Judas paid for his treachery?

Granny Matudia, her nightgown trailing in the dirt, rushed up to the scorned wannabe leader. No one stopped her. She grabbed Kumdi's khaki shirtsleeve, nearly ripping the garment off his body. The ancient woman was angry. "What brings you here with the enemy of our people? You are a piece of dung to do this!"

Kumdi tossed his head haughtily and responded, "It's none of your business old woman. Let go of me or I'll get Lord Hallworthy to shoot you."

Granny Matudia was by no means finished. "You ungrateful dung-for-brains boy," she spat. "I made sure you and your sister left the settlement with full bellies. Now my kindness is repaid by you leading the *umlungu* to us." With a force like no other pumping through her veins, Matudia, much shorter than her opponent, developed Herculean strength. She balled her fist and knocked Kumdi off his feet with one blow to his chest. Alan and his entourage watched in amusement and amazement at this old woman's power and tenacity.

Their laughter now danced amid the first rays of sunlight. But there was no mirth coming from the shamefaced Kumdi. He sprung to his feet and shoved Matudia so hard she fell backward. *Thud.* Her head hit the hard dirt. The matriarch groaned in pain.

Two women rushed to the matriarch and helped her to her feet. Although dazed, she wasn't badly hurt. But her eyesight was spotty, so she didn't see Kumdi coming toward her. He had dusted the dirt off his pants and was now facing off with her. "Don't you dare touch me ever again, old woman!" he bellowed smirking with satisfaction.

"You know Anele has stolen a child!"

Matudia shook her fist and hissed, "Next time you won't get up. You've betrayed your own kind. Twazli's Dark Ones will come for your miserable black soul."

Alan made an angry, guttural cluck. "Enough of this mumbo-jumbo crap," he growled. "Kumdi, go get them *now!*"

With their handguns raised, the deputies, who had been riding the horses, followed Kumdi. They entered Anele's house. Within seconds they exited empty handed. Kumdi shook his head. "There's no one in here, *baas.*"

Alan snorted his reply. "They're hiding somewhere. Search all the homes."

Anele whispered in Vimbela's ear. "Please don't ask any questions. We are in terrible danger. Listen to me carefully. Take Shiya and run like the wind to my father's dead rat tree. Can you remember the way?"

Vimbela, her teeth chattering in fear, nodded.

"Climb as high as you can," Anele ordered. "And stay there with Shiya until I come for you both."

A little voice piped up, "*Umama,* why do we ...?"

"Be silent, Shiya, if you know what's good for you," Anele said. "You'll be all right if you listen to me. Go with Vimbela and I'll come shortly. I promise."

Shiya's terrified eyes spoke volumes. She clung to Vimbela like bubblegum.

Anele kissed the girls on their cheeks and said, "Hurry. Please, go now."

Vimbela was shaking like a bush in the grip of a savannah storm as she climbed over the mangled fence. Anele waited until they were out of sight. Something made her nose twitch. She tilted her chin and sniffed the air. What was that smell? Could it be the rich aroma of her father's tobacco? Was he here with her? Did she believe in ghosts? Without a doubt! Anele closed her eyes and said silently, *"Ubaba, I can't see you, but I feel you are here with me. Please whisper in my ear and tell me what to do."*

An incandescent sun rose in the sky, bathing the former Hallworthy servant in a soft blue light. With her head held high and with spiritual courage from her father shrouding her body, Anele walked toward the unwelcome intruders. "I am here, Lord Hallworthy."

Alan spun around and swung his rifle. The butt hit Anele squarely on the head. She flew backward onto the dirt. For a spilt second she was overcome by *déjà vu.*

Alan flicked her scalp flesh off of his weapon and said, "Where is my child, kaffir? Don't look so dumb. You know damn well what I'm talking about."

Anele feigned innocence. "Lord Alan, I do not know what you mean. What child?"

The rifle's wooden stock slammed down again. A fountain of blood spurted from Anele's nose. "Don't act smart with me, you black bitch," Alan hissed. "You know damn well what I'm talking about. Where is my child? I know she is here somewhere."

Thank God, his snarling voice was a blur. But her inner voice was clear. *Spirits of the Underworld, end my life now. I can't let anything happen to my child.*

Alan straddled Anele. "Did you think I wouldn't find you?" he scoffed, nudging her mouth with the cold steel muzzle. "Has the cat got your tongue, black bitch? You want to *know* how I found out about you and my kid? Well, I'm going to tell you."

"Sorry to interrupt you, Lord Hallworthy," a police officer said. "Would you like us to continue searching?"

"God dammit, yes. Search every inch of the godforsaken place."

Alan refocused his attention. "Naturally, you don't know this but Maria—you know the Sicilian bitch you freed and hoped I'd never find—told me she'd given birth to twins." Alan tapped a finger against his chin. "Now, let me think. Could it be that someone I know helped the *wop* deliver? She couldn't have done it by herself! Maybe it was a black bitch named Anele who killed one baby and stole the other?"

Anele's mind snapped to attention. *Maria didn't give birth to twins! She couldn't have! Great God in the Spirit World, in my haste to save Shiya, did I not see the other baby? Had the twin fallen deeper into the compost pit?* She tried to sit up, but Alan's boot pressed down like a massive concrete block on her rib cage. At that moment she would have sold her soul to Twazli's creatures for a gun to shoot Alan dead. She would have done anything to keep Shiya forever safe from his evil ways. Anele's tortured mind knew age didn't matter to Alan and that Shiya would become another one of his victims. Many clouds had darkened Anele's life, but this was the most sinister. Helplessness tore apart Anele's heart. *I tried, dear God of the white people. I tried to protect her.*

Again, Anele struggled to rise. Alan's boot pressed harder into her rib cage ensuring she didn't. "Don't you dare move," he snapped. "I'm not finished." He inhaled sharply before continuing. "After Maria gave birth, you took the healthy child and ran away with it, didn't you? How do I know this? Ah! I can see by the look on your face that you're dying to know. Am I right?"

Anele's hate-filled eyes glared back at her former slave master.

Alan continued, "Maria thought she could get away from me. Wrong! I found the whore not far from my house, bleeding like a butchered pig. I'd have left her to rot if it wasn't for her telling me about my children. If it wasn't for Maria's psychiatrist in the state mental hospital where I dumped her, I would have dismissed her crazy story."

"Bastard!"

A rib bone caved in under the pressure of Alan's boot. Anele grimaced in agony. Alan resumed as if nothing had happened. "At first I didn't believe any of it because Maria is nuttier than a fruitcake. It was a cleaning man at the hospital ..." He gestured to Kumdi to come forward. "It was this man who verified Maria's crazy story."

The moment was Kumdi's. He grinned like a demented lunatic. Alan didn't break a smile. He shouted for all to hear. "Where is the *white* child? One of you better bring her to me, or I'll pick you off like flies."

The tribe remained quiet until the rifle's blast lifted the matriarch off her feet. Granny Matudia was dead before her body thudded to the ground. Paralyzed with fear, no one moved to help the old lady. But Anele begged him, "Please don't kill any more of my people, Master. They are innocent bush people, and they don't understand English. I've no idea why Kumdi would make up such lies. There's no white child here."

The next shot Alan fired nicked the side of Anele's ear lobe. Frothing at the mouth, Alan hissed, "You are a lying runaway bitch. For the last time, where ..."

Loud gasps directed his eyes to the east.

Leaping like a gazelle over obstacles, Shiya raced toward them. A wiggling green snake was clasped in her hand. She sprinted past Alan and the other intruders as if they weren't there, and released the deadly black mamba onto the earth. She hunched down and stroked her mother's battered face. Shiya's voice was tearful. "*Umama*, did the *umlungu* man hurt you? Do you want me to get the *Imikhuba*? The witch doctor will destroy the bad men."

Anele's agonizing physical pain was momentarily forgotten. She still had her wits about her. That was a comfort. She wrapped her arms around her precious child.

Alan's face revealed no joy at seeing his daughter. He bent to study his child and was amazed at how much she resembled him. The girl was tall, towering over most children her age. She had his blond hair, but not his blue eyes. Hers were green, reflecting Maria's Sicilian heritage. Shiya's nose and mouth were finely chiseled, like his mother's. Yes, she belonged to him. She would never be a *true* Hallworthy. Definitely not, his thoughts raged. But she would be his in more ways than one. As if reading this sick man's mind, Anele pulled Shiya closer and whispered in her ear, "Run, child, run. This man is going to eat you like a crocodile."

Shiya made a comical face and responded, "He's not *ingwenya*, silly *Umama*. He's not a crocodile. He is umlungu, a white man."

Alan smirked. His patience was strained. He snatched Shiya from Anele, threw her over his shoulder and marched to the jeep. She struggled violently to free herself, crying out, "*Vulela umlungu,* bad white man, let go of me ..." A backhand across her face sent the girl into a flood of tears, tearing Anele's heart from her chest.

Shiya was flung into the passenger seat. In a pitiful voice she begged, "*Umama*, get up and save me."

Exhausted from the emotional rollercoaster all Anele had left was a plea to the gods in the Invisible Kingdom. *Watch over this special child. Make this child strong with your spiritual serpent powers, for she will need them against this evil man. He will show her no mercy.*

A loud boom halted her prayers. With a tidal wave of willpower, Anele forced herself into an upright position. She couldn't see Shiya in the jeep. "Oh, no," she groaned. "The *bastardo* has killed her." She fell back against the hard earth and wept. Then a voice startled her. When she looked up through tear-filled eyes, she could just make out the shape of a stooped man standing over her. Twazli softly said, "Shiya isn't dead, Anele. But you will wish she were. I tried to warn you. But if it helps you heal, the *underworld* has heard you."

It was too late for any of his words.

"Twazli," Anele said, "I hope your flesh rots in the fires of the white-man's hell."

A second dark shape loomed over her. "It's true, Anele," Tekenya reaffirmed. "Your Shiya sits in the chair of the tin cart. I want you to know that I shouldn't have listened to the mouths of others. My heart now tells me otherwise. Will you forgive me?"

Anele closed her eyes against the sight of him. There was nothing in her heart to forgive. Tekenya had betrayed her when he asked for her to be stoned for spitting at Twazli. The contrite suitor knelt and stroked Anele's battered head. "You should have married me when I asked. I would have taken you and the child far from here, to Basutoland, where I was born. The *umlungu* would never have found you there."

A white policeman pushed Tekenya aside. "Out of the way, *kaffir*, or you're next!" Too weak to resist, Tekenya did what he was told. His arms hung limply at his sides as he watched Anele being hogtied, then dragged across the dirt and thrown into the back of the jeep. She landed on the body of Kumdi. His dead eyes were gaping toward the sky. A single gunshot to the back of his neck—execution style—marked his demise. Anele felt no anger toward Kumdi, only pity. She softly said, "I forgive you, Kumdi. Fly free and seek out my father. He will guide you into the Invisible Kingdom of Spirits."

Alan stuck his head out of the window. To one of the uniformed men, he smiled and said, "Thanks for your help. I couldn't have done it without you."

"It's been a pleasure to have been of assistance, Lord Hallworthy. And thank *you* for your most generous *donation*. If you ever need our help again, please don't hesitate to call my contact number in Nairobi."

Through his rearview mirror, Alan, a wry grin on his lips, watched the ex-cons and mercenaries disguised as police officers mount their horses and ride away. Alan chuckled. He had pulled off the perfect charade. He knew from experience the tribe would simply mourn their dead and resume their bush ways. There would be no outside investigation into what had happened this day.

Alan's vehicle sped from the kraal in a fog of red dust. The jeep drove over thorn bushes as if they were merely clumps of tall grass. High above, hidden under the canopy of baobab leaves, Vimbela clung to a broad bough. When the flap at the back of the jeep flew open and exposed Anele and Kumdi, she scrambled down and raced after the car, coughing and choking in the dust of the vehicle's wake. "*Umama*, where are you going?" she screamed. "Come back. It isn't my fault. I did what you told me. Shiya wouldn't listen. She climbed down the dead rat tree and ran. I couldn't catch her. She has the legs of a cheetah ..."

Vimbela tripped over a tree stump. Her temple struck a jagged root. She lay unconscious.

In the jeep a petrified Shiya was held in a vice grip on Alan's lap. She cried out, "*Umama*, Shiya wants you."

Alan dug his fingernails into her tender flesh. "That black bitch is not your mother. Do you understand? And you can forget that *kaffir* name. From now on, your name is ..." Alan scratched the stubble on his chin. "... Little Shit! Or better still, Little *Wop* Shit!"

A fire grew in the child's tear-swollen eyes. The grizzly in her stood up, and she attacked. "The witch doctor is going to kill you for hurting me and my *umama*. The *Imikhuba* can make his body invisible, you know. He'll cut your throat, and you'll die just like the cattle at slaughter time. Then the cook will boil your bones, and I'll eat you."

Alan's chest shook with laughter. But his mirth turned to fury when Shiya sunk her teeth into his leg and her small hands beat and clawed at him. Alan beat her so badly that the poor child's face looked like it had been put through a meat grinder. Before the pain sent her into a faint, Shiya said, "One day. One day, *umlungu*, I roast you alive for hurting me and my *umama*."

Shiya blacked out.

Shiya was a "special" child. She had unexplainable adult attributes that would be tested time and time again.

Had Anele's pleas been heard?

Yes.

But which one of the deities now looked over Shiya?

Only time would tell.

That afternoon the sun continued to bleach the earth. The jeep, carrying its two hostages, drove past the infamous gamekeeper's cottage and came to a halt at the edge of a sugar cane field. Alan opened the driver's door and got out to stretch his legs. Shiya, bloodied and bruised, had been tied up and stuffed between the driver's and the passenger's seats.

Alan went to the rear of the vehicle and lifted the flap. "Jesus!" he cried, swatting a swarm of flesh-eating flies. Kumdi and Anele were shrouded in an animated veil of black. Alan reached in, grabbed Kumdi's legs, and flung his body to the ground. To Anele he said, "You are next, black bitch. But I'm going to wait for the police to arrive and take you to where you belong—to jail."

Alan tucked Shiya under his arm and began walking. A few yards down the pathway, he lost his grip on her. Shiya rolled onto the dirt. In a flash, he grabbed her by the neck and squeezed. She gasped for air. Then, with the strength of the ungodly, she wiggled out of her wrist restraints and bit hard into Alan's palm flesh. "You little bastard!" he howled.

Her feet began to churn before they even hit the ground. Shiya ran into the dense sugar cane. On and on she fled, ignoring the sharp-edged leafstalks that sliced her feet like spears. Finally, with her lungs heaving and sweat streaking her dust-caked cheeks, she crouched in the thickest part of the foliage. A minute or so later, she cocked her head. What was that *whooshing* sound? Her imagination conjured up a leopard ... a lion ... a crocodile's tail. Shiya, terrified, tucked her head between her knees. When the pocket knife nicked the back of her ear she shrieked in pain. Alan stood over her.

"Did you think you could get away from me?" he mocked. Brutally, he yanked Shiya up by her left arm, wrenching her elbow out of its socket. Pain like stabbing hot knives ran up and down her arm. But not a sound escaped her lips. She knew her cries would only antagonize this cruel man further.

Alan dragged his silent daughter into a clearing. On a grassy embankment a black woman wearing an outgrown and faded maid's uniform stared at them. All she had been told was that she was to be there at three o'clock sharp. She had been waiting for over an hour.

Alan walked up to his servant and instructed, "Take this child straight to my house. Clean her up. I'll be there later. She only speaks Zulu. And Maekela, if she gets away, I'll murder *you!*"

Maekela nodded complacently and grasped Shiya's hand.

After Alan left, the kitchen servant looked over the child: darkened skin, emerald irises, puffy face. Cuts, welts, and bruises lined her features. A red ligature mark ringed her small neck. What on earth was going on? Who was this child? Why did she look like she had been attacked by a wild animal? While Maekela was sizing her up, Shiya was doing the same to Maekela. She couldn't help but stare with her one good eye at the young woman. Maekela's sparkling eyes were mesmerizing. They were as blue as the sky.

Shiya's survival instincts kicked in again. But the opportunity to flee was thwarted. Maekela's grip sent a shooting pain up the girl's injured arm. Shiya's eyes rolled backward, but she didn't cry out.

What Shiya couldn't understand was that this harsh act was committed by a *black* person. The villagers she had known and loved were kind, not hurtful. Her small feet raced to keep up with Maekela's long strides. She was deep in thought. As far as she knew, there were no green-eyed fieldworkers, housemaids, or foreigners on the property with that spellbinding eye color. But without a shadow of doubt, this girl child had *white* blood. But whose was the million dollar question?

Shiya had questions of her own. "What's your name? My name is Shiya, the Forsaken One, and I'm nearly six summers old. Where are you taking me? Why are you mad at me?"

"Be quiet. I can't think. This is all too much for me. I'm just a simple girl."

"What's a simple girl?"

"Shut up and let me do my job!"

"Let me go, *simple* girl. I have to find my *umama*."

"Do you want another beating?"

"No."

"Then be quiet!"

When the Hallworthy mansion came into view, Maekela stopped to catch her breath and inadvertently slackened her hold on the girl. Shiya took off like a bat out of hell—with Maekela hot on her heels.

Nearby, underneath a palm tree, Lamella—the old, black Hallworthy cook—was sneaking in a few minutes of shut-eye in a wicker chair, without permission.

If her owner had caught her, she would have gotten a tongue

bashing. Servants couldn't even take bathroom breaks without permission!

The din of high-pitched shouting rudely woke Lamella. "What on earth is going on?" she questioned. Could that be her kitchen helper, Maekela, running around in circles like a chicken with its head chopped off? Lamella yelled, "Maekela, have you gone mad? Get over here *now!*"

Oblivious to the old, black woman perched at the end of a chair, Shiya was having none of it. She darted behind Lamella. Her pursuer lunged. But in Maekela's efforts to snare the child, she tripped over Lamella's outstretched legs and did a nosedive. Shiya broke into a fit of laughter, but not for long. Maekela got up and snatched the girl with lightning speed. This time the servant's grip held like a steel clamp.

With a strong click of her tongue, Shiya cried, "*Nxe* (ouch)!"

"Serves you right!" Maekela answered. "You're going nowhere now."

The exasperated servant, with her hand fastened fiercely on Shiya's wrist, forcefully pulled the girl toward the kitchen door.

Lamella adjusted her Coke-bottle glasses. How she ever managed to see anything was a mystery. Her hand-me-down eyewear accounted for what she said next. "Maekela, where have you been? The table linens need to be ..." Lamella's dark pupils narrowed under the glasses. "When I'm talking to you, stand still. Who's that child? And where do you think you're going with her?"

"I'm taking her into the house."

"Maekela, you of all people know black children are forbidden inside."

Maekela huffed. Her hold on Shiya tightened. Shiya bit her hard, drawing blood. Maekela let out a shriek before complaining. "Why am I the one that has to deal with this wildcat child? Didn't you see what she did? This *white* kid bit me. My sister never gets orders like this from Lord Alan."

Shiya's protest cut her short. "Let me go, you nasty black *mamba!*" she screamed.

"Who is this child, and why do you hold a black child like a chicken's neck?" Lamella demanded.

"She deserves a beating," Maekela stated. "Lamella, this is not a *black* child. She belongs to the master, just like I do. And if she gets away from me again, he will kill me. That's what he said. I have to clean her. And I am trying to do just that."

But not only was Lamella's eyesight poor, so was her hearing. She scratched the bushy hair under her headscarf as if trying to remember a moment in time, the long-ago incident with young Anele. *Not again. No, not again. Black child bathed in my clean kitchen? Never again!*

Lamella voiced her discontent loudly. "Maekela, take her to the irrigation pump. Clean her there, if you must!"

Maekela puffed out her cheeks in exasperation. "Your old eyes deceive you, Lamella. Take another look at the child you think is one of us."

Cook removed her eyewear, then bent down until she reached Shiya's eye level. She gave the child the once over. Satisfied with her observation, she concluded, "What nonsense do you speak, Maekela? The child is as black as you and I."

Maekela clucked her tongue in frustration. "You need new eyes, old cook."

Shiya's head swung back and forth like a pendulum between the debating females speaking in a foreign tongue. With her free hand, Shiya reached for Lamella's prune-wrinkled hand. "Please, old lady, tell her to let me go. I have to find my *umama*, Anele. Bad *umlungu* men took her away from Tswanas …"

Lamella's eyes grew as round as dinner plates. Shiya took that as a positive response. Now her eyes searched hers. "You know my *umama*, old lady?"

"I …"

Suddenly, Lamella, Maekela, and Shiya froze like popsicles as they stood in front of the entrance to the kitchen. Lamella recoiled from Shiya as if the child had leprosy. Cook hadn't expected a visit from Alan's wife, but here she was. Her excess gardenia cream clung to her voluminous frame as she approached the trio.

Shiya stared at the chubby white woman whose appearance could have frightened frogs. Intuitively, she sensed this *umlungu* woman was no better than the *umlungu* man. Lady Corrie, her sausage fingers stationed on her wide hips, glared at Shiya and spoke in a language that again was strange to the girl's ears.

"Don't even think about bringing this *thing* into my home?" Corrie spat. "She is disgustingly filthy. Take her to the pump and clean her there." A string of other orders followed.

As soon as the sound of Corrie's shoes faded, Maekela let out a sigh of relief. She mocked her mistresses' instructions in singsong rhythm. "Maekela, make sure you check her for lice and fleas. Douse her with paraffin oil outside if you do find any nasty creatures. Scrub her well, cut her disgusting hair, and burn her clothes. I'll be back in an hour to see that you have done what I've told you to do."

Maekela couldn't get the irrigation hand-pump to operate. The handle was seized solid. No groundwater was going to come out of this old-fashioned contraption today. And the old wash house hadn't seen clean water in years.

The servant had little choice.

In the manor scullery, which had replaced the old wash house, Maekela removed Shiya's only item of clothing—a pair of cotton-woven panties—then lifted her into the deep enamel sink.

She proceeded to cut off Shiya's knotted blond curls with a pair of scissors. Shiya did not utter a sound, nor did Maekela. But when a hard-bristled brush invaded the girl's sore flesh, her chilling screams brought Lamella in from the back room. Maekela pointed to Shiya's elbow, swollen to the size of a cricket ball. Maekela handed over the sobbing child to Lamella's waiting arms.

Cook sat with the girl on a rocker outside the scullery, the same one that Anele had rested on many times. For a small child who had lost everything she loved, snuggling onto the cook's large lap felt blissful. Lamella lovingly looked into Shiya's eyes and spoke in a language she understood. "Old Lamella is going to make you better, child." She lifted the hem of her apron and said, "Dry your eyes, little one."

With her own eyes glistening with sorrow, Maekela stared at the black-and-blue child.

Lifting her forefinger, Lamella instructed, "Maekela go into the pantry and bring me an orange."

Shiya face turned happy. She was hungry. At last she was going to get something to eat. Shiya wrapped her arms around Cook's neck and kissed her cheek. "I like you, old lady." Lamella laughed, "And I like you too, Missy."

When Maekela returned with a huge orange, Shiya tried to snatch it from Maekela's hand, but Lamella grabbed the fruit first. "You can have it in a minute, child. But first, I need you to do something for me."

Shiya raised her sore arm as instructed. Cook placed the orange under the child's armpit; lowered her arm; and, in the wink of an eye, snapped the dislocated elbow back into place. Shiya passed out. When she awoke, she was being rocked gently. With her arm still throbbing, Shiya cried, "Old lady, make the pain go away."

"Hush now, child. It's going to hurt for some time, but it *will* get better, I promise you. Would you like the orange now?"

Shiya tore ferociously into the juicy fruit, devouring the skin and pips. Lamella forced a smile. "Child, I know who you really are. While you were *sleeping*, Lady Corrie came back and explained why you are here."

Lamella shrugged at Shiya's blank expression and said, "For whatever reason Anele took you to her home, you will have to, from this day on, forget about her. I know you are only little, but it's best you never mention her name again. She's been taken to Montclair prison, a very bad place. Nobody gets out of there alive, do they, Maekela?"

Maekela nodded glumly.

Lamella continued. "I knew your *real* mother. Lord Alan brought her back here shortly after she nearly starved to death in the bush, so he told me ..."

The sound of high heels clip-clopping across the kitchen floor toward the scullery entrance sent Shiya diving for cover under Lamella's apron. Snuggled against the cook's warm belly, she listened to Lady Corrie's harsh voice rising and falling like a storm-whipped tide. "How dare you black bitches disobey my orders by bringing this *thing* into my home. Wait until the Lord comes home to hear about this. You will all be in for a whipping!"

Then there was blissful silence.

When the coast was clear, Lamella lifted her apron. "You can come out now, child. The witch is gone. I can't keep calling you "child." What name do you go by?"

"My *umama* calls me 'Shiya.'"

"Anele chose well. It's the perfect name for you. Now, I have to tell you something, and I don't know how much of it you will understand. But you will have to realize that *you* are a white missy. You must put behind you the life you have led with Anele in the bush, because …" Lamella took in a deep breath "… because, little Shiya, it's never going to be the same for you ever again. You will have to live in *their* world. You will learn to hate the skin color of the ones who have raised you. But like us, your heart will burn with hatred for those who treat us like animals."

Over the course of time, Shiya would come to learn that unhappiness had no color in a country that judged worthiness by skin tone. Of course, she didn't know if she were white, yellow, or green. Nor did she know that her skin resembled a Middle Easterners', even though she had Alan's blond hair and Maria's green eyes. Her mixed-blood heritage, from her Sicilian mother and British father, would classify her as "colored" by the Afrikaner National Party's 1948 Apartheid laws.

After withdrawal from the Commonwealth in 1961, the Republic of South Africa was born.

When the next person entered the kitchen, Lamella clambered to her feet and dropped Shiya from her lap. The girl took one look at the man and fled into the scullery. She shot under the sinks and crawled into a hole that was no bigger than a mailbox slit. Stomping feet followed her. Alan's voice boomed into her hidey-hole. "Come out, you little shit, or I'll skin your hide."

To the servants' bowed heads he ordered, "Don't you say a word in *kaffir* language! The bitch *will* learn to speak the King's English. I don't ever want you talking to her in Zulu. Is that clear?"

With their chins nearly touching their breasts, the women nodded. The tension in the room was electrified!

"I haven't got time to deal with this," Alan grunted. "Get that little shit out of there and take her to the mistress. She's waiting in the sitting room."

Alan marched away.

"Please, come out," Maekela pleaded in Zulu. "Life is bad enough here without you causing the Devil in that man to appear."

"Is the bad *umlungu* gone?"

"Yes."

Shiya crawled out, covered in cobwebs. Maekela wrapped a kitchen towel around the girl's body and knotted it at her breast. She held Shiya's hand and led her upstairs into a place Shiya could never have imagined existed. The newcomer stared at the trappings of the white world, where strange furniture and even walls were covered in cloth more splendid than the witch doctor's ceremonial robe. Objects that were shining as golden as the sun and as white as the moon adorned the room. Her eyes finally came to rest on the mistress, who was sitting in a chair large enough to seat Shiya's family.

Alan's wife, Corrie, motioned for the servant to bring Shiya over to her. Corrie grabbed her swollen arm, and Shiya howled like a banshee. Clasping her hands over her ears, Corrie shouted, "Shut up! Shut up! If you don't shut up, I'll break your bloody neck."

Maekela begged Shiya to be silent. She complied, but Corrie's angry words, now in Zulu, tore into Shiya. "You're not going to come between my husband and me, ever. Do you hear me? He wants you around, but I don't. I'm not able to bear his children, but I'll be damned if I'll raise his bastard kid. I'm going to make sure you leave here, sent as far away as possible. Your real mother is a whore and is insane. I hope she rots to death in the mental asylum. And Anele ... well, I certainly don't wish her well." Corrie glared into Shiya's tear-filled eyes and finished with, "God only knows what is in *your* blood!"

Shiya clasped her hands over her ears and remained silent, fear rendering her mute. Many years would pass before she uttered another word to a white person. Not a sound would escape her lips through some of the worst ordeals a child could suffer.

Renamed "Lynette" by Alan, a name Shiya hated but kept for legal purposes, the girl kept the heinous events that she endured—at the Hallworthy Manor, at the convent for "colored" children, and at the mental institution—locked in the attic of her mind for most of her life. There the diabolical events stayed until she decided to record her life story for *her* only child, a daughter named Brianna.

In 1998 Shiya would exorcise the ghosts from her past and the accumulated horrors that besieged her by telling the shocking truth of her incredible life and her unshakable will to survive.

But deliverance would not come that easily.

Death is ugly for whoever fears it.

Scratched on a wall in cell number 3, Gestapo Prison, Via Tasso, Rome, 1943

PART TWO

Lynette Hallworthy-Martinez

"Slavery is founded in the selfishness of man's nature—

opposition to it, is his love of justice. These principles are

an eternal antagonism; and when brought into collision

so fiercely, as slavery extension brings them, shocks,

and throes, and convulsions must ceaselessly follow."

—Abraham Lincoln, *Speech at Peoria*
Illinois, October 16, 1854

## CHAPTER NINE

British Columbia, Canada, February 13, 1998, Forty-Eight Years Later

"Silence is an imprint of fear."
–Anonymous

L ynette (aka Shiya) released a tremulous sigh, and with the tip of her fingers brushed away the tears falling down her cheeks. *How,* she wondered, *can I bear this?* Eyes that usually sparkled with the hue of faceted emeralds stared dully out of the cabin window at a heavy, grim, and gray snowfall. The nasty weather had locked in the tender shoots of spring bulbs, which didn't help the emotional roller coaster she was on. She normally didn't operate in self-pity, but this was different.

I don't want to ... I cannot ... go through this ... not now!

Lynette was no stranger to fear, but *this* latest fright paralyzed her. It was the proverbial straw that broke the camel's back, although it felt more like a ton of bricks.

Fate had decreed her life would be a terrible struggle, but her tenacity throughout her painful childhood and adulthood had always outplayed the insurmountable odds. As a newborn she'd been discarded like a half-eaten mango. As a child she experienced unthinkable wickedness. But through grit and force of will, she'd not only beaten the odds, she had become a wealthy and powerful woman—a far cry from her humble beginnings. Even when her beloved husband, Lionel Martinez, had died, she had not allowed herself to wallow in grief. She was a natural survivor. But this time fate dealt her a hopeless hand.

Cancer.

Lynette buried her face in the palms of her hands. Now cognizant of her mortality, she anguished to a god she had never believed in. *Why me God? Haven't I suffered enough emotional and physical bloodshed? Haven't I had more than my share of hell on earth? I could have stayed burrowed in that foxhole of hatred and bitterness, but, oh, no, not me. I chose to fight. What do you want from me? Why are you doing this to me?*

Lynette knew her clock was ticking and she wouldn't live forever, but the frightful six-letter word spelled out a grim discovery for the fifty-three-year-old. She was more than stunned at the diagnosis, considering she hadn't needed to see a doctor in over twenty years. When she had gone to a medical clinic to get a prescription for stronger headache medicine, a brain scan was suggested. The results from the MRI floored her. They revealed an inoperable tumor growing quickly at the base of her brain. Now, not only was the cancer destroying her brain tissue, it had mercilessly fast-forwarded her body's clock. Up until yesterday she had loved life—felt youthful inside and out—but not today.

The slim, five-foot-nine Lynette, who resembled Meryl Streep, hadn't a gray thread in her blond, shoulder-length hair. Her sun-bronzed complexion, smooth as a baby's bottom, was the result of a skilled cosmetic surgeon who performed his magic over a year ago. Not an age spot, wrinkle, sagging jowl, drooping eyelid, or unwanted moustache could be seen.

But the furthest thing from Lynette's mind right now was looking attractive.

She had never before run from a fight, and, with all her might,

she'd tackle this foe, too. And she'd do it without undergoing che-
motherapy or taking the highly dosed steroids offered to her. But
the thing that sent icicles down her back was that cancer did not
observe a fair set of rules. This disease did not negotiate with the
good, the bad, and the ugly; the young and old; males and females;
black, yellow, brown, and white. One could rail and rant at it, plead
to it, and pray about it, but the outcome seemed a whim of fate, a
toss of the dice.

Some lived. Some died. Many suffered so greatly, they longed
for death. Others yearned to live.

Lynette exhaled loudly. She'd not be an easy notch on the belt
of this heartless illness. But she would not give up ... lie down ...
accept defeat. She'd keep swinging to the last gasp.

Lynette wasn't ready to die. Not yet. She had unfinished business.

From infancy she had exhibited a stubborn will to stay alive—to
live life not as a victim of circumstance, but as a winner. Not only
had she fought, not only had she survived, she had *triumphed*! She
had played life like a *Monopoly* board; often landing on the right
squares, avoiding a "Go to Jail" card. Her survival strategy had been
simple: Do not dwell on the past. Do not dream of the future. Stay
focused on the here and now. Until today.

Lynette turned away from the window and reached for the cord-
less telephone. She knew she would be bequeathing her daughter a
can of worms, but she was entitled to the truth. Lynette knew the
time had come to share with her only child the bombshell of her
"tell-all." It was a truth Brianna had long beseeched her mother to
divulge. But would Lynette's revelations be heartfelt?

Yes and no.

Lynette pressed "1" on the speed dial. When the voice mail message prompted her, she sighed with resignation. In a tone so soft it

was almost a whisper, she spoke. "Brianna, I'd like you to come out here as soon as you can. I want you to know that I'm so sorry I've let you down—not being a very good mother to you—but please understand that I love you dearly, my darling daughter, and always have. I'll see you in heaven … if such a place exists."

With the phone still clutched in her hand, Lynette stood unmoving for a very long time. As if in a trance, she stared at a small cassette recorder she always kept by the phone.

Lynette's heart-wrenching and soul-numbing narration would forever change her daughter's life—and what remained of her own.

 Brianna Elizabeth McTavish, Valentine's Day 1998

"The first part in healing is shattering the silence."
–Erin Merryn

The headlights of the blue Nissan Pathfinder were on high beam. They punched holes into the dank fog ushering in this romantic day. For the young woman driving on the slippery, snow-laden highway in the British Columbia interior, this day would bring about anything but romantic expectations.

With her hands in a ten-and-two position, Brianna gripped the steering wheel with such intensity that the skin over her white knuckles stretched to capacity. She felt the blood pulsating in her temples. The law student, age twenty-three, found it hard to concentrate on her driving. The lids above her velvet black eyes were heavy with worry and fatigue.

Breathtaking winter scenery whizzed by without Brianna's notice. She could think only of the unnerving words recorded earlier: "See you in heaven." The message did not sound like her cheerful mother. It sent icy chills down Brianna's spine. She had tried to call her mom back, but her message went to voice mail: "Please leave your number and a brief message and I'll get back to you. Thanks."

Brianna had recorded, "For goodness sake, Mom! Answer your damn phone! Look, I'm really sorry. I didn't mean to be so rude the last time we spoke."

No response.

Brianna had tried humor. "Mom, if you don't pick up, I'm going to drive all the way out there and kick your ass."

Nothing.

Brianna's normally emotionally grounded character had exploded. She had thumped her fist on the kitchen counter and had screamed, "Damn you, Mother! I have an important presentation to prepare for. I could do without this damn melodrama."

Silence.

Annoyed and worried at the same time, Brianna had flipped shut her cell phone—hard. It wasn't like her mother to give her the cold shoulder. Had something happened? Was she ill? Had she fallen and been unable to pick up the phone?

A stone-faced Brianna had glanced up at the wall clock, 10 P.M. It was late, but if she hurried, she could make the nine-hour trip, spend the weekend, sort this out, and get back in time for Monday's classroom appearance. In minutes she'd packed an overnight bag and was halfway to the underground parking of the high-rise she lived in when she had a sudden thought: *Oh, shit. I forgot about Roberto!*

Brianna's boyfriend, a first-year emergency room resident, was on a night out with his friends. He had immediately answered his cell and, with understanding, said, "Drive safely, Sweet Pea. Give me a call when you get there. Love you."

"I love you, too, Honey Bun. I'm so sorry about missing our Valentine's date, but I'll make it up to you when I get back."

On the last leg of her journey down the mountain highway,

Brianna's thoughts were as gloomy as the dismal weather. Was her mood caused by her mother ignoring her return calls? Or was it because of their previous telephone conversation a week ago? It had not ended well.

"Hi, Mom, it's me. Sorry I haven't called for a few weeks, but I've been up to my neck in papers and presentations. How are you?"

"Fine," came the short response.

"You don't sound fine," had been Brianna's response. "Are you mad at me?"

"No."

Something wasn't right. Brianna had fished. "What's up, Mom?"

"Nothing's up."

"I know you, Mom. Tell me."

"It's not something I want to talk about. Okay?"

A long, grueling exam preparation had overwhelmed Brianna's usual patience. She had snapped. "Oh, that's typical! Just like *you* to keep secrets."

"*What* do you mean by that?"

"You know something, Mom. You're the most secretive person I've ever met. Come to think of it, I don't know anything about you, your past or what you *really* did for a living. I'm not stupid, Mother. I know you're hiding things from me."

"I suggest you come out of your courtroom persona and stop this Gestapo-style interrogation so we can talk more civilly. My past is none of your business."

A lifetime of simmering curiosity mixed with resentment boiled into indignant, wounded anger. Brianna had been abrasive. "You've been lying to me all my life. Who *are* you? Who's my father? Why won't you tell me the truth about anything?"

After a second of silence Lynette had responded. "I'm your *mother*. You are my heart, my soul, my everything. If you want to have a future with me by your side … what am I saying? There is no future." Lynette's voice faded.

"What did you say, Mom?"

Brianna heard a long sigh, then a soft reply. "I'm sorry Brianna. I'm very tired. I'm going to hang up now before we both say something we will regret."

"Here we go again. Always ducking out and you're not going to answer my questions, are you?"

"What questions?"

Brianna had exhaled loudly through her nose. "Who *are* you, Mom?"

"Mata f---in' Hari."

A click, then silence.

Once again, Lynette had escaped her daughter's probing questions.

Brianna's inner voice told her, *By hook or by crook, I'm going to get the long-overdue answers—even if it means strangling her.*

Now traveling at excessive speed, Brianna could have kicked herself. Revealing her long pent-up anger had only antagonized her mother and caused her to draw back into her shell. With serious trust issues marring their relationship, Brianna, in the past, had tried to coax her mother into revealing the missing pieces of the jigsaw that was her life. Lynette had always remained tight-lipped. Brianna couldn't even begin to guess at the reasons for her mother's ongoing secrecy. She was about to be faced with the shock of her life.

As a top law student, Brianna prided herself on her ability to "read" people, but not her mother! Understanding her was like trying to get blood from a stone. The mother-daughter pair had always been incompatible.

Though she drove in four-wheel drive, Brianna's vehicle barely made it to her mother's isolated log cabin. No lights were glowing through the windows. Morning's cold, gray glow had not yet intruded upon the still landscape. Snow drifts mounded on top of the surrounding evergreens, bending their branches low, and piled high against the cabin's outer walls. *This doesn't look good*, Brianna thought, pulling into the familiar driveway. According to her mom, a local guy plowed daily when the snowfall was this heavy.

She brought her Nissan to a stop outside of the cabin's garage door, which was wide open. The silver truck her mother drove was missing, and there were no fresh wheel ruts. *Maybe the car's in for repairs? No. It's brand new, Dumbo! Maybe she's gone shopping? At seven in the morning!*

Brianna rummaged through her shoulder bag. Where was her spare key? Not finding it, she approached her mother's door and turned the knob. Surprise! The door opened. This was not like her mother, a super-safety freak. Lynette always kept her cabin, which was nestled in the quiet serenity of the Arrow Lakes Valley, bolted like a fortress, day and night.

Brianna stepped in and yelled, "Mom?"

Silence.

Her mother was not an early riser. "Oh, please," she implored whatever divinities might be listening, "let her be all right!"

Still wearing her snow boots, Brianna hurried toward the bedroom. "Wakey, wakey, Mom. Surprise!" she forced in a singsong rhythm as her fingers fumbled in the dark for the light switch. Brianna blinked at the sudden brightness. Her tall frame went rigid. There on the unmade king bed was a mountain of dry-cleaning bags. Shoeboxes were stacked high. Handbags and bulbous plastic bags littered the bed. Was it her mother's intention to have a garage sale? Brianna spotted a note in capital letters taped to a shoebox:

"Briana, please see that all this goes to charity."

"What the hell's going on here?"

With the laces of her boots flapping, Brianna darted from room to room on the upper floor of the two-story cabin.

Empty.

She flew downstairs to the basement, which was below the cabin's two stories.

Empty.

Where was her mother?

Not in full panic mode yet, Brianna headed back upstairs to the kitchen and flopped down heavily on a leather, padded stool set before the breakfast bar. She needed to think—to get her legal mind in gear. For that she needed strong coffee. Also, she was starving. She hadn't eaten a thing since taking off from Vancouver the night before. Though her thoughts were in turmoil, the large tin of Arabian coffee triggered a whimsical memory that prompted an involuntary smile. "Mom," she had asked. "Why do you always stick to this ultra-strong brand?"

"Because, my dear," her mom had answered, "it's dark and mystical, like I am."

While the coffee pot did its thing, Brianna went to the living room. She looked up at the thick, Douglas-fir beams bracing the ceiling. She had always loved, when allowed, to spend time with her mother in this cozy home. They had shared many luxury homes together before Lynette became an empty nester. Why her mother had decided to buy this modest home was a mystery to Brianna. As far as she knew, her mother was not poor. She had paid in full for

Brianna's tuition and her downtown Vancouver apartment, adorned with the best furniture. Even so, her mom had always been full of surprises.

In Brianna's eyes her mother was a fascinating person and a likeable character loved by everyone who crossed her path. She was also a prankster with a wicked sense of humor. She loved to tell "clean" as well as some "dirty" jokes, and delighted in pulling April Fools' Day capers on unsuspecting victims. Brianna was always her first target.

Brianna returned to the kitchen to pour herself some coffee. Her eyes wandered across the room; every kitchen item was neatly in its place. She had always suspected that her mother's organized homes had bordered on a compulsive disorder that helped her tackle and master life's challenges with the precision of a military strategist. Even her mother's culinary skills were exceptional. She could concoct a meal fit for a king in little or no time. And her mom was not a woman who would run from trouble. She always met it head on.

So where is she? Surely, Brianna thought, their disagreeable phone call would not have prompted her mother to run away. That was not the first time they'd not seen eye-to-eye; they were so much alike—stubborn and strong willed.

Brianna nervously fingered her uncombed hair. Should she file a missing person's report? She shrugged that idea off—much too soon to jump to conclusions. What else should she do? Drive around the small village in the hope of spotting her mother's truck? Could she have stayed at a friend's house? No. Her mother had never mentioned that degree of closeness to anyone in the hamlet. In fact, after Lionel's accidental death—a fall from a roof six months ago— a grief-stricken Lynette, or so folk thought, had become reclusive and rarely ventured out of her cabin, except to replenish necessary supplies.

Brianna released a regretful sigh. She had let her mother's fairytale romance and sudden marriage to Lionel fifteen years ago upset her. Back then the spoiled, selfish, eight-year-old Brianna cared not a fig that her single mother had been devoting herself entirely to raising her daughter.

On the day of her mom's wedding, Brianna rushed to her bedroom and slammed the door behind her. She threw herself onto the bed and thumped her pillow. Into the feathers she cried, "I wish you were dead."

The tempestuous eight-year-old remained unforgiving. After the wedding Brianna had a meltdown, a tantrum that could have easily belonged to a teenager. "I'm so mad! How could you, Mom! He's ten years younger than you are! All the kids at school are going to make fun of me."

Lynette avoided the anger trap but wondered, "Where has my sweet daughter gone and who is this emotional girl who has taken her place?"

The newlywed mother answered her difficult daughter with tears in her eyes. "Brianna, for the first time in a long while my empty heart is filled with the purest of love," she stated soothingly. "If you can't see it … can't find it in your selfish heart to accept my happiness, then I'm sorry."

"Fine," Brianna huffed. "If that's the way you feel, I'll go and live with my *real* father. Just tell me where he is. I know the lie you told me about him being dead is bull!"

Lynette's beautiful green eyes dulled with painful memories as she responded, "Your father doesn't know you exist, and, Brianna, I haven't the heart to tell him. For many reasons best left unsaid, he mustn't ever know. But you don't have to look far for a decent parental heart. It's right under your nose. The man I married *is* your father now. Be happy you have this wonderful, kind, and loving man in your life. Be as happy as I am."

Lynette tried her best to console her daughter with these words: "I wish I had a magic wand to erase the past and put things right for you, but I can't. There has been too much water under the bridge. The identity of your father is a secret that must remain untold."

The spoiled brat reacted as she normally did—with temperamental rage. "I hate you! I'm going to run away if you don't tell me!"

As the years passed, Lynette remained silent about Brianna's natural father, and Brianna finally accepted her mother's partner into her life. As it happened, Lionel turned out to be the best father any young girl could have had. He doted on her. He drove her everywhere she needed to go and spoiled her rotten. Often he gave her spending money behind Lynette's back, even though her mother held a more disciplinary approach to child rearing: You must earn your own money to appreciate how hard it is to make it.

Brianna became the envy of her classmates who thought her kind, muscular, Hispanic "father" was a drop-dead gorgeous hunk. On graduation day one of her teachers remarked, "If I didn't know better, I would say you were his offspring! You two look so much alike. And he's not that young. He could be your biological father."

Brianna's reflection was cut short by the phone ringing. Brianna, expecting an annoying telemarketer, waited for the ID display: "British Airways." Brianna let the call go to voice mail. "Good morning, Mrs. Martinez," the cheerful voice said. "This is Cheryl Lacey at

British Airways. Please call me regarding your flight to South Africa ..."

Brianna grabbed the receiver. "Hi. This is Brianna. I am Mrs. Martinez's daughter. When did my mother book this flight?"

"I'm sorry. I can't give out personal information."

"For God's sake, I'm her daughter, not some stranger. And I'm also a lawyer," she lied.

"I'm sorry. It's against policy to give out flight information without the traveler's permission."

"Can you at least let me know where in South Africa she intended to go?"

"Like I said, we can't ..."

Brianna hung up.

She slumped into a chair and stared into the steamy depths of her coffee mug. Why would her mother go anywhere without telling her, especially to South Africa? She recalled an earlier discussion, not long ago, when she told her mother, "Mom, Roberto and I are thinking about flying to South Africa—to go on a safari, soak up the sun, and try scuba diving. Why don't you come with us? It will do you good to get away. Pappy is gone, Mother. He wouldn't want you to spend the rest of your life grieving, now would he?" Lynette's face had tightened. "You two go, but you will never get me to go to that beastly place."

"What makes you say that, Mom, if you've never been there? You haven't been there, have you?"

Typical of Lynette, she responded, "No."

That was then. This was now.

Brianna needed to move her search forward. She went to her mother's basement office and checked through desk drawers for flight notes, a credit card statement, or *anything* else that would help solve the mystery of her mother's sudden disappearance.

She found nothing to bite on.

Brianna sat down at her mother's desk and began calling various airports in British Columbia. That also was unsuccessful.

She contacted local hospitals.

That was a waste of time. Her mother had simply dropped off the radar screen.

Calling the police crossed her mind, but it was still too soon to get that panicked. Brianna's eyes burned with exhaustion; she was too weary to think further. She went to the spare bedroom to lie down, hoping that, after a brief nap, her mother would arrive home safely. As she was removing her boots, she spotted a brown leather briefcase propped up against the night table. She picked it up and dumped its contents onto the bed.

"*Jesus Christ!*" she exclaimed loudly.

Several banded wads of crisp $100 U.S. bills—a total of $50,000—stared back at her. There was also a velvet drawstring bag. Brianna opened it. The gravity of the discovery finally hit home. It was surreal. "*Oh … my … god!*" Brianna stared not only at a Rolex watch but also at several gem-encrusted rings, a black pearl necklace, gold bracelets, gold and silver earrings and brooches—all adornments Brianna had never seen. She took little notice of the plastic folders containing legal documents or of the hand-held micro-cassette recorder and boxed tapes. She put her hands over her eyes to make sure she wasn't dreaming. After all, nine hours of driving on slippery roads could play tricks on a brain. Then bells started ringing. She remembered when her mother had said, "I want you to come to my home."

Brianna picked up one of the plastic folders and noticed a blue envelope bearing no name. She slit the envelope with a fingernail and pulled out the letter dated Wednesday, February 13, 1998.

Brianna's mind spat out the reality: *Yesterday!* It was a gut punch.

For the longest moment, Brianna stared at the handwriting. Her mother's usual confident style had formed, instead, the shaky letters of a little girl:

My precious daughter, if you are reading this, you must have received my message asking you to come urgently. I didn't want it to be this way. I wanted so much to patch up our differences in person. I don't blame you for being angry. I'd probably have responded the same way if I had been in your shoes. God knows, I never wanted to hurt you, Brianna. I've loved you from the day you were born. You are my pride and joy, the love of my life. You are a charming, intelligent, and witty human being. Thank goodness, you are emotionally grounded, not like your neurotic mother, who definitely has a few screws loose.

Gosh. I don't know where to start. This is the hardest letter I've ever had to write. You know I'm not an impulsive creature, but awful news has forced me to act. You see, my darling, I recently learned I have an inoperable brain tumor that will bring about memory loss sooner than later. My brain is dying and my memory cells will become fickle, unable to rejuvenate new growth. It's not only a condition of aging; it's a bitter curse, maybe a karmic debt. Who knows?

You don't know this about me, but I enrolled in medical school years ago at the age of nineteen. That tells you something! I completed three years and then gave it up because the sight of blood made me faint. Some doctor, right? And now, after being diagnosed with gliomas cancer, I, as a private patient, have been given the royal treatment because, thanks to my medical background, I am able to fully comprehend their medical terminologies. I haven't had to wait long in waiting rooms; I've had the best specialist at my disposal; and I have been able to obtain copies of my MRI scans. The absolute horror of this brain malfunction not only has dumbfounded me but frightened and numbed me. I didn't know how to tell you. At this moment in time, I know my brain cannot function without my voice, so I'm going to spill what's left in my memory bank before the well becomes completely dry.

Oh, honey, I never want to see the day when I can't recognize you, share birthdays with you, celebrate your marriage, or hold my grandchildren. I have so much to do before this blasted lump robs me of everything and everyone I hold dear.

At first, I thought maybe it wasn't such a bad thing to fade into oblivion, forget some ghastly memories of awful times in my youth, all of which turned me into a fighter, a survivor. I suppose if I hadn't suffered, I wouldn't be who I am today—a bloody tough cookie. Wrong! That was me before I got my bad news. Now, inside, I feel like the Pillsbury doughboy. My past has a dark side that I never wanted to share with you or anyone else. It was too terrible, too ugly. I did not want to spoil your pure spirit with such knowledge. The tapes I left you will explain everything, especially the reason why I'm now so passionately driven to return to the land of my birth—to search out the Zulu woman who saved my life.

I never intended to air my dirty laundry on those tapes. Before I was diagnosed—probably cosmic payback—they were to remain a secret that I acknowledged occasionally to remind myself of my origins and of how blessed I have become in my new life. But my ongoing secrecy has only served to invoke your continuing anger and suspicions. So, as precious time slips away from me, perhaps the hour has come for you to meet the mother you never knew. I hope you'll find it in your heart not to hate me, but to forgive me. Before I forget, please get in touch with airport security at Vancouver Airport to reclaim my vehicle.

"Vancouver!" Brianna exclaimed. Scrunching the letter to her chest, she wondered if she and her mom had passed like ships in the night on the Coquihalla Highway. That thought struck her like a sledgehammer as she read the last page of the letter.

I have left written instructions and my signed authorization on the driver's seat. If you have any trouble getting the truck, which you now own, call Mike Rodriguez, my lawyer. His contact numbers are on my office Rolodex. Mike has the power of attorney to deal with my affairs in my absence. I've also sent him a parcel containing items he needs to handle. Brianna, it's in your best interest to contact him. He is a wonderful human being, a trustworthy soul, and he has my permission to tell you everything you want to know about the remarkable man whose blood you carry. I know this won't mean much to you at this moment, but I loved your father with all my heart. I would have gladly given my life for him, but then he went and left me. The swine! But in one way it's okay, because in death, I'll be closer to my beloved forever.

Now, because the brain specialist couldn't give me a time line when my memory loss will start and eventually shut me down, I'm going to do all the things I should have done years ago. Once one gives up hoping, what does one really have left? Do I have a lot of catching up to do? Yes. Mostly, I'm hoping to find my foster mother, and, with a little luck, trace the whereabouts of my biological mother, as well. That's if they are both still alive. I'm sure you're thinking, *What the heck is she going on about? She told me her parents were dead.* I hope you will forgive this deception. My heart is heavy with sorrow as I say goodbye to you in this letter. I would have given everything I own to have hugged you before I left. I'll try to call you when I get there. But don't expect me home anytime soon, if ever. While I still have breath in my body and a mind that functions, I'll love and miss you. Be strong. You have finally met your mother, my precious daughter. Now I must search for and, hopefully, find my own.

Love from Shiya—that's my real name.

Brianna's mind was in panic mode. She put her hands over her mouth and rocked back and forth. Tears welled up in her eyes. She wanted to cocoon up. Her young shoulders weren't prepared to carry the heaviness of this burden. What should she do? Call Mike? She had often heard his name mentioned but had never met her mother's personal attorney. As far as Brianna knew, he resided somewhere in the States. She couldn't wait to meet him and ask him long overdue questions about her parents. She was also anxious to listen to the cassette tapes, but a pounding headache and a hungry, grumbling stomach postponed that idea. She knew if she didn't eat something soon, she'd be heading into a far worse state.

Feeling extremely lightheaded, Brianna headed upstairs to the main floor.

Once in the kitchen, she opened the refrigerator and saw that it was stacked full. There was enough food in there to feed an army. She shook her head wondering why her mother stocked so much food for one person. It was mind-boggling. Brianna spotted a note stuck to a pizza box: "Brianna, please take some of this food and freezer stuff back with you to Vancouver. Dump the rest in the compost for hungry critters. Unplug the fridge and freezer. Thanks."

Brianna gave up guessing.

Juggling a microwaved veggie pizza, a can of soda, and the recorder and tapes, Brianna set everything down on the walnut coffee table in the living room and sank into a black leather love seat. She bit into the pizza and forced herself to chew. It tasted like sawdust, but she needed the energy to think things through. She leaned forward and slipped the tape marked "Africa #1" into the recorder. She turned up the volume and pressed "Play." She heard her mother's British lilt as clear as a bell

> Brianna, I assume by now you have read my letter explaining that the only way I will ever find peace is by returning to the land of my birth, South Africa. Was I born free? Hell, no!"

Brianna's brows arched. She believed her mother to have been born in London, England. She refocused.

> What I have recorded is the unvarnished truth. You see, I never told anyone about my life in South Africa. I wanted to forget. But

every now and then, diabolical images haunt me through nightmares. I would have thrown in the towel years ago if it had not been for you and my amazing husband, Lionel. When I learned about this tumor, I wanted to crawl into a hole and never come out. But I know I must finally face my past so that chapter of my life can be closed with dignity, not regret.

Brianna, I'd like you to listen to an incredible journey. Although it has bled my heart, soul, and mind of happiness, I want you to learn why. I was abandoned by my Sicilian migrant mother, and the events that followed rendered me incapable of being a good mother to you. You have wanted to know who I am. Now you can find out. But I fear you will wish you didn't know.

Well, here goes. I believe I was born sometime in December 1945. The only person who knows for sure is an African woman named Anele Dingane. She is my foster mother. Apparently, she found me as a newborn, near death, after being buried alive under some corn husks.

Brianna's inner voice screamed, *Is this is for real?*
Her mother continued.

I don't know why my biological mother discarded me like a dirty rag, but I intend to find her and get the answer to this and other missing pages of my early life. The black woman who found me named me Shiya, an African word meaning "forsaken one."

Brianna listened intently as her mother stepped back in time and, through the clear eyes of childhood, described her happy years in Tswanas kraal up to the time of their abduction. Brianna barely breathed as the soft-spoken narration continued.

I'm surprised I can think so clearly, but I've always been possessed by uncanny powers of vision.... Whether my eyes are open or closed, it's as if he is standing before me now—Lord Alan Hallworthy, the wealthy South African landowner who is my biological father. He was an evil man who lacked any sense of humanity, morality, or kindness. Alan learned where I was from a young man named Kumdi, a wannabe Zulu leader. Kumdi told Alan that a white child was living in Tswanas, and the landowner put two and two together.

When Alan came to claim me, Anele and I were badly beaten, tied up, and taken away. As I wiggled free from Alan's grasp, he foamed at the mouth like a rabid animal. All I had left of Anele, the mother I loved, was a shred of colorful material that I clenched tightly in my hand, snatched from her clothing before he bundled me up like a meat parcel and threw me between the car seats. I will never forget Anele's eyes, wild like a trapped animal's.

Something told my child's heart that I'd never see my precious mother again, so I clung to that strip of cloth as if my life depended on it. I have it to this day. It is sealed in my gold locket, the same piece you wanted but I wouldn't let you have. I'm wearing it now, as I record this tape.

Brianna remembered well the antique locket that her mother had always refused to part with. Now she knew why. She swallowed against the lump rising in her throat and concentrated on what her mother was saying.

Brianna, when I look back … no, I don't have to *look* back. I am already there.

The tape whirred to a stop and began automatically rewinding. "Damn!" Brianna cursed.

Tape "#2" whirled into action. This time Lynette's voice was not as clear. Brianna turned the volume dial to "Max."

Brianna, I must warn you. What I have to tell you is very graphic. If you don't wish to hear it, fast forward or destroy this tape.

Brianna had to wonder what could be any worse than what she'd already heard. Her poor mother had been ripped from the arms of Anele. *The Bastard!* She screamed internally. *Oh, how I'd love to see that Hallworthy fiend squirming in the witness stand …*

The phone rang. The ID displayed "Unknown caller." With excited expectancy, Brianna answered, "Is that you, Mom?"

"I must have the wrong number," a male voice said before he disconnected.

Brianna grunted in disappointment, then stared blankly at the wall as though its plain surface would yield answers to her questions. But nothing could have prepared her for this tell-all. She had no clue that it would get much worse.

Brianna rewound the tape.

> If you have decided to listen to this, my dear daughter, the story you are about to hear is a true account of my life. According to some shrinks, five-year-old brains aren't capable of storing too much information. Well, I can prove that theory wrong. I remember everything, as if it were yesterday because I have been gifted with a photographic memory. My scumbag father stole my soul, and it took me a very long time to reclaim it. I have lived with my pent-up anger in a foxhole of hatred for too many years. My bitterness, a coping mechanism, I believe, became my crutch, protecting me from going insane.

Brianna remembered little about her own early childhood. But she didn't doubt that her mother, a woman who could memorize phone directory numbers, could remember early details that would have been lost to others. Brianna was all ears, which she would soon regret. The narration went on.

> The physical injuries caused by my father seemed insignificant compared to the unbearable pain in my heart. I longed for Anele;

the Tswanas village; my river playground; and even the nasty tasting mealie meal, a porridge mixture that bloated my stomach and gave me gas. We kids used to have gas passing competitions. Guess who won that game!

Brianna couldn't believe what she was hearing. This soul-numbing story was horrible enough, but her mother's throaty chuckle at the end of "guess who" tore at her heart.

Her mother continued.

You're probably wondering how I can find anything funny in any of this, but without laughter I couldn't have survived. In my five-year-old mind, I intuited that I would never return to the African bush and the natives I viewed as my people. How right I was.

At sunset on the day I arrived on the Hallworthy estate, after being cleaned up and shaven bald by Maekela, and after having my arm injury "fixed" by the old cook, Lamella, Alan marched me off by the scruff of my neck to an old cottage that had once been used for overflow guests. He hurled me like a rag doll onto a urine-stained, coil-spring mattress and told me in English and then Zulu that he'd chop me up if I tried to escape. I may have been small and young, but I was smart. I vowed that escaping would be the first thing I'd do after he'd gone. Somehow, I was going to find a way out of that putrid-smelling cottage.

Alan slid the outside bolts into their locked position, and I waited, listening for the sound of his retreating footsteps. I examined the filthy room. Other than the bed, the only other piece of furniture was an old, dust-covered Victorian dresser without a bottom drawer. Opposite the dresser was a barred, porthole-sized window. Could I slide my skinny body through the bars? I sure was going to give it a try.

I took off the clothing Alan's wife, Corrie, had forced me to wear: a long vest fitted for a ten-year-old. I had no worries about my hair snagging on the rusty iron bars because my newly shaven head was as bald as a newborn mouse's, thanks to Corrie Hallworthy's orders. When I think back, I remember Maekela crying while she carried out Corrie's demands. In fact, the entire time I was incarcerated, Maekela and Lamella continued to follow Alan's sinister orders, but not without sorrow in their kind hearts.

With one tug at a time, I dragged the bed to the window. That was a task that took some doing. The bloody thing felt as heavy as a ten-ton elephant. But somehow I did it. I climbed onto the bed rail and brushed away the thick cobwebs draping the window sash. I then rubbed as much spit as I could muster onto my skin and began pushing the bottom half of the window up. It did not budge an inch. I clambered onto the windowsill to push on the top half. It wouldn't budge either.

"I realized that I needed both arms to hold the sides of the frame in order to have a better go at it. But one was still very swollen, useless, from my elbow having been wrenched out of its socket. I was so frustrated that I could have chewed through the wood like a rat. I jumped down and went to the door thinking I might have better luck, but it was as solid and immovable as a tree trunk. I remember thumping the door with my good fist. I went to the bed feeling defeated.

Folded at the end of the bed was a moth-eaten blanket. Although the room was stifling hot and airless, I wrapped the blanket around my body. It felt comforting and smelled earthy, like the bedcover Anele had made me in Tswanas. Exhausted, I fell into a deep sleep.

An hour or so later I was awakened by the sound of creaking bolts, my cue to bolt. I flew off the bed and hid behind the door, ready to run. That was a waste of energy because the servant Maekela, who had dragged me into the manor and carried out Corrie Hallworthy's barbarous orders, was faster than I was. Her fingers latched on to my ear like a mosquito. "No you don't, Missy. I'll get skinned alive if you get away."

I struggled with her but I was no match. With her apron Maekela tied my good arm to the bedrail then sat down beside me. She said, "Little child, it hurts me to tie you up, and I'd like nothing more than to let you go, run free, like Anele let your real mother go. But I have a child not much older than you, and the master would take his anger out on me *and* my son."

Her lovely blue eyes stared into mine as she spoke. "Like the old cook, Lamella, I knew Anele well. I used to work with her in the kitchen. I missed her so much when she ran away. I still miss her dreadfully. Anele was a brave and a loving woman for saving you." At the mention of Anele's name, I burst into tears. Maekela untied my restraint and cradled me in her arms. "Don't cry, little child. Pray to the white God and ask him to help you."

Maekela began crooning a tune that I'd heard Anele sing many times. It was about freedom. We shared a lovely few moments until Lamella arrived, huffing and puffing as if she'd just finished a marathon. She said, "Lynette, how is this ever going to mend if you undo my good work?" She came over to the bed and examined my arm.

I stressed strongly, in a voice that even surprised me, "My name is *Shiya*. My name is *Shiya*."

"I know, child. But if they say your name is 'Lynette,' then it's 'Lynette!'"

I remember making a "yeah-right" face and then shrieking when Maekela tried to lift my sore arm. Though it had been throbbing for some time, I didn't know my elbow was out of the socket again. Had climbing the window done it? Or had Alan caused this injury again when he threw me onto the bed? While Maekela left the room to empty the pee bucket, Lamella got to work. She did her "orange surgery" again and snapped the socket back into place. I cried, but this time I didn't faint. I did not utter another sound until after Lamella pulled a metal tin from her apron, smeared its contents—some type of greasy ointment—on my inflamed elbow, and bound my arm with a strip of material she tore from the bottom of her skirt.

As young as I was, I was smart like you back then ... adult thinking. Not knowing I was white, I made up my mind not to speak a word to any *white* person. But I knew it was safe to converse with my *own* people. So I asked Lamella what was to become of me. When her facial expression scrunched up as if a swarm of mosquitoes were attacking her, I naturally continued to probe. "Why am I kept here like a caged leopard? Why does that *umlungu* man hate me? And the *umlungu* woman said she doesn't want me here on her land?"

I saw tears in Lamella's dull, but truthful eyes. "It's not for me to understand the workings of the white people's minds," she said. Intuition told me she was keeping something dreadful from me, but I had no clue what it was. I was to find out only too soon. The two women had to leave me to get back to the house to serve dinner at seven o'clock, or all hell would break loose.

Lamella hugged and kissed me goodbye and told me she'd see me in the morning, bring me breakfast, and check on my arm. Did Lamella feel tenderness toward me? Or maybe I was just seeing a substitute mother in Lamella. I don't know. But I didn't try to escape from the cottage again or sneak past these kindly women who took care of my most simple needs. They were my family now.

In hindsight I wish I had run as fast as my legs could carry me away from that foul cottage that destroyed my childhood innocence. The long, lonely days, the weeks and months having nothing to do but wait for Lamella's and Maekela's daily visits were driving me crazy. I longed to be in the sun ... see the creatures of the wild ... swim in the river ... climb up trees. But most of all, I longed for my mother, Anele. How was she? Did the people in the prison treat her well? Was someone like Maekela or Lamella taking care of her needs?

One evening, not long after my arm had healed, Maekela came with my supper. I could see she'd been crying. "Is something wrong," I asked? Her answer was painful. I wouldn't see Lamella any more. She had died in her sleep. And this time it was for real, not the lie Corrie had once told Anele. Back then Corrie's best friend needed a cook, so Corrie had simply shipped Lamella off to her friend and told Anele that the cook had died. Corrie only brought Lamella back to the Hallworthy manor after she had tried to run away.

I remember grabbing Maekela's hand and begging her not to die. The thought of Lamella being dead was bad enough, but the thought of Maekela, with her kind blue eyes, leaving me as well tore my young heart to shreds. Maekela promised me she wasn't going anywhere. As long as her employers wanted her to feed me, she would be there every day.

Maekela sat on my bed like she normally did, but this time she poured her heart out to me, as though I were an adult. She told me that she hated working for the whites, but she needed her job to help support her son, a year younger than I was. He was born a year after Anele left. At that time I wasn't aware of the horrible lives black women endured due to racial hatred. I tried to understand her plight as I waited for her to continue. "I had to give my baby to a fieldworker to look after him because I couldn't."

"Why?" I asked.

"Because Lady Corrie threatened to have my child sent to an orphanage. Servants are not allowed to have or even raise their children while they are in service. So I gave my son to Rose, a migrant Bantu fieldworker. She brought him up while I gave her my wages. That's why I put up with the awfulness. But I do see my son on my afternoons off. He thinks I'm his big sister." She sighed. "It's better that way."

"Where is his father?"

"We never speak of him."

"Why not?"

"Because, child, he is a bad man, possessed by an evil spirit."

I immaturely responded, "The *Imikhuba* can make your son's father vanish, if you want."

Maekela didn't laugh. She simply said, "You've got a lot to learn, child." She looked away from my intense stare and ended with a sinister overtone. "I hope and pray you never have to suffer this evil."

We spoke about many things that day. Not all doom and gloom. I told her about my happy life at Tswanas and my love of snakes and other creatures. She made a face when I mentioned "snakes."

Maekela then told me how her own mother, a Hallworthy fieldworker, had died from sunstroke, or so it was believed. And then she spoke of how Anele had become a substitute parent to her and her sister, Isona. We parted that day with love in our hearts for each other. She filled the huge gap in my sorry life. But could she save me from an orphanage? How long Maekela would remain *my* substitute mother was an unanswered question.

Days later I stood at the window searching the pathway below. I had no real concept of time, but two sunrises and sunsets had passed. Where was she? Had she died, too? I hoped not. Who would take her place? Would it be her sister, Isona? I prayed it wasn't Corrie. Four sunsets went by. No food, no water, and a full, stinking toilet bucket. I knew that I had to do something, or I would starve to death. Without a bad arm to hold me back, I managed to get the top half of the window open. But my fear of being permanently stuck between the rusty dividers sent me to my bed dejected. I fell asleep feeling cold, lonely, and hungry. I prayed to Namandla, Anele's Zulu God, to let me die.

Sometime during the black of the night I heard heavy footsteps. I ran to the door thinking that it was my dear friend. "Maekela," I shouted. The door was flung open and a flashlight blinded me. Then a strong hand grabbed my neck. Alan smelled as if he'd fallen into a vat of beer. He flung me on the bed. That night a little girl "died" in the dark, all alone with a monster!

Brianna knew she was about to hear something horrific. She closed her eyes and heard her mother's voice change into something childlike and frightened.

What happened that night still lives deep my soul, forever. I think I died that night, the night I was viciously raped.

Brianna threw up in her hand and raced to the bathroom, leaving the tape playing. As her head hung over the toilet, she screamed in between spasms. You sick "*bastard!* She was a *child*, an innocent little child." As awful as Brianna felt, how could she or anyone else truly feel the pain her mother had endured without having also experienced a stolen childhood, a robbed innocence, and sexual abuse? And for sure, rape survivors didn't have the support that there is today. But her mother had not let what had happened control her. And she had dealt with these things all these years, without letting on. What a remarkable feat, Brianna thought. The brute didn't kill her mother's essence. Reflecting on how special her mother was, Brianna recalled a verse from a prayer book: "Let the ungodly fall into their own nets; and let me ever escape them."

Although Brianna dreaded learning more, she had to find out what happened after that heinous night. She splashed her face with cold water and then walked slowly, as if she were attending a funeral, back to the room with the recorder. Her fingers felt like ice as she rewound the tape. The horrendous narrative was hard to listen to without feeling paralyzed. Her mother's sobs seemed endless. She continued.

> With blurred and pain-filled vision, I saw the shape of a woman with a long object in her hand. I saw it rise and fall. I heard the thud.
>
> Corrie stepped over Alan—semiconscious from the blow—like the piece of dung he was and came to my side. Never had I expected such softness from her or to feel her hot tears mingling with her words, "Oh, dear God in heaven!" she cried. "What has he done to you?"
>
> A veil of darkness closed my eyes.
>
> I awoke in an unfamiliar bed and found Corrie and a black man standing over me. Naturally, I knew nothing about incest, molestation, rape, or any of the other horrendous crimes committed against children.
>
> But as young as I was, I was able to deduce that whatever Alan had done to me, Corrie was going to ensure no one ever found out. Why else would she get a *black* doctor to attend to me? Later I

learned that Alan had used a hunting knife to cut my ...."

Brianna slammed her hand down on the "Pause" button.

After downing a generous shot of brandy, she stared at the tape recorder and cried silently. , *I thought I was your best friend. You could have told me about the pain you carried locked inside so long and so bravely.* Brianna's heart was breaking. She didn't want to hear what came next, but she knew she must.

I saw Corrie whisper something in the doctor's ear. He then bent down and stroked my newly grown hair. In Zulu he introduced himself. "My name is Dr. Mubani. How are you feeling? Do you have any pain?"

I shook my head. That wasn't true. I was in agonizing pain.

"Lady Hallworthy wants you to know how sorry she is for the terrible thing that was done to you. As soon as you are able to walk, she is going to arrange for someone like myself to take you to an orphanage, a new home, where you'll be taken good care of. She begs you never to breathe a word to the nuns of what has happened here. Can you promise her that? Keep it a secret?" Why he spoke to me like an adult is beyond me. And I don't suppose I understood the gravity of what had happened or why I was asked to keep it quiet, so I simply nodded.

The doctor set about repairing me. I looked away as he placed fresh gauze on my stitched privates. He then gave me an injection—an antibiotic, maybe. Who knows?

On the day my vaginal and rectal sutures were removed, Dr. Mubani, whose name was imprinted in my synapses, whisked me away from Hallworthy manor. He handed me over to a smiling white nun in a traditional penguin suit. I couldn't have known that the Angel of Mercy Convent was for half-caste orphans known as "colored." Couldn't they see I was *white?*!

Some years back I hired a private investigator. He went to South Africa at my expense and tracked down that black doctor. The then retired doctor was very willing to tell the investigator about that day in Corrie's house and of the day he had to take me to the convent. The physician asked the private eye to relay a message to me. He had not been able to rid his mind of the part he had no choice but to play. He wanted my forgiveness. What for? He was a victim like I was. Doctor Mubani died a year later. In his memory, Baragwaneth Children's Hospital now has two newly built wings to house the overflow of AIDS-infected children. I donated the money anonymously.

Brianna's thoughts hung like fishing weights. One thing she knew for sure was that her mother was the most soft-hearted person she'd ever known, donating vast sums of money to many worthy charities—tons of tinned goods to food banks, and meal vouchers and luxury blankets for the homeless. If someone came to the door with a sob story, her mother was there to help them. When it came to neglected animals, there was no limit to her support. Brianna's pleasant thoughts of her mother's generosity were overcome by a tragic one. She couldn't push out of her mind the picture of a hungry, emaciated little girl with stubby golden hair, green eyes wide with terror, and a small mouth crying out for help. Brianna made a silent plea: *Mom, please call so I can tell you how much I love you.*

But her mother was gone. All Brianna had left was a disembodied voice coming from a recording.

At the convent I underwent a barrage of clinical tests to determine if I was autistic or severely retarded. But I believe what puzzled the psychologist the most was my muteness. There was no doubt that I was a traumatized child, but even I have to question the motivation for being voiceless. Looking back, I believe I was being loyal to Corrie, my way of thanking her for taking care of me in those first awful days. I decided to "Speak no evil. See no evil. Hear no evil."

While I was recovering from my injuries, the best part of Corrie's guilt was the lollipops, chocolate cake, ice cream, and other foodstuffs a child of the African bush would never have known existed. I felt I owed Corrie my life, and the only way I could keep our secret was to remain closeted in silence. That charade was my downfall because the Angel of Mercy Convent viewed me as an aberration. I was denied an education. Mother Superior said I was a blighted thing of the Devil who had no use or ability for learning.

I won't go into lengthy details about my convent years, but those memories still hurt like hell. Even though the staff appeared to live and work harmoniously, I was never shown an ounce of compassion. There were no "angelic servants of God" in that ghastly place. "Devil's aides" is more like it! And the white priest who delivered Mass was definitely the Devil incarnate. The dirty bugger lifted his garb and flashed his penis at whoever had the misfortune to cross his path. He only did it to me once, and I punched him in the nuts. I then proceeded to pee on a bench, rip up some prayer books, and set the church on fire by tipping over candles. Of course, my "ungodly" behavior was reported, and this only fortified the nuns' belief that I was possessed by the Devil. Yippee! I was banned from the chapel.

Brianna's lips could not help but lift into a smile at her mother's antics, although her deep anguish could not be disguised. Tears still fell from her cheeks as her mother continued.

Nothing can compare to the daunting task of learning to read and write as an adult. It is an experience I wouldn't wish on my worst enemy.

Brianna frowned. Did she hear right? *Adult!* She rewound tape. There was no mistake. Just the thought of her well-read mother being denied an education was unimaginable.

The convent housed some older orphans, mostly pregnant teenagers. I was the only young child. What I saw there was nothing more than a cattle market—young mothers, some willingly and others reluctantly—handing over their babies. Many of those poor girls didn't have any choice. I believe that tax investigators finally shut down the convent a short time after I left, thank goodness. Those so-called "angels" were running an adoption racket for profit, with most of their clients living overseas. I don't mean to knock every convent across the globe. No, I'm just shredding this particular religious institution. Some of the nuns were sadistic. I took an awful lot of beatings, and even had a chunk of hair ripped from my head for stealing a slice of bread from the kitchen. I think I was eight or so at the time. But you want to know something, Brianna. Those miserable years locked away from the outside world were paradise compared to my next prison.

Brianna held her breath.

To my horror, shortly before my tenth birthday, I recognized the tall man who was being led by Mother Superior. He was flanked by two uniformed white men. The sight of Alan Hallworthy sent me scrambling up a large sycamore fig tree. I wet myself on the highest bough, and I was sorry the fluid didn't land on him. "Lynette, come down this instant," bellowed the nun. Oh, how I hated that name. Inside I was *Shiya* and would be until the day I died. "No, no, no," I yelled. The strong voice that exploded from my unused voice box took me and everyone below by surprise. Alan's and Mother Superior's mouths fell open, as if they were catching flies. The nun bellowed for a helper. When I saw the African gardener begin to climb up after me, I freaked out. "I'll throw myself out of this tree if you come any closer," I said in Zulu. He kept climbing. How was I to know he only spoke Swahili? I wrapped my legs and arms around the branch like a boa constrictor. The gardener would have to cut off my locked limbs before I'd let go. But Alan's evil command reached the heavens. "Go ahead, jump," he shouted, "and save me a bloody headache, you crazy *wop!*"

"I had played deaf and mute for some time, but I was neither. I had learned well *this* man's language. His words didn't sting me.

They gave me new fight. What should I do? What *could* I do? Fight the gardener? Fall from the tree? Come down and die all over again? When the gardener reached the bough below me and extended his hand, I had no choice. I climbed down. Alan shot me a look of contempt, whispered something to one of the uniformed men, and then left the scene. Was I glad to see the back of him! I thought he had come to take me back to the gamekeeper's cottage and abuse me all over again.

What I didn't know was that Alan Hallworthy was my biological father. As such, he had the legal right to commit me to an asylum. What was his motive? To shut me up for good! Who would believe the accusations of a crazy person? According to the court records obtained by the investigator, I was classified as "colored" and unfit for society. And I was to remain incarcerated for the rest of my natural life. One human being enslaved by another is as old as civilization and will probably continue until hell freezes over. Slavery runs the gamut—from working forced laborers unconstitutional hours in agricultural fields to the lowest of all, human trafficking in the sex trade. Women, girls, men, and boys were being forcibly placed in brothels. Enough of that! I have to get off my soapbox and continue my story before I lose my train of thought.

Skoemansdaal Asylum was a state-run institution, not far from Pretoria, the capital of South Africa. It was a sane person's worst nightmare. I'd had more than my fair share of horrors, but this place, which had once housed prisoners of war, beat the lot. When I arrived at the steel gates of the sanatorium, the building looked like something from *The Addams Family*. The grounds boasted a spectacular display of flower beds and well-kept lawns as green as my eyes. I remember gawking at an enormous three-tier fountain with cascading waters.

However beautiful the grounds were, they held no awe for me in the days, months, and years to come because the "loonies" hardly ever got to walk in the gardens. And if we were given this privilege, we wouldn't have known if the sun was shining or if the fountain flowed because the daily dose of potent tranquilizers they gave us kept most of us in a constant zombie state, some of us almost catatonic. I outwitted the pill-givers by hiding the tablets under my tongue and then spitting them down the toilet. I decided the only way I was going to survive in this godforsaken place was to act out an academy award winning role. "Look, nurse. I'm spaced out. I can't harm a fly. So please, please take me on a walkabout."

The day I arrived at the madhouse, the grim matron refused to register me. She argued that the institution housed only insane white adults and was no place for a colored ten-year-old, crazy or not. She also pointed out that they didn't have trained staff to deal with kids. After several frantic telephone calls, the problem was resolved thanks to a paid-off white judge. I was forcibly taken to the top floor and restrained to a metal cot, the only one in the attic. I was given nothing to eat or drink, and during the night I wet the bed. The next morning, I was moved to the second floor and locked in a large room with eight women ranging in age from twenty to ninety. I was the only child ever to be admitted to Skoemansdaal.

Years passed without a ray of hope of ever getting out of that dreadful place. Not only was I attacked by loony inmates, I was also sexually abused by the male and female staff members. There was one staffer that took sadistic pleasure in stubbing out lit cigarettes on my skin.

Brianna nearly choked on her saliva. She had seen the tiny pink welts on her mother's upper chest and, being curious, had asked, "How did you get those, Mom?"

"From a bad bout of chicken pox," her mother replied with tongue in cheek.

The taped narration resumed.

My silent prayers to be liberated from this hellhole came when an angel arrived at Skoemansdaal. Doctor Cecelia Harcourt. She was the newly appointed psychiatrist and the first female doctor ever to take the position. I will never forget the look on her face when I was ushered into her examination room. "Lord above! She's a *child*," she said. "What's *she* doing here? How old is she?"

"Fifteen, we think," the matron said, handing over my file to the doctor.

Cecelia's brows arched. "What you mean you *think*?"

"She doesn't have a legal birth certificate."

In those days, Brianna, producing a birth certificate was not mandatory, as it is today. According to convent records, which I'm positive, were falsified by Mother Superior, I was registered as "illegitimate." This was a terrible stigma in those days.

Although Cecelia did not speak a word when the matron offered further information, her body language spoke volumes. In fact, she shuffled in her seat more than I did. Finally, the doctor closed my file, looked at me through eyes brimming with compassion, and told the matron and the male nurse who had accompanied me to leave her office. The matron protested saying that I could possibly be dangerous. She couldn't vouch for the doctor's safety. "Rubbish," Cecelia said in her strong Yorkshire accent, as she got up from her chair and shooed them out. "Wait outside. I'll let you know when I'm finished."

With no staff in sight, the doctor bombarded me with questions. "Lynette, do you know *where* you are? Do you know *why* you were put away? Do you know your real age? How did you get vaginal and rectal tearing?' She shook her head when I didn't answer and said, "I don't know if you will truly grasp what I have to say, but I'm enraged that a young *white* girl has spent nearly five years in this adult facility."

I had withdrawn deeply in order to cocoon my body and mind from a world that inflicted terrible pain upon me, but I wasn't insane. As a matter of fact, I was sharper than a butcher's cleaver. I knew the motive behind Alan's haste to commit me. I was growing up fast and could spill the beans. His intent was as evil as the man himself. But there was something about the kindness in this woman's voice and eyes—a tenderness I hadn't known in years—that broke my long silence.

In between glasses of water that soothed my dead tongue,

words flew out of my mouth. In fact, they were tumbling over each over. I spoke of everything that had been bottled up for years. As the doctor listened to the trauma I had endured, I felt, for the first time, free from the wretched guilt I had been carrying, as if what had happened to me had been my fault. Now someone else could help me carry the heavy load. The doctor swore she would never let anything bad happen to me again. She hugged me and told me she'd come back tomorrow, even though it wasn't her official "shrink" day.

That night I cried myself to sleep. Only this time I cried tears of happiness. Someone cared about me. She was going to save me. She was my Angel of Mercy.

The next day, in Cecelia's office, I met my angel's cousin, Roland Giles Harcourt. He was fifty years old and a British Consular stationed in Johannesburg. Cecelia explained that she had broken medical ethics by telling him about my case. But, she stressed, it was the only way she would be able to get his help.

Roland said he had sought advice from a Supreme Court judge, a friend of his, about my situation and that this learned person promised to look into the matter. A week later Roland returned. It seemed the judge's phone call to Alan's lawyer paved the way to my freedom. Alan disowned me and the South African court released me from Skoemansdaal to my new legal guardians. I was ecstatic to be the ward of Roland and Cecelia Harcourt. Although I was terrified of all men, I was not afraid of Roland. Cecelia informed me that I would have to live at Roland's apartment, not hers, until she found an alternative, as she had accepted a new posting back in England.

Of course, Roland was against this living arrangement. It was not "proper" to have an attractive young teenage girl living with him in his flat, he complained, but as I had nowhere else to go, he finally relented. In gratitude, I cleaned his apartment and made sure that he had a decent dinner to come home to, which was hilarious. The poor man never once complained about the burnt offerings I set before him.

I felt myself falling for this older man, who was the kindest, most caring person I had ever known. A love affair with a minor was the furthest thing from his mind. But I didn't want to lose the only man I could possibly love.

On my sixteenth birthday Roland took me to dinner at a fancy restaurant. After the delicious lobster meal, Roland excused himself to go to the bathroom. As soon as he left the table, I sneakily drank the rest of his red wine. Oh, I remember it well. It was my very first taste of alcohol, and my brain loved the intoxicating feeling. Roland chastised me when he found not only his glass empty, but the wine bottle, too. I didn't care. I'm surprised I didn't pass out. I was so unsteady on my feet, Roland had to carry me to the car.

Back at his apartment, the warm, fuzzy sensations I was experiencing made me feel all grown up and stirred a part of my body I never knew existed. For the first time in my life, I wanted a man to love me in this way. Knowing what a gentleman Roland was, an old-fashioned man in the warmest sense of the word, he would never have laid a finger on me if I hadn't instigated matters. Shamelessly, I asked Roland to help me undress. The look on his face was priceless. "Good Lord, no!" he cried. But I persisted, and one thing led to another. Unfortunately, my adolescent fantasy turned to outright terror when he tried to make love to me. I screamed my head off. He understood.

After that I stayed away from wine, and neither of us allowed our thoughts to build romantic castles in the air. However, we became inseparable, much to the disdain of his fellow diplomats. Poor Roland came home one night and said that due to our living arrangements, his peers looked at him like a pedophile. "We can get married," was my simple solution. Oh, the foolish mind of a romantic girl! I had no birth certificate. Parental permission was needed to marry under age 21. And I was still legally his ward. I believe it was about this time that I was confronted with some stark facts.

Roland started having second thoughts. He snapped at me for the slightest things. His sexual body language was obvious, but that passion soon turned into cold hostility. I was young, not stupid! The time had come to part company, but where could I go? Johannesburg might as well have been in the Himalayas. I didn't know my way around and could not read the street signs with certainty. But my Maker had granted me attributes that would help me survive: an episodic memory (the instant recollection of autobiographical events: times, places, associated emotions, and other contextual who, what, when, where, why knowledge that can be explicitly stated), where I can mentally travel back in time to an event from recent or the distant past. But most of all I had acquired the craftiness of a professional thief.

Brianna, I had no other options. I stole a blank British passport from Roland's office, as well as a Home Office seal, a passport camera, and a large pile of cash from his home safe. I had watched him open it before, and my memory chip had stored the combination. Later, when Roland left the apartment to buy groceries, I packed a small suitcase and hightailed it out of there. Sensing it was best not to be seen in Johannesburg, I hurriedly caught the first train to Durban. I doubted Roland would report me. If anything, I thought he would be relieved. He had come under scrutiny by the Home Office and probably would have lost his job in time. Did he really love me? No! Did I love him? No! It was a schoolgirl's crush. That's all.

Carrying the clothes and stolen items on my back, I arrived in Durban. My mind was set. I knew it was more than risky, but I asked for directions to the Hallworthy Refinery, as it now was called. Under the cloak of darkness, I snuck into the servant's quarters and prayed it was Maekela who returned that night. It was! She and her sister Isona hadn't seen me since I was a child, and they were overjoyed, though my new age and appearance—five-foot-nine, cosmetics that made me look older, and long hair flowing to my waist—took some adapting to.

We had bonded in the past, and now we hugged and kissed like long-lost siblings. I brought them up to scratch. As I told my story, their gasps echoed in the dingy shack. And yes, they would help me, as much as they could. I gave Maekela some money and told her what needed to be done. However, I was concerned about Alan. Maekela told me he no longer came to the shack to order the sisters to do his bidding at the cottage. His sights were on newer, younger refinery workers, both white and black. Plus, he was currently away on business. I breathed a sigh of relief. But Maekela warned, "Don't wander outside during the day, in case you are seen by a curious fieldworker."

The money I gave Maekela was handed over to a black policeman. It paid for my forged paperwork. I became a twenty-one-year-old British citizen named Lynette Smith, an identity stolen from Durban Births and Deaths registry. The real Miss Lynn Smith, a nanny from Yorkshire, died three weeks before I handed over the blank passport for doctoring. I intended to fly to Great Britain and make a new start. Before I could do that, however, I had some unfinished business to attend to in this land of horrors. As I record this, Lord Alan Hallworthy rots in jail. I put him there. I had incriminating evidence—a personal journal belonging to Corrie. But I'll explain about that later.

Thankfully, I had enough money to buy a one-way ticket to London, pay for hotel accommodations, food, and other expenses—for a while. When I arrived in Great Britain, December 1962, I was shocked to see snow. It was the first time I'd seen such a sight, and the white stuff mesmerized me.

I found a cheap hotel but had another shock—registering. I couldn't write, so I made up a story about hurting my wrist. The helpful desk clerk filled in my details for me. That embarrassing incident made me determined to get an education. When I started at the Adult Learning School in London, I concocted another story: I was an orphan raised by missionaries in North Africa. They were deceased, and I needed an English education, not Swahili schooling.

I started working at night in a strip joint as a glass washer—the only employment I could find without too many questions being asked—and going to school during the day. It was a challenge, but I graduated from high school with honors in two years. Unbelievable! I was gifted, or perhaps cursed, for I rarely forgot anything, and some things are best forgotten. I surprised more than a few of the school's staff members. After a vocational exam, I was informed I could pick any educational field I wanted. I chose medicine. At nineteen, I entered medical school. After three years, I gave it up. Can you imagine a doctor who can't stand the sight of blood? Instead, I enrolled in a science course and worked for a pharmaceutical company as a formulator. That career choice didn't work out either. What did I really want to do for a career? And how would I accomplish it? Whom could I trust to set my lifelong ambition in motion? Peter Graham McTavish!

Brianna smiled. She had been very young when her stepfather, Peter, had passed away, but she had always been glad she had kept his British name and not changed it to "Martinez," as her mother had wanted her to do. Lynette continued.

The day I gave notice to my chemistry professor and my job, Peter nearly ran me over in the university's parking lot. He jumped out of his Bentley. "Are you all right? What an idiot I am! I should have checked my rearview mirror before I started to back out. Do you need to go to the hospital?" I assured him I was fine. He helped me up, collected the scattered contents of my handbag, and offered to take me to a hospital, just to be sure, but I argued, "A stiff drink will do the trick." Need I say more? Alcohol and I are not the best of friends, but this time when it happened, I didn't scream my head off.

Peter was forty years old, a wealthy landowner in Scotland who partnered mostly with pharmaceutical firms, and he had never married. I towered over him, but that didn't matter. He made up for his lack of height with charisma. He loved animals, as did I, and we hit it off well. I not only found a wonderful boyfriend, I also discovered a shrewd businessperson whose shady dealings made mine look like a saint's. I never did tell him the truth about my life, only enough to prevent him from prying.

In August 1970, at age twenty-five, I agreed to move into Peter's house, "Fairfield" on the Isle of Skye. That farmhouse had a lot of history. Allegedly, it was the house in which Flora MacDonald gave love and shelter to Bonnie Prince Charlie. It could have been folklore, for all I know, but leaving the horrors of South Africa and starting anew in Scotland inspired magical ideas. In the months following my move into Peter's home, I refused to marry him. I'll discuss why later. He wasn't upset with me, nor were his well-to-do parents. From the beginning of our relationship, I had felt only coolness from them. Certainly, they didn't approve. A year later, however, I caved in and agreed to become Mrs. McTavish—in name only.

Brianna pressed the "Stop" button. She needed to reflect. Serene, picture-perfect scenes flooded her mind. Not long ago she had stumbled upon some of her mother's photographs and had asked, "Mom, these are beautiful. When were they taken?"

"That's Fairfield House, where you were born. We lived there for the first few years of your life."

"Really!"

"Who is the man in the picture? Is he my father?"

"No, he is not. Put those blasted pictures away. I don't wish to see them, and I don't want to talk about it."

Wearing a blank expression, as if she, herself, didn't want to remember some things, Brianna reactivated the tape. Her mother's voice sounded happy.

I loved my new home in Scotland, but I soon became fed up with Peter's endless dinner parties, stuffy men, and boring wives. Also, I faced lonely times when my so-called husband went on long business trips overseas—"business" is what he liked to call them. That's when I decided to put my original plan into action. But in order to do that, I had to return to school, yet again! This time I enrolled in law school, wanting to specialize in immigration law. At Glasgow University I used my married name, not any of the fake ones I had used to get in to previous educational facilities. In three years I passed my exams with flying colors!

Brianna's eyelids shut momentarily, as if sleep had overpowered them. She had always believed her mother was a freelance journalist. Whenever her mother left for days on end, she had accepted this lie without question. "A good story has come up," she would say. "I need to make money, sweetheart, so I'll see you in a week or so."

Brianna also recalled the many times she'd been left behind with the live-in nanny. Lonely for her mother, Brianna often cried throughout the night. A tumultuous mixture of sadness and anger began to pound in her heart. Brianna continued to listen.

I began advertising my legal services in an overseas newspaper. It didn't take long before my private mailbox in Glasgow was full of requests for assistance, mostly from people who had problems with their visas or landing applications. Using our home as a legal base, I began filing the paperwork through the proper appeals channels. I was successful with most of the applications. Peter was upset, to say the least. "My dear, I fear this could bring undesirable people to the house. You must stop immediately."

Feeling shameless, I lashed back at him with the only thing I knew would shut him up—blackmailing him about a secret I had honored in our early days together. "If you don't let me live my life as I want to, I will tell your parents, friends, and your business associates that you are a faggot."

I know this is hard to believe, but we only made love that once, the day he had knocked me over onto my backside in the parking lot. He regretted making love to women. He told me his truth, and I told him a truth of my own: I hated sex. It seemed we would get along fine. Even now I regret my demeaning outburst that day and the name calling. He was such a gentle, kind soul, so good to me and to you. I knew I had hurt him badly, but he never uttered a word in his defense.

The next day Peter rented office space for me in a good part of Glasgow. The five-story, red-brick building housed medical specialists, shipping agents, and other lawyers. I had the top floor all to myself. After fitting out my spacious office, I hired a legal secretary and began to work. I loved my job, and I saw very little of Peter over the next few months. He traveled a lot and so did I.

One day I received a registered letter from Germany that intrigued me. It seemed that Gerda Düsseldorf had applied several times to enter England to visit her English boyfriend, but she had been consistently denied. Being a hopeless romantic, I traveled to Frankfurt to see if I could help her. Apart from her eye color, I was surprised to see how much alike we looked, and we were about the same age—twenty-seven.

I met up with Gerda in an open-air café. Immediately I warmed to the bubbly blond. She handed me the "no-way-are-we-going-to-let-you-enter-Britain" rejection document. I explained that I would need some quiet time to go over it. She gave me a phone number to call once I was ready. In the quiet of my hotel room I pored over a rather large pile of paperwork and learned that she was a registered prostitute, but this didn't seem a sufficient or legal reason for denial. Something told me it was far worse. I placed an international call and spoke to a friend of Peter's who worked for Interpol. It turned out that they had plenty on her. In the '60s Gerda had been registered as a Nazi sympathizer after being arrested at a swastika-wielding demonstration outside a university. I didn't want to buck the immigration system, but the British, especially the bureaucrats, weren't forgiving. And the German wars had left many with embittered hearts.

I called her when I was ready and arranged to meet her over dinner. I asked Gerda what had happened at the demonstration. She said in her naiveté she'd been brainwashed by her boyfriend at the time. She agreed that her stupidity had left her marked in the pages of history, like the rest of her country. Now she was paying a hefty price for a long ago teenage love. Her explanations had never loosened the strict British immigration rules.

I left an optimistic Gerda at the airport. I told her that I'd do everything I could for her. Her chances were slim to none, but I didn't tell her that. Upon returning to England, I filed an appeal application. As expected, Gerda was denied entry. That same evening I discussed her case with Peter. He, too, had no love for the Germans. He begged me to drop the case. I argued that the government should not hold Gerda solely accountable for the long-ago demonstrations when others with worse records had slipped through the British net of red tape.

I didn't sleep a wink that night wondering how I could help this poor woman. Part of me wanted to believe my reason was pure sympathy, but, in truth, I suspect it was my daredevil character—let's beat the British at their own game. I wasn't patriotic like Peter was. My adopted homeland was just a temporary stopover on my way to as yet undecided horizons. So I hatched a dangerous plan. I decided to take a risk for a woman whose only motive to enter Britain was love, not politics!

My decision to help Gerda was not an easy one to make. Even though I had everything a person would need to be happy, life was still a struggle for me. On one hand I felt bulletproof when I thought of helping another person in need. On the other hand, I was being continually attacked by emotional ups and downs. Yes, I was heir to a fighting spirit, but my painful childhood was still lurking in the corridors of my mind. I had not yet dealt with the shame that overwhelms victims of molestation. I had no one to trust, to open up to about the darkness that enveloped the "essence" of Shiya. As I kept the force of the traumatized child at bay, I made my choices and life went on.

I arranged to meet Gerda in a different German city.

On a sunny Friday morning in June I booked myself into a Berlin hotel and waited. As instructed by the registered letter I had sent her, Gerda arrived at the hotel wearing a maid's uniform that would enable her to blend in with hotel staff. Over a glass of wine in my hotel suite, I explained the plan I had hatched for her. I could tell she was nervous about it, but so was I. I had a lot more to lose than she did. We went into the bathroom, where I dyed her mousy blond hair a lighter tone, one that would match mine. Then Gerda put on the clothing I'd worn when I entered the hotel. Being large breasted, she had a problem buttoning up my suit jacket, but with an extra tug, we managed to fasten it. A pair of dark sunglasses hid Gerda's Germanic blue eyes. I was thrilled with the makeover. You couldn't tell us apart.

Gerda was ready. I gave her the airline tickets, my credit card, and my passport. We hugged each other goodbye. She left the hotel bound for London. Never once did I feel afraid that she might stay in Britain and leave me stranded in Germany. However, if the disguise backfired, we would be in the middle of another kind of ball game, and she would have to face the consequences alone, as we had arranged. She would have to admit theft, saying that a cousin who worked at the hotel had stolen my passport.

My heart flew on that evening flight with Gerda. With a "Do Not Disturb" notice hanging from my hotel doorknob, I spent a boring weekend watching awful German television and munching on various food packets Gerda had brought me. Peter was in Mexico, and I had informed my secretary and the household staff in Scotland that I was off to Egypt to see a client.

At around midnight on the day Gerda was to return, I heard three short knocks—our prearranged signal. Gerda rushed into the room, her face radiant. The reunion with her lover had gone well. Gerda never told her boyfriend how she had managed to get into Britain, and he never pressed the matter with her. They were just happy to be together. The love of Gerda's life was an invalid, paralyzed from the waist down from a motorbike accident. The couple paid me handsomely for their stolen time together.

After a yearlong fruitless battle to get Gerda permanent residence status, I decided to take matters into my own hands and do what was right. I smuggled her into Britain once more. Finally she was able to marry her sweetheart. They live together happily on a farm in Yorkshire.

For obvious reasons, I did not attend their wedding. We had agreed it was best for us to sever all ties. But because of Gerda, I discovered my true calling.

I was disgusted by the legal, bureaucratic red tape that

prevented some desperate, good people from entering England—families torn apart, political dissidents, people denied refugee status, women fleeing abusive husbands, and so on. The immigration system treated them as if they were lepers. These people would have had no chance in hell if I hadn't helped them. You must be squirming in your seat, Brianna, knowing that your mother is a felon who has broken the law more times than you've had hot dinners.

Brianna was more than numb. Her mother was the last person she would ever have suspected of criminal activity. To the contrary, she always went by the book, or so Brianna had believed. The law student's ears now became sharply honed.

I suppose I can say it's all in my past, but then I would be lying. The profits I made from my smuggling days have provided me with more money than I could spend in a lifetime, and now it's all yours. I had the bulk of the money transferred into your name. I've only kept what I will need. The account details are in the briefcase.

Brianna pressed "Stop" and shouted aloud, "How could you, Mother? Your cloak-and-dagger activities have risked not only your life but mine, as well!" Brianna paced the room, practically bouncing with indignation, anger, and self-pity. How could she return to the field of law with a clear conscience? She wanted to take the tapes and burn them, but somehow she couldn't bring herself to do it. Reluctantly, Brianna pressed "Play."

I found my calling, all right, and I loved every minute of it. I ran Operation Grassroots, my name for my operation, until a few years ago. I never met my clients personally, the Irish forger, or the helpers. Personal contact was taboo. I used pseudonyms, pay phones, and out-of-the-way mailboxes to run my undercover operation—until my best "coyote" got caught. I didn't trust anyone else, so I decided to take the risk myself. I'm sure you've watched many movies featuring Spanish-speaking "guides" running clientele between borders. I believe I became the first *gringa* coyote. It was during this particular stage in my life that I met your father. You always wanted to know who your father was, and now you will.

The recorder whirred, stopped, and began rewinding.

"Are you bloody serious?" Brianna shouted at the inanimate object in her hand. She reached for tape "#3."

Brianna held the recorder a few inches from her ear. She didn't want to miss one word of the revelation she had waited such a long time to hear.

In the summer of 1974, under a stormy sky, my plane touched down in Guatemala City. It was a short flight from Mexico City to Guatemala City, but it had been a long journey the day before from Scotland to Mexico. At the Passport and Customs desk, I faced a stern officer who chewed his gum like a cow masticates cud—in slow motion. "What is the purpose of your visit, Señorita Edwards?"

"Tourism," I replied, without blinking.

Under tanned eyelids, the man's beady eyes examined my fake British passport, then ogled my skin-baring, skimpy, almost indecent outfit: a short white mini skirt, matching sleeveless top, and stiletto sandals. I wore a large straw sunhat perched on top of my Farah Fawcett wig, one of many in my arsenal of disguises. I wore more makeup than a streetwalker, and had packed my luggage with piles of tourist brochures, colorful shorts, skimpy tops, several bikinis, and suntan oil, not that I needed it on my olive skin. Did I pass for a tourist? You bet.

With my passport tucked back into my bucket-shaped handbag, I headed for the exit. In the "Arrivals" area, I had to smile. Standing behind the guardrail was a chauffeur in an immaculately pressed uniform holding up a cardboard sign that read "Señor

L. Andrews." We both smiled as he led me to a black sedan with tinted windows. The engine was running and was parked in a "No Waiting" zone. A typical Hispanic man, wearing greased hair tied in a ponytail, was slouched in the back seat. "*Señorita* Edwards," a grinning Carlos Miguel Rodriguez announced to his employer.

"*Bienvenido*," Juan Dominquez greeted. "Welcome to Guatemala. I hope you had a good flight. Please, get in." Hesitantly, I slid into the car next to him. Extending my hand, I said in eloquent English, "I'm Lynette. We spoke on the phone."

"Juan Dominguez planted a sloppy, wet kiss on the palm of my hand as his penetrating brown eyes fastened onto my chest. His antics gave me an opportunity to check him out. I guessed him to be in his late forties.

"You're not what I expected, Señorita."

With a goofy grin, Lynette responded, "What were you expecting? A man?"

"Si."

"I know my voice is husky, but did I really sound like a man on the phone?"

"No. You are a very beautiful woman."

"Well, thank you, Señor Dominguez. And please, call me 'Lyn.'"

After the formal introduction and a little small talk, Dominguez came to the purpose of our meeting. "Did you bring the money, *Leeen*?"

"I tried hard not to snigger at the way he had pronounced my name. I tapped my luggage and said, "Of course! But before I hand over a penny, have you sorted out his release? Do you have his passport ready?"

"No. My contact is waiting for my call. And no, I don't have what you want, not on me. It's at my villa. Not far from here."

Uneasiness ran through my veins. Was this a setup? Was I about to be mugged?

"Señor, it was agreed over the phone that our business would be conducted in a public place, like this airport."

"*Leeen*," he said, 'I'm a government official. It is better we're not seen together. We can drive to my villa and do business in private.

Then Carlos can drive you back to the airport. Okay?"

Something on his body caught my eye. A tattoo was peeking out from under his crisp, cotton, short-sleeved shirt. I felt a shiver of fear. *Oh, shit!* Is really what I wanted to say, but instead I answered, "It looks like I don't have much choice. But let me tell you this: If I don't call my boss in a couple of hours, all hell will break loose. Do you understand?" His throaty laugh sounded like the rattle of an insane person.

"There is no need to be afraid. Nothing is going to happen to you. I am a man of my word." He patted my hand and added, "Please relax and enjoy the ride."

I wanted to throw up. Juan was not only a corrupt immigration official, he was also Mafia. The organization's symbol—an underscored marijuana leaf—was etched on his neck. *If something were to go wrong,* I thought, *nobody would find my body in this godforsaken third-world country.*

A few months earlier, back in London, I'd thought long and hard about accepting this particular assignment. Most of the "courier" jobs I'd taken in the past had been risky, but those dealing with Mexico and Central America were even more dangerous. Being relatively young and enjoying the "spoils" of my work—lots of money—I chose not to heed the warnings. While we traveled to his villa, I sat rigid on the back seat. I found it hard to concentrate on Juan's chitchat, especially his barrage of questions.

"Are you married?"

"No."

"Do you have a boyfriend?"

"No."

"How old are you?"

"Old enough!" I snapped.

"How long have you been doing this?"

"Too long."

"Why do you take such risks?"

"For the money, Señor Juan," was my final statement on the matter.

"I was relieved when Carlos announced we had arrived at

Juan's villa. The massive wrought-iron gates were hurriedly opened by a uniformed security man. Impressive rows of bougainvillea shaded the driveway leading up to his home. I was amused to see a salmon pink, adobe-styled house—an odd color, I thought, for a burly Mafia man.

Inside the villa a large wall-mounted mirror reflected an array of vibrant local artwork hanging on every available wall space. He ushered me into an adjacent room cluttered with modern furniture and tropical plants. The walls were painted the same shade of pink as the outside of the building.

I realized that only a woman could have chosen this decor. I hadn't noted a wedding ring, so I fished, "Your wife has excellent taste."

"Yes, she *did* have. But sadly, she died a year ago."

"Not wishing to pry further into his affairs, I uttered, "I'm sorry to hear that."

"Juan's sudden impulse took me by surprise. He flung his arms around me and gave me a bear hug. It seemed an eternity before he let go. "*Mi casa es tu casa, Leeen,*" he gushed. "Make yourself comfortable. I'll get Magdalena to make lunch. Do you like seafood?"

"I hadn't noticed a female presence when we entered, so I assumed he was referring to a housekeeper. "Juan, I love seafood. But I'm not hungry. I had a huge breakfast this morning. I would like something to drink, though."

"Would you like coffee, tea, or tequila?"

What I would have preferred was red wine, but "When in Rome …" I downed the tequila in one gulp. The tension headache I'd been suffering all morning vanished. I began to feel relaxed, not to mention a bit tipsy. I often humored friends by saying, "Two strong drinks and I'll be anybody's."

Sunk comfortably into the plush, pink-and-grey floral sofa, I took note of many intricately carved horse statues in various poses on pedestals. "I see that you love horses, Juan?"

"Yes. A passion I've had since I was a boy. I own several Aztecas, half Andalusians. Do you like horses?"

"I love them."

"That makes two of us," he smiled warmly. "I can show you my horses, if you like."

"I'd love to see them, Juan, but my time here is limited. I think we should get down to business."

"I dumped the contents of my luggage onto the tiled floor and then slit open the plastic coating under the material lining. I removed the money hidden beneath. "Twenty-thousand U.S. dollars, as agreed."

I watched as Juan thumbed through the crisp thousand-dollar bills.

"It's all there," I confirmed.

"You must love this man very much, *Leeen*."

"Good Lord, no! I've never met him. I told you on the phone that I'm only the go-between, a courier," I responded glibly. "When can Julio Sandoval be released?"

"About an hour after I make the call. My driver will take you to a safe place where you can meet."

"That's not a good idea. A return phone call from him will be enough."

"*Leeen*, I'm curious. If you've never met your coyote ..."

I interrupted. "He has a code, a password."

"And what code is that?"

"I'm not a *dumb blond*, Juan!"

"I apologize."

"Apology accepted. Now please make the phone call."

Unaware that I was fluent in Spanish, he spoke uninhibitedly during his phone conversation. When he returned to sit next to me on the couch, he said matter-of-factly, "It's done. My contact at the prison will have him ring here as soon as possible."

"Great. Can I have the passport?"

"I observed Juan remove a large painting and expose a wall safe. He handed over the blank Guatemalan passport. I'd hardly tucked it into the secret compartment of my luggage when the phone rang. I spoke to Julio—my coyote—who I had learned had been caught at the Mexico-U.S. border a couple of weeks ago.

He had been immediately deported back to Guatemala and had been languishing in jail until I was able to get him out.

His "client," an El Salvadorian teenager, had managed to escape. The boy's sister, a legal immigrant in the U.S.A, had coughed up five-thousand U.S. dollars to get her brother into the States. The money order had been cashed in England. One thousand was sent via Western Union to Julio. That "retainer" had disappeared—been "liberated" by an unscrupulous American border guard. Before embarking on the perilous journey, Julio had told the boy that if anything went wrong and they became separated, the young man was to use the two-hundred dollars hidden in his shoe, return to El Salvador, and await further instructions. During Julio's brief stay in the American detention camp, he was able to contact Guadalupe, the boy's sister, who was living in San Francisco. Julio gave her my London-based number.

The operation to reunite brother and sister had gone horribly wrong, even more so when I learned that Julio was no longer fit to do another "run" on behalf of the boy. He had suffered a severe beating from a deranged inmate while he was in jail, and the attack had left him with serious lacerations on his face and a fractured thigh bone. This awful turn of events had left my mind scrambling. I thought: *I'll have to do the job myself. No. That would be out of the question. If I were caught, a fractured thigh bone would be the least of my concerns.* The vision of what could happen to me made me shudder.

Another idea surfaced. Why don't I pay another coyote to smuggle the boy through the tunnel—a drug smugglers' passageway that snaked its way from Tijuana, Mexico, to San Diego.

I decided I couldn't risk involving an unknown person. I wondered if I could trust someone in the Guatemalan Mafia. I wasn't sure, but it seemed I had little choice. So now I looked at Juan closing the safe and said in his own language, "I need your help."

His mouth fell open. My fluent Spanish blew him away. He agreed to help me—for a price, of course. Was I willing to pay? Why not? I thought it wasn't *that* big a sacrifice. Long after his moaning ended, I lay naked in Juan's muscular arms.

"*Eeewww*," was Brianna's response. She didn't want to hear about her mother's sexual escapades. She wanted, instead, to get the identity of her father.

Brianna began gnawing her thumbnail.

Juan was sated. I had started off with a get-it-over attitude—count the mosaic tiles on the ceiling, and then get on with rescuing the poor boy waiting at the El Salvadorian border. To my surprise, though, I enjoyed myself. I had never been highly sexed, probably due to a psychological blockage caused by long-term trauma, and I'd assumed I would have to wear the effect of my abuse for the rest of my life. In situations like this, past ghastly sexual-abuse memories had always sent me screaming to the nearest bathroom to vomit. That's why my life with Peter was perfect. We had a wonderful platonic relationship, and I loved him dearly in a special way. Because he drank like a fish, though, he died of liver failure when you were three, Brianna. There are times when I can't think of Peter McTavish without feeling sad.

A contented Juan laid his head on my chest and devised a plan. He said he knew someone, a high-ranking government official in El Salvador, who owed him a favor. Juan would have him locate the boy and take him to a place where Carlos, Juan's driver, could pick him up and bring him to the villa. But it would be up to me to get the boy across the U.S. border.

I had promised myself never to mix business with pleasure, but I found myself warming up to Juan. He was not only a worthy lover and partner-in-crime, but he also turned out to be an excellent chef. I was ravenous. He served me a large, puffy omelette filled with every seafood delight you could imagine. Then he topped the whole thing with fresh garden herbs and hot rum. It was delicious. After the meal, we took a shower together, taking turns washing each other's backs. Then the romantic interlude came to an abrupt end.

"*Leeen*, I'm a devout Catholic. I'm going to evening Mass. My darling, would you like to join me?" I could have swallowed the soap!

"Hell, no," I said. "I haven't set foot inside a church since I was a kid, and I don't intend to change that for anyone."

"Ah, come on," he pleaded. "The church is over a hundred years old. You will be very impressed."

"No. The Catholic faith and I don't see eye to eye."

"Why?"

"It's a long story, Juan. I don't want to get into it."

"I promised my wife I would go to church every Sunday."

"That's nice!" The church conversation squashed any intimacy we were feeling. I got out of the shower wondering how this tough Mafiosi could be such a softie at heart.

"I won't be long, *Leeen*," he informed me. "In the meantime, if you like, you can take a swim. No one will disturb you."

That made no sense to me. What was the point of taking a swim in chlorinated water right after I got out of the shower? But what else was I to do while he was in church? An earlier rainstorm had passed, leaving glorious sunshine outside. Wearing a red-and-white polka-dot bikini, I followed Juan, who was dapperly dressed in a black suit and tie, to the piano-shaped pool. I couldn't believe how blazing hot the sun was at five o'clock in the afternoon.

Sitting with my legs dangling in the warm water of the beautifully tiled pool, I counted myself lucky. I had come a long way from my humble beginnings in Africa. I could now afford anything I desired. Apart from the Scottish house I shared with Peter, I owned a cozy two-bedroom, sixth-floor apartment overlooking the River Thames—which was later sold. I drove a Rolls Royce, had a wardrobe full of fine clothes, and ate at the best restaurants. Mostly, I loved the English races and hobnobbing with the rich and famous in the horse business. Once, without thinking, I introduced myself as "Hallworthy." The horse trainer smiled. "Are you related to the famous Hallworthy family of South Africa, by any chance?"

"Yes." It wasn't a lie, but I let those who asked believe that I had inherited a vast sum of money from the Hallworthy estate. Nothing was further from the truth. As a child I had mustered a strategy born out of the need to survive—*willpower*, an inner strength that flowed from an ocean of sorrow. But thanks to my

Mensa brain—not bragging, just a fact—I found a way to escape that dark place that trapped my body and soul.

I not only survived, I fought back. I refused to be a victim. I was going to be a winner. I kept self-pity at bay by helping people who were desperate and unable to provide for their families in their countries of birth—victims who were unable to get past the red tape of immigration bureaucrats. I helped them migrate to another country and earn a decent living. The El Salvadorian boy was one of those people. He had been working slave hours in peanut fields, earning, literally, "peanuts." Because he was unable to support his elderly parents and younger siblings, the teenager turned to his American sister for help. It took her over a year to raise the money to smuggle him.

There was no way I could abandon this boy.

Three days later, the boy, nearly nineteen, finally arrived at the villa. I stared in amazement at him. I'd seen many exceptionally good-looking Latinos, but this boy was more than handsome—he was drop-dead gorgeous. His ebony eyes glistened like the black pearls I wore around my neck. His long, curly hair, as thick as a horse's mane, hung loosely on his broad shoulders. With a flutter of his long eyelashes, he greeted me, "*Hola*."

"*Hola*, Leonel (Lionel) Martinez. I am Lynette. You'll soon be with your sister. I promise you."

Brianna gasped so loudly she nearly choked on her saliva. *Her stepfather!* Yet another falsehood! Her mother had told her that she had met Lionel on a trip to the United Kingdom. Brianna twisted a strand of her hair in anxious expectation as her mother's voice droned on.

Lionel's warm hug had been very gratifying. But it was his look of gentle sadness that threatened to make me cry. The time had come to say goodbye to my host. "Be careful, *Cariño*," Juan warned. "And may God go with you and the boy."

"Thanks for everything, Juan. I don't know what I would have done without your help."

He grinned mischievously. "You can repay me by coming back to visit."

"One day, Juan."

"Call me when you're safely across."

Although our relationship had been brief, I was going to miss Juan, but I knew I was never going to return to Guatemala—ever. Sunshine turned to dusk as I drove the rented, top-of-the-line Mercedes through the American checkpoint without incident. A couple of miles clear, I let Lionel out of the trunk and gave him a Pepsi. We celebrated like excited children—played tag, pinched each other, and danced on the road's hard shoulder.

"*Gracias*, my special *gringa* coyote," he said, flinging his arms around me.

"You are most welcome, my special Latino. Now, let's find a phone booth, call your sister, and tell her that we will be arriving by plane as soon as I can book a flight."

What he did next nearly knocked me off my feet. He kissed me full on the mouth and said, "I love you, *gringa*."

I turned scarlet.

He held my hand tightly all the way to San Francisco. I hate to think what the first-class flight attendant thought. Thankfully, I still looked too young to pass as his mother. I felt a moment of self-disgust. *What are you thinking?* I asked myself. *He's only a boy!* But this boy was more mature than any other man I'd ever known. We had a connection, intense chemistry, as though our meeting was meant to be, as though we were soul mates. Brianna, I'm talking about your *biological* Pappy, the man I eventually married.

Brianna nearly fell off the couch. She hugged herself and shouted, "No, no, no!" It can't be true! There was no way he was her natural father. She clasped a hand over her mouth, her mind shrilling: *Oh, this is not happening!* With a shaky index finger, she turned up the volume. Her mother's voice was sincere.

I'm sure you are reeling with shock. Yes, the man you hated for a while *is* your biological father. I wanted so many times to tell him and you, but I couldn't. You see, I didn't think our marriage would last, and if I had been right, *both* of us would have been heartbroken. Oh, I can imagine what's going through your head. "What about Juan? You slept with him, Mother!" But I made Juan wear a condom, and, I can assure you, it didn't break.

Your father died. I wasn't supposed to outlive him. At one point I even considered joining my soul mate via an overdose. But I could not do that. I had *you* to think of. Well, now you're all grown up and will soon be a successful lawyer, and I'll be joining the only man I've ever loved—from day one. But before I end this recording, there is one more confession I have to make ..."

Click. The tape ran out. This time Brianna didn't rush to insert the next one. Instead, she buried her head in the sofa's scatter cushions and wept uncontrollably. Some moments later, her chest heaving, she snatched a handful of tissues and wiped her nose and eyes. If only she had known, she would have treated Lionel better. A new flood of tears rolled down her cheeks. *I can't even go and tell my father that I'm sorry and that I love him because my friggin' mother took his ashes to El Salvador. God knows where my poor father's remains are scattered. Maybe Mike, mom's lawyer, will know.* Rage dammed Brianna's tears. The thought of her beloved mother keeping this secret was intolerable. Brianna could not stop the words spewing from her mouth: "*Mommie Dearest*! You are already dead to me!" Her attention was drawn to an ornate humidor sitting on the coffee table.

As ghostly fingers of cigar smoke swirled above her head, Brianna wanted to run from her mother's home and never look back, but she couldn't. As a non-smoker, she coughed, stubbed out the Cuban cigar, and, with a look that could kill, inserted the last tape. Her mother's voice sounded coldly indifferent.

It happened less than a year after I gave birth to you. Peter told me there was a black woman at the door who wanted to speak to me. I was surprised because there weren't too many blacks around the Isle of Skye. I led her into my office and closed the door. The woman rubbed her hands nervously. "My name is Marina," she said in an accent I immediately recognized. Her South African lilt was undeniable. "Gerda Düsseldorf gave me your address."

"I don't know anyone by that name," I replied evasively.

"Madam, Immigration is looking for my daughter and me. If they find us, we will be deported back to South Africa. My daughter and I hate the place like poison."

I asked her to explain.

Marina told me that they'd been hiding in Manchester with a friend, who just happened to be my old German pal, Gerda. Of course, I had great sympathy for the poor woman's plight, but I had to make sure she wasn't a "plant." Undercover immigration spies were as good at their jobs as I was at mine. Obviously, I grilled her. The personal details she relayed about Gerda could only have come from the source. I wanted to call Gerda, but thought better of it. Having determined Marina wasn't a plant, I loosened up and we talked about our similar lives in South Africa.

Her daughter in Manchester was the result of a brutal rape by three white police officers. I agreed to help the two women without further questioning. This time I didn't want money for my services. I had unfinished business of my own in that country. With Marina's help, there was a chance I could at last bury the nightmares of my youth.

Three weeks passed.

My Irish forger did a fantastic job on our new British passports. Marina and I were all set to return to South Africa. She wasn't happy about returning, but she knew she must. I wasn't going to help her if she didn't return the favor. So I hired a qualified nurse to take care of you at her home while I was gone, and I gave some excuse to Peter for my absence and yours. He didn't seem to mind that I was rarely home in those days. Perhaps he was even relieved. I suspect his new boyfriend was jealous of the woman who seemed to take precedence over him. A rather uncomfortable triangle had been developing.

On the long flight to Durban I told Marina about my life in the African bush and what Alan had done to Anele and me. She wasn't surprised. She had witnessed many South African horrors firsthand. But she was shocked when I explained how I was planning to avenge the wrongdoings. I thought she was going to back out, but, thank goodness, she didn't.

With a vendetta-driven heart I asked Marina to find a young black prostitute who was HIV positive. I didn't specify age, so I wasn't shocked when I learned Naomi was just shy of her thirteenth birthday. In most Third World countries, poverty is the diabolical crime, not prostitution. The promise of food, shelter, and costly antiviral medicine induced the girl to participate in my plan. Brianna, what I'm about to tell you is worse than a horror movie, so if you don't wish to hear this next bit, fast-forward the tape.

Part of Brianna wanted to hurl the tape in the trash bin, but what could be worse than what she had already heard?

Naomi was clad in a provocative dress I had bought her: a flashy red mini laced up the back. As instructed by me, she traveled by taxi to the Hallworthy manor and asked to speak to Alan, who still resided there. She told him she desperately needed work and would do anything. Of course the pervert couldn't take his lecherous eyes off the scantily dressed teenage prostitute. Alan lunged at her with the urgency of a wild beast in mating frenzy.

My plan was for a paid helper to take photos of Alan having intercourse with the young black girl, to catch the bastard in the act. My objective was to anonymously blacken Alan's name. He was an electoral candidate for Deputy President of South Africa, and all candidates had to follow certain legislative rules. Screwing a black prostitute was a cultural no-no; the act was my ticket to ensure the Devil never became a ruler in any form.

I intended to mail the lurid photographs to a black-owned

newspaper that would, undoubtedly, have a field day with the juicy scandal. But my planned revenge backfired horribly and shot my soul to hell. The explicit prints showed an asphyxiated Naomi lying naked in the hay, her neck compressed by ligature marks. She had been strangled with the clothing I had bought her.

Brianna lost it. She flung the recorder across the room, glaring at it as if it had come from the underworld. She screamed every swear word known to mankind. Then, with red eyes and a face as pale as parchment, she retrieved the recorder and continued listening, even though she didn't want to.

At Heathrow Airport I mailed the incriminating evidence tape to the District Attorney's office in South Africa and waited in Scotland for news. Subsequently, I heard from Marina, whose cousin had sent her an article from a prominent South African newspaper. At Naomi's murder trial, Alan Hallworthy had pleaded insanity. He was sentenced to a mental facility for the criminally insane for the rest of his natural life, which was prolonged thanks to the antiviral medication he received for full-blown AIDS. The bastard got what he deserved, and I got my revenge, but I'll never forget the price another soul had to pay for my vengeance.

I know it doesn't appease what I did, but I had Naomi's body, with the consent of her family, reburied on the Sacred Burial Hill near the Tswanas village. I plan to visit her there. At my request Marina periodically returns to South Africa to take money to Naomi's family, most of whom are infected with the virus. I pay for doctor visits and medicine. In fact, shipments of drugs are heading to South Africa as I speak.

I know my millions won't bring back Naomi, but while I still have breath in my body, I'm going to spend every penny I can to make things right. Some people consider me guilty. Others believe I am a hero. I'm not trying to justify my misconduct, Brianna. I am only trying to say that I have a good heart and that I tried to do good things. When I was trying to help people who were desperate and had no other recourse, my intentions were always free of guile and innocent of malice. I was a victim of brutal crimes, but I had no support or guidance. I was on my own.

I'm going home to die. It will be of my own free will. But before I do that, I'm going to try to make a difference in the lives of my African people. Yes, Brianna, *my* people! In my heart, I've always belonged to them. Don't hate me, my darling daughter. Please, love me for who I am.

On hearing her mother's final words, Brianna's eyes stared vacantly at the ceiling. After what seemed an eternity, she got up off the couch, went over to the fireplace, and stacked it with kindling. Then she struck a long barbeque match and lit the wood shavings. Soon the stench of burning cassette tapes filled the room.

She returned to the bedroom and placed the money and jewelry into the briefcase. She slid the damper on the fire to low, locked the front door, and climbed into her car. All she could think of now was Roberto. Before she started to drive, she made a call to him. "Roberto, it's me."

"Are you okay? You sound upset."

"Upset isn't the word for it. I'm on my way home."

"How's your Mom?"

"I don't want to talk about her!"

"Drive safely, Sweet Pea. Can't wait to see you and give you a big sloppy kiss."

Brianna "escaped" from Lynette's driveway.

## CHAPTER ELEVEN

# That Same Month, February 1998, Durban, South Africa

*"Be silent or let thy words be worth more
than silence."*
–Pythagoras

The Indian Ocean sparkled like sapphire gems as the British Airways airbus descended from clear, blue, sunny skies and made a smooth landing at Durban International Airport. The pilot informed the passengers it was five o'clock local time on this fine February evening. Shiya, now going by her African name, adjusted her wristwatch and prepared to disembark from first-class.

Wearing a pair of white capri pants, a pale-blue tie-back top, and open-toed sandals, she made her way to Customs.

"What is the purpose of your visit?" the officer asked.

"I'm here on a little business and lots of pleasure," she responded with half a smile.

He stamped her "authentic" British passport and waved her through.

In the "Arrivals Lounge" stood an elderly black man, the hardship of life written across his leathery forehead. He ambled toward her. "Are you Mrs. Lynette Martinez?"

"Yes, I am."

"Welcome to South Africa. My name is Kelingo, Mr. Durval's driver. He asked me to tell you that he is sorry he is not able to meet you, but he will see you later at the hotel. Follow me, please. I'll drive you to the Hotel Edward."

"How far is it from here?"

"Thirty-five miles, but I'll have you there in no time."

As Kelingo loaded her luggage into the trunk of the black, four-door Audi, Shiya sneaked a sideways peek at him. His back was bent. His face was as wrinkled and brown as a walnut. "Milk-bottle" glasses rested on the end of his stubby, broad nose.

He looks as old as the hills. He shouldn't be driving at his age.

A pain in her head caused her to cry out, "Oh, not now!"

"Are you all right, Mrs. Martinez?"

"Yes, I'm fine," she lied. The sudden onset of a blinding migraine distracted her thoughts about Kelingo's motoring skills, but not her distress. Severe headaches, double vision, dizziness, and trouble concentrating were, to name a few, symptoms of brain cancer. Despite her declining health, she coped. She was determined to see her objective through.

Shiya dry-swallowed two prescription capsules, something she had become quite good at, but she would have preferred to lie down, bury her head under a pillow, and sleep until the blasted headache subsided.

When the medication kicked in, she was more able to focus and, much to her surprise, Kelingo, aged eighty-seven, turned out to be a good driver. He handled the car well as he drove along the scenic route, Durban's Golden Mile, where the hotel was located.

As Shiya peered out of the car window at an Indian Ocean flanked by subtropical beaches of pristine, golden sand, she sighed. This breathtaking country held too much sorrow for her to appreciate its natural beauty. She both hated and loved this land that was her birthplace.

Kelingo adjusted his rearview mirror so he could make eye

contact. "I hope you don't mind me asking, but is this your first visit to South Africa, Mrs. Martinez?"

"No, Kelingo. I know this country pretty well."

Kelingo's eyes searched hers for an explanation, and she quickly diverted him from his curiosity. "How long have you worked for Mr. Durval?"

"Nearly fifteen years, Mrs. Martinez."

She had to ask. "I hope you won't be offended, but aren't you just a wee bit too old to still be working and driving a car?"

A broad smile crossed the old man's lips. "There's still a lot of life left in my old bones. There is no welfare state here, Mrs. Martinez, so I have to work. I'm a grandfather of twenty grandchildren who always need extra money for this and that."

Shiya felt a twinge of admiration for this man who should have retired long ago. "You said you worked fifteen years for him. What did you do before that?"

"As a child, I was a ..." he took a deep breath. The word "slave'" came to mind, but Kelingo thought better of saying it. After all, she was a *white* woman! "... from the age of six and on I worked cutting sugar cane. Then I got a job in a sugar refinery packing raw sugar into sacks. While I was at this factory, I met my present boss. He is the legal advisor to Lady Corrie Hallworthy, who owns the refinery."

Shiya felt her heart momentarily stop. She sucked in her breath noisily.

Kelingo's eyes met hers. "Do you know the Hallworthy family?" he asked cagily.

She turned away from his intense stare. "Not really," she replied convincingly. But her heart and thoughts raced like an Olympic sprinter, forcing her to take rhythmic breaths. *Yes, yes, yes! A young man named Kelingo had rescued Anele from the jaws of death, Maekela had told me.*

Was this old driver Anele's savior?

The coincidence was too much to ignore. She said, "Many years ago a young fieldworker saved the life of a little bush girl named Anele Dingane …"

She was nearly flung from her seat as the Audi came to a screeching halt on the shoulder. Kelingo looked as if he had seen a ghost. His skin drained of color, and his dark facial features turned a pale green. "How do you know of this?" he asked in a shaky voice.

"Are you the one who saved her?"

"Yes."

Shiya could have done handsprings.

Hurriedly, she got out of the car and seated herself opposite Kelingo. They talked for what seemed to be hours. Neither one believed this was a coincidence. Whoever or whatever pulled these cosmic strings offered another shocker.

"Anele Dingane *is* alive, Mrs. Martinez."

"You must be kidding! This is too much! Do you know where she is?"

"Yes. She's back home in Tswanas."

Shiya was blown away. Skeptically, she asked, "How do you know that?"

"I saw her there."

"Please explain?"

"Some years back I returned home to Mtunzini, which is not far from Anele's home, to visit my younger sisters, only to find that they had moved from our village to Tswanas kraal. You can imagine my surprise when I found Anele there. Of course, she was no longer the little girl I had marched off to the manor house. Also, it was no secret that she had been jailed at Montclair prison. I can't remember the whole story, but it had something to do with her stealing money and a white child." Kelingo paused long enough to look at Shiya and wonder, "You wouldn't be that child, would you?"

"Yes, Kelingo," she said softly, "I'm *that* child."

With clasped hands he said, "Great Spirit of the black people, please protect my aging heart from failure. I was told that Anele's *Shiya* was dead."

"Well, you were misinformed. As you can see, dear Kelingo, I'm very much alive and kicking. I'd love to continue this conversation, but please get me to the hotel. I have to phone my daughter. After that we can work out a plan to go home to Tswanas. Perhaps you can come by the hotel in the morning?"

Kelingo nodded.

The car came to a smooth halt outside the Hotel Edward. Kelingo's clasp of her hand was warm and tender. Shiya gave him a hug and then pressed a couple of hundred-dollar bills into his hand. She thanked him and said, "*Ngiyabonga*, Kelingo. You're a hero in my eyes."

"This is too much," he said, staring at the folded notes.

"Not too much for a loving grandfather. Buy your grandchildren something nice from me. And if you have any trouble exchanging the American currency, let me know. I can exchange them at the hotel."

"I don't know what to say …"

He was cut short by the arrival of the bellhop. With his metal name tag glinting in the sunlight, the black boy stood ready to pounce on her luggage. "Welcome to the Hotel Edward," the young man beamed.

While the bellhop placed her luggage on a cart, Shiya touched Kelingo's sleeve. "Goodbye, for now. And thank you for everything."

"It's been my pleasure, Shiya of Tswanas," he replied in Zulu.

Shiya's smile was as wide as the Nile.

She watched the Audi drive away and then followed the bellhop past the miniature palms that had been planted in enormous clay pots. She walked by Greek pillars and art deco facades as she passed through wood-and-glass-paneled doors into the cool air-conditioned foyer. She headed for the reception desk and said, "My name is Mrs. Lynette Martinez. I believe I have a suite reservation made by a Mr. Bryan Durval?"

"Good evening, Mrs. Martinez. Welcome to Durban and the Hotel Edward," the white desk manager greeted her. "Mr. Durval insisted that we provide you with our premier accommodation. We hope you will enjoy the presidential suite. It is on the seventh floor facing the sea. It has magnificent views of the Indian Ocean."

The suite was up to five-star standards. The four air-conditioned rooms were decorated in pastel colors and boasted dark wood furniture and rich floral fabric. The master bedroom contained a king bed adorned with the best of linens. Italian crystal bedside lamps were set on carved tables, and a huge, flat-screen TV dominated one wall. The bathroom design included an enormous whirlpool tub, a separate shower cubicle, and vanity mirrors running the length of one wall.

The hotel had gifted her with a bouquet of flowers, an enormous fruit basket, and a bottle of champagne. Against a wall sat a walnut bar cabinet filled with miniature alcoholic drinks, bottled water, and fruit juices. Shiya was more than satisfied with Bryan's hotel selection.

The bellhop, clutching his generous tip, closed the door behind him.

Shiya hardly had time to remove her footwear before the phone rang. "Hello, this is Shi- ... I mean, Lynette Martinez speaking."

"Good evening, Mrs. Martinez. Bryan Durval here. I'm sorry I couldn't pick you up at the airport. I got caught up in business."

"Don't worry about it. I got here just fine, thank you," Shiya said.

"Would it be too inconvenient if I popped over in, say, an hour and a half?"

"Sure," Shiya replied. "I'm looking forward to meeting you."

"Likewise," Bryan ended.

Shiya browsed through the Brasserie Restaurant's à la carte menu. The seafood section caught her eye. She lifted the telephone. "Hello. This is Mrs. Martinez in the presidential suite. I would like to order the *Agnolotti Cinesi* (fresh pasta squares stuffed with oysters, shallots, and ginger) and a bottle of your finest red wine. Please send them up to my suite."

Shiya hardly touched the food, but she did manage to drink two full glasses of wine. She walked into the bathroom to refresh her makeup, brush her long hair, and change into a lace-accented floral skirt and halter top. Italian leather sling-back sandals complemented her outfit.

While her heart played hopscotch, Shiya waited for her guest to arrive.

The lawyer was not what Shiya had expected.

Bryan Durval, age forty, was a physically imposing figure, standing well over six feet tall. His chiseled features were softened by sun-bleached hair and gentle aqua-green eyes. He was casually dressed in a khaki shirt, shorts, and brown leather sandals. Bryan's father, whom Shiya and Peter McTavish had met at St. Andrews Golf Club in Scotland, was extremely short, almost dwarf like. But his son was strikingly tall and handsome. Shiya was older now, but she was not dead! She felt his strong sexual magnetism pulling her toward him. But her internal voice chastised her. *Hussy! Lionel is hardly cold. You are here on business, not to get romantically involved! And quit drinking alcohol! You know how you get after you drink!*

Bryan shook her hand firmly, smiled, and said, "Pleased to meet you, Mrs. Martinez."

"Likewise, but let's dispense with the formalities. Call me Lynette, but not Lyn. I dislike abbreviations. May I offer you a glass of red wine, or would you prefer a cold beer?"

"No wine or beer for me, thank you. But I won't say no to a glass of water."

She handed him a bottle of Perrier and a glass tinkling with ice cubes.

"Bryan, how long have you been in practice?"

"Fifteen years."

"Does your father still work?"

"No. He's retired. I informed you of this when we spoke on the phone."

"You did! Darn, my memory is getting rusty! Then I'm bloody well stuck with you."

Bryan smiled and in a professional voice asked, "How may I be of assistance?"

He's a smooth one, Shiya thought as she reached for her handbag and removed a notebook. "I have itemized my instructions. But before we get down to business, I hope that I don't have to remind you of attorney-client privilege."

A frown crossed his handsome features. "Of course not," he said.

"Good. So I can tell you now that I was born here in South Africa. I left the country when I was a teenager."

"Really!" he responded. "You have a strong British accent. I thought you were English when we spoke on the phone."

Shiya didn't feel the need to explain or to tell him that English was her second language. "Before I discuss the list I've given you, I want you to know what prompted it—a wake-up call, so to speak. I have a tumor on the left side of my brain and have chosen not to undergo surgery. While I'm of sound mind, I have things to do, and quickly. There will come a time when I won't know my arse from my elbow, and that's where you come in."

Bryan tried not to show his surprise. Her coarseness didn't befit the articulate and classy-looking woman facing him. She also was very attractive. Before his good manners could stop him, he lavished her with a compliment. "I hope you don't mind me saying this, but you are darn good-looking for your age."

Shiya felt her face growing hot. "Well, thank you. But adding 'your age' doesn't make a woman feel youthful!"

Bryan, encouraged by her informality, leaned forward and asked roguishly, "Well, how old *are* you?"

"I'm fifty-three going on twelve."

Bryan chortled and then channeled his thoughts back on track. "Now, how can I help you?"

Shiya reopened her notebook. "I'd like to address the first item on my list: Lord Alan Percival Hallworthy."

Bryan's manicured brows knitted.

She noted his frown and smiled. "Yes, I do mean Alan Hallworthy, the plantation owner and former mayor."

"I'm afraid that would be a conflict of interest," Bryan stated. "I handle the affairs of Corrie Hallworthy, his wife. And you should be aware of this fact. If my memory serves me, you stated on the phone that you were an immigration attorney."

"Oh, don't preach the law to me. Do you want to know why I deliberately picked your family practice for my needs?"

His blond lashes flickered.

"I don't know much about you," Shiya said honestly, "but I know your father is as crooked as a pretzel."

Visibly shocked, Bryan glared at her.

Shiya, holding his angry gaze, said icily, "Don't look so surprised. Don't tell me you didn't know all about the theft—how your father amassed a fortune, how he owns homes here and in the Caribbean, and pays for a Learjet and an expensive yacht. All of those things aren't coming from a lawyer's salary. Your father made his fortune by cooking the Hallworthy books. He made a tidy sum swindling money from the refinery ..."

"Bullshit!" Bryan erupted. "I'm not going to sit here and listen to this!" He snatched his briefcase and marched toward the door. "I'm out of here, you crazy woman," he uttered without turning his back.

"I think you'd better sit back down, Bryan. I have to show you something."

With a curious scowl he turned around and faced her.

Shiya retrieved several folded ledger sheets from the back of her notebook, walked over to Bryan, and handed them over. In the back of her mind she was thinking: *It's like sending a thief to catch a thief! Come to think of it, wasn't there a movie with the same name? Was it the one with Cary Grant and Grace Kelly? Well, if it's good enough for Hollywood, the same plot will work for me.*

Bryan's golden tan faded. "How did you get these?"

"How I got them is irrelevant. What is relevant is your pledge to work for me now."

"If I do just that, how do I know that the information you have on my father is not going to go any further than this room?"

"You don't! But I will tell you this: once you have carried out my wishes, I will hand over the entire ledger."

Shiya knew she couldn't have held the two lawyers to ransom were it not for Maekela.

Years ago Shiya had contacted the Hallworthy servant. She not only had stolen the ledger for Shiya, but had also managed to get Corrie's handwritten personal journals, which Shiya brought with her on this trip.

With his shoulders rounded in defeat, Bryan said, "Okay. What is it you want me to do?"

"Let's sit down."

Shiya took a deep breath before saying, "First, I have to tell you that Alan is my biological father."

Bryan's expression was skeptical. "I don't recall seeing any Hallworthy children listed in *Who's Who*."

Shiya laughed. "You're not likely to find *me* in any book. I'm not even going to bother to have a DNA test done. I *know* who my father is! Would you like to hear the shocking truth?"

Now beyond surprise, Bryan bobbed his head.

Shiya, omitting only the most graphic sexual details, went back in time.

Bryan's face was so florid, he looked as if he were about to suffer a coronary.

"Are you okay, Bryan? Do you want something to drink?"

"I think I'll have that glass of wine now, a big one."

He downed the red wine as if it were soda pop and then leaned forward. As his eyes met and held hers, he disclosed information: "I followed Alan's trial closely. He only became mayor of Durban by paying off people over many years. And his powerful predecessors—grandfather Lord Nigel and father Lord Peter—were no better. They were all brutal slave owners who got away with murder. There isn't a 'free' black person in Durban who doesn't know about the diabolical history of the Hallworthy Manor, or hasn't had some encounter with the insane Alan. I'm sure all of the indentured servants he had kept locked away on his estate are now breathing a sigh of relief knowing he is the one who is locked up. He strangled that girl as if she were an unwanted kitten, without remorse. How many other times has he gotten away with murder? I shudder to think."

Shiya sighed deeply before responding. She couldn't get Naomi's pretty face out of her mind. Fighting back tears, she confessed, "You see, Bryan, *I'm* responsible for Alan taking Naomi's life. If I hadn't been so bitter and twisted, she'd be alive today. Or maybe not. You see, she was HIV positive when I hired her to go to the Hallworthy refinery and infect Alan. I wish I could take it all back, but I can't. The deed is done. But more than anything, I curse the new drug Kaletra, which I believe is an antiviral vaccine that's keeping my father alive."

Tears stung Shiya's eyes. "When I learned of my brain tumor, I asked myself, *What is my life worth*? Nothing compared to the deliberate taking of another's life. What I did was wrong. I'm no better than that bastard who sits rotting away in the mental hospital. He should have died years ago, but his symptoms didn't present until many years later. The Devil looks after his own. So many victims have succumbed to AIDS, but not him. I hate him like poison, but my moral compass has to be set back on track. I have to undo the wrong I've done or I'll never see the gardens of eternity. I'm not a religious person, but I do believe in hell. You may not agree with me, but it is my wish that you enter my signed admission of guilt into court."

Bryan shook his head in disbelief. His day had been perfect, until now. He was used to dealing with a mixed bag of criminals, including the insane, but this woman beat the lot. Such a classy person, he would never have believed it of her. A part of him wanted to release her control over him, and yet, he was filled with genuine sympathy. He looked at the woman who had bared her soul, knowing that Alan Hallworthy was behind bars because of his own sick actions, not hers. "Why on earth would you wish to spend the rest of your life in prison?"

"I owe it to Naomi. But I need some time before you put the wheels in motion."

Two hours passed.

Wrapped in a lover's embrace, they told each other secrets they would not have told a priest. Then Bryan's lips found hers … and time stood still.

Later, as daylight sneaked through the bedroom curtains, Shiya removed Bryan's arm from around her waist and gently nudged him. He opened his eyes, pulled her close, and murmured, "I wish we had met under different circumstances."

"You mean you don't *hate* me?"

"Of course not, sweetheart. You did what you had to do. And, by God, it worked. But on a serious note," he winked, "as your lawyer, I advise you to drop it. Alan's deviant behavior far exceeds anyone's capacity to forgive."

Shiya nodded in agreement. "You're right. Nothing will bring back Naomi."

Bryan, dressed and ready to leave for work, handed Shiya his business card. "I've written my private number on the back. I'm not in court today, so I can be here in minutes. I'll see you later, either way. We can sit down and arrange for you to go to Tswanas and see Anele."

"I feel like such a witch for treating you the way I did."

"Don't worry your pretty head over it. It's forgotten."

Shiya was left alone with a cautionary thought: *You didn't come here to have an affair. And what's with this cradle snatching?*

Shiya took a shower. Wrapped in a towel, she ordered breakfast. Lovemaking had made her ravenous. While waiting for her meal, she picked up a magazine and flipped through the pages. Her eyes came to rest on the glossy photograph of an Italian beauty advertising a "Never Fail Makeup" product. The model's seductive smile triggered a thought: *Brianna.* She grabbed the bedside phone and dialed out. A man's sleepy voice answered at the other end, and Shiya heard him say, "Bri, there's a woman on the phone who sounds like the Queen."

Brianna snapped awake and snatched the phone from Roberto's hand.

"Mom, where are you?"

"I'm in ..."

Brianna cut her off. "How could you just leave like that? I listened to your tapes, and I'm very angry. You could have told me yourself. To find out all this stuff this way is beyond words."

Shiya lowered her head. What reaction did she expect?

Brianna wasn't going to let her mother speak. She had something urgent to say. "Mom, come home, *please*. I'm devastated by all this. We need to talk."

"I can't."

"Yes, you can!"

"I thought I made it clear why I needed to come back to South Africa."

"You're in *South Africa!* Give me the number so I can at least call you regularly to see if you are okay."

"I'm staying at a hotel, but not for long."

Brianna, angry and worried to the point of despair, shouted into the receiver, "For crying out loud, Mom. I thought I'd always have stability, a safe place with you in my life, but I guess I never saw how selfish you are."

Shiya sighed. She could only imagine how her daughter felt. Her daughter's tirade hit her hard. Coolly, Shiya said, "Brianna I'm suffering enough by not having *you* in my life. And your attitude isn't helping matters. Stand on your own two feet now, and don't look back ..."

The line went dead.

There was nothing Shiya could do but end the conversation. It was getting out of hand. It was too late now to turn back the clock. But it was not too late for what she still had to do. She had waited the better part of her life to carry out her plan.

Shiya dressed quickly. Her ankle-length black skirt, cream blouse with shoulder buttons, and black flats made her look matronly. That's how she wanted to appear for her clandestine assignment.

She ordered a taxi and waited outside for it to arrive.

The East Indian cab driver opened the back door of his taxi, returned to the driver's seat, and asked, "Where to, lady?"

"I would like you to take me to Pinetown Mental Hospital."

"It's quite a ways from here and will be expensive."

"I don't care. Just take me there, *please*. This is a wait-and-return, so you'll make good money."

After an hour and a half's drive in total silence, the cab driver pulled up in front of a four-story, grey-stone building with barred windows. On the lawn were a number of disabled patients. Some sat in wheelchairs, and others, accompanied by nurses in red capes, strolled in the gardens. At the admittance desk Shiya wrinkled her nose at the overbearing smell of disinfectant. The air was almost unbreatheable. This was the last time, she hoped, she would ever have to walk into a medical facility of any sort.

The black attendant, with bifocals perched on her nose, looked up. "Can I help you?"

Shiya felt her heart pounding out of her chest as she replied. "A close friend asked me to check on her uncle, who is a patient here. I'd like to see him and pass on her message."

"What is the name of your friend's uncle?"

"Alan Percival Hallworthy," a pokerfaced Shiya said.

A deep frown creased the attendant's smooth brow. The nurse peered over the top of her glasses and stated, "Mr. Hallworthy, to my knowledge, doesn't have any relatives abroad. I don't know if your friend is aware of this, but he is in solitary confinement under court order, and the only visitor he is allowed is his wife. She visits him every day at three. I can telephone Mrs. Hallworthy and tell her that you are here."

An icy shiver raced down Shiya's spine, and then her nerves gave way. "I can't do this," she muttered as she walked briskly away from the desk heading for the exit doors.

The attendant rounded her desk and chased after her. Grabbing Shiya's arm, she said, "You seem dreadfully upset. Am I right in assuming that you gave me a tall story? You know Mr. Hallworthy personally, am I right?"

Shiya blurted, "Yes, I *do* know him. He is my father."

The nurse stared in disbelief. "That's hard for me to swallow, but I have to wonder why else you would make up such a pathetic story? Okay, come with me before the lunch staff come on duty. I'll let you see him—unofficially, of course."

They came to a door marked "144-A." A key from the nurse's waistband opened the steel door. There, sitting on a cot, eyes cast on the floor, was a wizened old man wearing a urine-stained, pale-blue hospital gown. Saliva dribbled down his chin. He didn't look up. Once more, Shiya's nerves gave way. She wanted to flee from the pathetic character who was her sadistic abuser.

Shiya nearly jumped out her skin when the nurse touched her arm. "Remember, you only have a few minutes, or I'll be in hot water! And listen to me, absolutely no bodily contact. He's HIV positive." To the inmate she shouted, "Hey Alan, you have a visitor." When he didn't look up, the nurse explained, "He's as deaf as a doornail, the old fart! You'll have to shout if you want him to hear you."

Shiya's hatred was locked in her heart, just barely contained beneath the surface of consciousness, yet pity was threatening to intrude upon her enduring rage. Shiya wondered how she ever could have contemplated forgiveness. It was beyond all human reasoning. She was conflicted.

Alan's gaze remained focused on the floor.

Every bone in Shiya's body cringed when the cell door closed behind her, leaving her alone with the madman. She wanted to scream "Let me out!" but reason rose to the surface. *What the heck! I've nothing to lose.*

She bent at her waist so she came face to face with Alan. Then she verbally went for his jugular. "You sick son of a bitch! You should have died years ago. But then, the Devil really *does* look after his own, doesn't he, you decaying bastard? Look at me, you evil shit!"

Slowly, Alan lifted his head.

"Do you know who I am?" she bristled. "You should. I'm your daughter ... you know, the one you raped when I was a little child. I promised you that one day I'd get you, and I did. I set you up. I sent in the incriminating Naomi tape that put you here! Why don't you die and go straight to hell where you belong?" Instead of feeling relief from expressing her pent-up rage, she felt ashamed for venting herself on a helpless old man who didn't know who she was.

But the venom oozing from her heart resurfaced. She slapped hard his sunken cheek. In a flash, Alan's bony frame lunged forward and, with surprising strength, gripped his daughter around the neck. His stranglehold pinned her to the wall. Shiya managed to kick over a small metal table, alerting the staff. Two burly male nurses entered and restrained Alan.

With livid finger marks bruising her neck, Shiya fled to the waiting taxi. She wept all the way back to the hotel.

Visibly shaken but in the safety of her hotel room, Shiya examined the raised marks on her neck. They were nothing in comparison to the welts gripping her bitter heart. She felt she'd rather die first then ever let this evil monster go free.

Later that day, when Bryan arrived with Kelingo, Shiya was thrilled to see them both, especially the old man. She had hardly closed the door behind them when Bryan said, "I must tell you that things have changed since you last lived here. The pendulum in South Africa has swung, and now we have discrimination in reverse. To be white is a great disadvantage in the African bush, so I don't recommend going to Tswanas Kraal."

"You're right," she agreed halfheartedly. "I don't suppose things have changed much. Apartheid is still alive in some black hearts. Not just here in Africa, but in the world in general. But after the entire white race crippled the rightful people of this country, can you blame them for wanting to retaliate? Personally, I could kill a few white folk myself."

With an expression of discomfort written on his face, Kelingo looked down.

"I'm just trying to protect you," Bryan said.

"Protect me! If I'm killed the money runs out, doesn't it, Bryan?"

He winced. "That was uncalled for. What I'm trying to say is …"

Shiya turned her back on Bryan and said to Kelingo, who was looking ill, "Kelingo, how would you like to earn ten times the money you make with Mr. Durval?"

Kelingo, shifting from one leg to the other, remained silent. Bryan saved his driver from embarrassment. "I'm certain Kelingo would love to escort you to Tswanas. I'm quite prepared to forego his services for a while to help you on this assignment. I know how important it is to you."

With her rage now dissipated, Shiya gently touched her lawyer's arm. "Forgive me for being so rude. I seem to be making a habit of it lately."

"It's okay. I've had worse flung at me."

"When can Kelingo and I leave?"

"As soon as I can make the necessary travel arrangements," Bryan replied in an exasperated tone.

"Great! Thanks."

Shiya went to her bag and handed Bryan an $80,000 Euro cheque to cover the expenses of hiring a helicopter pilot to fly her and Kelingo to what is now known as KwaZulu, "the place of the Zulus." The funds would also cover Kelingo's wages, Bryan's fees, and the purchase of various supplies Shiya wished to take with her.

After the men left, Shiya's veins throbbed with excitement. She danced around the room saying, "*Umama*, I'm coming home at long last."

Happiness bounced throughout Shiya's body. She went to the liquor cabinet, took out a miniature brandy, poured the contents into a glass, and toasted, "Here's to the final chapter of this story. To all of Anele's ancestors, if you are listening, I thank you for guiding me home. Bless you all."

The next morning couldn't have come fast enough for Shiya. She had hardly slept a wink, and now her stomach was jittery with excitement. She took a quick shower and packed her bags, making sure the photo album with pictures of Brianna and Lionel were within easy reach. She was about to leave the room when her scatterbrained memory nudged her. She lifted the telephone receiver and dialed an international number. The phone at the other end rang and rang, and then the voice mail cut in. "Hi, this is Brianna and Roberto. We are not here to take your call ..."

Shiya was disappointed. She waited for the customary "beep," then began. "Brianna, I was hoping to speak to you, but never mind. I want you to know that I'm truly sorry I let you down. But I have some good news. I've found Anele, and I'll be leaving today for the

African bush. Before I leave, I'm going to buy a cell phone, but I'm not sure it will work out there. I want you to know that I love you with all my heart. When this journey is over, I will be joining my beloved husband, your father. I know he's waiting for me in the Invisible Kingdom of Souls, and I don't want to make him wait too long. Please take care, my special child. I'll see you in heaven." She hung up and then rang the hotel desk to bring her luggage down.

In the foyer, a poker-faced helicopter pilot was waiting for her and Kelingo. "I'm Captain Johannes de Klerk."

Shiya extended her hand in greeting, but his hand was not forthcoming. She found his behavior odd, but chose to ignore it.

"Follow me, Mrs. Martinez."

They stepped outside into a glorious sunny day. There wasn't a cloud in sight.

They took a short car ride to Durban's executive airstrip. The hot, sticky airborne part of the journey seemed to take forever. Finally they landed on a dirt patch not far from Chief Naboto's resting tree. The giant leaves on the baobab tree whipped back and forth like ping-pong balls as the blades of the chartered helicopter rotated. Shiya was afraid of flying, so she felt more than happy when the helicopter settled on solid ground.

Shiya thanked the pilot, who had spoken hardly a word to her and not one word to Kelingo since they left the hotel. "See you back here in a month, Captain. Okay? And here's a little something extra for you," she said, handing him an envelope.

Johannes forced a smile and counted the South African rands. He was surprised to find nearly as much money as Bryan had paid him. *Bonus!* He tucked the money into the top pocket of his shirt. At first he'd been hesitant about this trip—too dangerous to land his operator-owned chopper in unknown territory. That snake in the grass, Bryan, had been persuasive though: "Look, man, the woman is loaded. She is willing to pay plenty. Take it. You need the cash. You have another baby on the way. Here's a map of the region. I've highlighted a suitable place to land."

Johannes—a former member of the apartheid regime's secret service hit squad—was glad to rid himself of the English woman. She was too la-dee-da for his liking. But worse was the old black guy sitting behind her. He'd been inappropriately familiar with her. Johannes made eye contact with Shiya. "I'm curious, lady. Why would a *white* woman," emphasizing the word "white," "want to come out to this place?"

Obviously, Bryan had paid him but had not given an explanation for her journey.

Shiya resisted the temptation to verbally smack him. This was the beginning of her new life, and she was ushering it in on a February morning with a racist boor?

Shiya held her head low as she scrambled out of the cockpit into eddies of swirling dust. Kelingo followed. She distanced herself from the whirling blades and waited for the pilot to unload the cargo Bryan had purchased from her list—several boxes of items for the village.

Johannes didn't budge from his seat.

Shiya scowled. Choking on a mouthful of reddish dust, she stepped up onto the helicopter and rapped her knuckles on the window. Johannes opened it a fraction and glared at her. "What do you want, lady?"

"I'd like my money back," she bellowed above the din.

"Hell, no!" was his curt response.

"I just paid you extra, well over the airfare, to help me unload!"

"You are crazy! I'm not lifting a finger to help a *kaffir*-loving woman. You had better get your stuff out or I'm taking off with it."

Shiya blew a gasket. "You rotten dirtbag!" she screamed. "I'm never going to use your services again."

Johannes's lips curled into a smirk. "You'd better hurry. My time is precious."

After some backbreaking unloading, Shiya gave Johannes the finger and received one back.

"Your days on this planet will be numbered," he bellowed before lifting off.

She paid no heed to his threat, but one day his parting words would come back to haunt her.

Safely away from the chopper, Shiya brushed dust from her white jeans. She wondered why she'd chosen to wear white when khaki would have been far more appropriate. Kelingo, dusting his own pants, sidled up to Shiya and said, "I'm sorry for the way that awful man treated you. I hope you understand that it's not my place to get involved in arguments between white people."

Shiya wrapped an arm around Kelingo's shoulders. "Good Lord, there's no need for *you* to apologize."

She could see by his look that his apology wasn't enough.

"When Nelson Mandela was appointed our president and apartheid was abolished, I was a very happy man. I had hoped things would improve between our races. Sadly, hatred in the hearts of both blacks and whites still festers. That's the way it is. It will never change."

"I don't believe it ever will," Shiya agreed. "Even while I lived continents away, I tried to keep up with the news over here. But I believe it's not the old apartheid ways that cripple this country now; it's your people—*black* people who are fighting and murdering each other."

"That's a fact," Kelingo sighed as he stared at the ground.

"Enough about this distasteful subject, Kelingo," Shiya said. "Let's get what we can carry and come back for the rest of it later.

I can't wait to see Anele." She was so excited, she felt like pinching herself. She couldn't believe that she was actually stepping back in time to the place she had lived the first years of her life. Unable to contain her emotions, she hopped and skipped. "Whoopee! I'm home, at last!"

Kelingo's old eyes smiled warmly. He, too, was happy to be in his homeland.

After a bit, Shiya asked, "How much farther?"

"It's not that far now."

"Okay. But there is something I have to do before we go on. These darn shoes are killing me."

Shiya bent down, removed the expensive sandals she was wearing, and flung them to the side of the dirt path. Whoever found them was welcome to them. Kelingo stared at the discarded footwear. "It's not wise to go barefoot here," he cautioned, retrieving the sandals and tucking them into his waistband. "Unless you have leathery old feet like mine that nothing can penetrate," he laughed. "There are lots of poisonous thorns, centipedes, and fire ants that would be happy to bite into your soft feet."

Shiya grinned impishly. "The buggers won't like the taste of my blood. My feet will just have to grow leathery like yours."

She skipped along the pathway like a sprightly teenager, until a stabbing pain halted her. "Ow! What the …!" She looked down at her foot—thorn barbs.

Without an "I told you so," Kelingo's experienced fingers plucked out the thorns. He then handed her the sandals.

Shiya, her footwear back on her feet, sprinted down a well-trodden path. Her green eyes danced with joy as she saw, at last, the tops of thatched roofs. A childhood memory flashed in her mind: the spanking Anele gave her for climbing over the kraal gate when she was four years old. "Shiya," Anele had said. "There are dangers out there that a little child knows nothing about!"

Is this where I left my heart? Shiya asked herself, after her reflection faded.

Shiya's presence at the gate sent the village dogs into a barking frenzy. With their teeth bared and their saliva pooling on their jowls, the dogs rushed the fence. Shiya shooed them off and fumbled with the rope hitch. When no one from the inside came to her aid, she looked back. Kelingo was nowhere in sight. Had he stopped to relieve himself? In her eagerness, she decided not to wait for him.

With unladylike composure, Shiya clambered to the top of the wood-slatted fence, lost her balance, and landed flat on her backside into a fresh cowpat. Spattered with manure, she was at first mortified, and then laughed to the point of tears.

Kelingo arrived and had no problem undoing the latch. He clapped a hand over his mouth to muffle his giggles. Shiya scowled playfully, "Please feel free to laugh your head off, Kelingo. I should have waited for you."

Kelingo, still smiling, offered his hand. "Let me help you up." He pulled her to her feet.

Shiya wiped her dirty hands on the sides of her jeans. "Oh, this is a fine way to see my family."

By now many of the villagers—mostly women—had surrounded Shiya and Kelingo. Some wore curious frowns. Kids pointed fingers at the visitor and sniggered. A stocky, elderly woman pushed her way through. "Brother Kelingo, my heart sings with your presence!"

Shiya couldn't stand the suspense a moment longer. "Kelingo, my Zulu is rusty. I haven't a clue what she's saying. But please tell your people why I'm here, and take me to Anele."

To the gawking crowd of twenty, Kelingo announced, "This is Mrs. Lynette Martinez. She has come all the way from America to see her mother, Anele."

Expressions of disbelief appeared, mostly on the faces of the elderly.

Kelingo continued, "Some of you older people may remember the white child who lived here for five years …" he paused for a second before he hit them with the revelation "… before she and Anele were stolen by the white man."

The loudest intake of breath came from a large-breasted woman with brows as creased as tram tracks. She elbowed her way to the front line, bent, and with remarkable strength lifted Shiya. "I didn't recognize you," she murmured against Shiya's cheek. "We have both grown old."

Shiya stared into the cobalt irises that were sunlit with emotion. Then it dawned on her, "Oh, my God! Is it really you, Maekela?"

"Yes, dear friend."

"Is Isona here, too?"

"No. Sadly, she is with our loved ones in the Invisible Kingdom. She was beaten to death by Lady Corrie not long after you left the estate as a child."

Shiya gasped. "What happened?"

"I don't want to talk about it. But I can tell you that she's doing a good job in the Invisible Kingdom. She's taking care of the village children we lost to disease, and my only child, a son. He was killed in a diamond mine explosion."

After the murder of Naomi, Maekela followed Shiya's advice—to get the hell out of Dodge. But not before obtaining Corrie's journals—the incriminating records.

"Oh, I'm so sorry to hear about Isona and the explosion. But darling Maekela, please take me to my mother," pleaded a tearful Shiya. "I can't wait another moment."

Before Maekela could comply, a tall old woman stepped between them, blue eyes also twinkling in the sunlight. "I've heard so much about the white baby my mother rescued. I'm thrilled to know you, my younger sister."

"I'm sorry. Should I know you? I don't remember Anele having another child when I was here."

"No. I was born before you were found in the cornhusk pit in the Valley of a Thousand Hills. I was raised in Kenya by Father Batuzi and his wife Nyasha. My name is Insikazi."

"Oh, my goodness," she gasped. "I can't believe it! Maekela told me that a child had been taken from Anele when she was a teenager! How did *you* find your mother?"

"It's a long story and I'd love to share it with you. We'll have some time to do that now, if you like, because you happened to arrive on the day *Umama* visits the grave of her father, my grandfather, who once was chieftain of this village."

"Show me the way to the burial place," Shiya urged. "I must see her. I can't wait …" She suddenly remembered her appearance and laughed. "Good Lord! I can't let my mother see me like this! Is there somewhere I can wash and change? I don't want Mother to think a cow with diarrhea has come to visit with her!"

Insikazi translated for the gawking crowd. Laughter rang out. Then the tribe dispersed as if it were an everyday occurrence to have an *umlungu* visitor among them.

"By the time I get water fetched from the river for you to wash," Insikazi said, "our mother," she smiled at the associated word "will be on her way back. Vimbela always brings her back before the sun sets. That will give you plenty of time to prepare."

"That name sounds familiar."

"Vimbela was your wet nurse, Shiya."

Shiya's smile stretched ear to ear. It was wonderful to hear her real name spoken again. Kelingo interrupted her happy thoughts. "Mrs. Martinez, do you need me for anything?"

"No, Kelingo. I'll be just fine."

"Before some animal gets to the food boxes," Kelingo informed, "I'm going with the boys to collect them."

"Kelingo, no more 'Mrs. Martinez.' Out here my name is Shiya— my true name. While I live here, the awful English name given to me is no more. I want you to call me Shiya. Okay?"

"I'm not accustomed to calling white people by their first name, but if you insist. 'Shiya' is a good African name."

Shiya's heart flooded with appreciation and love for this ancient man who had so willingly assisted her. And she found it delightful the way he pronounced her name—*Shee-i-ya*. But what Shiya couldn't see in his smiling, soft brown eyes was a hard glint of intended betrayal.

"Kelingo, when you bring back the boxes, you'll find one marked with a large 'C.' Open it and hand out the treats for the children. I don't suppose these poor kids have ever seen candy bars."

Kelingo's brows rose to his hairline. "*All* of them!"

Shiya laughed. "No silly. The kids will be hyperactive for days if you dish them all out. No, just give each of them a lollipop for now."

"A pleasure," Kelingo returned. "I can't thank you enough for your tender heart toward our people."

Shiya placed a hand on his shoulder and said, "You don't need to thank me, Kelingo. It is I who should be thanking you."

Kelingo bowed at the waist. "It has been an honor. In the white man's world, I was half a man, but here I am a whole man. I don't want to return to the legal firm, but it doesn't look like Mr. Durval will let me out of my work contract. I only have one year left."

"Maybe I'll be able to work something out with Bryan that will make that possible."

Shiya watched Kelingo head for the gate with a bevy of boys close behind him.

Anele's natural daughter handed a pail to one of the girls. "Go quickly to the river. Fill this pail and bring it to my hut. Go fast, Leticia." To Shiya she said, "Come. I'll take you to my hut. You can undress there. When the girl gets back, you can wash."

The two women strolled leisurely toward the cluster of a dozen or more grass-thatched huts at the far end of the compound.

Under the dung spatter on Shiya's cheeks was a healthy glow. Her illness was the furthest thing from her mind. All she needed to complete her happiness was Anele.

Insikazi pointed to two huts at the end of the mud-walled assemblage. "That one is mine, and the big one to the right is Anele's. Do you remember it?"

"Not really."

Anele had lived alone in her hut, Insikazi told Shiya, since her old husband, Tekenya, was snatched by a crocodile in the river four years ago.

Shiya shuddered. Her thoughts diverted to the girl who had gone to fetch water for her. *I hope to God a crocodile doesn't snatch her.*

Shiya was pleasantly surprised when she stepped into Insikazi's hut. Although the woman's living quarters were windowless and no bigger than a broom closet, the well-pounded soil was shiny and immaculately clean. In the center of the hut was a raised single bed covered in a colorful patchwork quilt. Oil lamps sat on small tree stumps that served as nightstands. Intoxicating aromas wafted up to Shiya's nostrils. "What *is* that glorious smell?"

"That is the oil from the black ironwood trees. I sprinkle it between the floor stones to stop the pests, spiders, ants, and dog fleas from getting into my bed and eating me alive!"

Shiya giggled like a little girl.

Insikazi made tea from crushed red leaves, and the half-sisters chatted happily. Shiya wanted to hear about Anele, but she did not want to appear rude, so she resisted the urge to rush the pleasantries. At last, when her patience was running thin, Insikazi told her about Anele. "Our mother is frail in body from being so long in jail, and her eyesight is poor, but her mind is sharper than the claw of an eagle. This you will find out ..."

They were interrupted by a visitor who entered the hut and introduced herself. "My name is Sister Bertha. I'm the schoolteacher. I was down at the river when word reached me of your arrival."

"Nice to make your acquaintance," Shiya said. Her eyes took in the nun's beauty—purple-black skin and eyes twinkling like onyx. The nun did not have typical Zulu features: a rounded face, broad flattened nose, long neck, or high forehead. Her features were the opposite. "You're not from these parts, are you, Sister Bertha?"

"No, I'm not. I'm Nigerian. I was born in a village very similar to this one."

"What brought you all this way?"

"It is a long story. Do you have the time?"

"Of course," she returned with intrigue.

"Not long after you and Anele left Tswanas, I volunteered to take the previous Sister's teaching position." A dam of memories burst forth as Bertha spoke at length, giving Shiya a vivid account of her life and her entry to Tswanas kraal. She finally ended with, "That's enough about me. I'm dying to hear all about you. Can I ask you how long you intend staying here?"

"For the rest of what remains of my life."

Sister Bertha frowned quizzically. She wanted Shiya to elaborate, and when she didn't, the nun decided it would be too impolite to question her further. Instead, she spoke of the progress her students were making.

Shiya found herself warming to the friendly schoolteacher. Yes, she decided, the nun appeared open minded enough to be trusted.

Once they were outside the hut, Shiya took hold of the Bertha's hand and said, "Sister, I'll let you in on a little secret that I hope you will keep to yourself for now. I'm here because I have a tumor growing on my brain that will shorten my life. So, you see, I've come home to reclaim my foster mother and my childhood before I have no memory of them."

The sister's dark eyes moistened. "I'm so sorry to hear that. If there is anything I can do, please don't hesitate to ask. And I hope we can become close friends. I'd like to make your stay here a happy one. Let me assure you, your secret is safe with me."

"Thanks, Sister. I'm looking forward to having some wonderful chats with you." Shiya glanced down and noticed Bertha's feet. Her patched black shoes had trod more miles than had been expected of them.

"Before you go, Sister, I've got something for you. Wait here a moment." Shiya dashed into the hut, retrieved her sandals, and handed them to Bertha. "We look about the same size, so I'd like you to have these."

"Oh, th-ank you," the nun stammered, clutching the footwear to her chest. Her eyes shone with gratitude. Then she dug deep into her tunic pocket and removed a small silver crucifix and handed it to Shiya. "And I'd like you to have this."

Shiya stared at the gift. "I'm sorry, but I don't want it. Don't try to put your beliefs on me! I've had more than my fill of Catholicism."

"I didn't mean …"

"And I didn't mean to be ungrateful. What I intended to say is, do good work for these people, but, please, leave me out."

The Sister smiled in a way that told Shiya this holy woman would not give up trying to convert her—just like the JWs who regularly showed up on her doorstep in Canada, her closed door.

What Shiya could not have predicted was that those very sandals would find their way, once again, back to her own feet.

As Shiya sat on the floor of Insikazi's hut, she felt perfectly at home. It was as though she'd never left this village of her youth, had never come to live in relative luxury. All thoughts of her Western life—creature comforts, her brain condition, and the loved ones she'd left behind—vanished from her mind as if by the wave of a sorcerer's wand.

This day was second in importance in her life, following the day she gave birth to her daughter, Brianna. Today she would meet the woman who had saved her from an awful death and gone on to become the only mother she had ever known.

The pail of washing water arrived.

Shiya removed her soiled clothing and washed her entire body with the lukewarm, muddy-looking river water. Then she donned the native attire Insikazi provided her with—full-length, cotton, gold-and-green caftan; a headscarf of the same material; large, metal-beaded hoop earrings; and a Cleopatra-style necklace. Shiya felt like an African princess.

Insikazi beamed her approval. "You are, once more, one of us, Shiya of Tswanas. Let's go see the woman you love."

"I hope no one has told her I'm here."

"Don't fret. I warned the whole village to remain silent."

With Insikazi walking at her side, Shiya felt nervousness kneading her stomach as she moved toward Anele's hut. Would her "mother" recognize her? Would Anele love her the way she had continued to love Anele?

Tired from her walk back to the kraal, the person Shiya had waited so long to find was lying on her side, facing the mud-thatched wall, and she was snoring. Shiya's heart thumped so noisily she feared it would startle Anele awake.

Shiya was barely breathing as she crept to the bed and knelt down. She was shocked by what she saw. Her foster mother was so thin that she appeared skeletal. Her backbone protruded visibly. Her skin stretched tightly over limbs that once walked, ran, and jumped. Shrunken sockets appeared where eyes once flashed with mischief, anger, or tenderness and shriveled lips suggested a mouth that once expressed pouts and laughter. Tenderly, Shiya touched Anele's arm and said in broken Zulu, "*Umama*. It's me, *your* Shiya."

Anele, with her thigh bones creaking, turned over. A croaky voice asked, "Who is it?" The tip of her nose wrinkled as she added, "I smell a strange scent not of our village."

Shiya couldn't wait for a translation. She enfolded Anele's bony face into her hands and gently kissed her on both cheeks. Anele's hands, now more bone than flesh, roughly pushed Shiya away. Then her eyes, dim with cataracts, stared long and hard. Finally, her fingers traced the face inches from hers. "*Namandla!*" she shrieked. "Great God of the Zulus, is it really you, my precious Shiya?"

Tears flowing down her cheeks, Shiya responded, "Yes, my darling *Umama*. Your Shiya has returned home for good." She took Anele's fragile form into her arms and rocked her gently. "I love you, *Umama*."

"I love you too, my *Shiya*."

Quietly, Insikazi slipped outside, leaving mother and daughter to share with each other their many lost years.

Shiya and her foster mother drew apart from their tight embrace when a portly, white-haired woman with sagging jowls entered the hut and plopped herself down beside them on the bed. The old woman patted Shiya's cheek. "You won't remember me, white lady, because you were so little when I was last in your life, but I'm happy to see that my milk has given you strong, tall bones."

Again, Shiya's limited knowledge of Zulu was tested.

Vimbela, now much older in body but not in mind, sat down beside Shiya and babbled away.

Anele translated.

Of course she remembered the day. How could she ever forget that day when she was yanked up a baobab tree to escape evil?

"Darling Vimbela," Shiya said while hugging the woman.

Vimbela was animated, flailing her arms, and jumping up and down. Then her shoulders sagged and the smile disappeared. "I cried lots of tears the day you didn't listen to me and were taken by the *umlungu* man ..."

Anele interrupted, "That's enough, Vimbela. I don't think Shiya needs to be reminded of that awful time."

"Yes, *Umama* Anele. I say no more words. I just came to see my baby, who is a big old woman now."

Vimbela's childish spirit raised pity in Shiya's heart.

"I want to thank you, Aunty Vimbela. Your milk did, indeed, make my bones strong."

Like the cat that got the cream, Vimbela grinned, but her smile dried instantly when Anele told her to leave the hut.

"Shiya and I have many more things to talk about. You may come back later, if you wish."

With pouting lips, Vimbela argued, "But *Umama* Anele, I want to stay with my baby. I don't want to go to bed."

Anele shot her a disapproving look.

Vimbela left, muttering under her breath.

The cloak of night descended quickly around the mother and foster daughter who were lying side by side on the narrow bed. Wrapped in each other's arms, too excited to sleep, they talked for hours. Anele confided that not a single day had passed without Shiya in her thoughts.

Anele revealed how she had lost her natural daughter to Father

Batuzi, and his so-called *wife,* and how, many years later, she and Insikazi were reunited.

"The Nigerian priest was not the religious soul he had made himself out to be. Insikazi was deathly afraid of her adopted father's volatile temperament. At aged fifteen she ran away from him, hitched rides from black travelers, and ended up in Durban, where she got a cleaning job in an accountant's office. About a month into her employment, her white boss accused her of stealing money from his office drawer. Of course, Insikazi swore her innocence. Her boss promised to keep his mouth shut if she would have sex with him. She refused.

"Once the boss's sexual advances were spurned, he called the police. The white magistrate handed down a ten-year sentence. Insikazi's incarceration took place at Montclair jail—the very same prison I was in.

In the courtyard one day I saw a girl with bright blue eyes … eyes I had never forgotten … Alan's eyes. His eyes had never left my tormented soul. Could it be my daughter, I thought? Or could it just be another one of Alan's offspring?

"You can imagine my shock when I learned the truth. Insikazi and I clung to each other. I begged for a transfer to Insikazi's jail block, but, of course, was denied."

Anele's soft-spoken voice hardened with anger. "I was willing to do anything to be with my own flesh and blood, but it wasn't to be. We caught moments together in the courtyard, but it would be many years until we could finally share a life together. After Nelson Mandela came to power—I thank the Great Spirits for this man—we were both released.

"I would have died before ever seeing Tswanas again if it hadn't been for the strength of my daughter. It took us many long, tiring days to reach here. But we made it, and I have her to thank for the long life in these old bones, a longevity that comes from my father's side."

A toothless smile creased her lips. "I'm doing quite well for an eighty-year-old woman, don't you think? We blacks don't stress over everyday things, like white folk do. That's our secret to long life."

Shiya couldn't find the words to respond. Suddenly, Anele began to cry.

"What's the matter, *Umama*?"

"I wish it could be washed away."

"What could be washed away?"

"I wasn't expecting to ever see you again."

An inner voice warned Shiya that if Anele divulged her secret, it wouldn't be pleasant news. But curiosity overruled logic. "You can tell me. I'm past hurting."

After a deep, labored breath, Anele began. "When you were a baby, our first schoolteacher, Sister Babavana, and I became very good friends. She would come by my hut each day after school ended. We would chat and drink tea. Although she had heard about you from village gossip, she was curious to learn the real facts about you directly from me. So I told her how I found you.

"One day after Sister had returned from a holiday, I was happy to see her, but she avoided me, which is difficult to do in an enclosed compound. When I finally demanded to know what was wrong, all she said was that I had lied to her. She went to the tapestry bag that she carried to and from the village and handed me a crumpled newspaper. I informed her that I couldn't read, so she read the article to me. It was about the skeletal remains of a newborn baby girl found not far from the Hallworthy property line. I didn't think anything of it until she came to the part about the baby being white, not black, as was first assumed.

The newspaper showed a map of where the child was found. I

knew the area well. It was the same place where I found you."

Shiya released a deafening cry. "Oh, my God!" she cried breathing into the palms of her hands. "There were *two* of us! Maria gave birth to *twins!*"

Anele clasped her hands over her ears when Shiya began to cry loudly.

Insikazi rushed in. "What is it that makes you howl like a hurt dog, Shiya? *Umama* looks scared half to death."

Shiya's eyes were vacant, lost in a forest of pain.

Anele's hands latched onto Shiya's face. "Look at me, Shiya. I swear on my father's spirit, you were the only one I found under the pile of corn husks."

Shiya's tongue was numb with shock.

Anele turned to Insikazi. "Make us strong tea. Use the leaves I collected from the red bush. We both could do with some tea."

Shiya found her voice. "I need a bloody drink, and I don't mean tea!"

"Would you like some beer?" Insikazi asked.

"Yes, that will do."

A shroud of silence hung in the hut until a large pitcher of beer appeared.

Shiya made an "ugh" face before draining a mug of the vile tasting alcohol—anything to wash away the horror, to knock herself out, to wake up to a new day in which the past was totally erased from her memory.

It wasn't going to happen.

Shiya, collapsed in an unconscious heap on the floor, was blissfully unaware of the strong arms of the young man who lifted her and placed her limp body onto Anele's bed. When Shiya came to an hour or so later, her sodden brain tried furtively to bring her back to earth. Were the voices she was hearing coming from inside or outside of her head? Through blurred vision she discerned two gray shapes moving toward her. She was cringing.

"It's all right, Shiya. Don't be scared," Anele reassured her. "This is Sliman, a Tswanas witch doctor."

Shiya instantly regretted bolting upright. The room was spinning like a top, and she feared losing her stomach contents. But there was nothing wrong with her voice. "Why in the world do I need a witch doctor?" she protested. "I got drunk on that strong beer; that's all. And if my childhood memory serves me well, the *last* person I wish to see is Twazli!"

Anele's laughter pealed like a church bell. "Shiya, it would be a miracle if Twazli stood here. He would be over a hundred. Sliman is Twazli's youngest son, and he speaks English."

"No disrespect, young man," Shiya said, "but I've long left my childhood. Boogie men are no longer part of my belief system."

Anele clucked her tongue. "Child, you are going to need this medicine man if you wish the cancer cells to leave your brain."

Bertha! If she had been in the room, Shiya would have slapped the nun for breaking her promise. Shiya indignantly said, "Mumbo-jumbo is going to cure cancer? Not even a bloody miracle will erase the tumor I have."

Sliman touched her cheek. "You'll never know, Shiya of Tswanas, if you do not put your faith in a medicine that has been practiced since dinosaurs roamed the earth."

That statement brought a smile. "Okay. You win. I'll try anything to be rid of the bloody awful headaches I have been having."

Illuminated in the warm glow of candlelight, Sliman bared no resemblance to Twazli, the nightmarish ghoul she remembered from the past. Unlike the father, his son had forsaken his predecessor's goat-pelt garb, white face paint, and dried chicken-feet earrings. Instead, he was well attired in a beige shirt and shorts. His cocoa-bean eyes, and teeth the envy of any toothpaste commercial, were set in a mahogany face. His features were not demonic or terrifying, but benign and reassuring. Shiya decided this spiritual young man wouldn't hurt a fly. Or would he?

Sliman gestured her to squat opposite him. When he smiled at her, she felt warmth spreading throughout her body. *Interesting*, she thought. *Am I bewitched already? Don't even think about it!*

Sliman directed her to place her hands in his. "I want to sense your spiritual color," he said with an air of authority.

Immediately, Shiya experienced a tingling, electric sensation in her captive hands. The feeling spread throughout her body progressively. Her muscles tightened, and she found she was unable to move. Strangely, though, she felt no fear. Suddenly, she was floating. Weighing less than a dandelion seed on a gentle summer breeze, she drifted toward Sliman. She wondered if his eyes were growing in size. They transformed into two huge, dark orbs that drew her in until she became fixed in their centers. Traumatic scenes from her life formed a disjointed collage, the product of a mad artist's brush. Then an undulating light appeared in the distance. Her mind floated toward the light like a moth to a candle. Never one to easily relinquish self-control, Shiya had sworn to herself never to be hypnotized for any reason, so she fought hard to regain control of her own will.

Shiya jerked to full consciousness. As her head swiveled, fuzzy images came into focus. She objected. "Sliman, it is bloody wrong to control another's will. No one has the right to dominate my mind. I don't want to be 'put-under.' Please don't ever try it again."

Sliman, who had a calm personality, softly replied, "It is the Gardeners of All Life who have chosen to shut down your brain by giving you the cancerous mass, not me. They feel that the vessel they bequeathed unto you has been disrespected—blighted—with rage for too many years. Your receptacle overflows with hatred and unforgiveness, Shiya. To drink in the light, you must first spit out these demons. They are more than your spirit can bear. Let go of them, Shiya of Tswanas. Don't take that persons shame as your guilt.

"I know it is not easy to forgive, but you must if … if you wish to remain mortal. The tumor that grows in your brain is a spiritual forewarning. If you ignore your demons of hatred and unforgiveness, you will succumb to them for eternity. If it comes as any solace," Sliman allowed himself the hint of a smile, "you are not entirely to blame. The tainted blood flowing through your body comes from the white evil that sired you."

"Well, that comes as no surprise," Shiya responded.

"Shiya, my all-seeing stones will help you fight your battle with the demons of darkness." Sliman placed several objects on the floor in front of them—three small, round stones composed of a crystalline material. One appeared to be an off-white color, another as black as ebony, and the third a smoky gray. Beside the stones Sliman placed a small, soft, brown leather pouch with a long drawstring. "Through these spiritual stones I am able to see a chain of many lives. None of your past lives have been good ones. Badness from ancient worlds has followed you through many reincarnations. Your inner self is fighting to erase that badness so it can be admitted into the Kingdom of Pure Souls."

Sure, Shiya thought. She prided herself on being open minded, but this seemed too far-fetched. But she decided to hear him out.

The seer continued. "The whitish stone is for light, the black is for darkness, the gray their battleground. All of us contain these three elements, and they are constantly at war. You are to place the stones in the bag I have provided and keep it by you at all times. Do not let another person touch them or the power of the stones will inflict their fury upon you."

Yeah, right!

"I will prepare some herbal medicine to put into rooibos tea. The mixture will turn your good cells into cancer-fighting warriors." Sliman got to his feet. "I must go now. But I would like to leave with you an Eastern saying: Do not let the sun set on your wrath, on this or any other night, for it will be your undoing, Shiya of the Tswanas." He turned to Anele and spoke quickly in Zulu and then bid the women good night.

Left with her thoughts, Shiya contemplated the happenings of the night. What harm could it do?

As instructed, she picked up the stones one by one, deposited them in the pouch, and placed the pouch around her neck. She then undressed and slid into bed beside Anele. Lying back to back with her foster mother, Shiya fell instantly into an exhausted sleep.

 Tswanas Kraal, the Homecoming

*"We will remember not the words of our enemies,
but the silence of slaves."*
—Martin Luther King, Jr.

Shiya opened her eyes and saw sunlight filtering through the door curtain. Anele was already up and not in the hut. She had probably gone to the toilet, a crudely-built latrine at the perimeter of the village. That was the same place Shiya needed, with some urgency. Grabbing a handful of tissues from her handbag, Shiya dashed outside. The sound of children sniggering alerted her to the fact that she was as bare as a peeled banana! *Too late*, she thought. *I'm sure I'm not the first naked woman they have seen. But maybe I'm the first* white *buck-naked one!*

The lavatory was unoccupied, and it stunk to high heaven.

Shiya squatted over the hole, pinched her nose with one hand and swatted the ever-present blowflies with the other. There had to be a way to improve this unsanitary place. She didn't know much about septic fields or tanks, but she could ask where the nearest town was so she could get building plans drawn up to have a proper toilet installed. If that plan failed, she would ask Bryan, who had promised to come and see her in about a month.

Without a care in the world, Shiya strolled back to the hut, waving at the villagers and keeping an eye out for Anele. Her foster mother was nowhere in sight.

Shiya opened her suitcase and removed clean underwear, a pair of khaki shorts, and a white T-Shirt. She'd have given anything for a long soak in a hot tub, a soft robe, and a pair of slippers, but, instead, she used baby wipes to wash her perspiration-drenched body. She'd barely zipped up her shorts when Sliman entered the hut, silent as a shadow. She'd have to get used to the custom of not knocking.

"Did you sleep well?" he asked.

"Like a log," was her cheerful response, "and for the first time in ages I did not wake up with a headache. Even though I kicked up a stink about hypnotism, it has done the job. I'm more than grateful, Sliman. Thank you."

With a satisfied smile curving his full lips, Sliman handed her an earthenware bowl decorated with obscure symbols. "I want you to drink this," he said. "Today, you start your treatment."

Shiya looked at Sliman and then into the bowl. What was in it? She took the vessel from his hand and stepped outside with it. Sniffing the bowl and peering at the reddish liquid inside, she made an "ugh" face. Insoluble particles were floating on top of the concoction.

"This looks like embalming fluid made up of scarab beetles!"

Sliman had inherited his father's laugh. He sounded like a braying donkey.

"It is an ancient herbal tea," he explained. "It has secret properties that will trigger your healing process."

This is utter madness, Shiya thought. She was about to hand the bowl back when her inner voice stopped her. *What if this ancient remedy really works?* She was reminded of the stepchild in the Madagascan proverb: If he doesn't wash his hands, he is dirty; if he does, he is wasting the water. Was she indeed wasting what precious little time she had left by not being with Brianna? Or would this vile-looking nectar be her unlikely healer? Her will to survive pushed her to pinch her nose and down the potion. Licking her lips, she turned to Sliman and said, "It's not that bad, actually. It tastes like honey, lovely and sweet."

Sliman gave her an "I-told-you-so" smile and said, "I'll give you a supply of the dry fermented leaves. You must first boil water, steep the leaves for half an hour, then wait until the liquid becomes cold. You are to drink a full cup three times a day: when you rise, at noon, and at sunset."

"How much do I owe you?"

"You owe me nothing. In my father's day you would have had to buy ten head of cattle, or sleep in his bed and ..."

"Ugh! I'd go into a coma before I'd do that!"

"And I wouldn't take you into my bed," Sliman laughed. "You are way too skinny for me!"

Over the next few days Shiya began to feel she was actually breaking free of the hate chains that had nearly destroyed her body, mind, and soul. Her ability to speak Zulu was improving. She assisted in the various tasks that supported village life, such as planting seeds and picking root vegetables. During the day she lived for the moment. But in the dead of night, Brianna's face haunted her. She missed her daughter dreadfully. What hurt the most was having no ability to make contact; the cell phone she had purchased in Durban proved useless. So under the shade of Naboto's baobab tree, with Sliman at her side, she wrote her daughter a long letter that resembled a mini-novel, telling Brianna about life in Tswanas and how happy she was to be there. She mentioned Sliman's medicine and magic stones and admitted that they seemed to be helping her. But she omitted that the young witch doctor and she were sharing special moments away from the kraal. Nothing improper had happened between them, and she did not want to sully their warm friendship with even a hint of suspicion.

Sliman and Shiya held hands and yakked about so many things: poetry, literature, her love of classical music, and her conclusion that modern music was "muck."

Two months flew by with no sign of the helicopter's return. This suited old Kelingo well because that meant he did not have to work through his signed contract duties with Bryan, but it did not suit Shiya. Why hadn't her lawyer turned up as promised? Had he changed his mind? Had she gummed up the works by sleeping with him? Had she been strung along by the smooth-talking Bryan?

Another month passed and Shiya's letters to Brianna piled up.

Although her daughter was never far from her mind, Shiya's days were never lonely. The five women—Anele, Insikazi, Vimbela, Maekela, and she—were one big, happy family.

Anele taught Shiya how to weave cotton for general clothing and school uniforms, and to sew hides.

Insikazi taught her how to milk the goats.

Maekela taught her how to play a game with numbered stones.

And Vimbela taught her how to weave baskets and make beaded jewelry.

As time slipped by, a patchwork of sights, sounds, smells and colors—sewn together with a generous thread of words—lead Shiya to feel she was in the healthiest condition of her life. It was as if the brain cancer had never existed.

On the last day of June she heard the sound of an aircraft flying over Tswanas. She ran to the landing area and was thrilled to see the familiar chopper, but not thrilled to see the face of Captain Johannes. Smugly, he said, "Look, lady, I don't ask questions. I don't know why Bryan didn't come himself. He just paid me to bring the supplies I have in the back."

Shiya bit her tongue to keep from saying, "For your information, you arrogant SOB, *I* pay *you!*" But to do so would only fritter away valuable energy.

"Did Bryan send a message or letter?"

"No."

"Did he tell you when he might be coming out here?"

"No."

"Can you wait while I run back to the kraal and get some letters for mailing?"

"No."

"You son of a bitch," she swore. If she'd had a baseball bat, she would have swung it.

Her village helpers had hardly gotten the last box out of the helicopter and onto the ground when Johannes lifted off. Shiya, growling like a pit bull, screamed out, "Damn you, Johannes. You're an asshole ... and so's Bryan!"

Stomping back to the kraal, she wondered how she was going to retrieve her personal belongings from Bryan, the ones given to him for safekeeping. He had her passport, bankbooks, checkbook, credit cards, and at least $50,000 in U.S. cash and $50,000 in other currencies. What was she going to do? How could she provide necessities to the villagers? Thinking Bryan would come at least once a month, she'd brought little cash with her. She ranted her concerns to Anele.

Anele's response was not one she expected. "Shiya, I hope you won't take this wrong, but we got along fine before you came with the fancy foodstuffs. We are simple people. We survive by our own means. It won't bother me if I never see white indulgences again."

Shiya exhaled loudly. "Why didn't you tell me this before?"

"I didn't want to hurt your feelings. I may be old and set in my ways, but I'm not senile. I know how much it means to you to pamper us simple folk. But once you start spoiling my people, especially the children, they won't accept you for who you truly are—a genuinely kindhearted person. They see you now as a supplier of fine things, and nothing more. I know you have a soft spot for the white lawyer, but I'll bet anything he's a bad apple. Remember, child, not everything is as it seems."

A visibly upset Shiya left the hut. She walked in the hot sun, hatless and shoeless, for what must have been miles. She was unmindful of the mosquitoes biting at her bare, sweating arms and legs. Had she been blinded by impulsive infatuation? If so, what happened to her usually keen legal mindset? It came as a shocking realization to her that she was susceptible to a charlatan's charms. How could she have been so trusting? And so darn stupid? She had to find another way to help the Tswanas people live a better life.

Fortune would smile upon her and present a new solution to her dilemma. As the saying goes, "Luck prefers a risk-based mindset." Did this proverb apply to Shiya? Only time could answer that question.

CHAPTER THIRTEEN

 August 1998

"Rented silence will not protect you."
–Anonymous

I t was the beginning of August, springtime in South Africa. The season brought a profusion of color and a hive of activity. Bees swarmed around the nectar-laden flowers—wild bougainvillea, dark-red aloe blooms, and intense yellow blossoms hanging from the ends of laburnum branches. On this fine spring afternoon, Sister Bertha, returning from a brief vacation in Nairobi, was accompanied by a young black priest, Father Samuel Ungobo. They entered Anele's hut. Shiya was delighted to learn that Samuel was a qualified pilot and had landed a borrowed two-seater, twin-engine aircraft three miles from the kraal. The priest and nun had walked the rest of the way to the village. Shiya couldn't wait to present her plan to him.

Without hesitation, Father Samuel agreed.

Five days later, after landing at a private Nairobi airstrip, Father Samuel drove Shiya in his dilapidated Volvo truck to the nearest International Bank.

Shiya—wearing a two-piece beige suit, Bertha's "loaned" Italian sandals and a ponytail at the nape of her neck—walked into the colonial-style building. Bank tellers and customers stopped what they were doing and stared at her as if she was an apparition. Not too many white customers frequented this rural part of Nairobi.

"I'd like to speak to the bank manager," Shiya said to the desk clerk sitting nearest the door.

"Certainly, Madam," was the respectful reply.

Shiya watched the clerk disappear into a side room. Within seconds a burly man attired in black pants, black tie, and a crisp white shirt emerged and walked toward her. "How can I be of assistance to you?"

"I'd like to withdraw money from my Swiss bank account, but I don't have my bankbook with me."

"Do you know the telephone number of the branch in Switzerland?"

"Yes."

"Then come with me. You can make the call from my office."

After providing the personal details necessary for security, Shiya was able to transfer one million dollars U.S. into her new account at the Nairobi Bank of Commerce. The delighted bank manager waived the cost of the phone call. Shiya came out of the bank smiling. She would, after all, live to enjoy her fortune, but at a price. She missed her only child. How she would love to talk to Brianna, and share her abundance of good news, and bring her up to date.

She could ask Father Samuel to drive her to Nairobi International Airport, do some ocean hopping, fly to Canada, see Brianna, and then return. Oh, she'd do absolutely *anything* to be with her daughter, to hold her in her arms, to tell her how much she loved and missed her, to convince her that she was only trying to protect her from the painful truth of her illness.

For an instant the thought of seeing Brianna buoyed her spirits, but just as quickly her mood sank. She had hurt her daughter so deeply with her deceptions that it seemed certain she would not get a good reception. She felt tears sting her eyes. Then she shrugged. Perhaps it was best to let sleeping dogs lie—at least for a while.

In a chilling twist of fate, Shiya's emotional pull to be with her daughter would get a chance to develop. Meanwhile, there was one person she had to talk to.

As though he had been expecting her call, Bryan answered his cell phone on the first ring. Shiya attacked him like a predator, leaving the lawyer little opportunity to defend himself. She spoke her mind, then, shaking with rage, slammed down the receiver in the public telephone booth. She would go back to Tswanas and forget she'd ever met him.

The trip home was a nightmare.

Gale-force winds buffeted Father Samuel's ancient, overloaded aircraft, bouncing it like a rubber ball in the sky. With her teeth clenched tight and not a paper bag in sight, Shiya worried she might lose her lunch—a large portion of fish and chips eaten at the airport cafeteria. Samuel's excellent navigational skills guided his laden craft through the storm to a safe landing. She released a huge sigh of relief and felt like kissing the ground.

Back in the kraal Shiya was surprised to be handed a package that Johannes de Klerk had dropped off only hours earlier. Bryan had not mentioned this during their heated telephone conversation, but she had given him little chance to say anything.

His stiffly worded communication began:

"Lynette, I'm returning your personal belongings. I also enclose a detailed account of the $250,000 retainer fee. I've honored my side of your scurrilous request, and I hope you will keep your promise to destroy the 'you-know-what.' Don't expect to see me again. Yours faithfully, Bryan."

In the days following his letter, Shiya barely gave the content of his letter a second thought. She had better things to do, like getting on with life in the wilderness. When the children were not in Sister Bertha's classroom, they surrounded her like moths to flame. They were delighted when she read them stories from popular children's books she'd purchased in Nairobi. She became their "sweetie giver." She played games with the children but refused to swim with them in the river. And she comforted adolescent girls who came to her and poured their hearts out. Most evenings, with oil lamps and candlesticks close by, she read to Anele historical accounts of the Anglo-Zulu war of 1879.

Anele interrupted, "You know, my father fought in that war. He was shot twice and survived. But one of my uncle's didn't make it home."

"I'm sorry to hear that."

While Shiya continued to bask in the love of her adopted mother, she worried about her declining health. Anele was incontinent, and sometimes refused to eat. One morning Anele latched onto Shiya's arm. "Would you take me to the sacred rock? I want to go when the first stars are out."

At night! Shiya's head screamed her concern. For all the love she had for her mother, this idea was a no-no. Shiya was terrified of bumping into a hungry leopard or one of the other deadly creatures the village children delighted in telling her about. So far she had encountered none of these beasts, but she had heard their hunting cries, which always sent the village dogs into a frenzied barking of their own.

Goosebumps rose on Shiya's arms. "Why do you have to go at night, *Umama*? Can't it wait until daylight?

Anele's chin jutted. "No, it can't. Night is the time to see the crystal bowl with diamond pinpoints of light—the souls of our ancestors."

"Ah," Shiya cooed. "You put that so beautifully, Anele."

"So you'll take me tonight?"

"Why not," she replied nonchalantly as she rubbed her goose-bumps.

With an oil lamp lighting the way, mother and daughter slowly walked hand in hand to the sacred rock, which resembled a large bird. They stopped frequently to allow Anele to catch her breath and to readjust the wooden crutch under her armpit. Just before they reached the rock, Shiya saw the red glowing eyes of a large cat. The hairs on her neck and arms stood straight up. Then bravado took over. She shouted, "Be gone, creature of the night. You won't like the flesh of either of us, for it's as tough as turtle shell and just as nasty tasting."

The "telling off" brought a throaty chuckle from Anele. Shiya's words were something her father, Chief Naboto, would have said.

They waited until the creature, probably a leopard, slunk into the dense shrub before they continued on their way. When the women stood side by side atop the spiritual rock, an aromatic scent mantled them. Many had sought out this sacred place to confide secrets, beg for mercy, and wait for loved ones to pay a visit from the netherworld. Anele raised her arms toward the heavens as if she were trying to snag a star. "Namandla, I thank you for bringing my

Shiya back to me. I want you to take good care of her now because I'm ready to join my family in your invisible kingdom."

Shiya gasped and grabbed her mother's shoulders. "No. You are not leaving me yet, *Umama*," she pleaded.

"Ah, child, it's time for me to go, to leave this mortal place. Namandla, the Great Maker, has sent me messages. Shiya can you see them?"

"What do you see?" Shiya asked tearfully.

"Look around you," Anele said lowering the lamp. "See the stonecrop plants, the miniature orchids? They have flowered. I can smell them. They have not done this since you were a child. This is a spiritual sign." Her hands groped over the jutting rocks, picked a delicate white flower, and reached out to offer it to Shiya.

With her arm still extended, Anele gently stroked the velvet petals. "This is the sign I have been waiting for. The spirits have come to take me to heaven."

"Please, don't say that, *Umama*. I couldn't bear the thought of losing you so soon."

In barely a whisper Anele replied. "My beloved Shiya, it is not that I don't love you. It is that I'm eager to join my father, mother, siblings, and my best friend, Lamella, who took care of me as a child. And I'd like to see Isona, who died giving birth to Alan's umpteenth child."

Sorrow welled within Shiya like a wash of brine. She could not bear the thought of losing Anele, the only mother she had ever known, a woman who had been lost to her for so long. But deep inside she knew that it would only be a matter of time, and that it would come soon.

"God of Africa," Shiya prayed softly, "please don't let my mother die, not just yet. I haven't been given enough time to get to know her again. But if this isn't to be, please do something for me. When you open your arms to take her, take me, too. I want to be with my mother for all eternity." A voice in her head interrupted her prayers, reminding her that selfishness was not a virtue. So she hugged Anele and whispered in her ear, "If that is your wish, *Umama*, then I have no choice but to let you go. God forbid I should be the one to hold you back."

"Don't worry, my child. I'll be watching over you. And when I'm gone, I do not want you to cry. I want you to go home to your daughter. She is the one whose love will make you strong in mind, not Sliman's tea leaves. Will you promise me this, Shiya?"

"I promise."

Shiya, clutching the little flower, silently accompanied her mother back to the kraal. She could not prevent Anele's passing, but she was thankful she had made the choice to return to South Africa when she did. The time she was spending with Anele was the happiest she'd ever known.

Shiya climbed into bed and snuggled next to her mother—watching her every minute, listening to make sure she was still breathing. Finally her drooping eyelids closed, and Shiya fell sound asleep.

The next morning, the sound of Anele's loud snoring was music to Shiya's ears. Her precious mother was still with her, and she thanked the Zulu god for hearing her prayer.

While Anele slept on, Shiya lit the single-burner propane stove—a purchase from Nairobi—and set about making a pot of tea. When she saw movement under the blanket, she called out, "I'm making your special Indian tea, *Umama*. Would you like some chocolate biscuits to go with it?"

Anele's muffled voice replied, "No, child, tea will do fine."

While waiting for the water to boil, Shiya sat on a chair and began singing a Johnny Mathis song, *"Let your heart remember ..."*

Halfway through the chorus her mouth went as dry as parched soil. Then, for no apparent reason, she began to shiver uncontrollably as a sense of foreboding flooded her body like a tidal wave, and then disappeared.

What did this mean?

Was this the day Anele would leave her?

Was Brianna okay?

Have the tumor cells in her brain regrouped? Have they readied for battle, prepared to shut her down for good? Forcing herself to remain calm, Shiya cocked her head sideways and frowned. *Strange,* she thought. *I can't hear the hustle and bustle of the villagers going about their daily chores.* She was about to investigate when she heard dogs barking.

"The dogs only bark like that when a stranger comes," Anele remarked, "or if they spot a leopard."

"I'll go and see what's happening," Shiya said.

Shiya couldn't believe her eyes as she approached the gate.

The snarling dogs made the advancing horses skittish, and the riders were none too pleased about entering the enclosure. Old Kelingo dismounted his brown roan and, with reins in hand, undid the gate hitch for Bryan.

Shiya greeted the old man first. "Hi, Kelingo. I was sorry to learn when I got back from Nairobi that you had returned with Captain Johannes to Durban." She finally confronted Bryan. "What brings *you* here? I don't take kindly to *white* people," she added mordantly, "and neither does *my* family."

"I had little choice but to come out here," Bryan replied coldly. "There are important matters to discuss that couldn't wait. I don't suppose many of these people surrounding us speak English, so I'll come straight to the point. My father received a telephone call from Judge Kubrick, a friend and colleague of his. It seems your unauthorized visit to Alan Hallworthy at the State Mental Institution has caused a serious problem."

With an impassive face, Shiya waited for Bryan to finish.

"Corrie Hallworthy is demanding an inquiry. It was in the news."

"What's in the news?"

"Of course, you couldn't possibly know, being stuck out here. Well, Alan Hallworthy tried to commit suicide. Corrie learned from her husband that your visit prompted his action. She blames you for his desperate state of mind."

"I wish he *had* killed himself," Shiya responded contemptuously.

Bryan's eyes sought hers. "The new district attorney is a close friend of Judge Kubrick's and my father's. My father has broken the law by repeating their conversation to me, but he is concerned about my welfare."

"I think your father should be more worried about the stuff I have on *him!* But I'll leave that alone for now. Anyway, there's no proof that I was there."

"Oh, yes, there is," Bryan replied. "The reception nurse, the male orderly, and the taxi driver have given sworn statements. With that proof in hand, Corrie has hired the best legal advice there is. Only yesterday a top prosecutor handed the affidavits over to the DA's office."

"Why are *you* so bothered about all of this? *You* didn't go to the institution. *I* did. They are after me, not you!"

"That's where you are wrong. I booked the hotel room, remember? And it won't take long for Corrie's legal team to find that out."

"Crap! You might have been followed out here."

"That should be the least of your concerns. To put your mind at rest, it's highly unlikely. I'm not stupid. I had a bush pilot drop me off on the outskirts of the game reserve. I traveled by a safari tourist truck to the border, where a prearranged horse was waiting for me."

Unconvinced, Shiya countered, "I really don't see what all the fuss is about. I simply visited my own father. That's all."

"You, of all people, should know about unauthorized visits without the court's permission," Bryan countered. "Alan is a convicted inmate, not just a patient. You, personally, are being held accountable for his suicide attempt."

"So, Counselor, where do we go from here?"

"Since I wasn't present when you decided to break the rules," he said coldly, "I can add nothing to the inquiry. If Judge Kubrick summons me to court, I will be in a very difficult situation. On the one hand, I'm bound to honor my original attorney-client privilege. On the other, I could be disbarred for withholding knowledge of your whereabouts. Surely, you can see my predicament."

"Bullshit! No judge is going to hold you in contempt if you simply say that you have no idea where I am. It's simple. No Lynette Martinez. No court case. Open and shut!"

"Lynette, I cannot in all conscience lie under oath."

"Well, what can I say, Bryan? I'm sure the cleared check will prove beyond any reasonable doubt that the retainer for your legal services was, in fact, not deposited into your law firm's account but, instead, into your personal savings account outside South Africa! How do I know that? I also have friends in high places, you asshole!"

Bryan was squirming in his riding boots. Shiya was about to make him squirm even more. "You are just going to have to brazen it out, aren't you? Otherwise, this hostile client-from-hell will turn tail."

Open-mouthed and speechless, Bryan glared at her, turned his back and mounted his horse to leave.

Shiya stopped him. "Let me put it this way. I not only can have your father prosecuted for stealing money, but I can put *you* in *his* shoes. Oh, don't look so surprised," she added as Bryan's blond eyebrows rose. "I know exactly how much you've squandered from my retainer fees. You were foolish enough to send me a *detailed* expenditure account. I think you were hoping that my tumor would rob me of discovering the false claims you've made. Some of the items you have claimed as expenses didn't happen, did they, Bryan?"

"I resent ..."

She cut him off. "I have an idea. If you want to keep your sorry ass out of jail, then this is what must be done."

Shiya outlined her plan. It was brilliant and daring and dangerous. A pasty-faced Bryan listened in abject silence. His eyes were round and unblinking. Not a muscle was twitching. He looked like a mannequin sitting on a mount. When Lynette finished, he exploded into life. "Are you bloody crazy? I'll never pull it off!"

"Yes, you will. You are one of the most cunning men that I've ever met. I hope you enjoy Switzerland, Bryan. Pack some warm clothing. It's friggin' cold there this time of the year!"

When the horse's hooves were out of her hearing range, Shiya sought the seclusion of Anele's hut. She could have kicked herself for her stupidity in going to see Alan. What was she thinking! But she had no qualms about coercing Bryan into criminal deception. If everything went according to plan, no one would end up facing a judge. And there was no doubt in her mind that her good friend, Gerda Düsseldorf, would help, without hesitation or question. She pulled a brilliant rabbit out of her hat at the last minute. But in the doing so, she'd made an enemy of the worst kind. Would Bryan betray her?

Only time would tell.

Across many oceans, Gerda, instructed by Bryan, booked the next flight to South Africa. From an airport pay phone in Durban, she contacted him on his private line. An hour later they met at a bar in a dingy part of town, and there Bryan handed over the decoys: the Martinez passport, a platinum credit card, and a cosmetics bag bulging with Swiss francs to cover expenses. Traveling on separate flights, Bryan and Gerda met again at a prearranged hotel in Switzerland. There she returned the documents and gave Bryan the canceled airline ticket she had used to enter Switzerland. She asked Bryan to give Shiya her love, and flew back to Britain using her own identity. With proof of Lynette's departure from South Africa to Switzerland, Bryan was home free, and so was his client-from-hell.

However, Bryan's client was not going to leave everything to providence. Shiya had an ace up her sleeve—a card she would play should her plan fail to throw Corrie Hallworthy's bloodhounds off her trail.

From under Anele's bed Shiya dragged out her suitcase. Beneath a section of lining, she removed Corrie's journal. Corrie had written down every sordid detail that had occurred to Shiya while she had been held captive. The notes did not leave a single felonious stone unturned. Page after page held the sequence of tragic and horrifying events, not only about Shiya, but also about Anele, the sisters Maekela and Isona, and many other nameless girls who had suffered at the hands of their tormentors throughout the years. This diary would serve to incriminate not only Lord Alan Hallworthy, but Lady Corrie, as well, should the need arise.

When Shiya had received the stolen journal many years ago, it had torn her heart to relive the past, but the handwritten entries enabled her to record in detail her childhood trauma for Brianna. Shiya glared at the journal resting in her lap. "Revenge is sweet, sayith Shiya," she whispered. She had vowed years ago that the

Hallworthys would be punished, would stand trial for their heinous acts. But she would have to wait for the outcome of her Switzerland plot. *Soon it will be all over*, she thought. *The door to my ugly past will be firmly closed.*

Shiya looked up to see Anele and Insikazi enter.

"How did the meeting go with your lawyer?" Anele asked.

"Not well, *Umama*. I'll tell you about it later, but first …"

"What do you have there?" Insikazi interrupted. "Is this a new storybook?"

"No. Good God, this is *no* storybook. This is Corrie Hallworthy's one-way ticket to hell."

Anele shuddered. That name still resurrected pain. Anele heaved a loud sigh and spoke to Insikazi. "Daughter, please leave. I wish to speak to Shiya privately."

Shiya read a few entries aloud. It was too much for the old lady. She put her hands over her ears and burst into tears. "Oh, my dear Shiya," she cried over and over. "We've both been treated so wickedly."

Mother and daughter clung to each other and wept, their tears a salve on their tragic pasts.

 # Farewell

"Say not in grief 'she is no more' but in thankfulness that she was."
–Jewish Proverb

When Bryan returned to Tswanas, he seemed a lot less tense. He was even a little friendly to Shiya when he gave her the good news. Gerda had been more than happy to help, he reported, and the plan had gone well. The District Attorney's office had dropped the case against her. Although she was relieved it was over, Shiya suddenly felt a nudge of guilt. She touched Bryan's hand. "I want you to know that I don't feel particularly glad about the precarious position I placed you and my good friend Gerda in. But I'm so relieved you're both safe. Of course, it's best we never see each other again."

"I agree," Bryan said as he remounted his horse. "I promise you that I will never betray your whereabouts to any party should a query arise in the future."

"Thanks, Bryan. No hard feelings. Okay?"

"None taken, *Mrs. Martinez.*" Bryan grinned, gave her mock salute, and, like in a scene from a Hollywood western, rode off into the sunset.

His jovial demeanor didn't fool Shiya, though. She knew by the way he had emphasized her married name that he hated her guts. She was, after all, the woman who had tried to destroy him, his father, and his family's good name. A man like Bryan would not be forgiving ever! He would seek revenge, and she would be wise to watch her back.

But for now, thank goodness, it was over.

Shiya rushed into the hut to tell Anele. "My name and passport details will be in every airport computer from here to Timbuktu, *Umama*. And until I can get a replacement, a forged one, I will have to stay here if that's okay with you. In one way it is a good thing as I don't want to give Brianna false hopes."

"Your absence will make her grow into a strong woman," Anele said. "Children shouldn't be pampered and protected by their parents. It's up to them to learn to walk a good path. If they don't, we mothers cannot be held responsible for their actions."

Shiya playfully pinched Anele's sunken cheek and said, "You are a wise old owl."

Later that day, as candlelight shadows created eerie shapes on the mud walls, Anele enjoyed the evening meal: a bowl of stewed hare accompanied with mealie meal pancakes. Shiya hardly touched her food. For some unknown reason, her stomach was in knots. She hadn't a clue why. She should be without a care right now, but the odd feeling she'd experienced some days ago rushed in again, setting her insides to shudder.

"Why aren't you eating?" Anele asked. "Is your belly upset?"

"The food is wonderful, but I don't feel hungry."

"Are you still worried about the lawyer man?"

"No. I don't know what it is that is bothering my mind." Shiya got up from the chair. "I think I'll make my red-bush tea. Maybe it'll give me an appetite."

After drinking her tea, Shiya announced, "I think it's time for my beauty sleep."

"Mine, too," Anele laughed.

Shiya shared a nightly cuddle with her mother. Normally Anele would have released a happy contented sigh, but tonight she stiffened her back and sat upright. "Shiya," she said in a soft tone, "all of a sudden a very strange feeling is flowing through my blood. I keep seeing the stonecrop flowers opening up before my eyes. I sense, dear daughter, that my time has come to leave this earth."

Shiya sighed and held the old woman tightly, as if sheltering her with her arms would keep her from leaving. "No, *Umama*," she cried. "Please don't say that."

Anele patted Shiya's hand. "Child, don't be scared. I just know that before the cock crows I will rise into the tranquility of the Invisible Kingdom, where souls are free of cumbersome gray-flesh vessels. My loved ones are waiting for me. But we will never truly be parted again. I will forever remain in spirit by your side."

Shiya's eyes began to tear. "*Umama*, I know your body is tired and your soul wishes to depart, but please don't leave me yet. Stay one more night. Okay?"

Anele did not reply.

Shiya, dreading the moment she would no longer hear Anele's raspy breath, forced herself to remain alert. She didn't want to miss a nanosecond of time with her beloved mother, but her eyelids had other plans. They grew as heavy as tombstones and closed the door to staying awake. Sleepily, she kissed Anele goodnight.

While deep in slumber, neither mother nor daughter heard the plaintive whining of the village dogs. Nor did they see the two men, wearing camouflage jackets with hoods pulled down low, stealthily enter their hut. With panther like grace, the men moved like shadows in the night past the spluttering beeswax candles sitting on an orange crate. They crept toward the bed. Captain Johannes aimed the nine-millimeter handgun, complete with silencer, and shot Anele and Shiya in cold blood at point-blank range. Then he and his black accomplice fled into the pitch black of night.

Shiya's breathing grew more and more shallow. She was barely alive.

Outside a buffeting wind began pummelling the trees and brush around the village. It swept through the compound and then entered Anele's hut. Its powerful breath lingered briefly over the injured women. Then, Ugwele, the sacred wind god of Africa, soared toward the dark heavens carrying the precious soul of Anele with him.

 The Witch Doctor's Ancient Ways

"Oh God, if there be a God, save my soul, that's if I have a soul."
–*Anonymous*

A full moon hung low on that tragic night.

In the hut next to Anele's, an aging man groaned. His internal plumbing was desperate for release, so he stepped outside to relieve himself. He noticed strange shapes lying outside Anele's hut and went to investigate. At the sight of the village dogs, white froth congealed around their rigid muzzles, Natu scratched his head. He bent and touched the neck of the pack's leader. The dog was warm to the touch, but not breathing. What's going on here? He glanced at the entrance to Anele's hut. The curtain door was missing. He found it lying in the dirt a few feet away.

The perplexed Natu poked his head into Anele's hut. The candles were extinguished, and he could barely discern the motionless shapes on the bed. He called out their names. When he received no response, he headed toward the bed and halted. His bare feet stepped in something sticky. Bringing his finger from the viscous liquid to his nose, he knew it was blood.

Natu dashed into his own hut, lit an oil lamp, and rushed back. A terrible sight greeted his eyes, and his hollering awoke the village.

Insikazi screamed in horror as she stared at the blood-drenched heads of her mother and half-sister. Who could commit such a brutal crime on defenseless women? She questioned. What kind of monster would do this? Somebody had to be very angry to do this. Who was the killer?

It wasn't long before Anele's hut was crammed with people who wanted to witness the grizzly scene. Sliman rushed in and elbowed his way to the makeshift side table where he grabbed a hand mirror. It fogged under Shiya's nose but not under Anele's, who lay huddled next to her stepdaughter in a final sleep.

"Shiya's alive. She's alive," the witch doctor repeated. "I need more light. Fetch more lamps and candles. Natu, get my medicine bag. Hurry, please!"

Natu raced to Sliman's hut.

Inside Anele's hut, women wailed.

Vimbela, in her simple innocence, leaned across and shook Anele's head. "Why do you not open your eyes, *Umama* Anele?"

Insikazi gently removed Vimbela's hand, now stained crimson with blood. "She can't open her eyes, sweet Vimbela, because our *Umama* now sleeps with the dead."

It took several moments for the realization to sink in. Then Vimbela began pounding her chest in grief. As she fled the hut, her sorrowful shrills shattered the darkness. She sunk to the ground and wailed. "Fly free now, *Umama* Anele. And my special baby, Shiya, please let the Ancient Spirit put his breath in your body. You must not die."

Back at the grizzly scene the visibly shocked Insikazi turned to Sliman. "Who could have done this terrible thing? Why would someone want to kill my mother and Shiya?"

"I don't know," Sliman replied. "But one thing I know for sure, the dogs were poisoned so the killers could get to the women."

"I am a light sleeper," Insikazi said. "I heard no dogs bark at all in the night."

"Ah! You wouldn't have. The killer knows the animals well. They do not fear him. He caused their mouths to close."

After Natu's second wife died, he sired a son in his aging years with his third wife, a teenager named Kalayonga. The nine-year-old boy, Zepsiweli, was small in stature and easily able to wriggle through the dense crowd. He sidled up to Sliman and, wearing a poker face, blurted, "I know who killed Anele and the white-faced woman."

"Explain, Zepsiweli."

"I saw the old man Kelingo and the *umlungu* man, the one who comes in the big bird that falls from the sky—"

Astonished by this allegation, Insikazi interrupted, "*Kelingo!* You are full of nonsense, boy. Why would he want to harm my mother or Shiya? He loved them."

Just then, Natu rushed in with Sliman's baboon-hide bag.

With the sharp point of a hunting knife, the witch doctor tried to determine how deep the bullet was lodged in Shiya's cranium. Feeling no metal on metal, he withdrew the knife and filled the hole with a mixture of muddy-looking ointment and ground aloe leaves. Then, with Natu holding up Shiya's head, Sliman bandaged it with long lengths of deer hide.

Gently, the men removed Shiya from the blood-spattered bed and placed her body on the dirt floor. The coldness would slow down her heart rate, the witch doctor told Natu.

Sliman squatted beside Shiya. With his knife, he cut the bag from around her neck. He spilled the sacred stones onto the dirt. They were bright turquoise. It was a great sign. Her spirit was not ready to fly away.

A burial woman touched his shoulder. "I've witnessed many deaths during my long time on earth, but none like this. I believe Zepsiweli. He speaks the truth. Kelingo is a traitor. He pretended to love his people and the woman who saved him from the white man's work."

"He belongs to the Dark Spirit now," Sliman responded. "He will squirm in the Fire God's breath for the rest of his life."

Sister Bertha pushed her way in, took one look at Shiya, and cried, "God have mercy!" With her index finger she made the sign of the cross on Shiya's forehead.

Sliman said nothing. Her gesture was touching, after all.

The nun turned to Zepsiweli. Taking the little boy's hand, she said, "Come with me. We will take the mule and go for help."

"Where are we going, Sister Bertha?"

"We will travel to the game reserve and find a white warden. Shiya is, after all, *white*."

"Is that wise, Sister Bertha?" Natu interrupted. "We will be blamed for Shiya's attempted murder. She is a *white* ..."

"No, no! No one is going to accuse us. We didn't shoot her. We have no guns here."

"You are wrong, schoolteacher," Natu argued. "The people of Tswanas might not have blasting weapons, but we will surely be marked for punishment."

Sister Bertha shook her head and sighed. No amount of reassurance would convince him otherwise. What's more, a tiny voice niggled at her: *maybe he is right.*

"Come, Zepsiweli," she said. "We have sad business to attend to."

The Sister led the boy out of the hut. He darted to the village enclosure which housed the tribe's one and only aging mule. Zepsiweli would walk alongside this animal while Sister Bertha became its passenger.

While the boy set about bringing the mule out of its stall, the nun filled a water container for them. She figured it would take about two hours to make it to the border of the game reserve and another hour to the warden's office which was situated on the northern border.

Anele's home emptied of all mourners except Sliman and Insikazi, who knelt beside her dead mother and whispered, "I know in my heart that you do not fly free. Please give me a sign that you remain earthbound?"

As though granting her plea, an eagle's feather drifted into the hut and spiraled onto the foot of the bed. The heartbroken woman picked it up, held it over her heart, and murmured, "*Umama,* your killer has not taken your spirit, only the vessel that carried you on this earth." She leaned forward and placed the feather in her mother's blood spattered hair. "I promise you, *Umama,* I will hunt down Kelingo, the snake he is, if it takes the rest of my life. I will kill him with my bare hands. I swear it to you, my beloved mother."

Insikazi joined Sliman on the floor. Wordlessly they huddled next to Shiya, wrapping their arms around her chilled body.

Sliman began chanting an ancient ritual. Insikazi squeezed her eyes shut when she saw a grotesque little manifestation climb onto Shiya's chest and breathe into her mouth.

 Winston Mandel Mandekana

"Silence is the real crime against humanity."
–Anonymous

Sixty-five year old retired crime reporter, Winston Mandela Mandekana, was a citizen of the United Kingdom. He was touring the Umfolozi Game Reserve and chatting with the warden when Sister Bertha and the boy arrived on the northern border of the reserve. Mandekana did not doubt the Sister's shocking story or her cry for help. His experience as an investigative journalist spurred him into overdrive.

Mandekana immediately instructed the game warden to inform law enforcement of the shootings. He then asked if he could borrow the Dodge truck parked outside the office.

Without hesitation, the warden handed over the keys, adding that there was a full jerrycan of gasoline in the back, should he need it.

With Sister Bertha sitting beside him, Mandekana set off in the truck for Tswanas Kraal, following Sister Bertha's directions. Trailing behind them, and obscured by the wake of the vehicle's dust, Zepsiweli sat atop the old mule. When he would arrive at the kraal was anyone's guess.

The drive to Tswanas felt short to Sister Bertha, compared to the walk and the mule ride she and the boy had undertaken to get to the reserve.

When Mandekana and Sister Bertha arrived at the kraal, law enforcement was already there. Standing behind the newly placed crime scene tape, the veteran reporter positioned his video camera, cleared his throat, and began. "Here, in Tswanas—a remote village in KwaZulu Natal, formerly Zululand—two people were reportedly victims of a brutal crime. They were shot execution style sometime in the early hours of this morning. One of the victims, Anele Dingane, a Tswanas tribeswoman believed to be in her eighties, died at the scene. The second victim, Lynette Martinez—a visitor from Canada—is alive but in critical condition ..."

A loud din overhead halted Mandekana midstream. He looked up to see an air ambulance preparing to land. How did it get there so fast?

As luck would have it, the ambulance happened to be flying over the game reserve when the game warden alerted law enforcement, who, in turn, alerted the pilot.

Mandekana waited for the dust and noise to subside before he continued reporting the information he had gleaned from a crime scene investigator.

"In a race against the clock, Martinez is being airlifted by the emergency response team's air medics and flown to Addington Hospital in Durban. As you can see behind me," the reporter moved aside so viewers could see the activity, "the man in charge of investigating these brutal crimes is Detective Pieter Marquand, a renowned CSI from the Special Crimes Bureau in Durban.

"No one knows yet what really happened here. Neither the police nor I have been able to get information from the villagers. They are uncooperative. Their silence is unclear. Baffling questions remain. Who *is* Lynette Martinez? What was she doing so far out in the desolate wilderness? Why were these women assassination targets? For now these crimes will remain a mystery. For the BBC I am

Winston Mandekana reporting live from Tswanas Kraal, KwaZulu Natal, South Africa."

CHAPTER SEVENTEEN
 Love, Hate, Guilt, and Revenge

"God is closest to those with broken hearts."
–Jewish Proverb

A continent and several time zones away, (nine hours ahead of Vancouver, Canada) Brianna, her stomach swollen as if she had swallowed a football, cuddled the best she could against Roberto's back. The mother-to-be was content.

Four hours earlier, over dinner in their favorite Japanese restaurant, Roberto had proposed and presented her with a platinum, two-carat diamond ring. "Will you marry me, Bri?"

"In a heartbeat," she had said, this time without hesitation. Why she had stubbornly refused his proposals before now was buried in her subconscious.

Roberto had leaned forward and stroked Brianna's protruding navel, which was visibly showing through her flimsy top. "You mean in two heartbeats," Roberto said playfully. Then in the same tone of voice, he scolded, "You're the most stubborn, independent person I have ever known. You should have agreed to marry me the day you found out you were pregnant." His face lit up. "Just think, in three and a half months, I'll be a dad. We will be parents."

The wide awake mother-to-be's joy was mixed with sadness and a huge dose of guilt. Tears rolled down her face because she couldn't share her happiness with her mother.

In the early days, after her anger over her mother's criminal disclosures had diminished, Brianna had thought of traveling to South Africa to find her. Roberto had squashed that idea. "South Africa is huge! It would be like searching for a needle in the proverbial haystack, Bri."

So she had moved forward with her life, not only for herself but also for the sake of her unborn child. But no matter how hard she tried, she couldn't erase the enormous *mistake* she'd made. Yes, the lawyer, Miguel (Mike) Carlos Rodriguez, had answered many of her questions, but he had also opened a dark door deep in her being, one she could never truly close.

Five months earlier, a weak February sun filtered through the lobby of the Denman Inn in downtown Vancouver. One of Mike's hands was waiting near the entrance doors, clutching a briefcase, and the other was tucked into the pocket of his gray, pinstriped suit. He sighed and checked his wristwatch: 3:15 P.M. Brianna was fifteen minutes late.

Mike, age fifty-three, had styled his long salt-and-pepper hair in a ponytail that rested on the starched collar of his immaculately pressed pale-blue shirt. Almost nervously, he scanned every female face entering and leaving the hotel lobby, awaiting his first meeting with Brianna. He had no clue what she looked like now. The last photograph Shiya had sent him was taken the day Brianna graduated from high school. In his briefcase was a courier package containing Lynette's heart-rending goodbye letter to him.

Mike and Lynette had known each other since 1974. It was a fated meeting. With her help, he had come a long way from the days he had worked as a chauffeur for Juan in Guatemala. She had funded his law studies, and he had passed the bar with honors. He had always kept in contact with her and thought of himself as her best friend. What baffled him most was why she had not confided in him. Why had she left the country without first calling him? Why?

Mike's thoughts crashed to a full stop. There was no doubt in his mind that the stunning young woman—wearing windswept, shoulder-length, black hair; a leather jacket; and chocolate-brown jeans—who was alighting from the mini-cab was none other than Brianna. He walked briskly out of the lobby door to greet her. "You must be Brianna? I'm Mike Rodriguez."

"Nice to meet you at last," Brianna smiled, returning his firm handshake. "I'm sorry for being late, but my car wouldn't start, and I had to order a cab. Let's go inside. I'm dying for a coffee."

Brianna sat opposite Mike in the hotel lounge. Sneakily, she took in Mike's Guatemalan features: dark skin tone, moon face, strong jawline, trimmed goatee, and black-coffee eyes. His Hispanic accent was sensual and reminded her of the Latino film actor, Antonio Banderas. Mike, too, was regarding the slim woman—the shimmering dark pupils, long black eyelashes, olive complexion, sturdy chin, and glossy lipstick covering full lips. Her singular flaw appeared on her lovely hands: fingernails that were bitten to the quick and as red as raspberry juice. She didn't strike him as being a nervous person, but her mother's vanishing act would be enough to cause anyone to bite their nails.

Mike had never understood Lynette's reasons for not letting her daughter know about Lionel, her biological father. In his opinion, it had been a heartless decision. Mike had gotten to know the gentle-mannered boy during the long drive back from the El Salvadoran border to Guatemala, where they met up with the woman calling herself "Lynette." He had not been surprised to learn that the couple had found each other years later and married. But keeping the truth from her daughter about the girl's biological father was beyond his comprehension. Mike had chosen never to raise the matter when he communicated with Lynette—something they did only by phone.

Mike looked at the clock on the wall. It was getting late. "I have a return flight to Seattle this evening, so we must get down to the unpleasant business at hand, I'm afraid."

Brianna, her fingers laced so tightly her knuckles turned white, watched Mike open his briefcase and place a legal-sized folder on the table. "Your mother has instructed me to handle all her affairs and relevant issues relating to you." Taking a typical lawyer's stance, he added, "Do you have any objection to my acting on her behalf?"

"Why should I? She hasn't left me much option, has she?" Brianna's tone was cool. Her mother's shocking revelations had unhinged her feelings for the parent she thought she knew. Did Mike know about the criminal admissions? Brianna harbored a suspicion that he wasn't entirely in the dark, but she had to ask, "Mike, how long have you known her?"

"I met her a long time ago. If it weren't for her, I would never have attended law school in the States or have the private practice I have now."

"She was *that* generous?"

"Yes. And I'm only one of many people your mother has helped. But I'll come to that later. I would like you to read these." He handed her some paperwork. "Please initial where I've indicated."

Brianna took her time checking over the documents that granted Mike the right to handle her mother's affairs. She initialed in the places he had marked and handed the paperwork back to him.

Mike said, "In your mother's letter to me, she deeply regrets leaving you on such short notice. She states that time is of the essence. May I assume you are now fully aware of her medical condition?"

"Yes."

"Your mother hopes her journey to the Republic of South Africa ..." he paused, unsure how much she knew. "Are you aware that your mother was born in Africa?"

"Yes."

"She also states in her letter that she has recorded certain information on tapes concerning past events. It's her wish that the tapes be handed over to me."

Brianna tossed her long hair, "Who's going to want them? The FBI, the CIA, the Mafia?

"This is not a matter to take lightly," Mike interjected. "In the wrong hands ..." He shrugged and shook his head. The answer was obvious.

"The tapes are legally mine." Brianna stated.

"Yes, I know that, but I am suggesting we use caution in this regard." He was walking a tightrope. Just how much had Shiya recorded? Had she revealed the smuggling operation? Had she named names, *his* in particular? He found himself shrugging. No. She was too smart to do anything that stupid.

But he had to make sure. "Brianna, how many tapes did your mother record?"

"I can't remember," she said glibly.

"Was I mentioned in the tapes?"

"Not really. At least I don't think so."

"Would you mind giving them to me?"

"I can't. I burned them. The stories she revealed were horrible. It made me sick to my stomach that she was subjected to and endured such atrocities.

Why didn't she tell me ... trust me? She had such courage. If only I'd known."

Mike continued to fish. "Were the tapes *just* about her childhood?"

"Yes and no. My mother didn't leave anything to the imagination."

"I'm sorry, Brianna. You may not wish to hear this at the moment." He straightened his black-and-gray striped tie. "But in the event of your mother's death ..."

Brianna's stomach lurched before she spoke. "My mother's not dead, is she, Mike?"

"Until I'm informed otherwise, your mother is still alive."

How, Brianna wondered, could she be so relieved to hear this but still be so mad at her mother at the same time? If her mother were here, she would hug her and *then* throttle her.

Mike came to the part he was sure would shock Brianna. "You will inherit in excess of $11 million U.S. when your mother dies."

"Holy catfish!" she gasped. Brianna could not have looked more shocked if she'd crammed all her fingers and toes into a live socket. Her mother had been frugal: bought a modest home in Canada, drove a plain truck, and, to Brianna's knowledge, had never once splashed money around, except for some appliances and, of course, Brianna's law studies. Most of the designer clothes her mother had left behind and rarely worn had been in her closet for as long as Brianna could recall.

Seeing her faraway look, Mike asked, "Are you okay?"

Brianna shook her head to clear her thoughts. "Just a little flabbergasted."

"In addition to the money you will inherit, there will be substantial sums from her investment accounts, and then all her personal possessions. Plus her home in Arrow Lakes Valley and the two houses she owns in Central America."

Brianna's eyebrows arched. "I didn't know Mom owned homes there. She never said anything about this on the tapes."

"She bought them for her husband's family."

"Ah, my father," Brianna sighed.

Expressionless, Mike said, "You know then?"

"Oh, yes. Did you know that Lionel was my father?"

"Yes. Again, I must stress that it was your mother's decision to keep your father a secret. Not mine."

"I can't even go and say hello at his graveside. Mother went and cremated his body and scattered the ashes. Is that correct?"

Mike crossed his fingers under the table and asked God to forgive him for the lie. "Yes. I did that for her. I laid his ashes to rest in the river where he loved to play as a child, not far from the city of Santa Ana."

Brianna, fighting angry tears, burst out, "That makes me feel friggin' great!"

Mike squirmed in the chair wishing he were anywhere else but in this uncomfortable situation. He had always been Shiya's puppet, but this time, she'd gone too far. His next words were ad lib. "It wasn't a planned love affair, Brianna. It just happened."

"I know about that. It was on the tapes."

"Then may I tell you my side of it?"

"Go ahead."

"In the summer of 1974 I picked up your mother from the Guatemala airport. She looked like a film star. She was tall and slim with long hair that shone like spun gold. The exquisite color of her emerald eyes melted me, as well my boss, Juan. We were surprised at how well she spoke our language. She was so intelligent, refreshing, and vivacious. She was absolutely delightful compared to the other foreigners we had encountered."

Brianna was tempted to let Mike know that her Spanish was just as good as her mother's, having taken it as a second language, but she kept silent.

"Juan instructed me to drive to El Salvador and collect Lionel.

This I did, not because Juan asked me to. I did it for the most cap-tivating woman I'd ever met. She risked her life to rescue a young man whose life was endangered by the political situation occurring there. Do you know anything about the war in El Salvador?"

Brianna shook her head no.

"Okay. I'll put you in the picture," Mike said. "In 1969 El Salva-dor was invaded by Honduras. Fueled by U.S. aid to the Salvadoran military, thousands of native teens were kidnapped by the soldiers and forced to enlist in the army."

"That's awful." Brianna hesitated as she thought about how much Mike must have admired her mother. "Am I reading between the lines here? Did you like my mother more than you are going to admit?"

Mike's cheeks reddened. "My dear, there wasn't a man in Gua-temala who wouldn't have fallen for your mother. I'll tell you a little secret, seeing that you are reading between the lines. Yes. I've always had a soft spot in my heart for her, but I have never told her. Lionel would have challenged me to a duel!"

"Are you married, Mike?"

"Ah," he said, noticing Brianna's eyes directed to his ring finger. "I forgot to put my ring on after my shower this morning. Yes. I've been happily married for many years. I have two wonderful sons. Alejandro is twenty-one and Ricardo is nineteen. If you like, it would be an honor for you to spend some time with me and my family."

"I would like that, but there's something I desperately need an answer to. Why did my mother not tell Lionel about me?"

Mike sighed. "After your mother's departure from Guatemala and the U.S., she sent me a large sum of money via Western Union. She wanted me to cross into the States and personally hand the cash to Lionel's sister for his upkeep. Being illegal, Lynette knew it would be tough for him to find a job. I knew she had more than a soft spot for that young man. One day I had to tell her that Lionel was engaged to an American girl whose father owned a grocery store and hired him without any questions. I remember your mother sobbing on the phone. It broke my heart. But she never stopped sending money. She even insisted on paying for his wedding. Sadly, Lionel's teenage wife died in a head-on collision only ten days after they were married. It was by pure coincidence that your mother and Lionel met up in the States."

"Can you bring me a large shot of tequila," Brianna asked a waiter passing the table.

"Sure," he replied. Then he turned to her companion, "And for you, sir?"

"I'm okay with the coffee, thank you."

Mike continued where he had left off. "Your mother was doing one of her "courier" jobs, as she liked to call them, and bumped into Lionel in Los Angeles. That was that. Having been separated once before, they were never separated again, until he died.

Tears welled in Brianna's eyes and spilled onto her cheeks. "Oh, she loved him more than she loved me."

"I doubt that. But if ever there was a true love story, this was it."

"But why on God's earth didn't my mother tell him about me."

"She was afraid of losing him. You see, even though Lionel was in love with your mother—and please forgive me for saying something so personal—she wasn't highly sexed. So she let Lionel *wander*, if you know what I mean."

"Good Lord!"

"So you see, Brianna. Your mother's deep insecurity about holding on to a much younger man was what made your mother keep your birth a secret. If she had told him about you, she believed that Lionel would have hated her and left her for another woman." Mike dug into his jacket pocket and handed Brianna an envelope. "This is the letter she was going to send to Lionel via me, when she found out she was pregnant."

"How did you get it?"

"She gave it to me for safekeeping."

Written in her mother's best handwriting was a note dated April 2, 1975, the day after she was born.

My darling Lionel,

I will be lost forever in the memory of our time together. My soul is in sorrow and my heart is in despair for a love that can never be. When the winds blow across the Scottish Highlands here in Great Britain, I will whisper your name in the hope that the wind god will carry it to your heart. Until we meet again in a world that has no mortal chains, I will see your eyes in our daughter. She is our love child. I will treasure her with all the love in the world. I will love you forever.

L

Brianna looked at Mike. "May I keep this?"

"Of course," Mike said. "I know it's not easy to do, but don't judge your mother too harshly. I know she will contact you or me. Even without her permission, I think you should know about the great family you have on Lionel's side. I'm sure they would love to meet you."

Brianna shot off her chair and flung her arms around Mike's shoulders. "You're a great guy. Thank you."

A blushing Mike rose quickly to his feet. "I have their addresses in my phonebook at home. Do you have e-mail?"

"Yes."

"Great."

Brianna scribbled her e-mail address on a paper napkin and handed it to Mike. In turn he handed her his business card. "I'll e-mail their whereabouts as soon as I get back to Seattle."

"I've missed having family, Mike. It was hard growing up as an only child, but even worse not having grandparents, uncles, and aunts."

"Your paternal grandfather, Jose Martinez, died some time ago, but your grandmother, Rosaria, is very much alive. She is a sweetheart. You are going to get on fine with her. And by the way, you have plenty of aunts. Rosaria gave birth to eight daughters, and every one of them is alive and kicking. Lionel was her only son."

"Wow!" she said. Brianna found herself staring at the handsome Mike. She downed the tequila and would forever regret her heart overruling her head.

"Mike, can you catch another flight? I've enjoyed your company, and there is still so much to talk about.

After three more drinks, she batted her lashes seductively.

At about 3 A.M. Brianna snuck back into the apartment she shared with Robert and quietly headed for the bathroom. She stood still under the cascading shower. Her tears mingled with the warm water. Feeling as if the world had stopped turning, she knew that no amount of water could erase her stupidity. *What you have done is irreparable,* her insides cried out to her.

The phone's shrill ring caused her to jump.

The bone-chilling, long-distance call would send Brianna into a downward spiral of hate, love, guilt, and revenge that would forever change her life.

 ## Brianna Arrives in South Africa

"When sorrows come, they come not single spies,
but in battalions!"
—Shakespeare, "Hamlet"

T he sun shone like a golden coin over the continent of Africa, but it was not a bright spring morning for Brianna. Her swollen eyelids were hidden under large sunglasses as she stepped onto South African soil for the first time. She had longed to visit this country: go on a safari, soak up the sun, scuba dive in crystalline waters, and try shark fishing for the first time, but now those dreams were no longer on the forefront of her mind. Her rambling thoughts dissipated when she saw a stocky man heading straight for her. He removed his black fedora. "Are you Brianna McTavish?"

"Yes, I'm Brianna."

"I am Detective Pieter Marquand. We spoke on the phone." The police official's eyes turned to the man at Brianna's side. "And you are?"

"This is my fiancé, Roberto Caldrese. Whatever you have to tell me you can say in front of him."

With an approving nod, Marquand gestured with a wave of his hand. "Follow me, please. I have a car waiting outside. We can talk on the way to the hospital."

As the car swallowed up the miles, Brianna learned in more detail the circumstances of the attempt to murder her mother and about the nun's long-distance mule trek to alert the park ranger who then radioed for help. In the detective's estimation, Shiya wouldn't be alive today if it hadn't been for the intervention of a witch doctor who had prevented further blood loss.

"Any leads as to who might have done this?" Brianna asked. "I just want to know who and why?"

"No, not yet, but I'm working on it."

"I hope you still have the death penalty here because it's important that whoever did this pays the consequences for these actions. Personally, I'd like to see them hang from the gallows." Mixed emotions of rage, anxiousness, and sorrow gripped her heart. *If I had my way, I'd see the bastards hanging by their balls!*

Marquand announced, "We're here now at Addington Hospital. Take the elevator up to the top floor. Your mother is in a private ward of the ICU unit. I've already notified my deputy that you are on your way. If you need me, here's my number," he said, handing Brianna a card. "Give me a call when it is convenient for you to talk some more. I've a couple of things I want to go over with you."

Brianna held Roberto's hand tightly and walked into the hospital.

"It's going to be okay, Sweet Pea. I'm here," he said.

Brianna took several deep breaths while fighting back tears. "Oh God, I don't know what to feel. Part of me is still angry at Mom, and the other part is breaking in half for her."

"I know, Sweet Pea, but you can do it."

The uniformed officer standing outside the emergency unit asked Brianna and Roberto for their IDs. After a brief examination, he pushed open the doors. A petite black nurse watched the pair approaching. "Are you here to see Mrs. Martinez?"

"Yes. I'm her daughter."

"I'll inform her neurosurgeon, Doctor Cohen, you are here."

In numbed horror Brianna stared at the unrecognizable woman who was her mother. She was swathed in bandages. A life-support machine beeped and intravenous plastic tubes gurgled into her nose, mouth, and arm. Even though her mother was alive, she looked to Brianna as if she were already in the first stage of rigor mortis.

Brianna rushed over to her mother's bedside and cried out, "Oh, dear God! What have they done to you?" She held her mother's limp hand and kissed it. "I'm here now, Mom. Everything is going to be all right. Please don't die. I love you with all my heart. I have wonderful news. I'm getting married. You must be at my wedding. And I have even better news. I'm twenty-three weeks pregnant. Mom, you are going to be a grandma."

Roberto stood silently at Brianna's side. No words from him could dull the pain felt by the love of his life. He slipped quietly away in search of the neurosurgeon. At the nurse's station, he asked, "Is Mrs. Martinez's doctor on his way?"

The nurse looked up from her paperwork and pointed. "He's here now."

Roberto headed toward the short man wearing a stethoscope draped around his neck. He introduced himself as a fellow physician and inquired after the patient's condition.

The surgeon's voice was soft with compassion. "It's touch and go at the moment. The next forty-eight hours are critical," he stated, handing over Shiya's medical chart.

Roberto read his commentaries and noted that the air-ambulance paramedics had to defibrillate her and that she had undergone emergency surgery to remove the bullet lodged at the base of her brain. Her head had been shaved. Her scalp had been peeled back like fruit. Her skull bone had been sawed, and a circular piece of bone had been removed—like taking the top off a boiled egg—enabling Dr. Cohen to remove the bullet. Miraculously, the projectile had lodged in a fibrous, tumor mass and had not damaged blood vessels or brain tissue. However, Roberto noted that the surgeon had not attempted to remove the carcinoma. He placed the medical notes on the counter and commented to Dr. Cohen, "It's a miracle she's still alive."

"Yes, I agree. Ironically, it was the tumor that saved her life. As you can see from my notes, it was too risky to try to remove it."

The professionals chatted about the differences in medical practices in South Africa and Canada. Then, thanking the surgeon for allowing him to check the records, Roberto returned to Brianna. He saw the lowered bed rail and found the love of his life lying on the bed with her arms wrapped around her mother. Brianna's face was wet with tears, and her hand tightly gripped the bed sheet. The sight brought a lump of pity to Roberto's throat. "You okay, Sweet Pea?"

"No, I'm not," she whispered.

Roberto pulled a chair closer to the bed, took his rosary beads from his pants' pocket, and silently began the ancient prayer *Hail Mary full of Grace.*

Brianna could only imagine what her mother would say to this: "Don't bother praying for me. I don't believe in that crap! And I'm beyond redemption!"

A nurse entered the room and scattered Brianna's thoughts when she shooed her off the bed. Brianna sat in a chair, rocking back and forth, never taking her eyes off the nurse working on her mother.

After checking her patient's vital signs, the nurse smiled at Brianna and said, "I'm told that talking helps when a loved one is in a coma. I remember one patient whose son sang to her every day for nearly two months. When she finally awoke, she said to her son, "For Pete's sake, no more! You can't sing to save *your* life, let alone mine!" That funny story prompted Brianna to smile, her first smile since arriving in South Africa.

"Well, Nurse, I can't sing, either. And even if I could, my mother hates my taste in music. She calls it 'muck.' And when she wakes up, she'd most probably—like that guy's mother did—give me an earful."

The nurse glanced at Roberto, whose fingers were thumbing through rosary beads. "That will also help," she added, and left the room.

A few minutes later a Caucasian woman holding a clipboard passed the black nurse and strode purposefully toward Brianna. "Good afternoon. I'm Mrs. Kloof, the hospital administrator. I'm told that you are the patient's daughter?"

"Yes."

Without the customary "I'm so sorry" and with pen at the ready, she said, "I would like some personal information."

"I thought Detective Marquand already did that."

"Yes. He has given me her passport details, but I need her medical information. Would you happen to know her doctor's name in Canada? What surgeries she's had? Allergies? Infections? Inoculations? Blood disorders?"

Brianna answered, "As far as I'm aware, my mother never had a day's illness until she was diagnosed with a brain tumor. I don't even know the name of her doctor. But I'm sure you can find it through the Internet."

"No childhood ailments?"

"Not that I know off."

"The reason I ask is that there is some severe vaginal scarring and long-healed bone fractures. Do you know how they came about?"

"I've no idea," Brianna answered glibly.

The woman's next question was to be expected. "Who is going to pay for her private care?"

"My mother's lawyer, Mike Rodriguez, is on his way here to South Africa. He will sort it out. This hospital does not have to worry about not being paid. My mother could most probably buy the place."

The poker-faced administrator left the room.

"Gee, Bri. You put that nicely," Roberto said with a ring of laughter in his voice.

The couple held hands and gazed out at the sea from the high rise hospital building.

Day turned into night.

Roberto encouraged Brianna to return to the hotel. It had been a long flight for both of them, and he pointed out that she and the baby needed rest.

Brianna wouldn't budge. "What if Mom dies while I'm gone? I'd never forgive myself. No. I'm staying put. You go, Roberto. Ask someone at the nursing station to call you a cab. Go to the hotel, and, if all goes well here, I'll join you later."

"Are you sure, Sweet Pea? I don't want to leave you, but I could eat a horse and go back for the rider, and then sleep for a year!"

"Off you go for that *delicious* meal. I'll catch you later."

"Would you like me to ask if there's a cafeteria here? I could go and get you a snack."

"I'm not hungry. Go now. I love you."

"I love you, too."

When she was alone with her mother, Brianna placed her warm hand against her mother's cold cheek. With steely resolve she whispered close to her mother's ear, "Mom, I'll find whoever did this to you and make them pay. I promise you that. I want you to know that you are my hero. I love you so much and can't bear the thought of never seeing you smile, hearing your laughter, or watching your beautiful green eyes sparkle with life. Mom ..."

For an instant Brianna thought she saw a facial tick, an eyelid flicker. Hope and joy overtook her. She studied her mother's face, looking, waiting ...

Her mother remained still and silent.

After midnight, jet lag overtook Brianna's exhausted body and mind. She climbed into the bed next to her mother. She didn't even feel the baby pedaling a bicycle across her womb, or feel the discomfort of burning heartburn rising in her esophagus. In a sleepy dream fog, she tried to visualize the face of her mother's attempted assassin. Was he white? Was he African? Was he ...

Brianna was rudely wakened by a poke to her arm. "It's against hospital rules for a visitor to get into bed with a patient," the night nurse said. "And I have to turn Mrs. Martinez over and change her dressings. You can wait outside, and we'll let you know when we are done."

"Do you have a spare cot to put in my mother's room? I don't want to leave her."

"No. That's against hospital rules."

"This would never happen in Canada," Brianna mumbled. She kissed her mother on the forehead and whispered "Goodbye, Mom. I'm going to the hotel. I'll be back in a little while. Hang in there. I love you, and don't you forget that."

Once outside, she inhaled deeply the cool night air, and then got into a taxi. "To the Edward Hotel, please."

She found Roberto snoring softly in the dark hotel room. She spotted a note propped against the bedside lamp: "Wake me up when you get back. Love you lots, my brave girl. Your Teddy Bear, Rob xxxxxx"

Brianna quietly undressed and climbed into bed beside him.

Roberto was out so deeply that he didn't feel her warm, naked body pressed against his back. She sighed. She craved that touchy-feely magic he was so good at. Sex would distract her from thinking about the hospital scene and what could lie ahead.

But that wasn't going to happen.

As soon as Brianna's head touched the soft pillow, she, too, was out flat. Neither of them heard the phone ringing in the other room.

Loud knocking woke up the pair in the morning.

Brianna glanced at the clock. "It's seven o'clock," she gasped. *Who could it be? Oh, God. I hope it's not bad news.*

She grabbed a white robe from the bathroom and rushed to the door while Roberto slipped into the shower.

Detective Marquand looked unforgivingly chipper for the hour. He noted her makeup-streaked face and tousled hair, and he apologized. "I'm sorry to disturb you, but we need to talk."

"It's all right. Come in," Brianna said, gesturing for him to take a seat. "Give me a moment, please. I just want to make a quick call to the hospital to see how my mother is doing."

She slipped into the bedroom to use the phone. The voice on the other end of the line informed her, "No change, I'm afraid."

"I'll be there as soon as I can."

On her way back to the detective, she caught a glimpse of herself in a wall mirror. *Oh, my God! I'm a mess!* She did a quick hand-comb through her tangled locks and straightened her robe.

"I'm sorry to have kept you waiting, Detective."

"How is your mother?"

"She's stable, but no change."

They sat opposite each other. Brianna couldn't help but notice his smug expression.

"I have some good news for you," he announced. "The interior police have an old black man in custody in connection with the shootings. He's singing like a bird."

"An *old* black man tried to kill my mother! Good Lord, why?"

"It seems that your mother created some powerful enemies during her short stay here. As I speak, a South African lawyer, Bryan Duval, whom your mother hired, and Captain Johannes de Klerk, the helicopter pilot who flew her to Tswanas in February of this year, have been taken into custody. The biggest surprise to all of us is that Lady Corrie Hallworthy, a social hotshot in these parts, has also been detained. They are all being charged with second-degree murder and attempted murder."

It took a split second for the name to sink in. "Corrie Hallworthy!" she shouted.

Marquand's eyes squinted suspiciously. "Do you know Lady Hallworthy?"

"I don't know her personally, but I have heard the name."

Peter's detective brain slipped into gear. "You need to explain."

"There's nothing to explain. I think I heard my mother mention her name once; that's all."

The detective's gut told him she was lying. "From Kelingo, the black man in our custody, we were able to deduce that it was Lady Hallworthy who arranged the shootings of both your mother and Anele Dingane."

"Why?"

"At the crime scene I found some journals belonging to Lady Hallworthy hidden in your mother's suitcase. How these diaries came to be in your mother's possession is a mystery. But I will tell you this, your mother paid Lord Alan Hallworthy an unauthorized visit at the mental institution where he is still incarcerated for the murder of a black prostitute many years back. It is my belief that when Lady Hallworthy found out, she blew her top ... because ... I don't know how to put this delicately ... apparently, from what I've read, your mother is Alan Hallworthy's illegitimate daughter."

Brianna, feigning surprise, blurted, "You've got to be kidding me! She told me her parents were dead!" She thought, *In a way, I'm telling the truth.*

"No, I don't think so. I ordered DNA tests on both Lord Alan and your mother, and I can say one hundred percent that she *is* his offspring."

Brianna's mind began reeling, and her stomach churned. Had that scurrilous Corrie written *all* the sordid details of her sick husband's appetite for young girls—including his own daughter? Brianna had learned through her studies that disturbed individuals—such as Corrie, who was probably a sociopath—often felt the need to document ghastly criminal behavior.

There was no doubt in her mind that Pieter Marquand now knew everything there was to know about her mother. As did she, but Brianna was not going to let on at this stage.

"I believe Lady Hallworthy hired the lawyer to get the job done," Marquand said. "But I also believe he got cold feet. According to Kelingo, Durval promised him and the helicopter pilot big bucks to carry out the executions. I'm pleased to say that less than an hour ago Bryan Durval was apprehended at Durban airport with a bag of cash and a one-way ticket to Switzerland."

An angry bull facing a matador could not have snorted with more derision. Brianna spat, "I hope they get the electric chair! But then even that is too good for those scumbags!"

Marquand didn't comment. Instead, he rose from his seat and said, "I have to go. I have a meeting with the DA. I'll keep you informed, Counselor," he said respectfully, even though he was aware she'd not yet sat for her final law exams. And he ended with sincerity,, "I hope your visit with your mother goes well."

"Thanks, Detective."

Brianna left for the hospital, leaving Roberto behind. Her reasoning? She wanted to be alone with her mother to tell her the good news. But the news had traveled faster than the taxi. The whole thing was a circus. Thronging the hospital was a mob of reporters, recorders, and cameras.

One journalist thrust a tape recorder inches from Brianna's mouth. "Miss McTavish, how do you feel about Lord and Lady Hallworthy being involved in the shooting of your mother and the death of her companion?"

"Will you be attending their trial?"

"What's your mother's condition?"

"Is she still comatose? Do you expect her to live?"

Brianna shoved her way past the horde the best she could. She pushed microphones out of her face and answered every question with a stern "No comment!"

Brianna was more than relieved when two burly security men rushed to her side. Using their bodies as shields, they helped move her past the frenzied journalists and the tape recorders that threatened to dislocate her jaw.

Brianna fled to the elevator.

In the hospital room the curtains were open and the morning sunshine was falling warmly on her mother's ashen face. Brianna went up to the cot and kissed her mother's clammy forehead. With elation, Brianna told her mother, "I've got good news. They got the buggers! You *have* to get well now. Don't you want to see them fry, Mom?"

Shiya remained unresponsive.

Brianna began singing an Irish lullaby—one her mother had crooned to her when she was a child. Brianna's tone-deaf rendition brought wincing from the nursing staff. Then a fully cloaked visitor entered the room. "Hello," she smiled, extending her hand to

Brianna. "My name is Sister Bertha. I've heard so much about you. I also loved your mother."

At long last, the blank spaces in her mother's life filled as the nun answered Brianna's many questions. Bertha ended with, "I'd like you to have this." She removed from her habit the same little crucifix she had once offered to Shiya. The nun said, "Pray for her, my child. Shiya is much loved by the people of Tswanas. They miss her dreadfully. There is someone special I'd like you to meet, the man who saved your mother's life." Bertha beckoned for Sliman to enter.

Brianna nearly winded the witch doctor with her hug. "I don't know how to thank you. You are my hero."

A broad smile crossed his mouth. With tears rimming his dark eyes, Sliman approached the bed, kissed Shiya on her lips, and whispered how much he missed her company, laughter, and feisty spirit. He talked of the loss he felt in his heart without her. There was no doubt, Sliman had fallen in love. He turned from Shiya to face Brianna. He took hold of her hands. Instantly, Brianna felt a tingling sensation, one she wasn't sure she liked. Quickly, she withdrew her hands.

Sliman looked into Brianna's eyes and said, "I would like to try something if it's agreeable to you?"

"Try? What?"

"It is not conventional medicine, so to speak."

"If it will help my mother regain consciousness, go ahead."

"I would like you all to leave the room."

"No way!" she protested. "I'm staying put."

The nun peered over the rim of her bifocals. She gave the witch doctor a disapproving look, but she nodded in compliance and left.

An icy shiver of uncertainty now ran through Brianna. Hugging her chest she watched Sliman remove a pouch from around his neck and empty a pile of stones onto the bed. The turquoise stones glistened under the neon lighting. One by one he picked them up and placed each stone strategically around Lynette's body. Then he rested his hands on top of her bandaged head, and began low chanting. Brianna swore she could feel the psychic vibrations.

After some inaudible Zulu incantations, Sliman spoke in English. "Shiya of Tswanas, feel the hands of the Great Spirit enter your broken body. Feel the warmth. Feel the love. Feel the healing. Open your eyes and come back to those who love you. Your time is not up on the mortal plateau. You must fight the hands that try to pull you into the place where evil spirits live. Your will to live is strong. I know this, because I have I seen it. Open your eyes, wild child of Mother Earth's creations."

He waited.

"Shiya, I know you can hear me. Your daughter is here. She is crying for her mother. An invisible umbilical cord ties you two together in this life and the next. If not for yourself, come back to earth for your beautiful daughter."

Nothing.

Brianna sighed. "I don't think my mother wants to live, Sliman. You see, I believe she wants to be with my father. She loved him more than me."

"No, sad child of Shiya," Sliman returned. "Your mother's love encompasses all. She no longer resides beside a silent ocean of sorrow."

Brianna gasped as the window flew open and a vagrant eddy whipped the sheets. A strand of Brianna's hair freed itself from her scalp, flew toward the bed, and flicked Shiya's face. Shiya's ashen pallor drained and was replenished by a healthy flush. Glued to her seat, Brianna's mouth fell open. She could not believe what her eyes were seeing. Was she actually witnessing a supernatural event?

Shiya's eyelids opened, and her sparkling emerald eyes stared at Brianna. The daughter stifled a scream of joy by clamping her hands tightly over her mouth. It was true! Her mother's eyes were searching, looking for something recognizable.

"*Mom!*" Brianna's ecstatic shout echoed throughout the room.

"My precious daughter, is it really you?" Shiya spoke nasally, the tubes in her throat and nose interfering with her speech. She looked at the IV in her hand, then at the bed, and then at the monitoring apparatus. "Why am I in the hospital? Did I fall or something?"

"Mom," Brianna almost laughed, "you didn't fall. You were shot."

Shiya looked at her daughter with disbelief. "Shot! Why? By whom? Where's my Anele."

A black nurse barged through the door and ended the questioning. "Mrs. Martinez, you are awake! I'll go and get the doctor." She turned and bustled away.

It was Sliman who broke the sad news about Anele.

Shiya's sobbing could be heard throughout the ICU.

Dr. Cohen entered the room, and before he could say a word, Shiya grabbed his white coat. "Take these blasted drips out," she demanded. "I've got to go home to Tswanas. My mother is dead. I have to see her before they put her in the ground."

"Mrs. Martinez," the neurosurgeon cautioned, "you are not in a fit state to leave this hospital. You have had a severe injury to the head ..."

"I know my rights," she argued. "Bring me the patient release form. I'll sign the darn thing, and that will get you off the medical hook. Okay?"

Brianna could have shriveled into a ball but chose, instead, to defend the doctor. "Mom, don't be stupid. The doctor is right. Get well first. Roberto and I will take you to Tswanas. You can put flowers on her grave."

The sour-faced doctor stomped out of the room.

"Who's Roberto?" Shiya asked.

"He is the man I am engaged to. He flew here with me. He's a great guy, Mom. You'll love him."

"You never told me about him."

"I met him the day after my *father* died," Brianna emphasized the word.

Shiya looked deep into her daughter's tearful eyes. "Oh, Brianna, I can't begin to tell you how sorry I am. I do hope that you will not hold it against me for the rest of your life."

"No, Mother. And I know that this is not the right time and place to discuss this, but I will never hold anything against you, especially after what I heard on the tapes. I understand now that you did what you had to do."

Shiya sighed with relief and then reverted back to her old self. With her eyes resting on Brianna's stomach, she blurted, "By the look of things, you should have a husband, not a fiancé. You look ready to drop."

"I've another three and a half months to go."

"Then you have definitely been eating for two," was Shiya's insensitive remark.

Brianna didn't bite back, though. A recent weighing had confirmed that she had gained more than twenty-five pounds, and she felt certain her crazy hormone imbalance was going to increase before the day was out.

Shiya released a noisy sigh of defiance. "Wild horses can't keep me from seeing Anele laid to rest. I owe her that much. Are you going to help me to get out of this hospital, or not?"

It was Brianna's turn to sigh, but with resignation. "I suppose I have to put myself in your shoes. What would I do? I'd probably do the same. Okay, Mom. I'll countersign the release forms. But I'd like you to come back with me to the hotel and rest while I make all the arrangements. Promise?" she demanded, wagging her finger like a scolding parent.

Shiya smiled. "I love you, Brianna. And I *am* thrilled! But I can't think at this moment."

"I love you, too, Mother. More than you will ever know. But if anything happens to you while you're in my care, I'll never forgive myself. And I'm not going to lose you a second time."

"Nothing is going to happen to me. I've never felt healthier. And I know who I can thank for that."

Shiya winked at Sliman.

"You are no longer a doubtful woman, I see," he laughed. "I'm glad to hear that. The art of black magic is a gift from the spirit world."

Sister Bertha, who had silently entered the room, shot Sliman a disdainful "you-are-a-heathen" look, but she said nothing. It was remarkable to Brianna that a black magician and a servant of Christian beliefs were standing side by side in this room. But she had long ago learned that fact is stranger than fiction.

The nun and the seer said goodbye to the mother and daughter. They had many buses to catch on their way back to Tswanas. Shiya offered to fly them back as soon as she could make a telephone call, but Sister Bertha spoke for Sliman and herself when she said, "We have our tickets and we must leave now."

"I hope Anele hasn't been buried already." Shiya said.

"No," Sliman replied. "I told the burial women to keep her earth vessel preserved until you could make it back to Tswanas."

"You were awfully confident, weren't you? But then, why am I surprised."

"See you in Tswanas, lovely lady." Sliman said. "We will celebrate Anele's passing with singing, dancing, and good beer."

"God willing," the nun responded.

After they left, Shiya turned to her daughter, whose eyes had flown like darts between Sliman, the nun, and her mother. "Now, bonnie lass," Shiya said, "it's time to make a move. Go and get the release forms from the not-so-happy doctor … get the nurse to remove these bloody tubes … pay the hospital bill. And please go and buy me some decent clothes at the nearest shop." Shiya sat upright and finished, "Let's get the hell out of Dodge! I have a party to go to!"

## CHAPTER NINETEEN

Anele's Funeral

"Oh what pain it is to part."
–*John Gray*

Monsoon rain clouds hung low over Tswanas on the day of Anele's funeral.

Six strong tribesmen hoisted the makeshift coffin, fashioned from the wood of gum trees, onto their shoulders. With their bare feet shuffling, they began the slow walk up the mountainside to the tribe's sacred burial site. Following in the pallbearers' wake, with African drums strapped to their waists, young boys pounded out a traditional tune for the dead.

As if attending a celebrity's burial, many villagers followed: Father Samuel, Sister Bertha, relatives of the murdered girl Naomi, former fieldworkers and servants from the Hallworthy estate, and, of course, the Tswanas tribe, and people from the neighboring Mtunzini Township.

Also in attendance were media from Canada, Great Britain, and South Africa, their digital cameras and video recording devices working overtime.

Winston Mandekana, the first to break the news of the shootings, was among them. The day he had bagged the story, he had used the oldest trick in the book to get it. He had lied. "I was born in Mtunzini, your neighboring village. I am one of you," he had proclaimed to the Tswanas villagers. "You can trust me. The white woman, what was she doing here? How is she connected to the dead woman, Anele Dingane?"

The naïve tribe gave him what he wanted.

His wired story was breaking news in London, England. The August edition of the *Mail on Sundays* headline read as follows:

```
African Woman Is Murdered for
  Saving the Life of a White
         Baby in 1945
      By Winston Mandekana

Lord Alan Hallworthy of South Africa
(a direct descendant of the deceased
Lord Nigel Hallworthy, a cousin of
Queen  Victoria)  and  Lord  Alan's
wife, Lady Corrie Hallworthy, have
both been named as persons of inter-
est  in  this  case  …  The  funeral  for
Anele  Dingane,  a  blood  relative  of
the Zulu King Dingane …
```

After the news release, the newspaper editor's office had been inundated with readers asking for a follow-up on this breaking story. The editor placed a cell phone call to Winston. "Get me everything you can," he ordered.

Winston responded that that would be nearly impossible. He couldn't get anywhere near the woman who survived this tragedy. She was flanked by Detective Marquand and several policemen at all times. He could only report what he was witnessing.

He saw Shiya and Brianna holding hands. They walked silently and unbothered between armed officers. The fuming reporters were held at bay with threats. They all had to tell their stories from a distance, through ultra-zoom video and digital cameras.

At the burial site the incessant hum of mosquitoes and other biting insects was soporific. Shiya was oblivious to the nasty pests attacking everyone's exposed flesh. Groggy from pain medication, she tried to focus on the coffin resting in the dirt below. She reached into the pocket of her black, full-length dress and pulled out a folded piece of paper. It was a poem she had written the day after she and Anele had returned from the sacred rock—the day the rare flower blossomed.

Shiya, with tears blinding her eyes and sorrow choking her throat, swallowed and then read what she'd written in English.

I tread the misty stairs, where there is no such word
    as "time."
We can all be together there. I know we will be fine.
And under stars unfurled, will echo out our laughter.
Mother dearest, Umama Anele, we will be as one in
    this world.
Rejoined in the thereafter.
I love you.
But I won't miss you because you will be forever
    locked in my beating heart.
So until we meet again in the Invisible Kingdom of
    Souls, you'll remain in my heart, dear Mother.

Sister Bertha translated for those who couldn't understand the English language. Dark faces beamed with appreciation for Shiya's poignant sentiments.

"Thank you, Sister," Shiya said.

"My pleas- ..."

The nun pointed, her mouth agape.

Brianna jumped back. "Oh, my God!" she shrieked. "I hope it's not dangerous?"

Before her eyes, undulating side-to-side, was the most dangerous and feared arboreal snake in Africa. It slithered out of the thick brush. The fast-moving, black mamba was highly venomous. Its 1.8-meter length continued to slither their way.

Detective Marquand drew his pistol from its holder. Shiya blocked his aim with her hand. "Put your gun away," she ordered. "He's not going to harm anyone. He has come to see me." Shiya turned away from the detective's "are-you-nuts" stare and calmly walked over to the snake, which was hissing loudly. She bent low, lifted the slender snake to her chest, whispered something to it, and then dropped it onto the coffin lid. The mamba disappeared under the wildflower wreath adorning the coffin.

Brianna verbalized what the detective was thinking. "Holy shit!" she shrieked. "Are you crazy, Mother? That thing could have killed you!"

"No, it wouldn't have. You don't understand, Brianna. Snakes and I are one."

"Now you're talking daft, Mom."

Sliman, standing to the left of Shiya, just smiled. But the biggest smile came from the mentally-challenged Vimbela. "Most beautiful daughter of Anele, *she* has heard your words. She will always be with you. See?" Vimbela pointed to the wreath. "*Umama* Anele sent you the black snake."

All heads turned at the sound of loud wailing.

There, standing behind the reporters, stood a tall, slim female wearing a heavy veil, long black dress, and gloves. She was flanked by what can only be described as beefy, foreign-looking bodyguards. She was sobbing uncontrollably.

"Who the hell is she?" Shiya asked Vimbela.

"I don't know, but she's not one of us. We don't wear such awful clothes."

Since no one seemed to know the woman's identity, Shiya walked away from the grave site and, with Brianna and the police officers following behind, she approached the woman ... who immediately turned to flee. Shiya grabbed her arm. "Excuse me. I don't want to sound rude, but who are you? Obviously you know Anele or you wouldn't be here."

The woman didn't reply. But Shiya could feel her piercing glare going right through her body.

"Who are you? Do I know you?" Shiya asked again.

A muffled voice replied, "I should be in that grave, not her."

"Good Lord! What on earth do you mean?"

"If it weren't for me, she wouldn't be lying in the cold earth."

"Now you've lost me."

"She not only saved you ... she once saved me."

"What the heck are you talking about? Who the *hell* are you?"

"I'm Maria, your *real* mother."

The woman's words didn't register in Shiya's fuzzy brain. "I'm sorry. What did you say?"

"My name is Maria Picasso Genovese. I'm your biological mother."

An overpowering emotion Shiya had never experienced before gripped her heart. She felt her legs give way.

Maria held her unconscious daughter in her arms for the first time. "I'm taking you home to Sicily. That's where we both belong."

"Over my dead body," Brianna hissed like a snake before she forcibly untangled Maria's arms from around Shiya. When she saw Maria's goons make a move, Brianna spat, "Don't even think about it! Just get here out of here before I yell for the cops." Oh, how she wanted to inform the tribe that it was *this* woman who had started the ugly ball rolling in 1945. None of these tragic events would have occurred if she hadn't discarded her child like an unwanted mattress. At this moment, Brianna would have happily watched the crowd stone the woman to death.

The whirring of rotor blades, Maria's aircraft taking off, was music to Brianna's ears.

In a twist of fate, the reverberating sound of a helicopter's rotor blades would be painfully resurrected in the not too distant future.

What comes around does, indeed, seem to go around.

 # Afterword

Diabolical slavery still thrives
after the 150ᵗʰ anniversary
of the Emancipation Proclamation

On September 22, 1862, in the United States of America, President Abraham Lincoln set the date of *freedom* for his country's three million slaves. The opening statement of the Declaration of Independence of 1776 reads:

"We believe these truths to be self-evident: that all men are created equal with the right to life, liberty, and the pursuit of happiness."

In 1865, almost 100 years after the Declaration of Independence, the Thirteenth Amendment extended this sentiment to "Negroes."

To this day, involuntary servitude is outlawed, and yet, *it still exists!* ***Why?***

"In its many dark forms, slavery did not die when America abolished it in the 1800s and Great Britain in 1834," says Lucia

Mann, author of *Beside an Ocean of Sorrow*, *Rented Silence*, *Africa's Unfinished Symphony*, and *A Veil of Blood Hangs over Africa*, the final book in the series. Mann's books are historical, African-set novels that explore British Colonial slavery in South Africa and the victims who survived the institutional brutality before and after abolishment.

According to the United Nations, there are more than 37 million slaves worldwide, a number that represents more than twice the number of those who were enslaved over the 400 years that transatlantic slavers trafficked humans to work in the Americas. *Why?*

"Today, many slaves are forced into prostitution while others are used as unpaid laborers to manufacture goods bought in the United States, Canada, and globally," Mann says. "It's almost impossible to buy clothes or goods anymore without inadvertently supporting the slave trade." *Why?*

Fifty-five ghastly, sobering, little-known facts about modern day slavery/human trafficking

1. Approximately seventy-five to eighty percent of human trafficking is for sex.

2. Researchers note that sex trafficking plays a major role in the spread of HIV.

3. There are more human slaves in the world today than ever before in history.

4. There are an estimated 27 million adults and 13 million children around the world who are victims of human trafficking.

5. Human trafficking not only involves sex and labor, but also organ harvesting.

6. Human traffickers often use a Sudanese phrase "use a slave to catch slaves," meaning traffickers send "broken-in girls" to recruit younger girls into the sex trade. Sex traffickers often train girls themselves, raping them and teaching them sex acts.

7. Eighty percent of North Koreans who escape into China are women. Nine out of ten of those women become victims of human trafficking, often for sex. If the women complain, they are deported back to North Korea, where they are thrown into gulags or executed.

8. An estimated 30,000 victims of sex trafficking die each year from abuse, disease, torture, and neglect. Eighty percent of those sold into sexual slavery are under twenty-four years old, and some are as young as six.

9. Ludwig "Tarzan" Fainberg, a convicted trafficker, said, "You can buy a woman for $10,000 and make your money back in a week if she is pretty and young. Then everything else is profit."

10. A human trafficker can earn twenty times what he or she paid for a girl. Provided the girl was not physically brutalized to the point of ruining her beauty, the pimp can sell her again for a greater price because he has already trained her and broken her spirit. This saves the future buyers the hassle. A 2003 study in the Netherlands found that, on average, a single sex slave earned her pimp at least $250,000 a year.

11. Although human trafficking is often a hidden crime and accurate statistics are difficult to obtain, researchers estimate that more than 80 percent of trafficking victims are female. Over fifty percent of human trafficking victims are children.

12. The end of the Cold War has resulted in the growth of regional conflicts and the decline of borders. Many rebel groups turn to human trafficking to fund military actions and garner soldiers.

13. According to a 2009 Washington Times article, the Taliban buys children as young as seven years old to act as suicide bombers. The price for a child suicide bomber ranges between $7,000 to $14,000.

14. UNICEF estimates that 300,000 children younger than 18 are currently trafficked to serve in armed conflicts worldwide.

15. Human traffickers are increasingly trafficking pregnant women for their newborns. Babies are sold on the black market, where the profit is divided between the traffickers, doctors, solicitors, border officials, and others. The mother is usually paid less than what is promised her, citing the cost of travel and the creation of false documents. A mother might receive as little as a few hundred dollars for her baby.

16. More than 30 percent of all trafficking cases in 2007 to 2008 involved children sold into the sex industry.

17. Western presence in Kosovo, such as NATO troops and civilians, has fueled the rapid growth of sex trafficking and forced prostitution. Amnesty International has reported that NATO soldiers, UN police, and Western aid workers "operated with near impunity in exploiting the victims of the sex traffickers."

18. Lady Gaga's *Bad Romance* video is about human trafficking. In the video, Gaga is trafficked by a Russian bathhouse into sex slavery.

19. Human trafficking is the only part of transnational crime in which women are significantly represented—as victims, as perpetrators, and as activists fighting this crime.

20. Global warming and severe natural disasters have left millions homeless and impoverished, which has created desperate people who are easily exploited by human traffickers.

21. Over 71 percent of trafficked children show suicidal tendencies.

22. After sex, the most common form of human trafficking is forced labor. Researchers argue that as the economic crisis deepens, the number of people trafficked for forced labor will increase.

23. Most human trafficking in the United States occurs in New York, California, and Florida.

24. According to United Nations Children's Fund (UNICEF), over the past 30 years, over 30 million children have been sexually exploited through human trafficking.

25. Several countries rank high as source countries for human trafficking, including Belarus, the Republic of Moldova, the Russian Federation, Ukraine, Albania, Bulgaria, Lithuania, Romania, China, Thailand, and Nigeria.

26. Belgium, Germany, Greece, Israel, Italy, Japan, the Netherlands, Thailand, Turkey, and the U.S. are ranked very high as destination countries of trafficked victims.

27. Women are trafficked to the U.S. largely to work in the sex industry (including strip clubs, peep and touch shows, massage parlors that offer sexual services, and prostitution). They are also trafficked to work in sweatshops, domestic servitude, and agricultural work.

28. Sex traffickers use a variety of ways to "condition" their victims, including subjecting them to starvation, rape, gang rape, physical abuse, beating, confinement, threats of violence toward the victim and victim's family, forced drug use, and shame.

29. Family members will often sell children and other family members into slavery; the younger the victim, the more money the trafficker receives. For example, a ten-year-old named Gita was sold into a brothel by her aunt. The now twenty-two-year-old recalls that when she refused to work, the older girls held her down and stuck a piece of cloth in her mouth so no one would hear her scream as she was raped by a customer. She later contracted HIV.

30. Human trafficking is one of the fastest growing criminal enterprises because it holds relatively low risk and high profit potential. Criminal organizations are increasingly attracted to human trafficking because, unlike drugs, humans can be sold repeatedly.

31. Human trafficking is estimated to surpass the drug trade in less than five years. Journalist Victor Malarek reports that it is primarily men who are driving human trafficking, specifically trafficking for sex.

32. Victims of human trafficking suffer devastating physical and psychological harm. However, due to language barriers, lack of knowledge about available services, and the frequency with which traffickers move victims, human trafficking victims and their perpetrators are difficult to catch.

33. In approximately 54 percent of human trafficking cases, the recruiter is a stranger, and in 46 percent of the cases, the recruiters know the victim. Fifty-two percent of human trafficking recruiters are men, 42 percent are women, and 6 percent are both men and women.

34. Human trafficking around the globe is estimated to generate a profit of anywhere from $9 billion to $31.6 billion. Half of these profits are made in industrialized countries.

35. Some human traffickers recruit handicapped young girls, such as those suffering from Down syndrome, into the sex industry.

36. According to the FBI, a large human-trafficking organization in California in 2008 not only physically threatened and beat girls as young as twelve to work as prostitutes, they also regularly threatened them with witchcraft.

37. Human trafficking is a global phenomenon that is fueled by poverty and gender discrimination.

38. Human traffickers often work with corrupt government officials to obtain travel documents and seize passports.

39. Women and girls from racial minorities in the U.S. are disproportionately recruited by sex traffickers in the U.S.

40. *The Sunday Telegraph* in the U.K. reports that hundreds of children as young as six are brought to the U.K. as slaves each year.

41. Japan is considered the largest market for Asian women trafficked for sex.

42. Airports are often used by human traffickers to hold "slave auctions," where women and children are sold into prostitution.

43. Due to globalization, every continent in the world has been involved in human trafficking, including a country as small as Iceland.

44. Many times, if a sex slave is arrested, she is imprisoned while her trafficker is able to buy his way out of trouble.

45. Today, slaves are cheaper than they have ever been in history. The population explosion has created a great supply of workers, and globalization has created people who are vulnerable and easily enslaved.

46. Human trafficking and smuggling are similar but not interchangeable. Smuggling is transportation based. Trafficking is exploitation based.

47. Sex traffickers often recruit children because not only are children more unsuspecting and vulnerable than adults, but there is a high market demand for young victims. Traffickers target victims on the telephone, on the Internet, through friends, at the mall, and in after-school programs.

48. Human trafficking has been reported in all fifty states, Washington, D.C., and in some U.S. territories.

49. The FBI estimates that over 100,000 children and young women are trafficked in America today. They range in age from nine to nineteen, with the average age being eleven. Many victims are not just runaways or abandoned, but are from "good" families who are coerced by clever traffickers.

50. Brazil and Thailand are generally considered to have the worst child sex trafficking records.

51. The AIDS epidemic in Africa has left many children orphaned, making them especially vulnerable to human trafficking.

52. Nearly 7,000 Nepali girls as young as nine years old are sold every year into India's red-light district—or 200,000 in the last decade. Ten thousand children between the ages of six and fourteen are in Sri Lanka brothels.

53. Human trafficking victims face physical risks, such as drug and alcohol addiction, STDs, sterility, miscarriages, forced abortions, and vaginal and anal trauma, among others. Psychological effects include clinical depression, personality and dissociative disorders, suicidal tendencies, PTSD, and Complex PTSD.

54. The largest human trafficking case in recent U.S. history occurred in Hawaii in 2010. Global Horizons Manpower, Inc., a labor-recruiting company, bought 400 immigrants in 2004 from Thailand to work on farms in Hawaii. They were lured with false promises of high-paying farm work, but instead their passports were taken away and they were held in forced servitude until they were rescued in 2010.

55. According to the U.S. State Department, human trafficking is one of the greatest human rights challenges of this century, both in the United States and around the world.

Millions of Modern Day Slaves Need Our Advocacy

If we fail to address this plague of crimes against humanity, we'll never be able to bring an end to the unconscionable, heinous trade in human flesh.

WHAT CAN WE DO IF WE SUSPECT A
CASE OF HUMAN TRAFFICKING?

- **Catholic Sisters congregations:** (888) 373-7888.

- **Victims hotline and online tips reporting:** The *Modern Day Slavery Reporting Center*, created by Mann, is a Web site that makes it easy for third parties to report suspicious activity by clicking "File a Report." This section allows visitors to volunteer information. www.ReportModernDaySlavery.org

- **Federal Bureau of Investigation, report human trafficking:** (888) 428-7581. This number can be used 9 A.M. to 5 P.M. EST to report concerns to the FBI. They also offer plenty of information about human trafficking on their Web site.

- **Various easy-to-find anti-trafficking organizations:** Type in "human trafficking" on any online search engine, and several sites will appear promoting various methods of combating modern slavery. The important part, Mann says, is to follow through on an interest to help.

"Although I have a firsthand account of dealing with national prejudice and human slavery, many other people are compelled to help victims of human trafficking because freedom is a universal desire," Mann says. *"Any individual can make a difference in someone's life. That is the motive behind my books. I want victims to know that, like me, their tragedy can become their triumph."*

T OGETHER LET US TIRELESSLY
PURSUE THE FIVE A'S:

- **A**wareness
- **A**cknowledgement
- **A**ction
- **A**bolition
- **A**ccountability

WE ARE MAKING A DIFFERENCE!

www.LuciaMann.com

Help Report Modern Day Slavery
www.ReportModernDaySlavery.org

 # About Lucia Mann

Lucia Mann, humanitarian and activist, was born in British colonial South Africa in the wake of World War II. She now resides in British Columbia, Canada. She retired from freelance journalism in 1998, and wrote her books to give voice to those who have suffered and are suffering brutalities and captivity.

Visit www.LuciaMann.com and www.ReportModernDaySlavery.org for more information on how you can help alleviate the scourge of modern-day slavery.

www.ingramcontent.com/pod-product-compliance
Lightning Source LLC
Chambersburg PA
CBHW030812260626
47169CB00001B/288